A Theta Alpha Gamma Story

POSTER Boy

Anne Tenino

Riptide Publishing
PO Box 6652
Hillsborough, NJ 08844
www.riptidepublishing.com

Cover Art by L.C. Chase, lcchase.com/design.htm
Editor: Sarah Frantz and Rachel Haimowitz
Layout: L.C. Chase, lcchase.com/design.htm

ISBN: 978-1-62649-131-1

First edition
April, 2014

Also available in ebook:
ISBN: 978-1-62649-130-4

A Theta Alpha Gamma Story

POSTER Boy

Anne Tenino

For all the Gavins I've known.

Table of Contents

Chapter 1

"So . . ." Toby began, balancing his beer cap on the side of his index finger before flicking it toward the trash can with his thumb. The idea was to get the thing in the garbage, but he failed. Failure was totally his oeuvre lately. "What's the gossip?"

"You'd better clean that up," Sebastian said. "Brad won't appreciate it if he finds it on the floor."

As Toby picked up his offensive litter, he couldn't help the small snipe that slipped out: "He's got you trained well, doesn't he?"

"Yes, he does," Sebastian agreed mildly.

"Sorry." Toby returned to rest his butt on the kitchen counter next to his friend's. "That was uncalled for."

"It seemed a bit out of character for you." Sebastian tipped his bottle up for a swallow, eyes on the social activity in his kitchen. "I was under the impression you approved of my relationship with him."

"You know I do. I've just been feeling . . ." *Left out.* "On edge lately."

"Your thesis isn't coming along well?"

Gah. Thesis. *Shudder.* "What would make you think that?" Had Sebastian been spying on him? With as much time as the dude spent working on *his* thesis, it would seem impossible for him to keep tabs on Toby.

"Because you avoid the subject at all costs."

It was only circumstantial evidence, but Toby didn't bother trying to refute it. "I'll have you know I sometimes lie awake half the night worrying about writing my thesis." Not much of a defense, but he couldn't help it—the writing of a thesis took inspiration, and lately he'd been feeling uninspired.

Clearly, lack of motivation wasn't a problem for Sebastian or their friend Paul. The few times he'd hung out with them this academic year, Toby'd seen how obsessed *they* were with finishing their master's degrees and immediately got hung up in worrying about how obsessed he *wasn't*. If they weren't so busy with their research already, he might have had to actively avoid them.

"Are you considering not finishing?" Sebastian asked, eyebrows inquiringly high.

Toby sighed. "I'm not going to drop out, I'm just . . . reevaluating my research so as to find the proper stimulus."

"Procrastinating." Sebastian nodded. "I see. Do you even want your master's?"

"I don't know." He rubbed his forehead, trying to massage out a better answer. "I'm getting the degree for the usual reason: out of a sense of obligation to my mother."

"You certainly fooled me," Sebastian mused. "Up until this term, I thought you were getting the education for its own sake."

"Nope, just an overdeveloped sense of duty." He *had* wanted the education, though. When he'd been in Tarragona last summer, studying the basilica his thesis focused on, he'd been certain he'd tear through this last task. But once the school year began and he didn't have the structure of a regular class load—either teaching or attending—he'd somehow found it harder to work on the thing. He'd barely managed a defensible thesis statement, and he certainly hadn't managed to start defending it. "Actually, I *was* interested, but for some reason, having to prove the depth of my knowledge is, I don't know, chafing now. So chafing, in fact," he continued, turning to his friend, "that I'm going to change the subject. What have you heard recently about Theta Alpha Gamma House?"

Sebastian quirked his lips in that amused way he had. "You don't want to go ask one of the frat boys currently in my living room?"

"No." Toby waved the suggestion off. "You know how they are—they're happy to come to these parties you and Brad have and drink the free booze, but the fratbros prefer this amicable separate-but-equal layout. TAG boys in the living room, gay boys in here."

"Oh, *they* like to preserve the separation, do they?"

Toby decided to assume that was a rhetorical question.

"It's not entirely segregated," Sebastian pointed out. "Some of the fratkind have ventured onto our savannah, if you'll notice. Kyle, for instance." He gestured toward the Theta Alpha Gamma president in the opposite corner of the kitchen. Kyle was talking to two other TAG brothers, but one of them was Sebastian's own boyfriend, Brad, who had the distinction of being both gay *and* a frat boy, therefore multiethnic, and possibly trans-species. Not to mention the catalyst for this weird social mix of frat boys and gay guys that had sprung up—somewhat like a fairy ring—on the Calapooya College campus.

"In spite of their accepting ways and their token gays, those frat boys are still most comfortable when we keep our distance. They'll appreciate me getting my information from you, and God knows I'd prefer it."

Sebastian tilted his head to one side, regarding Toby for a moment. "So what do you want to know?"

"Oh, tell me about the whole darned fratastrophe."

Sebastian snorted a laugh. "Nice neologism."

"Why thank you. I've been looking for an opportunity to use it." Toby offered up his smuggest smile and rewarded himself with a swig of beer. "Actually, I'm up-to-date on the initial events. Collin stayed with me after the fire, and I was with him when Kyle called about the bomb the following morning. I just haven't heard much since."

It was the subsequent investigation he had no clue about. The things that had happened *after* Collin, his last single friend—the last guy who didn't immediately think about his partner when Toby called to see if he wanted to hang out—had defected and gone over to the dark side. Joined the ranks of the leg-shackled. Fallen in love and renounced the single life.

Gotten himself a boyfriend, in other words. The fact that they'd had a friends-with-benefits agreement only added to Toby's sense of loss. Not a major loss—Toby hadn't been in love with the dude—but the loss of a good friend.

"Well," Sebastian said, reminding Toby they were in the middle of a conversation. "I suppose you know they're still investigating whether the fire was set by the same perpetrator who planted the bomb."

"That's more than I've heard," he responded, the words slipping out before he could stop them. Not that they were horrible words, they simply sounded a little bitter. Or forlorn. Or utterly uninformed. "Do they have any idea of a motive yet?" It was the first question that popped into his head. He was all about changing the subject—or at least diverting attention from his lackluster mood—tonight.

"The current theory"—Sebastian gestured with his beer bottle—"is that TAG was targeted because of that new, gay-friendly membership policy."

Toby stopped mid-drink to ask, "Really?" Although why was he surprised? History was full of people persecuting others for being queer or otherwise different.

Sebastian's smile went sour, twisting down. "It's Collin's uncle's theory, as it turns out. He's president of the TAG alumni association and fought the policy change in the first place."

"He'd have a stroke if Collin came out." He knew all about Uncle Monty. The guy had his nephew totally under his thumb.

"Actually . . ." Sebastian held up a "point of order" finger. "As of Wednesday night, Collin *is* out. Not to his uncle, only the frat, yet still."

Okay, that did it. Toby had been officially disenfranchised. He understood it; in the past, when he'd been in relationships, he'd done it unintentionally. But until this point in his life, he'd never felt quite so outside of things. It all left him feeling like the boy who couldn't swim, so pretended he had something else to do while his friends all went to the pool.

Thank God he was a generally optimistic person, because otherwise this might really be getting him down.

He pulled out of his musings at the end of Sebastian's explanation of Collin's big reveal to the frat brothers. "Unintentionally, Tank outed him, but the only one who was surprised was Collin when he found out all the guys knew already."

"Tank did it, huh? Interesting . . ." Tank was one of the TAG members truly comfortable with the gay boys. He'd even been in the kitchen earlier, socializing. Maybe it was because he was so utterly alpha male he didn't feel threatened. "Collin did hang out with me quite often. It might have given the fratbros a clue." Well, that and the dude was one of those guys who had to work at being butch.

"Collin and Eric first got together the night of the bombing, am I correct?"

"Yeah." Toby took a swig from his beer, forcing himself to relax a couple of mysteriously tense muscles. Eric was clearly a better match for Collin than Toby had ever been, or ever thought to be.

His convenient-sex relationship with his friend had died a natural death the night before, anyway; when Collin had come over to Toby's place looking for "comfort," it had become apparent very quickly that the coddling he needed had more to do with cuddling than with copulating.

"If I were a more sentimental sort," Sebastian mused, eyes trained across the room on his boyfriend, "I might find the way they got together romantic."

"I'm sorry to be the one to break it to you, but you've become the sentimental sort."

Sebastian didn't try to deny it; instead he smiled as if he found himself amusing. "I have, haven't I? To be honest, I recommend it."

Toby chugged the rest of his beer before answering. "Well, I believe we've seen the last of the single gay frat boys. Guess I'm screwed."

"I meant I recommend a relationship." Sebastian took his eyes off of Brad for the first time in minutes and tilted his head toward Toby. "But since you brought it up, TAG has acquired another gay frat boy—Tank's 'little' brother."

Toby pictured the huge—albeit perfectly muscled—TAG member in question. "How little could a brother of Tank's be?"

"Not very. Although he *is* shorter than him."

Which could still make him tall enough to have to duck under doorjambs. "Is he as beefcake-calendar-worthy as his big brother?"

"Why yes, he is." Sebastian smirked. "He's also newly out."

"Mmmmm." Toby rocked back on his heels, thinking. Maybe this new frat boy would be interested in some explorations of the sexual kind.

"He's possibly even virginal," Sebastian added with a gleam in his eye. They knew each other's proclivities well, after all. "Although not totally inexperienced. I know you have that predilection for the innocent young things."

"You make me sound like a pedophile. And how do you know he's not totally inexperienced?"

Sebastian's playful amusement melted away. "Brad made me promise not to spread it, but the guy had a traumatic coming out. He was a starter on the Avalon College hockey team, and his coach received some irrefutable evidence of the guy's orientation and kicked him off the team. He transferred to Calapooya a week into the term."

"Well that utterly sucks," Toby muttered.

Sebastian *hmmm*ed an agreement, and they spent a silent minute or two letting the party happen around them while contemplating the unfairness of life.

At least, that's what Toby was doing. Feeling sympathy and that other thing that often came along with it, sinking into his chest, hooking him like a hungry fish. *Interest.* Not necessarily attraction—he hadn't even seen the kid (although if he was Tank's brother, there was a better than average chance he was good-looking)—but the combination of inexperience and personal distress got him every time. He was a sucker for a guy who needed some comfort. And Sebastian knew it.

He sighed. Not in resignation, more in acceptance of his nature. "I'm probably going to take one look at him and want him, aren't I?"

Sebastian's amused smirk had returned. "I'd lay money on it."

ΘΑΓ

"This party is kind of a sausage fest," one of Jock's new frat brothers said to another. Jock squinted up at them from the chair he'd claimed in Brad's living room and tried to remember their names. The dude on the left was easy—it was Jules, the TAG secretary. But the other guy . . . either Turbo or Flounder. He didn't have them straightened out yet.

"You must feel right at home," Turbo/Flounder said to Jules, cluing Jock in. Definitely Turbo—only a week at the frat and Jock had already figured out that guy liked to mess with Julian.

"Oh, uh . . ." Jock waited to hear what weak comeback Jules would come up with. "No offense."

Oh yeah, totally lame. Didn't even make sense. Neither did the way he was looking at Jock . . . Unless the "no offense" comment had been directed at him?

"You know," Jules fumbled, obviously speaking to Jock, now. "There's nothing *wrong* with, well, sausage fests. I mean, you know, parties where there are lots of penises. Um . . ." He turned bright red while Jock just stared at him.

"Why would I be offended by that?" Jock finally asked. He had to say something, because he knew how easy it was to intimidate with a stare. He'd honed it to instinct at this point, and Jules's fidgeting was a sure sign that Jock was glaring at him like an opposing teammate.

Turbo shifted, clearing his throat. "Ignore him, man. He's just freaking because you're gay and he thinks he needs to treat you differently or something. You know, 'be sensitive.'"

Jock should probably be appreciative that Turbo at least tried not to be a dork, too, but the flare of annoyance in his gut wouldn't let him shut up. "You guys can stop being all careful around me anytime now."

"It's not because you're gay," Jules protested, throwing a glare Turbo's way before turning back to Jock. "It's what you *went through* because you're gay."

Fuck me. Jock rubbed at the throbbing that had started in his temple. "Seriously, can we not talk about it?" Maybe playing on their delicate fucking sensitivities would shut Jules up.

"Oh, yeah, totally." Jules assured him, waving his palm in Jock's face. "We can not talk about it ever. I mean, we want you to be comfortable, you know? And if not talking about *what happened* makes you comfortable, we can not mention it, like, forever."

Turbo was shaking his head in disgust, but Jock's thoughts went down a more violent path—picturing his fist pounding Jules's skull until the dude's brains leaked out his ears.

"We're here!" a female voice sang out just then, saving Jules from imminent death. "The party can start." It was Ashley—Kyle's girlfriend, who he'd met a couple days before—and a bunch of her friends. Sorority sisters? Whatever, there was a gaggle of them already, and more coming in the door.

"Sweet," Jules crowed, voice cracking. "The babes are here. I dunno about you," he said to Turbo, "But I'm not sleeping alone tonight." Then he was gone.

"He's sleeping alone the rest of his life unless he gets a clue," Jock said.

"Word," Turbo agreed, holding his fist out for a bump. Jock obliged, and for possibly the first time since he got to TAG, he had a moment where he felt as if he belonged. Then Turbo went off to talk to some chick, and Jock went back to being the village queer or whatever he was to these guys.

"Dude!" Ricky shouted, drawing Jock's attention. Ricky'd broken his leg in the fraternity fire by falling down the stairs (Gomer said something about an exploding water heater, but Jock made it a policy to not believe half of what the guy said), and he was still in a wheelchair. He had the biggest cast Jock had ever seen, and it poked straight out in front of him like a battering ram. Ricky mostly used it like a cattle prod, moving people out of his way. And to punctuate his statements. "I'm telling you—they're reopening registration just for us, all we gotta do is find a place to stay," he said excitedly to the guys sitting on the couch.

Danny and Gomer were there. Jock didn't know them that well yet, but he knew the third dude well enough: Noah, the sophomore who'd hinted around that he'd like to spend some alone time with Jock. So far Jock hadn't taken him up on it. What was that saying about shitting in your own sandbox? Hooking up with a TAG dude had to be a bad idea.

As Jock was watching, Noah asked, "How're we gonna find a place to stay in France?"

They were going to France?

Ricky bugged his eyes out at Noah, as if he was the stupidest creature on earth. "Not *France.* Provence."

"Provence is *in* France," Danny said.

"Are you sure?" Ricky asked, squinting suspiciously.

"Yo, Kyle!" Danny yelled over his shoulder toward the kitchen. "Kyle! Mr. President, sir!"

Kyle poked his head around the corner. "What?" He tapped his fingers on the doorjamb, looking around the room. "Which one of you said my name? What d'ya need?"

"Me." Danny raised his hand. "Is Provence in France?"

Kyle did that slumping thing people did when they were annoyed. Then he rolled his eyes to make it more obvious. "Yes. It's in France. Don't ask me shit you can look up on your phone—that's why they call them *smart.*" He disappeared from view before they could ask him more.

"See? Told ya," Danny said, leaning over Gomer to get into Ricky's face.

Noah pulled Danny back to his side of the couch. "Whatever," he said, cutting off a comeback from Ricky. "How're we gonna find a place to stay in France?"

Danny grinned, lifting his butt off the cushion and digging in his back pocket. "Duh. Ask our smartphones."

"But we don't know French," Gomer said, brow wrinkling up. "Don't you gotta know the language to do a term abroad?"

"Not for this program," Ricky said, balancing on his back wheels and grinning like a maniac. "They'll even give us credit for learning French."

"I *need* language credits," Gomer said. He dug his phone out of his pocket too. "Did you guys know English doesn't count?"

Danny laughed at him and punched him in the arm. "Good one, man."

Gomer blinked a few dozen times, then shrugged to himself and went back to his phone.

"Hey, man," Danny said, leaning toward Jock to tap his knee. "You wanna go to Provence for spring term with us?"

Fuck no. "You guys are going to France? With who?"

"The international studies department. Or maybe foreign languages." Danny screwed up his face. "Pretty sure it's the first one, though. They're gonna let us register later because of being homeless and all."

"We aren't homeless," Noah said.

Danny ignored him. "Maybe getting the frat house blown up has a silver lining."

"TAG House didn't blow up, dude, it only caught on fire. It was just a bomb *threat*," Ricky said, wheeling his chair closer to poke Danny with his cast. "And I lost my leg."

Danny scowled at him when Ricky poked him with his very-much-present cast.

"Sounds cool, but I can't guys," Jock said, cutting off the inevitable argument about whether Ricky had actually lost a limb or not. "You go on and have fun without me though." Maybe all the guys would go, and he'd have the frat to himself. *That'd be so sweet.* Peace.

Fucking Tank. Jock had joined this frat because his big brother, Tank, was a Theta Alpha Gamma brother, and Tank had really wanted Jock to join. Pretty much begged him. And since Jock had already fled Avalon and enrolled at Calapooya because his big brother was there . . . A lifetime of hero worship couldn't be ignored.

In the time he'd been here, Jock had discovered a lifetime of hero worship couldn't cancel out the anger he felt toward Tank. The anger he hadn't even really copped to until he was with his brother all the time. Being with the frat guys brought it all into focus, almost too sharp a picture. They all knew he was gay because, before Jock had even met the dudes, Tank had fucking announced it last spring, months before he was outed to his hockey team.

In spite of everything Tank had done for him, Jock was having a hard time getting over that. Even knowing why Tank had done it and figuring out TAG was a safe place, it still gnawed at him. Like, made him prone to biting people's heads off and imagining pounding Jules's brains out of his ear canals. He usually didn't have a hard time controlling his anger—fifteen years of hockey had trained him to keep his cool—but it had been unpredictable since he'd gotten here.

Longer than that, even—since before he'd gotten kicked off the team. Since Coach Schnigglehoeffer had his little rant over the You Can Play representative wanting to talk to the team about partnering with his pro-LGBT organization. The Dean of Athletics had made Coach give the guy his say, but Schnigglehoeffer had spent equal time afterward spouting off about homosexuality being "of the devil" and swearing he'd never had a "faggot" in his locker room and never would.

"I guarantee you've had a gay guy on your team, Coach. Probably more than one," Jock had interrupted mid-rant, not even thinking it over, his voice dripping with contempt. That was it, wasn't it? The moment he'd lost control over his anger. It was also the moment when Coach had put a target on his back.

"Bro," Tank said from behind Jock, making him jump. Shit, he'd spaced out everything going on around him and gotten lost in his thoughts. Another thing he didn't used to do much of. "C'mon into the kitchen and hang with us there," Tank suggested.

Shit. He'd worked up a pretty strong aversion to the guy's voice. Every time Tank spoke, Jock could swear the hair stood up on the back of his neck. He passed a hand over his nape, checking for bristling. He couldn't tell—it was all too short to lie on his skin back there anyway.

"Jock," Tank said louder.

Oh yeah, might've felt some hair jump there.

He hid his sigh and tilted his head up and back. "Yeah?"

"You'll like the guys that hang out in the other room better." Tank grimaced toward the couch, where one of the frat boys was spitting a loogy into someone's unattended beer while typing into his phone.

"Why will I like them better?" Would his brother admit the real reason?

"'Cause *I* like them better than most of these guys." He leaned his thigh against the back of Jock's chair but kept his eyes on the guys in front of them.

Jock slouched further into his seat. "You just want me to come in there because those dudes are gay." Tank thought that gay guys were his peeps. It wasn't that Jock disagreed, it was just that all the overprotective crap from his brother lately made him want to have a little fit and roll around on the carpet with the dude, wrestling out some frustration. Make his brother understand he didn't rate the sympathy.

Except Tank was huge—six and a half feet and mostly muscle, even bigger than Jock himself—and had always won matches when they were kids, and Jock knew for a fact that the rug at their feet was soaking with beer.

Tank's heart's in the right place. Or whatever.

"Sorta." Tank nodded. "But we aren't all gay. I'm in there and so're Kyle and Ashley."

Jock shrugged.

Tank leaned closer to him, saying in his ear, "I don't like seeing you mope out here."

Jock clenched his teeth. This was why he'd moved out of Tank's room at the frat—he was sick of being managed all the freaking time. "I'm not moping."

"Yeah? So what *are* you doing?"

"Watching. And even if I was moping, I can if I want to." He didn't stick out his tongue, only stopping himself by taking a swig of his nearly forgotten beer. *Ugh.* He kinda hated the taste now, plus it was warm. He associated it too much with that night. The last party he'd gone to, come to think of it.

"I'm just looking out for my little brother," Tank said quietly.

The guy was showing him more patience than he deserved. Jock took a second to try to find that objective, icy part of his mind, and got just enough. "Sorry, Beau," he muttered, nudging the coffee table with the toe of his sneaker. Even though Tank hated it when Jock used that name, he also knew his brother would understand that's what made it a sincere apology. "I'm just, I don't know. Adjusting."

Tank ruffled Jock's hair. If he knew how much less guilty and more irritated it made his little brother, Tank wouldn't do that shit. But Jock gritted his teeth and bore it.

"C'mon, bro. Let's go into the kitchen. There are some people there you haven't met."

Jock looked over at his frat brothers again. Noah had his tongue clamped between his teeth, typing carefully into his phone, thumbs so huge and stubby it looked like he was trying to text via chicken wings. Ricky was doing wheelies, and Danny was throwing peanuts at Julian, while excitedly telling the guys, "Yeah, getting out of this country is a real opportunity to develop the Beer Terrorist Response Team away from, you know, prying eyes and all."

Across the room, he could just hear Jules—talking way too loudly—telling some chick, "I'm a member of Mensa!" right before a flying nut hit him in the eye. As Jules shrieked and clawed at his face, the girl fled.

He probably did need to meet some new people. "Okay, lead the way."

ΘΑΓ

In the kitchen, Tank immediately got called over to answer some question of Kyle's and didn't introduce Jock to anyone. Which was fine with him. He trailed along behind his brother, then propped up a wall near—but not too near—the group Tank was now a part of and started scoping out the people in this room.

There were some guys he'd never met before, but they all looked older. More like Sebastian's friends than his frat bother Brad's. One guy looked kinda familiar, and Jock inspected him for few minutes (balding, blue eyes, linebacker build, bubble butt) before he remembered meeting the Calapooya softball coach. The coach was standing next to a Sebastian-type. Glasses, grad-student goatee, superior look on his face—he made Jock's skin prickle in irritation from ten feet away. The way Coach Gardiner kept casually touching Sebastian-clone, they had to be a couple.

Okay, so that was kinda cool, that the softball coach was gay, too.

Whatever. He shoved that thought away, focusing on something else. Brad caught his eye. He was one of those dudes Jock had clicked with immediately. Not, like, romantically or whatever, but platonically. He'd only known the guy a week, but Jock trusted him more than anyone else in the frat, so he didn't even try to deny it.

Brad was doing something over by the sink, and Sebastian was next to him, talking to someone else Jock didn't know. Another mystery man. When that dude turned a little more toward him—in profile now—Jock's skin prickled in a whole different way, sweeping down from his head, preparing him for something. Mystery Man leaned against the counter, legs crossed at his ankles. Relaxed and having a good time. Shortish wavy hair that looked black in this light, and deep, dark eyes with thick brows and lashes, plus a perfectly angled jaw with heavy stubble. His hands were stuffed in his jeans pockets, biceps relaxed but obvious under his short sleeved shirt, veins outlining and enhancing their shape.

There was nothing about him that was special in any way, as far as Jock could see, but still . . . there *was* something about him. Maybe it was that smile, or the expressiveness of his face, or the way a thin slice of pale skin with a few curly hairs was visible between the hem of his shirt and waistband of his jeans, but he totally caught Jock's attention.

Maybe it's because you're horny, and he's the only single gay guy in the room.

Then the dude laughed, head tilting back and neck stretching out, the sound rolling toward Jock and drenching him like a sneaker wave, and it didn't matter what made him so attractive. Jock would give anything to run his teeth along the line of his throat, hearing that guy moan in his ear while Jock worked his fingers into his pants.

While Jock stood riveted, the mystery man's conversation with Sebastian wound down. He began surveying the kitchen, turning to look at each grouping, each movement of his head making Jock's neck tighten up a little more. He straightened from where he'd been leaning, trying to find a more comfortable position. Then Mystery Man's gaze swept over Jock like headlights picking out an animal on the side of a road, halting there. When their eyes connected, it pinned him in place, heart banging against his breastbone, unable to move. Either trying to blend into the background or let the dude get a good look at him.

He *did* want to be noticed, didn't he?

Mystery Man smiled, a very lazy, confident tilt of his lips, eyelids lowering. Jock swallowed.

Okay, if he wanted something to happen—*yes, yes, I do*—he should maybe give an answering smile. Before he could though, the guy's eyes flickered down Jock's body, cataloging him, making him tingle everywhere, and all Jock could do was sway, shoulder brushing the wall, trapped in some kind of sexual magnetic stasis field, blood rushing in his ears and an echo of his heartbeat in his dick. He could feel the gaze sliding down his neck and across his chest, following the contours of his torso. His lungs forced in a breath when the guy's attention concentrated on his groin, lingering there a few seconds, then worked back up to Jock's face.

Jock parted his lips to take in more air, and immediately the dude focused on them, his own nostrils flaring. He blinked once, slowly, then zeroed in on Jock's eyes, quirking his brow.

Oh yeah. Whatever that eyebrow was asking, Jock was saying yes.

Not whatever *he wants*, his alarmist self chimed in, stopping him from responding immediately.

"Dude," Brad said from right next to him, and Jock all but jumped, swinging his head around and breaking the connection with his mystery man. "Did you meet Toby?"

"Who's Toby?" He blinked a few times, trying to clear his vision or his brain. Come back to reality after a major lust high.

"That guy eye-fucking you from across the room."

Jock gaped. "How did you see that?"

Brad snorted but didn't answer, other than crossing his arms over his chest.

Jock leaned closer, lowering his voice. "Tank didn't catch that, did he?" His brother kept mistaking him for a virginal little sister and getting all protective. Tank would totally try to stop him from hooking up. If he decided to.

"No, but he's not stupid, just straight. You keep it up and he'll notice eventually."

He glanced at the guy—Toby—again from under his lashes, but Toby had started another conversation with Sebastian, no longer watching him. "I don't think he's that interested," he muttered. Lying.

Brad laughed. "Uh, yeah. He is." He eyed Jock sideways a second before adding. "I don't know what you're looking for, but he gets around. I mean, he's not really a player, but he kinda thinks he is."

Jock cast another glance at Toby, and this time the dude was looking at him, locking onto his gaze and smiling. Jock held it for a second before glancing away. He couldn't just not have sex for the rest of his life because of one bad experience, right? *Gotta get back on that horse.* He shifted his weight, then shifted back. "So, he's not, like, trustworthy?" he asked Brad.

"Trustworthy?" Brad frowned. "I mean, he's safe and all, and he doesn't jerk guys around. I dunno, I could ask Sebastian, I guess."

"Forget it," Jock said quickly. "I'm being dumb."

Brad shrugged his eyebrows but said, "If you just wanna get laid? He's the dude to do it."

Laid. Jock adjusted his shoulders, trying to loosen up his chest. He didn't know Brad very well, but he had a gut feeling that when Brad got "laid," he was the receptive partner. So . . . was that what he meant?

Fuck. Who did he ask about this shit? He'd thought Collin might be someone he could talk to, but that was a dead end. The guy was either with or thinking about his new boyfriend all the time. Jock shifted his weight, trying to figure out what to say next. He didn't want to talk about that, but he did *sorta* . . .

Brad scratched behind his ear, then shoved his hands into his pockets. "When I first came out, I would have liked someone to talk to about it. I mean, I was kinda stupid—didn't even figure it out until I was twenty-one—and then the only guy who knew was Sebastian, which was cool, but he was my boyfriend, or close enough at the time." He snorted. "Then Ashley figured it out."

"Kyle's girlfriend?"

Brad's mouth twisted up in an unamused smile. "She was my girlfriend first."

Jock felt his eyes widen, and tried to get them to be cool about it. They ignored him.

"Yeah." Brad scratched again. "She's good to talk to, but there's tons of stuff I couldn't tell her about—she wouldn't've known the answers even if I'd wanted to ask her. Uh, so I guess I'm saying, if you want someone to talk to and Collin's not a—"

"Have you ever been with anyone but Sebastian?" Jock squeezed his eyes shut, trying to unsee what he'd just asked or something useful like that. "Sorry, dude."

Brad laughed. "No worries. Yeah, I've been with another guy, but . . . shit. It's a long story, I'll tell you some other time." Brad gripped Jock's shoulder when Jock started to say he didn't need to know. "Seriously, I'll tell you some other time, like, when it's just you and me. It might help or something. I dunno." Brad dropped his hand and straightened, glancing around the room.

Jock did the same, standing silently next to Brad a few seconds and letting the air pressure equalize or whatever needed to happen after a conversation like that. He studied Ashley, over talking with Kyle and Tank, trying to figure out if he'd ever have been able to date a girl. He'd never had to even fake it, because hockey kept him so busy he didn't have time, or so he'd claimed. He'd slept with a few, just to be sure and to bolster his secret. But if he'd stayed at Avalon and tried to keep his closet door shut, how long would he have been able to go without finding a beard?

"Hey Brad, are you going to introduce me to your friend?" someone asked, and from the way heat flashed all over Jock's body, he knew who it was before turning to see. And of course there stood the guy he'd half-hoped it wasn't.

Brad smirked. "Sure, Toby. This is Jock." He caught Jock's eye a second, but Jock got totally distracted from whatever silent communication Brad was trying to make when Toby stuck out his hand, holding it inches from Jock's belly, waiting for him to shake it.

It took him a second—he had to fight the urge to wipe any potential sweatiness off on his thigh first—before he put his palm against Toby's and entered into a whole new kind of silent communication. A touch that soaked into his skin and spread nervous energy up his arm. "Um, hey," he managed. Toby was shorter than him, about at Jock's chin, but his shoulders were broader than Jock had expected.

Toby didn't shake. Instead he held Jock's hand, fingertips sliding up past the ball of Jock's thumb to his inner wrist. Tapping out secret messages where Jock was especially sensitive. "Nice to meet you."

Jock lifted his eyes, looking into Toby's deep brown ones, connecting the two of them together like before, but with the added charge of skin-against-skin and Toby's voice still echoing in his ear. Jock swallowed. "You too."

Brad coughed. Well, or laughed. Jock dropped Toby's hand immediately and shoved his in his pocket. Grinning, Brad hiked a thumb over his shoulder. "Um, hey, I better check and see if the guys in the living room need anything."

Fuck. "You don't need to—"

"Go right ahead, we'll be fine here," Toby said, smiling.

Chapter 2

Well, that had been a pleasant thrill. Touching Jock had lived up to all of Toby's hopes for an instant lust connection. It had been quite a while since he'd had this sort of immediate, bodily reaction to someone, and the thought of what could happen later nearly had him salivating.

Assuming Jock was into it. But why wouldn't he be? He was male, it was sex, and he was clearly interested judging from the heat of their eye contact earlier.

Except the guy was utterly tongue-tied. He couldn't meet Toby's gaze for more than a second or two at a time, and he seemed almost scared. *This'll be a challenge*, Toby's libido whispered, rubbing its hands in anticipation—it did love the innocent young things. Toby reined himself in, ignoring the warm currents of attraction circulating in his belly and groin, fed by his proximity to this tall, built blond boy. Not blond, light brown.

He could do this. Ease this guy's nerves now, and then later he could work them up again. *Begin with small talk.* He racked his brain for an innocuous conversation starter. All he could think of was what Sebastian had said about the guy, and none of that would ease either of their nerves.

Oh, except, "I understand you're Collin's roommate at TAG."

Jock nodded, and was that a slight eye roll? Perplexing.

Possibly a subject change would yield more of a response. "So you're new to Calapooya? You started at the beginning of winter term?" What would he ask next, *What's your major?* If the guy didn't take the bait soon, Toby might be reduced to commenting on his size. Jock didn't stoop to hide his height, and his shoulders were straight and thrown back naturally, showing off a hell of an expanse of chest. His pecs filled out his T-shirt, but it wasn't tight everywhere, not a check-me shirt, just a shirt. Toby'd kill to peel it off the kid. With his tongue.

Focus. Something was off. Years of doing the hookup dance with various guys told him that, but Toby couldn't figure it out. He felt as if Jock was one of those optical illusions psychology professors tortured students with—was he looking at an old woman's profile or a young woman turning her head away? He couldn't get Jock's body language to make sense, not until the guy tilted his chin, highlighting how tense the muscles in his neck were. Then the picture resolved itself. Jock wasn't simply nervous, he was wary. Toby took a step back under the guise of leaning against the kitchen table and turned so they weren't exactly facing each other. The response was immediate—Jock's shoulders relaxed and his expression loosened up.

"I started winter term a week late," he finally responded to the question Toby had forgotten he'd asked. He crossed his arms and focused on something to his right. "I had to leave my last school sort of unexpectedly."

Oh, I know. Sympathy twanged one of his heartstrings. "Yeah, I might have heard something about that."

Jock gave him a sidelong look, one side of his mouth twisting up. "I bet you did." His smile grew—not into anything truly amused, but more in recognition of the humor in Toby's cautious response.

Progress. "So, what do you think so far?"

"Of Calapooya College, or of Theta Alpha Gamma?" Jock focused on his feet, nudging the linoleum with the toe of his sneaker.

"Both, or either. Whichever you feel like answering." He'd thought Jock was about to really loosen up, drop his defensive posture, turn to Toby, but something in what Toby had said had the opposite effect. Jock's face went blank and he dropped his head further, jaw clenching.

"S'all right," he said to the floor.

Toby had an urge to tilt Jock's chin up with his fingers, but he knew that would only make the guy more skittish. He didn't want to spook the kid, plus it would be much more satisfying to coax a welcoming, unguarded response from Jock through earning his trust. All the hottest hookups began with trust. And an off-the-charts lust connection.

Toby's charm almost failed him, but a new conversational gambit presented itself just in time. One of the straight fratbros wandered into the kitchen. Jock's attention was caught by the dude, and for a split second, Toby thought he was about to be dissed—that Jock would latch onto his TAG brother as an excuse to get out of this awkward *tête-à-tête*. But instead, Jock's lips tightened up and he shifted, turning more toward Toby and away from the beer-seeking frat boy.

Ah-hah. "Sometimes I find myself hanging out with all these TAG guys and I wonder what rabbit hole I fell down."

A short laugh burst out of Jock, and he grinned. *Verrry nice dimple in that cheek. Just one?* But by the time he'd turned fully toward Toby, the dimple had died down. Toby'd have to conduct some more research to determine the presence of other sexy-cute features on Jock's person.

"Yeah, Theta Alpha Gamma has to be the weirdest frat on the planet. I mean, I only started college in the fall," Jock said, shrugging one shoulder self-consciously. "But I was in a frat for a couple months at Avalon College—that's where I went fall term—and it wasn't anything like this. TAG's like one of those old sitcoms they show on cable, with the canned laughter and the really cheesy jokes delivered by people with lower than average intelligence." When he'd finished, Jock looked as surprised as Toby felt at how much he'd said.

Had to keep the ball rolling though. "You're Tank's little brother, correct? You two must be close if you joined the frat."

"I guess." Jock leaned closer, speaking out the side of his mouth while scoping out the room. "He's making me bananas."

Toby moved in toward Jock, well within the "friend" boundary, but more because he felt pulled there than by design. "If my brother lived within a few hundred miles of me, I'd kill myself. Or preferably him."

"Is he older?" Jock turned his head, his pale blue eyes meeting Toby's again, and in spite of the mundanity of their chitchat, Toby could feel that overwhelming attraction that had drawn him from across the room. A physical craving to get even closer.

When they hooked up, it would be fucking incendiary. *If. If we hook up.*

"Nate's my twin, but he was born first, so I suppose the answer is yes."

Jock's face went slack in surprise, then he got that brow-tightening curious look people did when they wanted to ask but weren't sure they should.

Toby smirked. "We aren't identical."

"Oh, so he's not . . ."

"He's not gay."

The nerves resurfaced. Maybe it was the simple mention of "gay," but Jock straightened upright fully, using their half-a-foot height difference to distance himself. He nodded, glancing around the room for a few silent seconds. Toby decided to see what Jock would do, if he would come up with something to say. Eventually he did. "I like my brother, but since all this shit happened, he's acting like I'm, I dunno, his virginal little sister. He keeps trying to protect me. It's wearing me out." He dropped his arms, shoving his hands into his jeans.

And how virginal are we? was on the tip of Toby's tongue, but it was beyond obvious Jock wasn't that kind of flirty, casual hookup material. A guy like this took finesse. He was young and newly out. Just a fledgling gay.

My favorite. Toby's lungs seized up at the prospect, then shuddered in a breath. "I have a similar situation with my brother. God knows why he thinks I need his guidance," Toby said unthinkingly, focused on the physical, caught up in the renewed, eddying undercurrents of sex flowing through him.

"Your brother thinks you're virginal?" Jock asked, dazzling Toby with his grin. *Yes, two dimples, one in each cheek.* "We might've just met, but even I can tell you're into sins of the flesh."

A laugh welled out of him, catching Toby unaware. "Um, no, he's not delusional, just meddling." He smiled, once more revising his estimation of the jock, Jock, in front of him. Definitely some kind of optical illusion, one that Toby couldn't decipher yet, but he was motivated to try even harder. The kid had everything—he was inexperienced, struggling, *and* had a great personality. "I'm the poor grad student while he's the well-paid career wonk. Apparently that entitles him to tell me how I'm wasting money. But not just money—the *government's* money." When Jock's forehead wrinkled up, Toby explained. "He thinks my tuition is covered by grants and loans. I haven't had the heart to tell him it's mostly fellowships, and since Calapooya is a private school, it's mostly private money." He leaned closer, stretching up toward Jock to stage whisper, "Nate's a *Republican.*"

"That's, like, a sin against the grad student belief system, isn't it? You win, your brother sucks worse."

"I win," Toby repeated, watching Jock's lips curl up into an answering smile. He had Tom of Finland fantasy lips—full and pouty, but with very male angles. This kid was just smoking hot, and he was staring into Toby's eyes, smile melting into something more intent and pupils widening. Toby reached out for him, running a hand along Jock's forearm, downy hair giving way under his fingers. Jock's lips parted, and Toby could hear the breath he took. Or maybe that was the air he'd sucked into his own lungs.

Then suddenly Jock jerked away from Toby's touch and glanced around the room, face paling. As if they'd been caught doing something wrong and all eyes were on them. *From that little touch?*

It *had* gone completely silent, but not because everyone was staring at them. No, everyone was staring at the door, where the man of the hour was standing next to his shiny new boyfriend—Collin and Eric. The ensuing silence was broken after a few seconds by Collin pulling out the awkward turtle maneuver—stacking his hands on top of each other and twirling his thumbs—and then the happy couple began making the rounds. Toby wasn't that interested—he'd already met Eric, and this weird trend toward domestic bliss among his friends was starting to irk him. He shook it off and refocused on Jock, hoping to pick up where they'd left off.

But judging by Jock's expression, that wasn't going to happen, not right away. "Shit," the guy muttered.

"You don't want to see Collin?" Toby inched forward, keeping their space intimate and conversation low in spite of Jock's mood change. Hoping to recapture the previous connection.

Jock shrugged, mouth turning down. "It's not that, it's just everyone keeps checking on me. Like, they're all making sure I'm not about to freak or something. Any second he's gonna come over here and, like, inspect me." He sighed. "I guess it's better than Tank riding my ass."

"They're just worried, right?" He said it automatically, on sympathetic autopilot, but the words brought him up short and made him rethink. "I'd be annoyed too." Okay, *that* he meant.

"Thanks," Jock muttered. He was studying the floor again, drawing designs on it with the toe of his sneaker. His hands were shoved so far into his jeans pockets Toby thought they might be around his knees. He was the epitome of abject teenage angst.

This kid is so *young.*

Jock could be his Brad. Just like Sebastian had—a smoking gay-naive frat boy who worshiped him the way Brad did Sebastian. Not necessarily the loving, sappy part, but that way he physically perked up when Sebastian glanced at him with that smile he only ever gave Brad. Seriously, that expression was sex on airwaves. Toby could almost get a contact hard-on from it.

"Hey," Collin said, coming up on Toby's right side, new boyfriend in tow. "What are you guys talking about?"

The stiff falseness of Collin's smile made Toby's stomach sink. "Oh, hey," he returned, giving his friend the expressional equivalent of hanging a sock on a doorknob.

Collin's glance flickered to Jock and back to Toby, his brows rising into his hairline. "This is Eric," Collin said, stepping into the space between Toby and Jock and turning to look at his beau. "You remember Toby, probably."

Toby smiled and held out his hand to shake. "Yeah, we've met. Sorta." He smirked at Eric, and the dude smiled back, tipping his chin in acknowledgment, because what could he say? He'd been so hot for Collin that night at the Slaughterhouse he'd never even seen Toby.

"And this is Jock, my new roommate." Collin said, looking at his boyfriend. "He's *Tank's little brother.*" Yet clearly, he was addressing Toby. Jock had called that right—Collin did his self-appointed cock-blocking like a pro, separating them physically and warning them off with looks and repeated mentions of Tank.

Toby wasn't ready to retreat though. At least not until Tank showed up and glowered at him. Backing off for the time being began to look like a good idea—Tank communicated his unwillingness to converse further with Toby through a series of grunts and growls. Toby didn't speak fratbro hubris, but the meaning was very clear. And the guy didn't get that nickname for being small and weak.

At Tank's arrival, Jock had subsided back into his mostly uncommunicative self, almost shrinking. These guys were freaking stifling him. Forget hooking up; the kid couldn't even socialize without Collin and Tank wanting to chaperone, could he?

"Soooo," he said, rocking back on his heels, trying not to look too scornful. "I guess I should be moving along too, huh?"

"Uh-huh," Tank vocalized, nodding. He'd lowered his brows so far they almost obscured his nose.

Saying something snarky would definitely be inappropriate. Toby bared his teeth at Tank—who said smiles were friendly?—and gave his farewell. "I wouldn't want to give anyone the wrong impression and thereby besmirch your little brother's reputation or anything."

Tank gaped while Jock snorted laughter, jerking his head up, dimples flashing, bright eyes meeting Toby's for one last potent shot to his libido. Toby had the momentary sense of standing on the edge of a cliff, swaying, about to fall over if he didn't catch his balance, but then it passed. He steadied himself, winked at Jock, and sauntered off.

ΘΑΓ

Tank cajoled Jock into the living room again—apparently he only wanted his little brother in the kitchen if no one was going to be attracted to him. No big, he might need a break from the flirting and stuff, because for a minute there he was pretty sure his skin was going to overheat and sweat would start steaming off of him.

He didn't want to be that fucking obvious. They may all figure he and Toby would hook up, but he'd like everyone to pretend they didn't, thanks.

But as soon as he wandered into the living room, Danny twisted around on the couch, saying, "So, saw you talking to that friend of Sebastian's. Uh, you know, you can bring him back to your room and no one will freak or anything."

No fucking way was he going to give the guys a clue about his sex life. He didn't need them weighing in, or even knowing if he got any. If he went back into the kitchen to find Toby now, all the guys on the couch would know why—they were all peering at him, eyes wide. Like curious baby owls or something.

So instead he grabbed his jacket and walked back to the frat. The *temporary* frat—the fire at TAG House had caused too much structural damage for the building to be occupied, so the guys had been forced to move into the third floor of a vacant dormitory on campus. Jock had fallen into the welcoming bosom of Theta Alpha Gamma just three days later. He was tempted to say the fire and bomb were omens of his arrival, but everyone always thought it was all about them, and it never was. Probably the same applied to him.

Still, he should've run back to Avalon the second he found out about that. Or once he met some of the guys.

Whatever. He sighed, heading for his too fucking small bed. The fucking *room* was too small. Too small for him alone, not to mention two guys. Of course, Collin was never there, he was always with his boyfriend. It wasn't like Jock wanted a companion or anything, but it would be nice to not feel abandoned. He'd never really had a gay friend, or at least not one that had a clue about how to go out and, like, meet guys or something useful. (Although Max could give a hell of a blowjob.) Coming to Calapooya and joining TAG was supposed to fix that, but Collin was a bust.

Brad's my friend.

Yeah, but the dude wasn't here, was he?

No hockey coach screaming you're a pussy, and you turn into a whiner.

Okay, that was it, no more whining. Things'd be better tomorrow. And next time he had a chance with Toby, he wouldn't let those fuckers scare him off.

ΘΑΓ

Shortly after they met, Jock bailed on the party. Toby didn't know when it happened, or why, but Brad made a point of telling him.

"Yeah, he was beat." Brad shrugged, but the way he watched Toby belied his supposed disinterest. "Guess he didn't have a good reason to stay."

Oh, ouch. That *hurt.* "Why are you telling me this?" he asked, losing a fair amount of his social veneer.

"'Cause you looked interested," Brad said baldly.

"I *am*." And it was true—he was downright fascinated, and even those few minutes of conversation with Jock had led him to thinking about the possibility of something beyond just sex. When was the last time he'd met a guy who made him think that way?

"No worries." Brad gave his shoulder a bro-slap. "You'll get another chance." Then he wandered off, with Toby staring after him, trying to figure out what he meant. Did the guy intend to make sure he and Jock had another meeting in the future?

Regardless, tonight's festivities had lost a lot of their luster.

The problem with the party was that it wasn't huge. It was only twenty-odd frat boys, more than half of whom Toby had no interest in, and twenty-odd sorority girls. The few people he did have an interest in were all in the fairy-tale kingdom of coupledom, AKA the kitchen. That was suddenly the last place he wanted to be.

He should go back to his apartment and work on his thesis.

Too tired. I'll put in a full day on it tomorrow.

Toby ended up in the living room, getting steadily drunker and having surreal conversations with various frat boys. None of whom were nearly as hot as Jock, and all of whom had a bizarre and ardent belief in something called a beer terrorist.

"You gotta watch out for them, dude," a guy who Toby thought might be named Danny said. Maybe-Danny was sitting next to him on the couch, leaning toward Toby, one arm braced along the back of the cushions. So intent on conveying his warning that he'd violated the straight-boy-personal-space rule by about a foot. "If you give them an opening, they'll strike," he said with all the fervor of a true disciple about to handle poisonous snakes. Or maybe something even more dangerous, such as a wine cooler.

I wonder what he'd do if I kissed him? Toby thought idly. He didn't care enough to find out. "Beer terrorists, huh?" He lifted his own bottle to his lips, about to take a drink, and suddenly it was ripped out of his hands, a few drops sloshing onto his T-shirt. "Hey!"

Maybe-Danny had it, holding it tauntingly at arm's length, eyes shining with the light of a zealot. "See? They're a real threat, and they'll strike when you least expect it." He nodded emphatically.

Toby mimicked his nod, holding his avid gaze. "I believe you. They're very much a threat." The only menace here was this fratbro's puny mental prowess.

The dude studied him a second longer, and then he gave Toby his beer back, expression settling into satisfied lines. He'd made his point. "Yep. A *real* threat. But don't worry," he added *sotto voce*. "We've got a plan for, like, thwarting them."

Toby grasped his nearly full beer, tugging to make sure fratbro would actually let him have it. The guy's grip loosened, and Toby stood up. "Well, time to find another one."

Maybe-Danny frowned. "Your bottle's almost full."

"Yeah . . ." Toby shifted his eyes around, casing the joint, then leaned forward to stage-whisper, "I'm stockpiling in case of a terrorist attack."

"*Duuuuude.*" Danny's brows flew up his forehead. "Smart move, man." He pointed his index finger at Toby, thumb cocked like a pistol, and "shot" him, winking at the same time.

Apparently he approved. Toby smiled in farewell and carefully backed away.

Somewhat to his astonishment, he outdrank and outlasted every one of the fratbros. He was lying on the couch, concentrating on being one with gravity and not flying around the room along with the wildly revolving walls, when Brad appeared, carrying something. Toby closed one eye to better focus on him, and the blurry image resolved into a walking smirk holding some fabric and what looked like a large bowl.

"'Zat?" Toby asked.

Brad lifted the bowl. "This is for you to puke into." He bent over and set it next to Toby's head.

"Though'ful of ya."

Brad straightened up and shook out the fabric. "This is a blanket so you don't get cold." He snapped it out and let it settle over Toby, drifting down on him, sheltering his alcohol-sodden form.

"'M I sleeping here?"

Brad nodded. "Or passing out."

Toby sighed. Then hiccuped. "The service here's excellen'. Have to remember this place."

Chapter 3

One nice thing about not being young and eternally horny (as opposed to youngish and horny most of the time, as Toby found himself at the ripe old age of twenty-four) was that he'd become more discerning. He might have decided to not pursue a guy like Jock because he'd been bailed on like that, but sometime in the middle of his morning-after shower at Brad and Sebastian's place, Toby's backup sexual response system kicked in—the Libidinous Mistake Detection Network.

Usually it warned him (too late) when he'd slept with a guy he probably shouldn't have, but it had moments of real usefulness, such as now, when it was telling Toby that Jock was worth another attempt. The kid was skittish, understandably, but Toby would swear he was attracted. Something else might have scared him off last night. Initiating further contact might be worth the attempt.

At least that's what he thought until he walked into Brad and Sebastian's kitchen, wearing only the pair of sweats he'd had in his backpack, hair still dripping, and noticed the computer sitting abandoned on the table. The chair in front caught his attention, pushed back and askew, giving the impression that whoever had been sitting there had gotten up and left in a rush. So of course he looked to see what had made Brad or Sebastian go flying off.

Shock jolted him when he met Jock's eyes on the screen over a stranger's condom-wrapped dick. The image filled up Toby's entire field of vision, interrupting the feed from his other senses. But when the rush of heat that had slammed into him started to subside, other stimuli started to filter in. He could smell the coffee anew, and soak in the coolness of the linoleum under his feet. And sounds drifted in from the living room. Footsteps.

Brad walked into the kitchen as Toby was still staring at the image of Jock, trying to puzzle things out. He stopped short, pale and frowning mad.

Toby lifted his hands up, palm out. "I didn't mean to. It was there and I came in—"

"S'okay," Brad sighed, running a hand over his head. "Just fucking sucks."

All of a sudden the picture didn't look so hot. It looked like a good way to out someone. And the knot in Toby's stomach just knew that's what had happened. If someone had sent it to some people, like a guy's coach? *Oh no.* His heart plummeted in his chest, felled by the tragedy that was Jock getting outed. *Poor kid.* "*This* is how he got outed? Where did you get it?" And why was Brad looking at it?

"Someone sent it to everyone in the frat. Probably the same someone who put copies of it all over the locker room at Avalon College."

Toby blew out a breath, a lump in his stomach settling into his gut. "That's horrible."

"Yeah," Brad muttered. He headed over to put the screen to sleep, then toward the counter where he picked up a cell phone and texted someone.

"What are you doing?" Toby couldn't imagine Brad would do something like spread this further.

"I'm getting ahold of Ashley. She'll be able to find out faster than anyone if other people were sent the picture. At least, she'll be able to do it without exposing him further."

Toby nodded, still staring at him. "She's a very useful female."

Brad rolled his eyes, then his phone buzzed in his hand. Ashley answering, Toby assumed. More texting ensued, and Toby stood there watching for long minutes, heart aching for Jock all out of proportion for how well he knew the guy. But it was tragic. Any gay guy would empathize, right? How good had the kid been at hockey? Toby didn't know, but somehow he had the impression Jock was really good. Like, professional career potential good. And now his whole world had been ruined by one stupid mistake. One time letting a guy he trusted—it had to have been a boyfriend, right?—take a picture.

"What can I do?" he heard himself asking.

Brad looked up at him, eyes wide. "Huh?"

"Can I do anything to help?"

"Um." Brad scrunched up his brow. "Be his friend?"

Toby waited for more.

"That's all I've got." Brad frowned, then went back to his texting.

After a few more minutes of being ignored (admittedly for a good cause), Toby drifted out of the room to find his pack again. He dug out the shirt he kept for emergency gym trips (but that never got used except as emergency post-shower-at-some-guy's-house clothes), threw his dirty garments in, said good-bye to a distracted Brad, and left.

Chapter 4

Jock had never been a black dude that Politically Correct White People pandered to, but when all the guys in the frat were sent the picture of him sucking that dude's dick, he suddenly got how it might feel.

It felt like being stifled under a ton of eager frat boy "sensitivity." It wasn't that he didn't appreciate the support, and all the guys swearing they'd keep it on the downlow, and telling him they really didn't care (even if he didn't believe them). It was that when Kyle had patted him on the back and said, "I just want you to know we're taking care of this," it made Jock's skin crawl where Kyle touched him, even through his sweatshirt.

"Taking care of *what*?"

Kyle screwed up his face. "Of making sure nobody in the frat leaks that picture. You don't need the whole world seeing it."

Jock stared at him, trying to figure if Kyle was that naive, or if he was that cynical. He nodded, finally, once he figured it was Kyle's problem. Because that image was like a guillotine blade hanging over him, about to slice through his neck. It was only a matter of time before he lost his head. Under other circumstances, he might've been touched by the way his frat brothers thought they could protect him. Now, though, he was irritated to the point of being pissed off at them. None of them blamed him for it. They all thought he was a *victim*.

How would they all feel if they knew how that shit really went down? Because seriously, he'd put himself in that position, and let that guy take the picture—did they think he hadn't noticed the phone in the dude's hand? Or the flash going off?

It was all right, though, because Jock spent most of the afternoon in Brad's spare bedroom, blaming himself.

Too bad that when he'd escaped to Brad and Sebastian's, Tank had insisted on coming with him for support. Every sympathetic, protective thing Tank said got all over Jock's last nerve, and he had to grind his teeth to keep from biting his brother's head off. As soon as Brad showed Jock the extra bed, saying, "Just chill out, dude. You need it," Jock had responded by shutting the door on them. He'd apologize for being rude later. He was too fucking exhausted to deal now.

Judging by the way the sun was coming in the windows, it was late afternoon when he decided he couldn't avoid everyone forever. May as well face the shit he'd created. Shoving himself out of his hidey-hole, he found Brad alone in the kitchen.

"Hey," he said to the dude's back.

Brad was standing at the counter, doing something to vegetables, but he looked over his shoulder and smiled. "Want something to drink?"

Jock shrugged and balanced on one foot to rub his instep with his big toe. He didn't know *what* he wanted.

"I can make coffee."

Jock squinted. "It's, like, late, right?"

Brad indicated the microwave clock with a tilt of his head. *4:26.*

"Nah. I don't even like it anyway," he admitted a second later.

"You want a beer?" Brad asked, wiping his hands on the dish towel he'd tucked into his waistband, then dropping it on the counter. "Sit down and I'll get you one."

"Okay." Why did everyone think beer made things better? *Whatever.* For now, he made his way over to the kitchen table, half-sliding—sock skating—on the slick floor. "Where's everyone else?" Like his brother?

"Sebastian went to the library to work, and Penny called and convinced Tank to go do something with her."

"She did?"

"I might've talked to Ashley and got her to tell Penny to distract your brother." Brad snapped a bottle cap into the garbage can, giving a fist pump when he scored a basket.

"Thank fuck," Jock sighed, pulling out a kitchen chair. "How did you know I didn't want him here?"

Brad snorted and set a beer in front of Jock's place, then sat himself down with another. "'Cause you wince every time he opens his mouth."

Jock winced. "Shit. Is he pissed?"

"He hasn't noticed. He still thinks you need him. I had to work pretty hard to convince him you were okay here with just little old me, even *with* Penny offering him fuck all to get him to leave."

"Thank you. Shit. Seriously, *thank you*."

"He's really getting to you."

"Everyone is. I mean, not you, I dunno why." Jock took a long swallow of his beer to shut himself up, forgetting it kinda nauseated him now. He couldn't help the face he made in reaction.

"You want something else?" Brad asked.

"No." Jock picked at the label on his bottle. "I drank a lot of beer that night. When I hooked up with that guy in the picture." He yanked the corner too hard, and a strip of paper tore off. He kept mutilating it, peeking to see Brad bunching his brows up and watching Jock's hands.

"So that's how that guy got the picture? You were wasted."

Jock's throat closed up, so he nodded, swallowing to try to move the blockage. This was his chance to tell someone what really happened, and he was going to fucking do it, even if his heart *was* climbing up his trachea with a grappling hook. But when he tried to take a breath for the words, he choked on it, falling into a hacking fit.

Brad leaned toward him, elbows on the table. "Dude, you don't have to tell me about it. Let's talk about something else," he said over Jock's racket.

Jock coughed once more before he could croak, "Okay."

Brad nodded and looked at him expectantly.

Jock took another chug of his beer and nearly hacked that up too, eyes watering.

"Or you could veg in front of the TV, or something else."

"I wanna talk," he said quickly, swiping at his eyes. "Tell me what you didn't last night at the party. About being with another guy." He took another swallow of beer, forcing himself not to react, nervous about bringing up the subject, but Brad half smiled at him. Then he stood up and started talking.

"Sebastian was the first guy I hooked up with," he said, reaching up to open a cupboard door.

"He *was*?" When did this other guy show up then?

Brad pulled out a wineglass. "After the first couple of times Sebastian and I hooked up, Collin jumped me in the shower."

"*Collin*?" Jock started to take a reflexive—or maybe emphatic?—drink of beer, but then his stomach objected so he set it down. Shit, he'd already drunk three-quarters of it.

Brad smiled with nostalgia or something. "Yeah." He slid a half-full bottle of wine out from behind the toaster, pulling out the cork. "He sucked me off. I didn't even really want him to, but, you know."

Oh yeah, he knew. "He had his mouth on your dick."

"That." Brad nodded, bringing the glass of red he'd poured to the table and placing it in front of Jock.

"Um, wine?"

Brad shrugged as he sat back down. "Hey man, you're gay. You're totally allowed to like wine and think beer sucks. Maybe I'll even make a quiche for breakfast in the morning and you can enjoy that, too."

"Guess there're benefits," Jock muttered. "So, um, about Collin, does Sebastian know?" He had to, right? Brad wouldn't tell him if his boyfriend didn't know, would he?

"Yep." Brad drained his beer, then grabbed ahold of Jock's. "We weren't, like, exclusive then, so he was okay with it." He grinned, but to himself. "At the time." As much as he'd seemed willing to say already, Jock still got the feeling he shouldn't ask. Too personal. Talk about sex? Whatever. Relationships? Not without an explicit invitation.

And shit, the wine was pretty good. Jock had had it at family dinners and stuff, but he'd never really *tasted* it, he guessed. Or something. He took another swallow, and as it went down he could feel it warming him up. Not like whiskey or liquor—because of course he'd tried that stuff; it was more mellow. It made the lights in the kitchen buttery and the darkening sky outside the windows seem serene. *Silent Night*–ish. Man, if he could think poetic shit like that after two swallows of wine and three-quarters of a beer . . . had he eaten today?

"Listen dude." Brad startled Jock. "Like, uh . . ." He scratched behind his ear a second. "Okay, thing is, everything I know about having sex with guys? I learned from a guy I was having sex *with*."

Jock nodded, half-afraid this would go where he hoped it would, and half-afraid it wouldn't.

Brad lifted up his palm. "Which was cool, don't get me wrong."

Jock shook his head and held his breath.

"But, you know, it might have been nice if there was someone else I could ask about, uh . . . everything the porn on the internet doesn't teach you."

Jock gulped some wine. "Does it hurt?" he spit out.

Brad twisted up his lips, like he was trying not to smile. "Only if you want it to."

Huh?

"I mean no, not if you're with the right guy, and he takes his time and knows what he's doing."

"Um, so, if you're the guy who's doing the doing? Like, how do you know you're doing it right?"

Brad straightened out his expression, then stood up and got the half-full wine bottle, plunking it down between them. "'Kay, here's the thing, I'm a total bottom." He fell into his chair and took a drink of the beer formerly known as Jock's.

Jock poured himself more wine. "Um, I kinda thought so."

"Yeah?" Brad lifted his brows. "Good. So you haven't done that, right? Fucked anyone."

"No." He swallowed, turning his glass by the stem. "I haven't, you know, been on the receiving end either. Just, uh, blowjobs and stuff."

"I figured. Okay, so, I'm gonna get kinda technical, I guess. Clinical. You can handle that?"

Jock nodded, carefully watching his fingers. He had a lot of scars on his knuckles. More than a guy holding a wineglass should have.

"I don't have to tell you to wear a condom, I guess."

Jock smiled over that for the first time in ever. "Yeah, there's pictorial evidence that I know better than to go without a condom."

And then Brad launched into a sometimes gross but totally fascinating description of everything that needed to happen, could happen, and should happen—"If it doesn't feel good to either of you, stop"—when guys fucked. Jock gave up being kinda embarrassed about it when Brad explained what could happen if the bottom wasn't really clean, because shit, the only thing more horrifying would be watching a baby being born.

"My friend Max says it sucks. Bottoming," he said once Brad had imparted all his technical knowledge. Max had also offered to prove it to Jock, but Jock had barely been into the friends-with-occasional-benefits relationship he had with the guy. Max wasn't someone Jock would have hung out with if they hadn't figured out each other's secret sexual orientation.

Brad snort-laughed. "Not for everyone. Goes back to the knowing what you're doing thing." The front legs of his chair thumped to the floor. "Or maybe it's about being with the right guy."

"The right guy."

Brad tilted his head and raised a brow. "Going home with Sebastian my first time wasn't an accident."

"You picked him."

"Fuck yeah. He's hot." Brad glared.

So disagreeing would be a bad idea. "Intellectual guys make me itchy," Jock said.

Brad glared another second or two before melting into a smirk. "Toby'd scratch that for you."

"Yeah? I'd totally let him."

Brad nodded. "He knows what he's doing. Just make sure you know exactly what you want. Go with your gut."

Fuck. "My gut . . . um, doesn't want to . . . you know."

"Your gut doesn't want to take it up the ass?"

Jock choked on the wine he'd been—nervously—sipping.

"Hey," Brad said, snorting. "Don't get all delicate and shit on me."

"Sorry," Jock wheezed.

Brad picked up his beer bottle, then set it down again. Then he did it again. He was making a design with the condensation rings, Jock realized. He did it for a while, until it looked like he'd been drawing in water with a Spirograph, before finally asking, "Why are you afraid to bottom?"

Jock thought about disputing the "afraid" thing, but they'd both know that was bullshit. Now he just had to decide whether to give the real reason. That took more thought than Brad was willing to wait through.

"There are ways to prepare to make sure it doesn't hurt."

"No." Jock shook his head, the idea of admitting fear of pain more upsetting than the real reason. "It's, like, um . . . Idon'twannabethegirl."

Brad blinked at him a few times, screwing up his face, then mouthed the words before repeating them. "You don't wanna be the girl."

Jock chugged what was left in his wine glass, which wasn't nearly enough. He grabbed the bottle, yanking out the cork.

"You don't want to be the girl?" Brad asked, jabbing his finger into midair, like he needed to point out the words as he said them.

Jock swallowed. "Yeah," he croaked, bottle poised to pour, but not quite at that tipping point—waiting with bated tannins to see how mad Brad would be.

His mentor shrugged, tilting his chair back again and crossing his arms over his chest, setting his jaw. "I don't think it's an uncommon fear, dude."

Jock poured wine all over the table. "I thought you'd be pissed," he said, unable to do more than watch while Brad snagged a dish towel from the counter behind him and sopped up all the burgundy liquid.

"Maybe, if I thought that being a bottom made me a *girl*, I would be." The way he growled that out, Jock didn't think he was entirely *un*offended.

Jock shot up, grabbing the towel and dropping to the floor to get the puddle that had dripped onto it. "I don't think you're a girl. Look at you, man."

"Yeah, look at me." Brad huffed. "I'm a guy who lets my boyfriend fuck me. *However* he wants, *whenever* he wants."

Jock peeked from under the table to see Brad glaring at him, arms crossed over his chest, and considered his options. It wasn't like he couldn't take Brad. It was that he didn't want to. "I'm sorry."

Brad sighed, falling back into his chair. "It's okay." He ran his hand through his hair a couple of times. "You gotta work out your issues with being femme or passive or whatever it is yourself, but I'll tell you one thing—no one bottoms *all* the time." He ran his hand across his face before correcting himself in a mutter. "Well, almost no one."

"Okay." Jock stood up, because kneeling at Brad's feet—even if it was to clean up the mess he'd made—was too weird. At least, while they were discussing this it was.

Brad flicked his eyes, looking quickly over to his side as if throwing away what Jock had said. It reminded him of when girls flipped their hair.

Dude, seriously, stop comparing Brad to chicks.

"And how much a guy flames isn't a reliable indicator of whether he's a bottom or a top, plus a lot of guys are versatile." Jock must have looked as stupid as he felt then, because Brad added. "It means they'll do either, depending on the circumstances."

"Oh." Well, that was . . . informative.

"So, if you don't want to bottom because it emasculates you or something, what does that say about the guy you're fucking?"

"Uh . . ." Jock wiped up some residual moisture from his wine with the toe of his sock. "I dunno."

"'Cause if that makes the dude you're with the 'girl' and that's cool with you, the fuck are you doing with a guy anyway? Go be het—tell 'em it was all a stupid drunken mistake. Rohypnol, I don't know. But being straight would make a lot of your troubles go away."

"It's not that simple, man." He nearly kicked the table leg, but not only did Brad have a bunch of good points, it would hurt his toes.

Brad shrugged, or at least Jock saw his shoulders jog in his peripheral vision. He couldn't quite look right at the guy. Hopefully Brad would shut up now and stop making Jock feel like a douche bag, but he had more to say. "No, it's not that easy. It's something you better think about, though."

"Duh," Jock muttered, then dropped into his chair again, slouching down.

"Yeah, so, anyway, Toby's versatile."

Jock jerked upright and met Brad's eyes. "Yeah?"

Brad smirked, raising his brows.

Jock shook his head, standing up for some reason. To pace, maybe? "Um." He shoved his hands into his pockets, yanking his waistband down too far, so he had to hike his sweats up before asking, "If I wanna, you know, top, do I have to tell him that up front?"

Brad looked at him levelly. "You gotta make sure he knows somehow, before things get *really* awkward."

"Shit," Jock muttered. How did he do that? "Probably won't see him again anyway." Maybe it was better, because if he saw Toby again and the dude still had that effect on him, how long would it be before he'd be offering up his virgin ass or trying to explain he wasn't going to? But if he did see Toby again . . . if they had a one-night hookup, maybe he could work it out so he didn't even have to field the "bottoming" question.

Brad tipped his chin. "Don't be so sure about that. Next time we have a party or something, you'll bump into him."

"What are you, my pimp?" As a joke it was kinda weak, but thank fuck it made things a little less awkward.

Brad grinned. "Just consider me your ass broker." Then he got serious again. "You know, once that picture hits Tumblr or wherever, you'll have more offers than you can take on."

Jock sighed, slumping against the counter. Thank fuck he wasn't the only one who realized it was inevitable. "Yeah, well, I guess I'd like to get a little more experience under my belt before that happens."

"I feel you, man." Brad nodded.

"Brad?"

"Yeah?"

"Thanks. I mean, really. Thank you."

ΘΑΓ

The frat brothers adjusted pretty fast to the trauma of seeing Jock in flagrante delicto. Actually, they barely seemed to notice, because right after the picture was sent to all the guys, they found out who'd set the frat house on fire and then tried to bomb it, and it had nothing to do with anyone being gay. Collin had ended up in the middle of it somehow, and Jock could totally understand why Collin wanted to stay at his boyfriend's house every night instead of coming back to the frat-dorm. Dude needed to get away from it all.

Besides, he was getting used to having a room to himself. He was even getting over his itchiness around the guys, and he'd stopped grinding his teeth whenever Tank spoke to him. He only did it about half the time now.

After a few weeks of nothing cropping up, he even started to think—*maybe*—that the asshole he'd blown that night would be happy with the damage he'd already inflicted. Maybe Jock could conduct his life in some kind of privacy now.

It took some thinking, but after a while Jock twigged to the fact that if he met a guy—Toby, say—at that gay bar Brad had mentioned, the Slaughterhouse, none of his frat brothers would ever know. Did Toby go to that bar? He might need to ask Brad about that also.

Because if he was going to go for it, he might as well with a guy who knew what he was doing.

Plus, he couldn't get Toby out of his head.

Even taking a study break, lounging on a couch in the TAG common area one afternoon before midterms, pretending to be asleep, Jock's thoughts kept drifting toward the guy. Brad had picked Sebastian, he'd said, and if Jock was going to pick someone for his first time, he'd pick Toby.

"So, dude," Danny said loudly. "Jock, dude."

Shit. He'd been successfully ignoring the other guys in here with him. Danny and Gomer were on the couch across the rickety coffee table from Jock, while Turbo was alternating between propping his hip on the back or leaning over it, getting in their faces. Ricky still had his wheelchair, and he was still trying to do fancy tricks with it that mostly involved popping some kind of wheelie.

"Dude, you awake?" Danny asked.

Fuck. "Yeah?" Jock asked, shoving himself up to sitting.

"You wanna go to Provence with us next term? Only a couple more weeks to register."

Jock was still trying to decide how to say "no" for the most effect when Danny went on.

"Yeah, dude, it's gonna be cool. I'm working on some, like, drills and exercises we can do. Really pull the BTRT together, make us a unit. You'd be a great addition to the team, man. We'd love to have you." Danny nodded earnestly, leaning over the coffee table.

"Uh, what's the BTRT?" Maybe he should've just gone and googled it.

"Oh, yeah, that's shorthand for Beer Terrorist Response Team. I just try not to say it too often 'cause some of the guys're kinda, you know, opposed to the idea of it. Kyle says if we don't drop it, he's going to push through a resolution to make the formation of militias against TAG rules." Danny screwed up his face. "I don't know how he thinks that's gonna stop us—we're not a militia, we're just a bunch of guys who want to join together into a small fighting unit in case any serious shit goes down. Mark my words, dude, someday the frat's going to thank us."

"Uh-huh." Had his eyes glazed over? He was pretty sure his brain had.

"So, you gonna think about it? Coming to France? Joining the team?"

"Oh, sorry Danny. I gotta stick around here next term. You know, settle in a little. I can't . . ." Jock ran a hand across his face, trying to think up a real reason.

"Can't what?" Noah asked, sitting next to him. He was the one dude who Jock felt like he could be really friendly with, once he'd negotiated past the not wanting to get anything going with another TAG guy thing.

"I can't spend spring term in France."

"You don't wanna go? If it looks like they'll find a decent place to stay," Noah said, nodding at the guys across from them. "I'm gonna think about it."

"Been there," Jock said, shrugging. He'd been with his family and with a touring hockey team in high school.

"You don't like it?"

"What? No, I like it, but I'm not burning up to see it again."

Noah opened his mouth to say something else, but the elevator opened just then and Julian spilled out, reeling like he'd been drinking. He stumbled into the middle of the common area, the whites of his eyes flashing. "It's over," he croaked, then he sank down onto the threadbare throw rug someone had put on the floor.

Noah's face screwed up in confusion, and the three frat boys across from them sat stock still, thumbs poised over their phones.

"Huh?" Jock asked. No one else looked like they were going to further the conversation.

Jules's hand flew up into the air, flailing in counterpart with his words. "Stacy dumped me!" He dropped his arm, resting the back of his wrist on his forehead and exhaling a shuddering sigh.

"Drama queen," Noah said under his breath.

Not very illuminating. "Who's Stacy?"

"Keep up," Noah said before explaining. "Stacy's his 'girlfriend.'"

Jock was still trying to puzzle out the air quotes around "girlfriend"—maybe she was the inflatable kind—when Jules began wailing again. "Not anymore she's not!"

"Did she dump you because you're a freak who thinks one date makes her your girlfriend?" Turbo asked.

Jules shot upright, digging his fingers into the rug and yanking it into his fists. "It was *two* dates," he spat out.

"Still, might've been premature to call it, dude." Danny nodded sagely, then threw a quelling palm up. "Not that I'm judging you or anything, I mean, now that I have this sensitivity thing sorta figured out. I'm just saying, is all."

"Your sensitivity isn't helping," Jules moaned, flopping onto his back again. Jock winced when he heard the *thunk* of the guy's skull hitting the floor.

Danny stood and looked down at Jules. "So, what did she tell you? She gave you a reason for breaking up, right?"

Jules sniffed and laid the back of his hand over his forehead again, seeming to wilt.

"She said I'm—" Jules gulped, voice breaking when he continued. "I'm not *butch* enough!"

Ricky screwed up his face. "It took two dates before she saw *that*?"

"There's a quick fix," Danny announced, index fingers pressed to his lips and hands steepled under his chin. When Julian turned to him hopefully, Danny regarded him like a lab experiment, nodding slowly before intoning, "Come to France."

Jules wrinkled up his whole face. "What? *France*? Why?"

Danny nodded. "For spring term. If you learn to speak French—if you *soak in* the Frenchness of it all—she'll be begging for you to come back."

Jules's eyebrows began to lift, as if the shroud on his machismo were wafting away. "You think?"

Danny nodded, standing in front of him and pointing, drilling Jules into place with the strength of his finger. "You say *anything* to her in French, and who gives a flying fuck if you're butch? You can speak with an *accent*."

Jules gasped in wonder, like he was buying this line of bull. Jock rolled his eyes along with his head to look sideways at Noah, whose lips were pressed together. Either trying not to laugh, or simply disgusted.

"An *accent*," Jules breathed.

"Oh, my, God," Noah whispered. "Yeah, I'm going to France. I *have* to see this go down."

"And there's our next team member, dudes," Danny announced, beaming at the guys on the couch.

Chapter 5

"Would you be able to meet us at the Slaughterhouse tomorrow night for a drink?" Sebastian's voice asked as soon as Toby answered his phone.

Usually, when his friends did something as a group, either Brad or Collin instigated it, or it happened accidentally. Arranging social outings had never been Sebastian's thing before, and the fact that was doing so now put all of Toby's instincts on alert.

"Unless you're too busy with your research, of course," Sebastian continued when Toby didn't answer.

Toby's fingers tightened on his cell until it creaked in protest. "Oh, I've made quite a bit of progress, I could probably take a night off." From fretting about how much he hadn't done. Two thousand words was nothing, but it was all he'd managed so far, no matter how many hours he spent trying to motivate himself. Maybe he should use fewer alcoholic incentives.

Sebastian sighed into his ear in that annoying, knowing way he had, but he pretended to believe Toby. "Would you like me to take a look at it?"

"Um, maybe when it's more polished," Toby prevaricated. Sebastian's silence expressed all the skepticism Toby'd been hoping he wouldn't. "So, a drink tomorrow night? Any particular reason?"

Everything changed in Sebastian's tone. "I've been busy lately. I want to reconnect with my friends."

"Oh, of course," Toby nodded at the phone, underscoring how much he thought Sebastian was lying. "What time should I be at the Slaughterhouse?"

"About eight," Sebastian said, then Brad's voice in the background filtered through the line. When Sebastian started speaking again, his tone had changed right back to his typically irreverent one. "Brad's asked me to inform you that Jock will be there."

"Will he now?" Toby smiled. He would have agreed to meet his friends anyway, just to figure out what was up with Sebastian's uncharacteristic behavior (and, yes, avoid his thesis), but add in Jock and he was *so* there. He'd been waiting for this opportunity. After finding out the sordid details of Jock's outing, Toby had decided he should back off. The guy needed time. He just had to trust an opportunity would arise.

And looky here! An opportunity. One might even call it an invitation.

So, yeah. He'd be there with bells on his nipples and condoms in his pocket.

But before then, there was the small matter of emailing his advisor, Louise, and letting her know that due to difficulties with his research . . . or maybe a dead laptop? But she'd just suggest he should go to a campus computer lab. No, definitely blame difficulties with his primary source research for the missing partial rough draft of his thesis. She'd cut him some slack, and really, she might appreciate not having one more thing to look at during midterm week.

Suuuure she will.

Maybe after some quality time with Jock, he'd actually get inspired to write up a killer draft.

Toby wasn't surprised when he arrived at the Slaughterhouse Sunday night, took one look at Brad, and immediately saw evidence of a significant relationship event occurring between him and Sebastian. A chain encircled his neck, a small lock holding it together at the base of his throat. Sebastian was wearing a similar chain, although longer and mostly hidden under his shirt.

Well now, wasn't that interesting? It would be gauche—and less fun—to ask outright. Toby'd have to approach this in a more roundabout way.

For the time being, he greeted Collin—who was boyfriend-free; it turned out Eric had to work tonight—Paul and Trevor, and finally Brad.

"Where's your friend?" he asked Brad. No point in pretending he wasn't there to see Jock.

Brad pursed his lips like he was trying not to smile. "He'll show up later."

Toby nodded and went to get himself a beer. Since the first order of business was on hold, he'd spend some time investigating developments. He began by standing next to Sebastian and eyeing the dude's necklace, not hiding his scrutiny from his friend. Sebastian smirked in that special way he had, one brow arched, as if daring Toby to try to make him give up his secrets.

After many seconds of silence and drink-sipping, Toby lobbed the first volley. "I see you and Brad have both taken a sudden liking to jewelry." It was a minor feint, sort of like the USS *Enterprise* sending a probe into a gas giant.

Sebastian tipped his chin once in acknowledgment.

Definitely worth more scientific inquiry. "It's strange, but other than the fact that Brad's necklace has much larger links, yours looks almost like the one he's wearing."

Sebastian took a leisurely sip of his drink, then set it on the bar. "I gave Brad that chain."

"Oh. And he gave you a matching one I suppose?"

"Why yes, he did." Sebastian smirked more broadly, idly scanning the bar—a certain sign of obfuscation.

Toby tilted his head to one side—the equivalent of touching épées and shouting "touché" between them. "Brad's is much shorter than yours, it seems. Almost like a choker . . . or perhaps a collar."

Sebastian stuffed his hands into his pockets, rocking back on his heels, eyebrows flying high.

Mm-hmm. "The lock that holds his closed reinforces a certain impression one might get from a chain like that."

"Oh? And what impression would that be?"

Gotcha. "The impression that he's your boy."

Sebastian sidestepped closer to Brad, resting a palm on his boyfriend's back downright possessively. When Brad turned, Sebastian smiled at him in what had to be the sappiest manner Toby had ever seen on the dude's face. Which wasn't very sappy, since it was Sebastian, but by the same token—it was *Sebastian.* "Well, he is my frat boy after all."

"Yep, I am," Brad agreed, then they stood there a few seconds, looking at each other in that way that Toby found both fascinating and a little repulsive. He just didn't *get* it. Or rather, he'd never had it with anyone. Which suddenly seemed like a gaping loss in his stomach, but how could he miss something he'd never had?

Because they have it.

Finally, their special moment ended, and Sebastian returned some of his attention to Toby.

"I take it this means you're in it for the long haul," Toby said. He was happy for them, really. So happy his diaphragm felt weak and overworked.

Sebastian smiled just as smugly as he had been all evening, as if he alone knew the secrets to both eternal life and the preferred lube of the Sacred Band of Thebes. "My relationship with Brad? That's exactly what it means. We're permanent."

And then—God help him—Toby realized he'd been wrong about the special moment being over when Brad nuzzled against the side of Sebastian's head, saying something in his ear that made Sebastian's eyes sharpen or brighten or possibly crystallize. They changed somehow, in some way that men who *weren't* in love couldn't find adequate words for. But Toby didn't have more than a couple of seconds to even try, because Sebastian dragged his boyfriend closer, so that all Toby could see of them was Brad's back and Sebastian's fist in his hair.

Why the hell did Sebastian invite us here for a drink if he's just going to mack on his boyfriend all night?

Duh. To show off their matching neckwear.

Yep, he was happy for them. Sure, he'd own to feeling a tiny bit excluded, but that's what happened with people. They began to pair off. Toby's sense of not quite measuring up was natural, and nothing a few minutes of talking to Paul— Scratch that, Paul and Trevor were walking across the bar, making their way to the door, Trevor's hand half on Paul's back and half on his ass, while he looked down into Paul's face and beamed at whatever he was saying.

At least Collin had come without his man tonight. Toby turned toward the barstool Collin had been sitting on to find him still there, texting into his phone, smiling softly. Toby recognized the expression, because it was exactly the same one Toby had just seen on all his other—coupled-up—friends' faces. The glow that wasn't all light reflecting off Collin's screen.

He needed another drink. Or to leave.

"'Scuse me," someone said, bumping into him from behind. Toby didn't have to turn to see who it was, because some sort of heated electrical message leapt from that body to his when they touched, even through clothing. *Jock*. They still had that crazy lust connection, even weeks later. It buzzed along between them like high-tension power lines. He nearly gave into his urge to lean back into the hard body behind his.

He turned around before giving in to the temptation. "Hey there," he said through his most charming smile, the one with that special glint in his eye and just enough tooth to be welcoming but not predatory.

But when he really focused on Jock, the image he'd been trying *not* to conjure up, oh, all the time flashed across his mind: the one of Jock on his knees, sucking off some other guy, staring up into the camera. Even while it stirred some interest in Toby's loinal region, it made him queasy. That image was so wrong, on so many levels. And he'd cut off his right arm to be the one to have taken it, which was like a whole heaping pile of smelly, steaming wrongsauce on top of utter rottenness.

He needed to rethink taking Jock home with him. Whether Jock thought so or not, he was vulnerable. Plus Toby wanted to take his time with Jock. Get to know him better. An urge he'd only fully recognized now that he'd seen the guy again.

"Dance with me," Jock said, eyes faltering and almost dropping Toby's gaze. At the last second he found some courage and continued to look down at him.

Toby stalled. He couldn't just flat out turn Jock down, but by getting to know him better, Toby'd been thinking on a personal level, not a physical one. Dancing—especially gay club dancing—was entirely about the physical. "You dance? You don't seem the type."

Jock smiled, dimples poking his cheeks. "I can only do it when I'm drinking."

"I see." Toby nodded and leaned closer, until he could smell the alcohol on Jock's breath, blended with one of those cleanish, bracing scents laced with a subtle thread of sex that the athletic boys always seemed to like. Shampoo or body wash? *Mmm, body wash*. He'd love to help Jock apply that. Someday in the future. "And how did you get served here?"

"Fake ID," Jock said shortly, shrugging one shoulder, cheeks darkening.

"You're one of those polite, well-mannered boys, aren't you?" Toby could feel his grin growing. He shouldn't tease like this, but it was too tempting to fluster Jock further, see if he could make more color bloom on his skin.

"What d'ya mean?" Jock scowled at him. Angry confusion, brows lowered.

"You're the kind of guy who feels guilty for having a fake ID, aren't you? Let me guess—because your daddy taught you not to lie?"

Jock's scowl drifted away, replaced by a pouty lower lip. "My mom. She taught me table manners too," he confessed. "I always know which fork to use."

"My mom too," Toby said. It was a simple thing, but it led to a *moment*. Not a Brad-and-Sebastian-in-love kind of moment, but a few seconds of staring into each other's eyes, caught up in recognizing they had some kind of serious link between them. Not just the connection of two guys who happened to like their mothers, but lust and extreme interest and something else he couldn't put his finger on. *So intense.* He cleared his throat. "I'm not sure it took, though." Total lie—he could balance peas on the tines of his fork with the most haughty European. He glanced away a second and tried to take the conversation back to flirty banter. Or something. "This place is kinda lively tonight."

"Well, yeah." Jock shrugged one shoulder. "End of the term's coming up."

"Are you ready for finals, then?"

"Pretty much." He nodded. "How about you? Is it worse as a grad student?"

"I'm not taking any classes right now, just working on my thesis." *Or not.*

"You don't have to teach classes?"

Toby gestured with his pint glass, preparing to explain. "Different schools have different programs. Calapooya doesn't let you teach any undergrad sections unless you're in your final year of your master's, but I taught more than my load the first two terms, so I don't have to teach any this term. Some schools expect you to teach the minute you start, and a few don't let you teach any, you just get to be an aide or whatever. That's what Sebastian was doing for Brad's ancient history series."

He'd thought he was giving Jock a small tidbit of information, but it turned out the guy didn't know as much as Toby'd assumed. "That's how they met?" Jock asked. "Huh. Hot for teacher?" He smirked.

"Something like that." Toby smiled, wondering how incendiary it would have been if he'd met Jock that way.

"So . . ." Jock cleared his throat, then said something that Toby didn't catch over the sudden blast of music. It must be nine—that's when the Slaughterhouse cranked up the techno. One thing about living in a smallish town, the local gay bars had to cater to multiple groups.

Toby leaned forward, back into Jock's personal space. "What did you say?"

"Do you normally wear glasses?" Jock said in his ear, breath brushing Toby's neck. *Shiver.*

Then the question registered. Great, the thick frames made him look dorky, didn't they? Damn his weakness for fashion. "I just started again. I've always had bad vision, but my eyes haven't been tolerating the contact lenses lately, so . . ." He shrugged, but it had to have been obvious he'd forced it.

"I like them." Jock smiled down at him, ducking his chin after a second. "You make a really hot hipster."

Toby came uncomfortably close to fanning himself. "Thanks." God, couldn't he do better than that? "If I don't dance with you, what will you do?"

Yeah. Flirty banter fail.

Jock jerked back, deflating the cozy bubble they'd created. "If you don't want to dance with me, just say no," he said quickly, then his Adam's apple bobbed. "So you heard about it, huh? The picture."

Saw it. "Yeah." Toby's brain scrambled, trying to regain its footing and fix what his nerves—nerves? Seriously?—had ruined.

Jock nodded, breathing deeply through flaring nostrils—it was audible over the music. "I get it," he said, starting to turn away.

Which was when Toby got it. "No." He grabbed Jock's forearm, squeezing into the hardness of his muscle. "I want to dance with you." *Really want to.* They could talk more later, right? Spend some time seeing if there was more between them than lust. Which there was, he believed, because they'd had that moment.

Jock didn't respond, just stood frozen, jaw set. Toby slid his fingers down the inside of Jock's arm, imagining they were tracing faint blue veins, until he reached Jock's hand, then gripped it. Tugging him toward the dance floor. Not pulling, because Toby'd fucked that up and Jock still needed to be able to refuse, regardless of who asked whom to dance. But after one nudge from Toby, Jock clasped their palms together and took the lead, dragging him along.

He didn't hesitate when they hit the linoleum tile that served as a dance floor, spinning Toby around and pressing against him, back to front. Toby started moving automatically, falling into the gravitational pull of Jock's body without thinking, while Jock matched his rhythm to Toby's, any hesitation or uncertainty Toby'd sensed before melting into the thump of the beat. He'd expected Jock to be more circumspect—the way the guy had jerked back from him at Sebastian's party, he'd gotten the impression that Jock wasn't used to any sort of public displays.

But it was crowded, and the Slaughterhouse played techno dance stuff nonstop during "club" hours, assuming their college student clientele didn't want anything else. They *had* to be this close together, or the other gyrating bodies would pull them apart.

The feel of Jock's groin in his back distracted him. Jock was hesitant, Toby could tune into that now. Not quite grinding them together, closer to intermittent rubbing. Ships kissing icebergs in the night. Toby raised his arms and slipped them around Jock's neck. If he didn't let his fingers run through Jock's hair, he'd be using them to grip Jock's hips and yank him flush against his ass, because, fuck, he could feel the guy getting hard, even with this unsustained contact.

He didn't know how long they danced. One song bled into another and he got lost in the movements and the slide of his clothes against Jock's, with the tantalizing hints of what was underneath. At least three songs played before he admitted to himself they were definitely hooking up. But that didn't mean they couldn't have more later. Why not start tonight with a bang? *Heh.*

So he gave in and let the night progress.

By the time Jock took his hand again and pulled him off the floor, he was soaking in sweat. The thought that a lot of what drenched him probably came from Jock himself gave Toby more than the usual thrill, leaving him grinning like an idiot, nearly laughing, and following thoughtlessly. He didn't come to his senses again until Jock halted suddenly in a pool of shadows a few feet from the exit.

Toby watched as Jock's back heaved with his breaths, trying to figure out what was going on. There was a breeze near the door, drifting into Toby's lungs and clearing out some of the fog that the thumping beat and the heat and scent of Jock had created in his senses. Toby stepped closer to Jock, running his other palm down his ribs. "Are we leaving?"

Jock turned to look at Toby questioningly, mouth moving like he wanted to answer but couldn't quite form words. His Adam's apple bobbed, and his grip on Toby's hand started to loosen. Toby didn't think, he reached up and cupped the back of Jock's neck, pulling himself up to take Jock's lips between his own and trace along them with the tip of his tongue. He found that little dip in the very center by feel, that pendulous part of Jock's upper lip that he'd been unconsciously certain would taste like candy. Gumdrops or jelly beans.

It tasted like sex. A little salty, just on that edge of gamey—the taste that one could never quite claim to like, but couldn't stop wanting. A little too close to the primitive for the modern man's comfort, but something he craved nonetheless. And Jock's tongue sliding along his *felt* like sex. Slick and muscular. Sweaty, musky sex with a porn-worthy soundtrack. *Oh fuck yeah.*

"Yeah," Jock agreed with the voice in Toby's head, even though Toby wasn't quite done kissing him. "We're leaving. It's gotta be your place, though, 'cause I can't take you back to the dorm with me."

Toby laughed, which ended his attempts to kiss Jock again. "My place. I'll drive."

Chapter 6

As soon as they left the bar, Toby leading the way to his parking spot, the cold air hit them. It was mild for February in Oregon, but not so mild they weren't shivering. He stopped and turned to Jock, glancing back at the bar. "Did you bring a jacket?"

Jock's hands were jammed in his jeans' pockets, and he was hugging his bare arms close to his torso like that could hold in his body heat. "No."

"I've got an extra hoodie in the car." He'd left stuff at too many bars over the years to bring them in anymore.

Jock nodded his clenched jaw but didn't make any comments about the likelihood of Toby's clothes fitting him. Was he nervous or cold?

Investigation was called for, so Toby pulled up a flirty grin. "I'm sure I've got something extra large for you."

A laugh burst out of Jock, complete with flashes of dimple.

Okay, even if he was nervous, he wasn't irredeemably so. Everything was still a go. Toby started toward his parking spot again. *Everyone has a first time.* But *was* it Jock's first time? Toby irrefutably knew that the guy had *some* experience; maybe he had more than the picture and his swings between confidence and uncertainty suggested. *Unless he's really good at Photoshop.*

Forget it. A guy his age would have had to have spent all his teenage years holed up in his bedroom learning graphics programs to be that good at it. And clearly Jock had been out of his bedroom, at least to spend some serious time in the gym. Besides, why mock up a picture like that of *himself*?

Maybe someone else is really good at Photoshop.

Get a grip.

"Um," Jock prodded him verbally, clearing his throat. "This is yours?"

The vehicle he was currently standing next to and staring at sightlessly? "Yeah, sorry. Thinking."

Jock was too big for Toby's hoodie *and* Toby's little car, which added a special air of awkwardness even before he started rapidly tapping his fingers on his knee. The five-minute drive stretched out endlessly, giving Toby even more time to think.

Why are you so nervous? It's not your *first time.*

Because, duh, his first time had sucked. Neither one of them had known what they were doing, and it'd hurt like hell. He hadn't bottomed again for months and months after that, convinced it sucked.

Chill. You've done this lots of times. He *had* been with an inordinate number of innocent guys. Wasn't that at least part of what attracted him to Jock? That and his intelligence, wit, and that air of hurt. He wanted to make sure this was good for Jock.

If it was even Jock's first time.

If he even wanted to fuck. Or bottom if they did fuck. Which Toby had totally been assuming, but Jock might be thinking other things altogether, which Toby could totally provide, and even *wanted* to provide. Was more in the mood to provide, really.

Jock yanked on the too-short sleeves of the sweatshirt Toby'd given him. Then he cleared his throat.

"Are you sure about this?" Toby asked. If he didn't start the conversation, this would get too weird to save. He knew himself too well to think he could bluff his way through, pretending it wasn't awkward.

Jock jerked. "Why wouldn't I be sure?"

Toby shrugged and concentrated on getting them the last few blocks, but after he'd parked in front of his building and shut off the car, he turned to the passenger seat instead of getting out. "Listen, um, you need to tell me . . ." He fiddled with the gearshift knob, trying to decide which way to approach this. Or waiting for Jock to pick up the thread.

Jock shifted his legs, hitting his knee against the underside of the dashboard.

You're the experienced one, dude. "What do you want? I mean, I was assuming you wanted to fuck—"

"I do."

Well, that was definite. "We should probably talk out a couple of things beforehand." He took a huge breath. "Like, is this your first time? I don't have to know—"

"Yeah," Jock croaked. "I've been with a couple of girls, but . . . I'm sure I want to be with you."

I want to be with you too. Toby leaned closer to him, settling his palm on the top of Jock's thigh. "Come inside with me. We'll work it out."

"Yeah." Jock met his eyes, and something pulsed between them, lighting and clearing out the cobwebbed corners of Toby's mind, where a few doubts about doing this were lingering. "Let's go."

Toby got lucky. In spite of not checking first—which he usually did when he brought guys home—his roommate wasn't around. Larry always tried to talk to the guys Toby was with, but the way he did it had the air of someone trying to communicate with a remote and undereducated tribe of savages, asking probing questions that he assumed they'd find inoffensive. Larry was working on his master's in social anthropology, and Toby had begun to suspect he was writing a thesis on the mating habits of The Geighs.

They shared an apartment in one of those old wooden rooming houses probably built by some young late-nineteenth-century widow to keep her solvent after the untimely death of her husband in a mining accident. There used to be many bedrooms and few kitchens or bathrooms, but at some later point someone had cobbled together spaces to create six apartments with bizarre layouts. The door to Toby's opened into the kitchen.

"Do you want something to drink?" he asked Jock, thinking of it mostly because he walked right in and immediately saw the fridge. It would help chill Jock out.

"Um, do you have any wine?"

"Wine? Yeah." He just needed to find it. Most of the gentlemen he entertained in his room didn't ask for wine. Well, Collin did sometimes, but he usually brought his own since he seemed to find what Toby had around inferior. "White or red?" Hopefully he either had some of each, or Jock would pick what he did have.

"Whatever."

Unzipping his hoodie, he walked over and began the ransacking of the cupboards, trying the one over the fridge first, where the wine was most likely to be. It wasn't that they might not have any; it was that Larry the Breeder always had some (because it made him suave, Toby supposed), but in that inconsiderate way he had he was forever storing it someplace new—almost like he was hiding it. It made it difficult for Toby to steal a glass or two on occasion.

It was when he'd moved on to the spice cupboard (another affectation of Larry's) that Toby realized Jock had come to stand right behind him. The subtle field his body generated interacted with Toby's and made it hard for him to concentrate on his search. "Sorry, this could take a minute," he murmured.

"S'okay," Jock said back, voice low. "We can talk about whatever else you wanted to talk about while you look."

"Oh." Not how he'd imagined this conversation going. For starters, he thought he'd have to initiate it. "I just needed to know, like, what you want. Like, do you want me to fu—"

"I want to fuck you."

Toby dropped the jar of oregano or weed or whatever he was holding on the counter. From behind him came the mysteriously sexy sound of unzipping. It lasted too long to be a fly, but Toby couldn't figure it out before Jock's hands had come around him, comically short sleeves of Toby's hoodie riding up his arms. Then Jock's chest pressed against his back, and Jock's voice fell on his neck. "Would you let me do that?"

Toby was in danger of thinking this whole thing had been a scam—Jock wasn't some innocent, uncertain boy—but then he felt Jock's Adam's apple brush his ear as he swallowed, and noticed Jock's white-knuckled fingers, gripping the counter to trap Toby's body. "I'd let you do that," he whispered, pushing his hips back into Jock's as Jock pressed into him, dick making itself hard and obvious. "Do you still want wine?" he asked as he reached up behind him, searching the back of Jock's neck for that seductive tickle of stubble on his palm. With his other hand he took off his glasses. He had a feeling they were about to get in the way.

Jock's lips moved on Toby's skin as he said, "No. I think you only have rosé anyway."

Opening his eyes—he'd closed them?—Toby realized the bottle was sitting right in front of him on the counter. "Looks like it, huh?"

"Yeah." Jock's breath started coming shorter as he rubbed what felt like a monster dick against Toby, widening his stance or somehow making himself just short enough to grind into the top of Toby's ass. "Where's your room?"

"Fuck." Toby shoved harder against Jock's groin. "Was your cock that big at the club?"

"'S far as I know," Jock said, curling one of his hands—which felt as surprisingly large as his prick did—around Toby's hipbone, digging his fingertips into the flesh of Toby's groin, centimeters from his dick. "Are we doing this here?"

"No. My room. Let's go."

In spite of the initiative Jock had taken in the kitchen, Toby still had some weird idea that he was conducting this excursion to the next stop on the sexploration train. But Jock took control immediately once they made it to Toby's room, pressing him up against the still-open door and slamming it shut at the same time. Toby managed to grab a handful of shirt before Jock's mouth was on his, forcing his lips open and thrusting inside. He had to fight to untangle his fingers from the fabric and catch up because his knuckles were pressing painfully into Jock's breastbone. Then he fought to breathe around the force of Jock's kiss and the way he stroked inside Toby's mouth, nearly to his throat, too overwhelming to taste, other than a hint of the wine Jock must have had earlier.

Gives great body check. Check.

He should have expected this kind of aggression, but he was unprepared for Jock's strength. Yeah, the guy was uncertain sometimes, but as soon as he got over it he took charge. Filled up all the space in Toby's head and senses, grinding his hard-on into Toby's stomach as he fought to get the hoodie off, then pulling Toby against him with an arm around his waist, fingers splayed wide on Toby's back, kissing him even harder. Could lips bruise? *Doesn't matter. Worth it.*

And the boy could really kiss, with those wet-dreamsicle lips wrapping Toby's and a tongue that might just rival his dick for girth. He was huge *everywhere*. Not just the size of his body and the physical intensity of him, but the way the lust flowed out of him, wrapping around them both. Jock manhandled him like he'd never experienced before.

So Toby let go of his expectations of the uncertain virgin, and took advantage of said virgin's size. He wrapped his arms around Jock's shoulders, and thighs around Jock's hips, climbing him, trying to break the kiss long enough to tell him *bed*. Jock gripped Toby's skull, not letting go of his mouth, shifting to palm his ass. Maybe to hold him up, but the way Jock's pinky curled around and pressed into the hard seam of Toby's jeans had him moaning. He could feel the echo in Jock's throat.

And then, thank *God*, Jock lurched, moving toward the bed, his hard cock bumping and sliding along Toby's while he stumbled across the room. Toby fisted Jock's hair, wrenching his head to a new angle to go deeper into his mouth, knocking them off course, but it was necessary to express how fucking transcendent it felt to touch like this. How much he'd been looking forward to it. Dying for it. And he had, hadn't he?

They definitely had more than lust to explore together, because in his experience, simple lust was *never* this satisfying.

Jock dropped him—or threw him—onto the mattress. Toby landed on his back, legs dangling off, arms wide, staring up at Jock, who stood at the foot of the bed staring at Toby dazedly, lips huge and wet and red. He'd look so much better—hotter—naked. Sitting up, Toby reached for Jock's fly, the small noise Jock made when Toby touched him sending more prickles across his skin.

Toby took his time, unsnapping and unzipping, watching the way Jock's abdomen jumped under his touch and listening to his ragged, stuttered breathing. When he left Jock's fly hanging open to reach under the hem of his shirt, a soft, disappointed "uh" escaped. But it was quickly superseded by hitching lungs when Toby trailed his fingers up Jock's stomach, tracing the grooves and hard angles, working up to the beautiful pectoral mounds. To trace the bottom curves of them, then palm the muscles, thumbs teasing Jock's nipples. He was rewarded with a groan.

Toby stood, forcing Jock back a step, fingers digging in so he wouldn't go too far. While Jock tried to help, Toby worked the T-shirt over his head. Then he bent forward to lick into the notch at the base of Jock's throat.

"Oh fuck," Jock murmured, twisting. At first Toby thought he was trying to step away, so he bit lightly in warning. He wasn't stopping *now*. Jock hissed and froze, then squirmed more. Trying to get the shirt Toby'd abandoned behind his neck down his arms. Nibbling his way down Jock's chest, he reached behind Jock and yanked it off, freeing Jock's hands just in time for him to grab Toby's head as Toby licked across his nipple. "Oh shit, that feels . . ."

"Good?" he asked, talking with his mouth full. It could be excused under the circumstances.

Jock grunted, hips jerking forward when Toby used his teeth.

Definitely more exciting than Toby's own first time with a guy. Jock's reactions amazed him. Made him feel like it was his first time, too. Whenever he introduced Jock to some new sensation, he could feel it flooding his own nerves, and his body's reactions mirrored Jock's. When he shoved his hand down Jock's jeans and into his briefs to knead his ass muscles, they both pushed forward, grinding into each other. When Toby wiggled his fingers between their bodies and traced the shape of Jock's dick the first time, Jock's groan shuddered in his own lungs. They both worked Jock's pants over his hips, Toby dropping onto the edge of the bed and Jock still standing, swaying in front of him, hopping on one leg and then the other, until he was almost naked.

Toby halted when confronted with plain white briefs bulging out at him, a wet spot spreading across it. He'd thought they were way past the point of no return, but this was somehow it all over again. He looked up, waiting for some kind of okay.

Jock stared down at him, mouth hanging slack, sucking in air, sweat beading on his forehead. "Yeah," he rasped.

So Toby dug his fingertips into the waistband and pulled Jock's briefs down in one vigorous yank. Hard, hot dick slapped him in the cheek, which some guys might have seen as a reprimand, but Toby saw as an incentive. He grabbed it, fisting Jock's shaft—as big around as he'd hoped—holding it so the dark pink head looked straight at him, pre-cum oozing out the end. Then he stuck out his tongue and licked it off.

Jock's knees buckled in Toby's peripheral vision and he pitched forward onto the bed, half-crushing him. Toby never let go, though.

Jock shoved up on his elbow, gripping Toby's jaw and holding him still for a kiss while working his dick through Toby's fingers and against his thigh. Then he pulled away. "You get naked."

"Make me," Toby said, smiling. Taunting.

Grinning, Jock let go of Toby's jaw to pull up his shirt. He didn't take his time undressing Toby, and Toby didn't encourage him to. He wanted his clothes off as much as Jock did. No more foreplay; they needed to get to the fucking.

In seconds he was naked too, pulling Jock over him. But Jock resisted, sitting back on his heels. He looked over at the nightstand, swallowed, turned back to Toby, then the nightstand again.

Okay, yeah, maybe Jock was a tiny bit of a nervous virgin. It wasn't as if Toby would forget protection. He reached over, feeling with his fingers for a condom while watching Jock's inexperience almost get the better of him. His brows lowered, and his lips dipped into a slightly angry pout.

"Hey," Toby said softly. He didn't let the smile he felt at the freaking endearingness of Jock's uncertainty show as he sat up, holding the condom between them. Not giving Jock's anxiety any more time to work up, he ripped the package open, grasping Jock's dick with one hand and rolling the condom down with the fingers of the other. Stroking a couple extra times. "To make sure it fits." He could finally grin when Jock's hips lifted up toward his hand.

Toby didn't waste any time after that. He grabbed the lube and lay back down, squirting some out and reaching under himself, sliding a slick finger into his ass.

"Aren't I supposed to . . ." Jock trailed off, staring down at what Toby was doing. Then he clamped a hand on Toby's knee, shoving his leg wider, licking his lips, dick thrusting up. An unconscious, primitive reaction, Toby'd bet. *Possessive.* Jock watching him made the somewhat clinical task of stretching himself sexy as hell. As if his fingers were Jock's, sliding inside him, twisting around.

Enough of that. He stopped. "C'mere." Gripping Jock's biceps, he guided him forward until Jock was hovering over him, kneeling between Toby's legs, propped up on his arms, fists on the bed bracketing Toby's ribs. Frozen other than his gasping breaths. His muscles trembled under Toby's hands, maybe with the strain of holding himself up like that, but Toby thought it was because of what they were about to do.

"Ready?" he whispered.

Jock gulped, then nodded. But he didn't move, except for his eyes, pupils huge and glassy, gaze drifting down Toby's body. Toby took the opportunity to admire the guy who was about to fuck him. Give thanks to the sex gods for this perfect specimen of masculinity. Broad shoulders slicked with sweat, beautiful, sculpted chest narrowing down into slim hips, and every muscle ever invented lovingly wrapped in smooth skin.

So fucking perfect. And I'm his first. How did he get so lucky? He swallowed the lump growing in his throat—the enormity of everything it meant to let Jock inside him. Overwhelmed with an unfamiliar sense of gratitude and possibility. *Definitely more than just sex.*

Jock's eyes tracked every move as Toby lifted his legs, gripping the backs of his knees and spreading himself open for him. He huffed heavily a couple times, grabbing his dick at the base, finally tearing his gaze away from Toby's offered ass to meet his eyes a split second before looking back down. "Now?"

"Yeah," Toby whispered. He was so freaking eager for this he didn't think Jock could go fast enough to hurt him. Still, he said, "Take it slow." He wanted it to last.

Jock wanted to feel Toby around him, gripping his cock. Like, learn the texture of him without a condom, but that would be stupid, so Jock put the idea out of his mind and took one more look at the body splayed open beneath him, waiting, before he got down to business.

Toby had chest hair, which Jock had never thought about, but now he didn't want to ever *not* think about. He'd devote every jerk-off session from here on out to furry guys. Swirls of dark around the nipples that spread to his breastbone and then down until it widened across his stomach, thickening into a whole nest where the goods were kept. Toby's dick bowed up from his stomach, pointing in a perfect curve to his belly button, weighty and veiny and glistening at the tip. His balls, two lopsided little spheres in a sac crowning the shaft, were thrusting up like they wanted Jock to notice them, wrinkling tight in anticipation. A line ran down between them, a continuation of the one that started on Toby's chest, until it swirled around his asshole, brown hair sprinkled all over, obscuring it in some places and slicked down with lube where Toby'd trailed it when he'd fingered himself open.

Hottest thing he'd ever seen in real life. Jock's prick drooled like a bloodhound inside the condom, begging to go off leash. He gripped the base tighter, partly to keep himself in check and partly in preparation, and directed it until the latex nipple brushed Toby's hole, making it flex in reaction. Like it wanted more.

He gave it more. Fed the head of his dick into Toby's ass, pushing harder when Toby told him to, until it opened for him and swallowed the first half inch or so. "Oh fuck." Better than a chick or a fleshlight. So hot and tight and slick—even if he couldn't touch it with his bare skin.

"Yeah," Toby agreed, sucking in a breath. "Don't stop."

He was way ahead of him, already working on getting that next inch in there, then another, watching himself disappear inside Toby with a sense of awe. Like he'd performed that age-old magic trick of hiding the salami without any foreknowledge. He slid back out just so he could see himself burying his dick in Toby's ass all over, then did it again, working up a rhythm. So much more than the simple mechanical act of sex. If he'd had any doubts about whether or not he was gay, fucking a guy would have cleared that right up. But he'd had no doubts, and that made the experience even more mind-blowing. Validation of everything he'd thought about himself, maybe even everything he'd done to be here now.

Toby laid his hand on his own dick, stroking it in time with Jock's thrusts, eyes squeezed tightly shut and face contorted as if he were in pain. That must mean Jock was doing it right and then some, because Toby started grunting and urging him on breathlessly, digging fingernails into Jock's flank.

Please let him come before I do, he prayed to no one in particular. He'd maybe thought this would be one of those things where he'd get off too fast and have to help Toby out after, but now, looking down at him, watching Toby take his dick like this, Jock needed to see his partner come all over his own belly and know it was driven by his cock shoving into him.

Toby's eyes flew open just when Jock thought he couldn't make it any longer, that the explosive friction of stroking into hot slickness would make him blow before Toby was ready. But Toby gasped, mouth hanging open, and his whole body arched up toward Jock's before he started spilling cum onto his abdomen, the muscles of his ass squeezing Jock tight.

"*Fuck* yes." Jock planted his hands next to Toby's head and bent over him, pretzeling Toby's spine, taking his mouth and filling him fully at both ends, losing control over his nuts. Dumping cum into the rubber and a shout into Toby's throat. Shaking so hard he nearly came apart at the knees and elbows.

He couldn't stop kissing Toby, even after he'd filled the condom—not Toby, like he wanted to so much it made him ache—and the last of the aftershocks died. Even after Jock was mostly limp, his hips ground against Toby's butt cheeks as he sucked on Toby's lips.

So, yeah, it was fantastic. Better than he'd hoped. He didn't want it to end. But finally he *had* to pull himself off of the dude—his arms were shaking too much to hold him up—and throw himself onto his back beside Toby.

"Jesus, fucking, Christ," Toby panted. "What just happened?"

Jock laughed so hard he lost the breath he'd managed to catch in the last few seconds. "If you don't know, we're both fucked," he gasped out.

Toby chuckled along with him, rolling over and tossing his arm over Jock's chest, pulling himself closer, until he rested his head on Jock's shoulder. "No, *I'm* fucked. I may not be able to sit all day tomorrow, but that was worth it." He pulled the condom off of Jock carefully, twisting the end and leaning across Jock's body to drop it over the side of the bed and turn off the lamp on the nightstand. Then he settled back in, head under Jock's chin and fingers splayed over one of his pectoral muscles.

That was when it got a little weird.

What should he do now? Pat Toby's back or something? Was this postcoital affection? Another thing he hadn't thought about before. Did he like it as much as body hair? Toby's gusting breaths felt good on the skin of his chest, like caresses, and Toby's hair tangled in the stubble of Jock's jaw like velcro. Attaching them. So he bent his arm the other way, palming Toby's back and pulling his warmth a little bit closer. Toby slid his leg across Jock's thigh and sighed vocally, slumping against him.

"Good first time?" Toby asked in a mumble.

Jock snorted. "Uh, yeah." Did anyone's first time suck?

"Mmm." Toby nodded, or possibly just made his head more comfortable against Jock's neck. He mumbled something else before rolling over and grabbing a blanket from the other side of the bed, throwing it haphazardly over both of them. Only covering about half of Jock's body, but it was enough. Then, Jock was pretty sure, Toby fell asleep.

Jock stayed awake forever staring into the dark, thinking about nothing in particular. More alive than he'd been since . . . he didn't know.

Thank fuck he finally had that out of the way, and he hadn't even had to field any questions about taking it up the ass.

Chapter 7

At two-something in the morning, Toby woke up to find Jock sitting on the edge of the bed. "Hey," Toby murmured, yawning and scooting closer to run a hand down Jock's naked back.

"Hey." He didn't turn, even when Toby touched him. "Where'd my jeans end up?"

Could he really want to leave? Toby'd thought they'd had a good time, and he'd have liked more of it. He had to be misreading this. "If you're just going to the bathroom—"

Jock shook his head. "No, I need to head back to the dorm."

Well, that was pretty clear. "Oh, yeah. Of course." A thump on the wall told him Larry was home.

"Um, your roommate's straight, huh?" Jock asked, head tilted down like he was searching the floor. Except he was too still.

"Shit," Toby muttered, sitting up himself. "Did Larry bring a girl home? I can't believe I slept through it." Usually he liked to give color commentary through the wall. Larry'd probably freaked Jock out. That bastard was such a thorn in Toby's side.

Jock shrugged, his shoulders moving jerkily. "They were mostly quiet. I wasn't sleeping."

So, like, he'd been lying here awake the last hour or two? Toby didn't want to read too much into it, but it all contributed to the sinking feeling in his gut. The one telling him Jock wasn't interested in a repeat visit. He stifled a sigh and forced his voice to sound friendly. "I'll give you a ride, it's a couple miles to campus from here."

"You don't have to," Jock said, glancing over his shoulder, spine relaxing now. Because he knew Toby'd let him leave? Then he stood, muscles flexing and gliding in the moonlight, all his actions smooth and coordinated. No wonder he could dance—most big guys didn't move that easily. He had to be fast on his skates, too, didn't he? Toby'd thought hockey players tended to be smaller than that. He watched the show as Jock walked to the foot of the bed, unself-consciously naked, frowning at the floor. The frown cleared and he bent over. When he stood back up he had his briefs in his hand.

God, don't cover that up, Toby's libido whined. "You could stay if you wanted." *We could fuck the night away*. Or suck, or any number of things. Many times.

Jock looked at him, face blank for a second, then his eyes flickered to the wall behind Toby's head. *Larry*. "I don't really want to run into your roommate over cereal in the morning."

So maybe it *was* just jitters over being newly out? Either way, the guy was clearly leaving. Toby slid out from under the comforter, not anywhere near as confident as Jock was. He hadn't thought about it while they were fucking, but he wasn't as fit as he used to be. Surreptitiously he looked down, and yes, his stomach totally pooched out, nary an abdominal muscle to be seen.

Suddenly Jock's hand landed on the exact spot on his body that Toby was inspecting. "I like all this hair. It's hot."

Really? He'd been thinking he had too much on his gut, but if Jock wanted to disagree, he wouldn't argue. "Thanks. But I'm nothing close to as sexy as you are." Good lord, did he sound as bashful and awkward to Jock as he did to himself? This was the most disorienting postcoital experience of his life, bar none, and he couldn't figure out how to get it back on track. Self-confidence had never been a major issue for him, just small bobbles here and there, but he'd never misread a guy this completely before. *What. The. Fuck?* Had he been imagining that spark beyond lust?

"Thank you." Jock slid his hand around Toby's body, combing his fingers through the curls there and then squeezing him in a sideways half hug. "And thanks for making my first time fantastic." Then he kissed Toby's cheek.

That was the moment Toby definitely knew their hookup had been a one-off. An experience never to be repeated again. He forced himself to meet Jock's eyes. "Happy to oblige. Everyone's first time should be good. Now I'll drive you back to campus—it's part of my full-service deflowering package."

Jock grinned at him, tilting his head down for a soft kiss on the lips—a friend kiss, no tongue, just platonic affection. "I like you. You make me laugh."

Toby coerced his face into a smile. "I like you too." Much, much more than Jock realized. Too bad the feeling wasn't reciprocated.

Hooking up was easy, at least now that he'd jumped that first hurdle. The half-dozen blowjobs and handjobs he'd managed to score before had been more accidental than intentional, and most of the time he'd only sort of enjoyed them because he'd been so freaked about getting caught. After Toby broke the ice for him, Jock managed to get laid three times the next week. He was starting to think that he'd been ignoring a lot of signals from gay guys over the last couple years. All he had to do was go to the Slaughterhouse, stand around and check out all the guys on offer until he saw one he liked, then make significant eye contact. After that, the other dude did everything. None of them changed their minds when he said he wanted to top, either. As far as he could tell, *everyone* wanted to bottom.

The third time kind of ruined it for him, though. It was the Monday a week after he had gone home with Toby, and by then he was starting to recognize some guys from the bar on campus. And some of them recognized him. In the break between his math class and his late-afternoon lab he went to the Beatnick Café in the student union to get a latte before finding a place to study. When the barista handed him his drink, he refused to let go after Jock had wrapped his fingers around the cup.

Jock scowled at him, and he smiled. "Hi, I'm Kenny. I've seen you at the bar."

Ahhh. "Yeah?" He smiled back.

Kenny let go of the cup slowly, brushing his fingers against Jock's. "My shift here ends at four."

He'd never really made an assignation with a guy on campus before, but glancing around the café, he could see no one he knew, or anyone watching them. And Kenny was cute—huge smile, carefully mussed blond hair, and the svelte twink body type. He probably didn't have any chest hair, but a quick survey assured Jock he'd have abs. The apron the dude had on covered them up, but no one wore a shirt two sizes too small if they didn't have the goods. "I get out of chem lab at 4:25."

Kenny rested his hip against the counter, leaning closer to Jock. Close enough to spark up that subtle electric charge two attracted bodies created when in proximity. "Mmm, and where do you usually go after chem lab?"

"Well, today I plan to stand out front of Miller Hall, looking for company."

Kenny straightened, looking at him from under his lashes. "Maybe today you'll find some."

The forecast looked good, didn't it? Jock smiled at him one more time, making an obvious scan of Kenny's body again—he'd finally clued into the fact that that was sort of like a good-bye handshake in the language of pre-fuck flirting—and went to dump a packet of sugar in his drink. When he set the cup down, he realized Kenny'd written his phone number on it, too. Hedging his bets.

Yeah, hooking up was *easy*.

Kenny wanted Jock to fuck him, and his eyes lit up in a very gratifying way as he watched Jock get naked in his dorm room, tongue captured between his teeth as if he needed to keep it from going rogue. Jock's original estimation was right, the guy did have abs. No body hair, though—not *anywhere*. Jock had been with a chick who'd waxed her pubes, and he'd seen it on guys in porn, but for some reason he hadn't expected to encounter it in real life. As he was first entering Kenny, for a fleeting second he thought he might actually be with a girl and nearly went soft.

"Something wrong?" Kenny asked, arching to push his hips just a little closer to Jock.

He shook his head and finished the job. Kenny's tight ass made it easy. It just wasn't as hot as Jock had hoped. In truth, none of the three other guys he'd been with had been quite as good as Toby. Lack of experience, maybe, his and theirs.

Afterward, when he was sitting on the edge of Kenny's tiny bed, looking for his clothes, Kenny decided a little postcoital chitchat was in order. "So, what did you think of Toby?"

"*What*?" Jock nearly ripped his briefs in half. "What do you know about that?" He waited, stock-still, refusing to turn and look at Kenny. Where did this guy get off, talking to him about Toby? If the dude thought he had the right, he was dead wrong.

"I saw you leave the Slaughterhouse with him," Kenny said in a perfectly normal voice. At least, as far as Jock knew it was normal, based on their very short acquaintance. "He's a dreamy fuck," he added with a sigh.

"I wouldn't know," Jock said, standing and yanking his underwear up his legs.

Kenny either ignored Jock's conversation-killing tone or didn't notice. "You should totally take him for a spin if you get another chance. He *really* knows how to use his hips. I mean, he doesn't just shove it in and race toward the finish line, he takes the scenic route."

Jock's head got caught in his shirt, or he might have responded to that. Probably inappropriately. When he finally got untangled, Kenny was staring at him, eyes huge and mouth gaping. "Uh, not that there's anything wrong with hard and fast. Sometimes that's exactly what you want, you know? Especially for an early-evening quickie."

Early-evening quickie. Was that supposed to refer to *him*? Jock dropped onto the bed, shoving his feet in his shoes. "Dude, I'm not that interested in discussing my sex life with you." He stood up again and scowled down at the figure still lying in the bed. Why the fuck would Toby waste his time on *this* guy?

"Well, now," Kenny said softly. He sat up, sheet falling off his chest and showing those abs Jock had thought would be worth seeing. "Don't get all protectionist, sweetheart. You can't conduct your adventures someplace as small as Calapooya and think no one's going to notice, especially if you get around. Everyone will know you and I hooked up."

Oh this little *prick*. "Are you saying you're going to make sure of that?" Jock's fists balled up at his sides, so he shoved them in his pockets. Until he needed them.

Kenny just rolled his eyes. "No, I'm saying people saw you walk into my dorm with me. I'm saying you met me in front of Miller Hall when about a hundred other students were passing by."

He flashed hot, then cold. Holy shit, he'd *known* he shouldn't have hooked up with a guy on campus. Now fucking *everyone* would know, wouldn't they?

Kenny went on, making it worse "I'm *saying* the girl on shift with me at the café totally knows what I was doing when I gave you your drink."

Anybody who didn't already know he was gay could figure it out from this one fuck. So much for it being his business. Were they gonna start keeping tabs on who he slept with? *Gay Hookup Bingo.*

"It's not the first time I've met a guy that way." Kenny smiled coldly, batting his lashes. "I'm sorry, sugar. I hope you didn't think you were special."

Jock dropped his head, trying to get his temper under control and make the knot in his chest dissolve. "Yeah, I get it." Like he fucking cared what this prick thought of him? "You're not special either. And I need to get going."

Kenny huffed. "Yes, you do." Just when Jock was leaving the room, he added in an almost admiring tone, "Thanks for the totally banging fuck."

He didn't know for sure, but that sounded like a backhanded compliment to him.

Chapter 8

Toby didn't get the partial draft of his thesis done the week after midterms. In truth, he'd barely managed another 2,000 words. It was asinine to blame it on what had happened with Jock, but he could trace his inspiration-killing ennui right back to that moment when Jock had said "Thanks for making my first time fantastic." He hadn't needed to add, "Now that I've popped that cherry, I'm going to go out and find other guys to fuck," because it had all been right there in his voice.

He couldn't think of anything else that kept him staring at the screen and/or his research for hours on end, not really accomplishing anything. He'd start working, writing along, and suddenly find he'd lost his train of thought and the last paragraph didn't make sense.

Once he even found he'd referenced the "Visijocks" instead of "Visigoths."

Hello there, textbook Freudian slip.

He never should have assumed they'd start something more serious from that one night. All evidence pointed directly to Jock's having just gotten *out* of a traumatic relationship. One serious enough that he'd trusted the other guy to take a picture of him and *not* share it around. He probably needed a break from emotional entanglements for a while. He needed some time to learn to trust again.

A relationship where they didn't fuck?

Maybe the ex wasn't into it.

Maybe he should stop thinking about it.

That turned out to be impossible. This sense of lost opportunity clung to his shoulder like an organ grinder's monkey, no matter how hard he tried to dislodge it. The little bastard kept beating off, too.

Or possibly that was him.

He got some relief from his preoccupation with Jock when Professor Louise Van Veenen, graduate advisor extraordinaire, summoned him to her office for a meeting. Toby spent exactly no time wondering why.

Obviously, he was about to be called to carpet.

When he got to his advisor's door at ten in the morning on the appointed day, his lungs were working like he'd walked up all four flights of stairs instead of having taken the elevator. Louise's door was ajar, but he knocked before pushing it open. "Professor Van Veenen?"

She swiveled her desk chair around to face him with narrowed eyes. "I'll assume, by your using my title, that you know I'm not happy."

He gripped the jamb. "Because I'm one minute late?"

She shook her head very deliberately. "Because you're a *week and a half* late with your work on your thesis."

He teetered in the doorway. "Technically, I think it's not a true half week until tomorrow."

"Don't even try that crap," she said, giving him The Palm. "You're a history major, math is your weakness."

"Since when is keeping track of my days math?"

She looked down her nose at him, even while sitting at her desk. "Toby. Sit down."

He picked his way carefully across her tiny office—roughly the size of one half of a dorm room—avoiding the teetering stacks of books and carefully skirting the floor lamp she insisted on keeping, even though it had a habit of leaping in front of students who were trying to navigate their way to her single armchair.

He made it without mishap.

Louise swiveled to face him again, regarding him levelly for a long moment. "Tell me precisely how much of your draft you have *written.*" She tapped her temple with an index finger. "Not how much you have planned, but words on the screen."

Toby clasped his hands between his knees, interlacing them studiously. "Um, not quite five thousand." If he counted notes still waiting to be transcribed from cocktail napkins.

Her sigh made him flinch. "I don't see how you can possibly finish this quarter based on the work you *haven't* done so far. It might be time to ask yourself how committed you really are."

Toby snapped his head up to gape at her. "I'm almost finished."

"Not with your thesis you aren't."

"With school!"

"Not with your thesis you aren't," she repeated, giving him bug eyes.

"I'll get it done, I'm just, you know . . ." he gestured in the air, hoping that would explain things.

"Can you really finish something *quality* in time?"

Highly unlikely. At least if he intended to sleep anytime in the next three weeks. "I have to—I don't have a fellowship next quarter." He hadn't needed it, since he'd essentially be done, but he couldn't pay full tuition next quarter without it, and short of explaining to his mother he wasn't going to finish his thesis *this* term. . . . Very much not an option. "Um, I can't take until the end of spring term to complete it?"

"You could." She nodded, but something about how she exaggerated the motion didn't sit right with him. "But stay on fellowship money? No. The history department doesn't have it in their budget, especially when you aren't teaching."

He leapt on that, because explaining away another term was much easier than telling his mother he wasn't going to finish at all. "I'll teach a class. Two." He *liked* teaching. Felt more motivated when he was teaching.

"All the teaching fellowships are *taken*, Toby. It's nearly spring break, and you know how competitive the positions are."

"Don't I have seniority or something?"

She gave him The Look. A sort of tilted-head, under-the-eyebrows look, with a "puh-*lease*" curve to one side of her mouth. "I'm *not* telling some poor student that he's out of funding because my slacker thesis candidate was too busy partying to finish on time."

Toby groaned and fell back into the chair, letting his arms dangle over the sides. "What am I going to do?" He'd have to come up with tuition on his own, which definitely meant calling his parents. He could try and talk to his father, but Dad always told Mom everything. The man could never keep a secret from her. Could Toby get a job? Kenny at the coffee shop had said something about needing another employee in the mornings. How much did baristas make anyway?

"There is one possibility . . ." Louise began, and Toby jerked his head up to see her tilting her head and looking at him like a cat sizing up a mouse.

He raised his eyebrows and threw out his hands, spreading his fingers wide. "Well? Speak!"

Her lips twitched almost imperceptibly at the corners, giving Toby the distinct impression that he was being set up. Hopefully whatever she was setting him up for wasn't going to be too horrible. "The satellite campus in Provence has a situation, and they're quickly running out of time. They need a resident advisor for a group of students who've had to arrange off-campus housing in a *gîte* between Saint-Rémy-de-Provence and Arles. There's apparently a 'pool house studio apartment' for this advisor."

Toby blinked at her. "Provence?" Her air of manipulating him into some onerous task was all out of proportion with sending him to France. "What's the downside?"

"You won't get a stipend," she said. "But your living expenses will be covered, including meals."

Toby took a breath, centering himself, because he knew there was worse—Louise always led with the good news. "Go on."

"You'll have to get your international driver's license; it's too remote for any public transit, and you'll be responsible for getting the students to campus every day. The facilities where you'll be staying will provide a van adequate for the purpose. You might also want a car for your own use."

Toby did some quick calculations, mostly about how much he'd need to ask his parents for. "I could probably handle that." His own vehicle sounded like an "emergency credit card" expense to him.

"I'll have to cut some kind of deal with the International Studies department head. And someone will have to convince them you're a"—she curled her fingers in air quote formation—"'responsible party' and are capable of keeping these kids in line."

It was a fantastic deal. If he could get it. "So . . . would they consider me a 'responsible party'?"

She tilted her head. "If someone vouches for you, I'm sure they would."

"Would 'someone' be you?"

She raised her brows at him, smiling for the first time since he'd arrived.

"Okay, so what do I have to do?"

Louise chuckled. "Nothing really, except finish your thesis while you're there and drive those students into Saint-Rémy every weekday. I suppose *technically* you'll be responsible for keeping them out of trouble. And of course you'll owe me a favor. Now, do you want any more details or should I see if I can arrange it?"

He was tempted to say yes on the spot, but that wouldn't be something a responsible party would do. Responsible parties asked for all the terms before signing the contract. "Details, please." How many more pertinent facts could there be?

"The students going are members of that frat house that burned down."

"Theta Alpha Gamma?"

She nodded.

"Oh God," he muttered. That was a mighty fucking pertinent fact.

She gave him a sympathetic squint, reaching to pat his knee. He couldn't get over the feeling that she was suppressing a smile.

He bent over, tunneling his fingers into his hair and resting his forehead on his palms. Best position to weigh out the pros and cons. Having to finish his paper was neither a pro nor a con, because he had to do it either way.

Maybe Jock is going.

That would be a horrible reason to go. He'd essentially be chasing after the dude, and that wasn't something he did. He needed to make a decision based on the facts available to him. *Pros first.* If he went, he wouldn't need a job and would have to sponge off his parents less. He could have his own place, even if small, and not have to live with Larry the Breeder another term. And the crowning pro: he'd be in his favorite part of France (out of the parts he'd been to).

What were the cons? The fratbros. That was it.

He sat up and nodded firmly. "Okay, I'll do it."

ΘΑΓ

Because he was a good son, Toby called home within a couple of days of his quasi-disastrous meeting with Louise. He was such a good son, in fact, that when his mother answered the phone—because she would pick up once she saw it was Toby calling instead of letting

Dad get it—he planned on *not* hanging up and calling back repeatedly until his father answered.

Besides, she knew that trick. So he'd made himself comfortable on his bed when he was alone in the apartment, took a few calming breaths, plastered his most insouciant smile on his face, and dialed.

"I suppose you still have that unfortunate predilection for boys?" Toby's mother asked after the obligatory greeting stuff.

Toby sighed theatrically. "Yes, Mom. I have to admit I do, no matter how hard I try to find girls attractive."

She snorted. "Thank God. Your brother has more girls than I can handle. Now, how much money do you need and for what—your father will want to know that part."

"Who says I need money?"

"You're a grad student, honey, every time you call you need money."

"Are you saying I only call you when I'm financially strapped?"

"I'm saying that no matter why you called, you ask for money at some point."

This was good. Witty banter. He could totally deal with this. "Oh. Well, that's much less insulting." Unfortunately, he made the mistake of not filling the silence afterward with chitchat.

"So, how much?"

Toby took a deep breath. "Enough for a ticket to Marseille and a rental car for three months." He was pretty sure he could handle the rest.

"Mmm," she said. "Need to do more research for your thesis? You know, if you'd gone directly into a PhD program like I wanted, you probably wouldn't feel this need to do more work than the subject requires."

God. A dissertation would fucking *kill* him. He'd never make it through that—he'd only done the master's because he'd been hoping once he was done he could segue into something that she'd see as an acceptable substitute for an academic career. Then he'd never have to face her disappointment over having *two* capitalist offspring.

"It's unnecessary," she continued, totally oblivious to his discomfort. "Once you're at Berkeley, you'll have more research than you can handle."

"I didn't apply to Berkeley," he blurted, cringing when he heard what came out of his mouth.

A shocked black hole of silence was his response. But his mother abhorred a vacuum, so she wasn't quiet for long. "Where *did* you apply then?" Her upset was very apparent in the way she clipped off her words. Not anger, but disappointment.

Toby cringed further and considered conducting the rest of this phone call under his bed. Instead he pulled a comforter over his head, rolling onto his side and tucking the cell protectively between his shoulder and his ear. "Nowhere."

It sounded like he'd knocked the wind out of her.

"I'm sorry," he said over her tortured gasping for breath. "I'm thinking about taking a year. For some independent study. In Provence. That's what this trip is about." Oh, he was a shameful son, wasn't he? Although he'd managed to keep her from asphyxiating.

"So you're taking a leave of absence? Toby, I really think you should finish first."

"I'm not taking a leave," he said quickly. He could at least give her some of the truth. "Louise and I met and we both felt it would be beneficial for me to spend a little more time on my thesis." *Yeah, that's the way it went down.* "But since there weren't any teaching fellowships available for spring term, I took this resident advisor position at the Provence campus."

She bought it. She even complimented him on finding a position that would allow him to continue working toward his educational goals. "You can leave a few days early and go to Tarragona," she said at one point. "I'm certain that basilica deserves more study."

Toby squeezed his eyes shut and shook his head, but he didn't object verbally.

After a half hour on the phone with his mother, she'd booked him a plane ticket, promised him money for a rental car and incidentals, and thoroughly shamed him. He was a wrung-out mess, lying on his bed staring stupidly out the window at the gray cloud ceiling while his mother gave him lots of advice and admonishments. Ending with, "And Toby? Keep your nose clean over there."

"Pardon me?"

"I mean it," his mother contended firmly. "I know all about you and your little peccadilloes, so watch it. You need to focus on your studies at this point, not your social life."

Well, since most of his sexual energy was wrapped up in a guy who wouldn't even talk to him, that was one thing he could promise. "I will, Mom."

Toby checked the roster as soon as he received it a week and a half before the end of winter quarter, but there was no "Jock" listed as going on the trip to Provence. Well, presumably there were lots of jocks—possibly all six of the guys going were athletic meatheads—just none *named* that. But Jock wouldn't be his real name, would it? Of course not—who stuck their kid with that kind of burden? "River," "Stone," or "Moon Unit," sure, but "Jock"? If parents were going to go in that direction, wouldn't they swing all the way to the dark side and label the kid "Bubba" or "Butch"?

So what was his actual name? In spite of racking his brain, he couldn't think of Tank's last name (likely because he'd never bothered to find out), and nothing leapt out at him as being the obvious progenitor of "Jock."

He was left with two choices: give up or ask someone who'd know.

He texted Collin.

What's Jock's real name?

Collin didn't text him back for*ever*. But Toby distracted himself by working a few more hours on his thesis. He wasn't writing it now so much as re-outlining. Talking with his mother had focused him—he'd finish it because he was too close not to, but he wasn't getting a PhD.

Definitively deciding that had somehow liberated him, and he found himself able to look at the subject more clearly than he had since he'd been in Spain. Which allowed him to see how utterly he'd fucked up the stuff he'd already written. He'd spent the last week or so reorganizing his research and restructuring his arguments, his newfound detachment allowing him to obsess about the damn thing less and simply work more.

His phone dinged at him just as he was about ready to take a break.

Meet me at the Beatnick Café at 1:30 and I'll tell you his name.

Toby texted back, telling Collin he'd be there, the whole time wondering if this was a social appointment or a ransom demand. Would his friend expect something in return before coughing up the name?

As it turned out, Collin did—he insisted on chastising Toby in exchange for the information.

"I cannot *believe* you slept with Jock," Collin said as soon as he sat down. They were almost the only people in here.

"I cannot *believe* it took this long for you to find out I hooked up with him." Toby glanced up at the counter to see who the barista was, but no one was there at the moment. "I cannot believe you think it's such a freaking tragedy. He didn't seem to feel that way." Not until afterward.

Collin scowled. "I cannot believe you're the resident advisor for the TAG guys going on the trip."

"Sad, but true." He sat back in his chair, crossing his arms. "Now answer my question. The one I texted you hours ago."

"I cannot believe you got together with him and you don't know his real name." Collin shook his head.

"What, you know the full legal name of every guy you've ever gone home with?"

Collin huffed, eyeing him. "I'd make it a point to find out the name of a guy I really liked. Who I wanted to see again."

"Who says I want to see him again?" He pretended great interest in the espresso menu hanging over the counter. As if he didn't know what he'd order. Should anyone ever show up to take his order.

"I cannot believe you're trying to pretend you aren't really into him."

"There seems to be something wrong with your belief system. You should probably get that checked out. His name is . . .?"

"You really are into him, aren't you?" Collin asked, dropping his scolding tone.

"Yes." He gave up prevaricating and sat forward, meeting his friend's eye. "It's so very unlike me."

"You've had relationships before."

"Ah, maybe that's the issue then—you see, I don't *have* a relationship with Jock." Toby forced his lips into a smile. "I had a one-night stand, and when I invited him to stay longer, he refused. Since then, I haven't seen even a glimpse of him, thereby making it impossible for me to ask him his real name. I decided chasing him down was beneath me." And too pathetic.

The people sitting across the room from them got up and left. The place was empty now except for the two of them. "Gavin Gervaise," Collin said after a moment of silence.

"Gavin? He doesn't look like a Gavin." Gavins were slender and sometimes a bit femme, an impression reinforced by their long, wavy hair. And they played in rock bands, didn't they? Or wanted to. Oh, and they looked good in leather.

Jock would look utterly *hot* in leather, but not the way a Gavin would.

Collin shrugged, pursing his mouth. "That's his name though. His middle name is Jacques, which is how he got tagged with 'Jock.'"

"Huh." Toby didn't need to reach for the messenger bag he'd hung on the back of his chair and search out the roster. "Well, there's no Gavin going on the trip, so I guess he's escaped being in close quarters with me for three months."

Collin waved that off. "Okay, seriously, stop with the selfless sacrifice shit. That is *so* like you. Remember the night the frat burned and I stayed with you? You wanted to comfort me. You didn't care about not fucking, you were happy to hold me instead because I needed it."

What, like it was a character flaw? "That's not true. I was very upset about not having sex. It just seemed inconsiderate to complain."

Collin huffed. "Please."

"Please," Toby repeated after him. "Can we not discuss this anymore? I'm ready to move on to another subject now."

"Fine," Collin agreed. "Let's talk about the frat brothers."

Toby groaned but didn't actually protest. It was better than the alternative. Besides, other than ascertaining that the one with the cast—Ricky, according to Collin—would have it off before he arrived in France, he didn't really listen. Something about the kinds of trouble he needed to look out for from them, and behaviors Collin ominously termed "warning signs."

"Are you even listening to me?" Collin asked.

"Um," Toby conjured up his "thoughtful" expression. "No, I wasn't."

Collin threw both hands in the air. "Seriously, you have to keep an eye on these guys. The potential for asshattery among them is exponential. You can't imagine."

"Uh-huh." How hard could it be to stay a couple steps ahead of the stupidest of the fratbros? In an earlier period of human history, Toby's ancestors would have already culled them from the herd.

Someone coming out of the storage room in the rear of the shop caught his attention. An employee. "Finally."

An employee he recognized.

"What?" Collin craned his head in the direction Toby was looking. "Oh, no . . ."

"I cannot *believe* you didn't tell me Kenny was working," Toby whispered furiously.

Collin grimaced, so that meant he'd heard the gossip too—that Jock and Kenny had hooked up. Considering Kenny's carefully nurtured slut princess image, this wasn't the first time they'd been with the same guy, but it was the first time Toby wasn't indifferent to it. It didn't help that Kenny was one of those guys his Libidinous Mistake Detection Network hadn't warned him about until it was too late.

"He wasn't here when I came in," Collin responded, keeping his voice low. "He must have just started his shift."

"Oh, hey guys!" Kenny called, waving and walking toward them.

"Quick, text my phone and I'll pretend someone summoned us or something," Collin hissed.

But it was too late. The chair next to Toby was pulled out and Kenny plopped into it, smiling far too brightly in his face. "You haven't been in for a while."

"Hey, Kenny. I guess I tend to come in when you aren't working," Toby answered.

"I'm sure it's not by design or anything," Collin said sweetly. Toby'd had no idea he could go all cat girl like that.

Kenny acknowledged Collin's comment with one of those "die, bitch, die" smiles, then turned a pouty lip on Toby. "If I wasn't so cute I might think you were avoiding me."

Collin snorted.

"I'd never avoid you." Toby forced his most winning grin, nudging his friend under the table. Seriously, he didn't need this drama.

"So, boys, what are you talking about?"

"Nothing much," Toby said.

Kenny's smile went sly. "I could swear I heard you mention that hottie, Jock."

Toby physically recoiled. *I can't take this right now.*

"Um, excuse me?" Collin snarked. "Your ears deceive you."

But Kenny ignored him, lowering his voice to say, "That guy? Was a totally lame lay."

Toby gaped, and Collin choked.

"What did you think of him?" he asked brightly.

"I *think*," Collin snapped, "that he just walked in and heard you."

Chapter 9

When Jock walked into the Beatnick, he heard his name. Not like someone calling to him, but like he'd come up in conversation.

The picture. Why else would anyone be talking about him? It had to be out. *It was only a matter of time*. Through the sudden pounding in his ears, he turned his head toward that side of the café, trying to hear more.

The only people in the place were Collin, Kenny, and . . . Toby. Sitting together. And Kenny had just said something else—too quietly for him to catch—that made Toby's jaw drop and Collin's nostrils flare. Then the prick sat back and asked Toby, "What did you think of him?"

Jock's stomach lurched, and he had to swallow down bile before he could say, "Let's get out of here," to Noah.

Too late. "Hey Collin!" Noah waved across the room. The only fucking oblivious person here and Jock had to be with him. Then his friend abandoned him by the door to go join their frat brother, leaving Jock with a reverberating pulse and a decision to make. And he would have gone for the easy way out—through the door—if Toby's eye hadn't caught his right at that moment.

It was just like the first time they'd looked at each other at the party. An almost physical link. But this time it was more clash than connection. Discordant. *Everything's wrong*. He should be sitting next to Toby, not that prick. Then they could be talking about Kenny instead of *them* talking about *him*.

One good thing—they probably weren't talking about the picture.

Still staring at Jock, Toby answered Kenny's question in a voice that carried all the way to the door. "He was shockingly good for me. Best I've been with in a long time." Then he stood up and walked over to stand in front of him, never breaking eye contact. "We weren't talking about you," he said quietly from less than a foot away. So close Jock could feel the space Toby's body took up and the subtle way he disrupted Jock's personal boundaries.

"I heard my name," Jock said.

Toby grimaced. "That was all Kenny. And what I just said. But we weren't, you know, comparing notes. He'd just sat down before you came in."

The wave of icy-hot relief that rushed through him from the crown of his head was all out of proportion with the situation. Or at least that's what Jock told himself. He crossed his arms over his chest, stepping back from Toby. "Whatever."

Toby's Adam's apple bobbed, and he broke their eye contact. "Noted. I won't do you any favors in the future."

"I'm being a dick, sorry," Jock blurted, then felt the tips of his ears get hot. "I mean, thanks. For saying . . . that." He nodded his head toward the table Toby'd been sitting at, noticing for the first time that Kenny was watching them intently.

For a half second, Toby touched Jock's arm—the back of his wrist, just below the cuff of his bomber jacket. "I meant it."

"Thanks," Jock repeated, sucking in a deep breath and looking into Toby's brown eyes for a second longer before giving in to his more craven self and turning to head out the door.

He'd taken the path halfway back to the frat before he heard footsteps come pounding up behind him on the asphalt. "So," Noah panted. "You and Toby, huh?"

Jock grunted and tucked his chin closer to his chest.

"He's pretty hot," Noah said.

Jock threw a sideways glare at him and caught the dude grinning. *Fucker*. "Shut up."

"Sounds like he's kinda into you," Noah went on cheerfully.

Jock broke into a jog, listening to the asshole he left behind laugh.

As he took his impromptu run back to the dorm, he couldn't stop thinking. About Toby, and why he'd avoided the dude—because, yeah, he totally had—and what might happen if they got together again. What Toby might eventually want from him, because the dude wouldn't bottom forever, right? That's what Brad had said.

All of those trains of thought led to one truth he'd hoped to avoid awhile longer: he might not have it in him to man up and be the girl.

At just after six in the morning, Jock lay in bed awake but trying to pretend he wasn't when his phone beeped at him. Did he really need to look at it? It was probably Tank texting him to see if he wanted to go lift weights. They were both cursed with the early riser gene. He could work out with Tank—it passed for quality time spent together, but Jock got away with barely talking to his brother.

When he picked up his cell though, *Max Abrahamson* glowed up at him. Jock scrubbed his eyes to make sure he was seeing the name right.

Dude, you need to get online as soon as possible and do some . . .

Do some what? He hated that his phone truncated texts.

He'd hardly heard from Max since he left Avalon, and he'd figured that was pretty much it for them. They'd only become friends because they'd discovered each other's secret sexual status. That had been Jock's first lesson in gaydar or whatever: he could check out all the straight boys he wanted and they never noticed, but the gay boys caught him scoping them out right away.

What the fuck did Max have to tell him that was so important he'd text this early? Except it was after nine there. Shrugging, Jock typed in his passcode and the full text floated up from cyberspace, in stark white on green, bringing along with it a coldness that clutched at his lungs and made it hard to breathe.

Shoulda known, he thought to himself as he read. Because, duh, Max had a stake in Jock's public queerness, didn't he? They'd hung out together a lot, publicly. So Max'd find it important to let him know ASAP if word got out.

Dude, you need to get online as soon as possible and do some damage control or something. It's hit the media. http://annetenino.com/college-hockey-player-outed/ . . .

Jock's heart shrank in on itself as he fell back on the bed, touching the link Max had sent with a finger that seemed suddenly bigger than his whole phone and twice as unwieldy.

"Gay NCAA Hockey Star Outed, Cut From Team" read the headline on the page that popped up.

Well, at least it was accurate. He scrolled past the slowly loading picture and scanned the text.

"A promising young center from Avalon College's Knights, Gavin 'Jock' Gervaise, was recently cut from the team for serious misconduct related to his social activities, but new allegations have surfaced that the decision to cancel his scholarship and athletic involvement was motivated by the discovery of his sexual orientation . . . received a photograph depicting the young student athlete in a compromising situation—sent to us by snail mail . . . neither Coach Schnigglehoeffer nor Gervaise have responded to repeated attempts to contact them for comment . . ."

Fuck my life. But God bless his instinct not to answer his phone when he didn't recognize the number. Except then he would have had some advance warning.

He found the thing he'd been hoping would never get out near the bottom of the article. "Rumors abound of an NHL team scouting the young player, but none of our sources will name names. 'I can't tell you, he didn't want it getting around,' a friend of Gervaise's who wished to remain anonymous informed this reporter." Fingers shaking now, he scrolled back up to the top, holding his breath. *Thank fuck.* It was the official team picture of him in his jersey looking intimidating. Reputable news outlets—even minor ones—wouldn't put the "compromising" picture on their site, would they?

Not that that would stop it from showing up on Tumblr.

It took Jock a couple of tries to get a legible message typed out to send back to Max, but he wanted the fucker to have no doubts about his feelings. *I know you're the "anonymous" source, motherfucker. No one else knew about the scout outside of the coach. And what the fuck kind of "damage control" is it you think I can do NOW? Douche bag.*

He kicked off his blankets and jumped out of bed, nearly shoving his laptop over backward when he flipped up the screen. It took mere seconds to type his name in the search bar—no quotes or anything—and a page of hits popped up. Scanning quickly, the only bright spot he could find was that they were all "pink" news blogs, even the first one Max had sent him. So he was all over the gay blogosphere—he counted thirty-two of them—but he hadn't hit mainstream media or even the hockey blogs.

Yet.

Christ, he could *not* just hide out here and wait for that to happen. He was a sitting duck for his frat brothers to come knocking at his door to offer their acceptance and sensitivity, and as soon as that happened, he'd probably lose it and break someone's face. He had to get the fuck out of here.

He did the only thing he could think of—threw on track pants and running shoes, intending to head off for Brad's house.

Unfortunately, when he opened the door to his room, his brother was standing right there, fist raised in the air about to knock. The expression on his face made it sickeningly obvious that he knew.

"Why didn't you tell me?" Tank asked.

"How did you find out?" Jock asked at the same time.

Tank took a deep breath and blew it out slowly. "Someone emailed me with a link."

Jock gripped the doorjamb. "Who?"

"It doesn't matter, but… Why didn't you tell me about the scout?"

"That's what you care about?" He stared at his big brother. "I just got seriously fucking exposed, and that's what you care about?"

"I care about it all," Tank said, reaching to lay a hand on his shoulder. "But I didn't know about the scout. It seems like the kind of thing you'd tell me, bro." And there it was, the reflection of hurt in his eye.

Fucker. Jock clenched his jaw, chewing on his teeth a second before biting out, "I didn't want anyone to know."

Tank pulled back, his whole face wrinkling up in bewilderment. "But I'm not just anyone, I'm your brother. You've always told me everything. We've always worked out your career goals toge—"

"I don't want to have a fucking career in the NHL as the gay guy," he bit out.

"But they're pro-LGBT now, bro. The You Can Play campaign—"

"I don't want to be the pioneer!" Jock exploded, his jaw unclenching violently, getting in his brother's face. "The first gay guy who plays? He'll be a fucking *token*, Tank. Nothing will matter except that he's gay—not talent or leadership or personality or *anything*. He'll just be the first faggot to go pro!"

Tank's mouth flapped, brow scrunching until it nearly covered his eyes. "But they were *scouting* you because you're great, you've *got* the talent. They were scouting you and you didn't tell me. I could have *helped* you."

"Helped me *how*?" He came damn close to punching his brother, just to knock some sense into him. "Helped me stay in the closet? Pretend to be straight? That's the only way I could play *just to play*. But how long could I hide that when I didn't fucking *want* to anymore? I want to fuck whoever I want to fuck, and no one has the right to tell me I can't do it, and I want people to think it's *normal*. I'm not a *cause*, I'm a good player who happens to like dick!"

"Exactly!" Tank pounded his fist into the palm of his other hand. "And if you'd fucking *trusted* me enough to tell me about the scout, I would've backed you—"

"*Trusted you*?" Jock found himself screaming into his brother's face. "Why the *fuck* would I trust you? The last time I told you something I wanted kept secret, you told your entire. Fucking. Frat! I wasn't outed last term, *bro*. I was outed months before that by *you*!"

In the ringing silence, the sound of someone's door opening echoed around them. "Uh, guys?" Danny said.

They ignored him.

Tank swallowed, backing off a few steps, the whites of his eyes showing. "You said it was all right. I mean, after I—"

"Of course I fucking did! You're my big brother, and I worshipped you." Jock charged out of his doorway, toward Tank, making his brother flinch back more. "But you really think when you came home last summer and told me you'd announced my big secret to your frat that I didn't fucking feel like you'd knifed me in the back? Because I *did*, Beau." He was spitting, he could see it flying through air between them, so he pushed himself forcibly back, down the hall, yelling at Tank from a distance, barely noticing other doors opening around him.

"I told you that in the first place because you were the one person I could trust, but you blew it, didn't you? When you told me you fucked it up, and then you were all apologetic and fucking *crushed* about it? I tried to let it go because you've *never done anything wrong*. Not to me before." *Ouch*, he'd punched himself in the chest, but he continued, because now he could finally let it all out. All that shit they'd *both* made happen. "I couldn't believe it, you know? I thought it must not be as bad as it *felt* like it was. Like, when you swore I could trust these guys not to spread it around? I tried to trust that, but all the fucking sudden it could get out there, couldn't it? *Anyone* could let it slip at any time, just like you did, and then where the fuck would my career be, huh?"

Tank didn't have an answer. He just stared, white-faced and gasping. In the same kind of pain Jock had known for months, and if his brother wanted to share in his "career"? Then he got to share in this, too.

"I guess that's how much you cared about my career. And about me." Jock sneered, knowingly twisting the knife in his brother's gut. "You know what I believed in my whole life? Hockey and you. Mom's a religious freak, and Dad makes fun of it behind her back, but I didn't need to put my faith in them because I had my brother and that fucking ice rink. And then you pulled that shit and all the sudden I didn't have you, did I? I couldn't trust *anything*."

"I don't . . ." Tank flapped his jaw a couple more times. "I didn't mean to tell them."

Jock huffed, curling up his lip. "I've heard that from you before. It's not good enough." He turned before Tank could respond and walked off, not seeing where he was going, just leaving. Done. The guys parted for him—where had they all come from?—but no one tried to talk to him as he slammed open the stairwell door and pounded down the steps, two beats of his heart to every footfall. He kept track automatically, focusing on the physical and pulling himself out of his head. *Two more flights, round the corner, grab the rail, race down the next set, grab the rail, almost there.* Slipping into the white noise of the purely physical. Running through the fog, across the grass as soon as he was outside. Running away.

He didn't come to until he found himself panting, bent over and trying not to puke. Soaked in sweat and mist. When he could finally straighten up and focus on his surroundings, he was surprised to immediately recognize where he was, even though he'd only ever seen it at night. He'd stopped in front of Toby's apartment building. Why the fuck had he come here?

Safety.

He scanned the parking area, sucking in breaths and shaking out weak legs. But Toby's car wasn't there.

He's not here for me either.

Get a grip, dude.

He had to walk all the way back to campus. Too tired to run. No one lurked in waiting to torture him more. No idiots in the stairwell, no one hanging outside his room. The whole place was eerily quiet and deserted, as if everyone had gone underground until Jock got over his fit.

He truly appreciated that. Maybe these guys weren't so bad.

But of course when he unlocked the door to his room, Tank was sitting on Collin's bed, head bowed, hands clasped between his knees. He didn't even look up when Jock walked in and stood in front of him.

"How'd you get in?"

Tank cleared his throat, still showing Jock the back of his head and exposing his neck. Maybe that should make him look vulnerable, but since his brother's neck was nearly as thick as his skull, it didn't. "I called Collin and he let me in. He also told the guys to leave you alone."

Jock planted his hands on his hips. "But not you?"

"Yeah." Tank glanced up, then returned to his omega-wolf pose. "He told me I should leave you alone, but I had to talk to you. I need to apologize, bro. I know you probably don't want to hear it right now or see me or anything, but you gotta—"

Jock's hand on the back of Tank's head shut him up like magic. "I know."

"No you don't." Tank said, lifting his head and fully facing him, eyes red and puffy. "Or maybe I need to say it, I dunno."

Jock swallowed the lump in his throat and nodded for his brother to go on. He owed it to the guy—Tank never cried, and God knew Jock hadn't over this whole fucking thing.

"I'm sorry," Tank whispered. "If telling those guys had anything to do with why you let that guy take the picture—"

"No." Jock shook his head. "It had nothing to do with it. I was talking shit before. I was pissed because this has been—" He yanked himself away, walking over to the windows and gripping the sill, staring out at the light gray sky and the dark gray buildings and trees.

"You didn't deny it," Tank said from right behind him.

Jock rested his forehead on the cool glass, and it sent a chill through his whole body, down his back. He was still wet from his run and there was a breeze over here . . . but that had nothing to do with how cold he felt. He shook his head.

"So you did? You let that guy take the picture? Knew he'd spread it around?"

He had to squeeze his eyes shut to do it, but he nodded yes.

His brother's arm across his shoulders broke him. He hadn't cried over any of the bones he'd fractured over the years, or when that guy's blade sliced open his thigh, or either of his concussions, or when he'd been kicked off the team, but he cried now because Tank still had his back. Even after Jock had betrayed him. "I couldn't just *quit*," he choked out. "I had *prospects*. I had to—"

"Shhh." Tank forced him away from the window, turning Jock around so he could hold him. The only person in the world whose arms were stronger than Jock's and whose shoulder was at the right height for him to sob into.

"I'm—I'm sorry."

"Nothing to be sorry for," Tank said, his voice raw. "You did the best you could. Only person who needs to forgive you is you."

Jock laughed in the middle of a sob, blowing snot all over his brother's chest and neck. "That's really understanding of you, Beau. You've been hanging with too many queers."

"Yeah, some of my best friends are gay."

When Jock had pretty much cried himself out, his brother tucked him into bed—seriously. And Jock let him. He let Beau arrange the blankets under his chin and everything. "Thank you."

Tank smiled, his eyes even redder and puffier than before. "I owed you."

Jock shook his head, but he was too tired to argue. Half-asleep. "I'm missing my political science class," he mumbled.

"I'll write you a note."

Jock snuffed a half laugh out his nose. "I need to be alone. I don't care if it's Collin wanting to get in here, I don't want to see *anyone*.

Maybe ever again, but at least until tomorrow." He rolled onto his side, blinking at his brother. His eyes hurt, and he just wanted to close them. "Keep 'em all away from me?"

"'Kay," Tank said, patting his head and standing. "You got it, bro. Take a nap."

He nodded, closed his eyes, and immediately dropped off into sleep.

ΘΑΓ

Jock woke up to find the world had gone dark and silent. The sun had set and the frat boys were all snug in their beds, he assumed. The clock claimed it was after one in the morning, which meant he'd slept most of the day away. No wonder he was groggy and disoriented.

Just not actually sleepy. He lay in bed a while, staring at the patterns the campus lights made on the walls of his room, trying to convince himself he didn't need to know. But like a suicidal moth drawn to a bug zapper, he couldn't seem to stop himself from getting out of bed and opening his laptop.

He started with email. There were forty-seven, which sounded manageable until he noticed who they were from. A national LGBTQ rights magazine, a couple of reporters from Massachusetts, tons of bloggers, some local news and talk shows, and a major sports cable channel.

Oh, and a bunch from his former friends who he hadn't heard from since he'd left Avalon. He found one from Max, one from his cousin Lea, and a couple from Danny (with stuff about France and beer terror in the subject lines). He deleted the rest without opening them, and saved the few he hadn't for later reading. Then he went searching.

It was everywhere. Not the biggest story on the internet, not on the landing page of any national syndicates or anything, but word was out. And people had made comments. Reading those would be a horrible idea. He fought the temptation for long minutes, but he'd been on the edges of the limelight (at least, the local limelight) long enough that common sense won out. If some numbnut's comment about his inability to put a puck in the net pissed him off for days at a time, he really didn't need to find out how comments about where he was putting his dick would affect him.

Jesus, I can't believe I'm this important to anyone.

He sighed and clicked back to his email. Ten more had come in since he'd been searching, and the first one was from something called "Out Scout." Maybe it was because he'd denied himself the pain of reading whatever vicious things internet trolls had come up with to say, but he opened the email and read it.

Out Scout was a nonprofit "committed to furthering the cause and concerns of LGBTQ high school and collegiate athletes." They wanted to help him sue for reinstatement to the team. No surprise—his parents were still pushing him to sue, but Jock didn't see how he could win. Lots of people had seen him drinking that night, and that right there was a violation of his agreement with the athletic department. He could have been dismissed from the team just for that alone. Forget that no one ever *did* get in trouble for drinking, the point was that Schnigglehoeffer had grounds.

Plus there was the whole issue of him letting it happen because for whatever reason he'd been incapable of saying, "I don't want to go pro." He'd fucked that pooch. Jock rubbed his eyes, the bright screen in the dark room making his vision go wonky. But he didn't turn on the light or stop reading. Instead he opened the next email in his queue.

It was from another nonprofit, but this one wanted him to give inspiring talks to kids. He deleted it after the first two sentences, because he was about the last person who should be a role model.

The third one was from a guy whose name he didn't recognize that wanted Jock to "fist, fuck, and felch" him, in that order.

He'd never needed brain bleach so much in his life.

It was the next two that really killed him. One was from the goalie of the Avalon hockey team, and the other was from the second-string center.

Luc, the goalie, thought Jock had gotten fucked over, said some shit about Schnigglehoeffer being a prick and a bigot, and told Jock he should keep in touch.

Mark, the second-string center, thought Jock was a pussy who "took it up the ass," and blamed him for the shit-talking the Knights were fielding from their opponents. Jock trashed the email before reading Mark's list of insults.

He hadn't been close to anyone on the team, not yet, but for some stupid fucking reason, their opinions mattered more than he'd expected. And yeah, he'd expected some flack from them.

Whatever. Better get used to this kind of crap.

Clenching his jaw, Jock held down the power button on his computer until the screen went black, then stared out the window until sunrise. Long enough to watch a large van with a satellite dish and the logo of a local news affiliate decaled on the side pull into the parking lot nearest the frat. He ducked, low enough so he could still see but not be seen (even if his lights were off), and held his breath. *Maybe some other newsworthy shit hit the fan.*

He kept hoping that right up until the cameraman and reporter were camped in front of the dorm, and the second news van was pulling into the lot.

Stooping, he ran away from the window and out into the hallway, straight to his brother's room.

When Tank answered his pounding, Jock didn't even have to say anything. "I already saw the media dudes. No worries, bro, we have a plan," his brother said, then shoved past him and yelled, "Operation Hockey Boy is a go."

As doors opened and guys started to spill out, Jock had to let the wall hold him up because his legs couldn't anymore. He may ridicule these guys for calling emergency meetings over hangnails and posting a guard on the beer fridge, but he knew he could count on them.

As the day wore on and he was escorted by a phalanx of TAG brothers from class to class, he realized not only could he count on them, but he didn't find them annoying anymore. Maybe it was blowing up at his brother, or knowing that they all pretty much figured he'd chosen to be out, but every time Ricky took out a reporter with a deft clubbing of his cast, Jock appreciated their support without suffering the usual backlash of irritation.

He still had plenty of anger, though. Within twenty-four hours, the campus was a minefield of satellite vans and reporters who'd pretty much ask anyone questions, and he totally got why celebrities sometimes went crazy and beat the shit out of paparazzi. If one more douche bag with a microphone popped out from behind a fir tree and started shouting questions, he'd go all Kanye West on their ass.

"Why is this such a big fucking deal?" he asked Kyle's girlfriend, Ashley, at one point. Not that she had any special knowledge—she just happened to be walking next to him when he got fed up and snapped it out.

She did have some insight, though. "Because you won't talk. If you'd have a press conference or somet—"

"No."

"I thought not." She nodded. "That's what we figured your response would be." Her sorority sisters were part of the operation, too, distracting reporters through whatever means possible, from flirting to pantsing a running camera person. He'd seen that with his own eyes and laughed until he nearly puked.

The third day was what did him in, though. It was a little thing that pushed him into action—for some stupid fucking reason, he listened to his voice mail.

He pretty much didn't let himself look at the online stories about his outing, he deleted most of the thousand-plus emails he got every day without doing more than seeing who they were from, and he'd muted his phone because it rang all the time, just checking occasionally to see if someone he knew had left a message.

He didn't mean to listen to the one from Jim, executive producer for No Socks Productions, but the one Danny had left him before that went on so long that he'd lain down on his bed, phone cradled to his ear and zoned out. Next thing he knew, he had Jim's way too jovial voice telling him he thought Jock had a very "cinematic" mouth, and that he'd *love* to pay him an "obscene amount of money" to recreate the scene that had gotten Jock outed in the first place. While filmed by his crew for the "premier gay hipster-porn outlet on the internet," of course.

Jim liked to pepper his statements with Jock's name. "We're an all-class production, Jock, I assure you. We could also talk *bukkake* for some really serious dough. I'm sure I don't have to tell you, Jock, there are a lot of guys who'd get off on nutting on an athlete of your standing. There's a market for any kinky shit you wanna get up to, Jock, as a matter of fa—"

Delete. Delete, delete, delete. For a split second he was afraid he'd cracked the screen on his phone from poking the icon so hard, and that he'd need to get a new phone on top of dealing with the regular clusterfuck of activity his life had become . . .

New phone number. He didn't have to keep the same number. Why hadn't he thought about that before?

He didn't have to keep *any* of it—not his email address or his social media accounts or anything. He grabbed his laptop off the window, ordered a new phone online, opened a new email account, then started in on the other shit. Each time he closed an account he felt a little bit freer. Facebook, Twitter, and Tumblr—not looking at any posts, of course—were gone, and he didn't even want to start new ones.

He may have done this to his life, but that didn't mean he had to listen to what everyone else thought about it.

Now if only he could do something to delete the media circus. He jackknifed out of bed, landing on his feet when he realized he *could.* Or at least, he could remove himself from their presence.

As long as it wasn't too late to register for spring term in Provence.

Chapter 10

Toby left for Europe halfway through finals week, relieved to get the hell away from the constant reminders of Jock and his situation, and swamped by guilt over being relieved. Collin had told him that Jock was bearing it all "stoically," and that Brad and Tank had organized the guys so Jock wouldn't have to go anywhere without some kind of bodyguard. Toby caught sight of him a couple times, surrounded by angry, frowning fratbros, with a string of newscasters scurrying along behind, shouting.

He'd thought, for a day or so after their meeting in the café, that there'd been some renewed interest there, but Jock hadn't made any further attempts to talk to him after that, so Toby'd gone back to his holding pattern. Waiting for his bruised heart to heal, the whole time wanting to reach out and offer whatever he could to ease the pain of the sexiest frat boy God had ever created.

Which pretty much left him with hoping that the place the guys had rented would be conducive to "getting away from it all."

After three days in Tarragona, Toby picked up his rental car and spent a long afternoon following the Mediterranean to Provence, then turned inland to find out what kind of housing the fratbros had saddled him with.

They'd done good. The *gîte* was beautiful. It was actually a *bastide*, one of those fortified houses that were actually farming complexes with a main residence and multiple outbuildings. Exactly what Americans thought of when they imagined renting places in the European countryside. This one was a mixture of stone and plaster, the plaster areas painted that mellow shade of pale ochre Toby always associated with Provence: bleached-out sunflower. That was his name for it, at least.

The front door of the house swung open just after Toby parked in front of it, and an utterly stereotypical French farmwife walked out.

She was wearing jeans instead of a dress, but otherwise she had all the necessary features. Large nose, lined yet attractive face, dark, graying hair in a bun, determined set to her lips, not fat but definitely well nourished. Toby got out of the car to greet her, stepping into the mild warmth of early spring in southern France. Even now at late afternoon, the sun was exceptionally brilliant. He'd forgotten that since the last time he'd been here. Sunshine in this part of the world was simply *different*, as if it were made up of alternate hues of the rainbow or something.

He blinked away the brightness and stepped forward as the woman came toward him, holding out his hand to shake. "Madame Bouvinet? *Je m'appelle* Toby."

"Welcome!" She beamed at him, then got right down to business. "I will have you drive around to the back, yes? It will be better to park there." He breathed a silent sigh of relief that her English seemed so good. It would make it easier on the guys.

Following her directions, Toby found a second, smaller building with a gravel parking area in front of it, more like what he'd expected—not as quaint or as old, with some touches that were clearly for expedience rather than beauty. But still plastered with bleached-out sunflower, ringed by plants, and set behind a patio with a sitting area. "This is where the—what do you call them again? The boys who are part of your 'Greeks society.'"

"Uh, fratbros," Toby said unthinkingly, caught up in the glimpse of perfect blue pool water behind and to the left of the place. "We're separate from the main house?"

"*Oui*. I will show you."

The setup was pretty utilitarian, but also very French. Hopefully this was what the guys were expecting, rather than some kind of resort. The furniture was cheap, the floors were tile of course, the walls sometimes met at crazy angles or had warped surfaces, but it was in actuality awesome to his eyes. Two bedrooms on the top level, a third long skinny one tucked in under the eaves off an oversized landing in the stairs, and a large, open, timber-vaulted main floor with a kitchenette at one end and a single bathroom that was reached by stooping through a hobbit-sized doorway under the stairs. Toby checked out the television (huge), the Wi-Fi (functioning), the weight room the guys had insisted they needed (taking up half the main floor), and the laundry facilities on the back porch. "This is great," he said, smiling in some relief. From the rear of the house he could see down into a small village below the hill the *bastide* occupied.

Madame Bouvinet nodded, then motioned to the left. Toby followed her finger to a smallish, roundish in-ground pool with lots of teak lounge chairs on the flagstones surrounding it, and beyond that a teeny, tiny little hut. "You are the resident advisor, yes? That is your *cabanon*."

French wasn't his best language, but he could swear *cabanon* meant something like "shed" rather than "pool house." Oh, it was cute, and as he traversed the deck to get a better look at it, he realized it wasn't actually built for a garden gnome. More like a regular gnome. Assuming they were a little larger than the other variety, but to be truthful he didn't know. Much like the bathroom in the main building, he had to duck through the doorway. He did it, holding his breath the whole time, seriously concerned about what he'd find.

It took a few seconds of rapid blinking to adjust to the dimmer interior after the brightness of the late afternoon. When he could see, he breathed a silent sigh of relief. Yes, it was tiny inside, but it wasn't as bad as it could have been. Tall enough for his five feet eleven inches (and possibly even for someone as big as, say, Jock). When the door opened or closed, it would brush the linens of the double bed shoved against the far wall. There was a bathroom closet with a sink, a toilet, a drain in the floor, and a shower nozzle mounted in one wall. To round out the amenities, a broad shelf cantilevered out from one wall with an electric kettle sitting on top of it and a small fridge underneath. Shoved up next to it were an old-fashioned water cooler and two barstools.

Madame Bouvinet insisted on giving him the tour, standing between the bed and the counter, turning and pointing as she explained what was perfectly obvious.

"It's wonderful," he said after a minute of her explaining how the cabinets set into the walls had been cleverly fashioned by her son, and how the two "rather adequate" windows were new.

It *was* wonderful. It was his own tiny space, filled with light let in by the disproportionately large windows and wafting with the breeze through the open doorway. Looking out of it, Toby had that same view down into the valley that the laundry porch did. From the cast iron table and chairs set up in the small gravel area in front of his *cabanon*, he could watch the wind or the sky or the small cars crawling out of the small village.

He wanted to get his stuff, throw it on the bed, and dig out the carafe of wine he'd stopped at the *supermarché* for. He'd also bought olives, sausage and cheese, bottled water, and an *alpillette*—the small local version of a baguette. He could lie on his bed or sit in his patio set while he ate. Then he'd watch the sun sink slowly, maybe swim even if it was far too cold still . . .

"—meals will be in the main house, *petit dejeuner* and lunch only." Madame Bouvinet was prattling on, but she stopped suddenly and turned to him. "You are tired, are you not? *Bon*. I will give you the keys and leave you. You have something for your dinner?"

Toby assured her he did and went to get his stuff out of the car. He did the minimum possible, simply pulling out his food and wine, something to change into, and a book. Nothing erudite or academic. Science fiction.

Tomorrow would be early enough to go through the newest material he'd collected for his thesis and work it into his outline. Get into the right mindspace for writing before his charges arrived. They'd be showing up over a couple of days, and by design or by accident, Jock's plane came in last.

Three days later, the night before the first of the bros showed up, Toby got half-drunk and all philosophical, butt settled on one chair out in front of his place and feet up on the other. He was doing well—already he'd completed a decent introductory overview of his paper, and he felt like he had his ducks in a row to finish this damn thesis. As for his other duty while here, time would tell if herding the boys would suck as much as he worried it might. Really, though, how bad could anything be when he got to spend the next almost-three months here?

This place fucking rocks.

As the plane made its descent into Marseille, Jock caught glimpses of the city, the Mediterranean, and the French countryside. He had to crane his neck, looking over the heads of the other passengers, because he'd snagged an aisle seat. Mostly he caught flashes of sky, but he confirmed that it was all as sun-drenched as he remembered. He'd have liked a window seat, but being six-four made that torturous. At least with an aisle seat all he had to worry about were his legs getting run over by a food cart.

He was so fucking relieved to be getting out of the United States. Not so much the US, but the attention he'd been getting there. By the time he'd left, things had cooled down, but he'd been getting even more of the kind of attention he most wanted to avoid: the people who wanted him for their cause.

Three months in a foreign country sounded perfect. Except for the part about Toby being there.

Because of course Toby was going to pick him up at the airport. Which was no big, right? So what if they were going to be together a lot for the next few months? So the dude had popped his cherry (sorta); that didn't mean they had to have any sort of, like, future sexual interactions.

But the tension in his shoulders wasn't listening to him, so he used the trick of focusing on his immediate problems and ignoring (potential) future problems. He stood in line at immigration, mentally bitching about how slowly it moved and fidgeting with his passport. Then he fought his way to the baggage carousel for his suitcase, wheeling his luggage cart right through customs after that, passing bored-looking agents who waved him on.

Focusing on the present worked right up until he got to the frosted glass sliding doors that marked his official entry into France. When they parted—reminding him of a theater curtain even though he'd never been on a stage—fate kicked him in the nuts. Toby was standing front and center, smiling and laughing with Noah, surrounded by the rest of Jock's Theta Alpha Gamma brothers.

What, they all had to come see Jock and Toby's reunion? And what was Noah doing being all friendly like that?

No one noticed him. Well, not no one, but Toby didn't, not right away. Not until Noah jogged Toby's elbow with his own, and a smiling, bright-eyed, laughing Toby turned to him and immediately sobered up.

I never should have come.

Whatever, too late now.

Jock set his jaw and kept walking forward, until he was engulfed in bro-hugs and a chorus of greetings, yet burningly conscious of Toby hanging at the back of their small crowd the entire time. The guys moved around him in a swarm, jostling for position, different faces and voices coming at him, but he didn't really register who said what until he came face-to-face with Toby. All the activity around them continued, but static held them both in place, looking at each other across a small stretch of industrial carpeting.

Toby stood there, hands shoved in his pockets, dark hair flopping over his forehead and framing his deep brown eyes. Still mostly expressionless, just a slight curve to his lips that Jock couldn't interpret. Up on one side of his mouth and down on the other.

"How was your flight?" Toby asked after a few seconds of silence.

Jock shrugged and glanced over the guy's head. "Fine. Long."

"You hungry? We have a two hour drive back to EuroTAG."

"EuroTAG?"

Toby's lips tilted up a little more, in a tiny smirk. "That's what the fratbros are calling it," he said just loud enough for Jock to hear. Then he jerked his eyes away, scratching his temple with an index finger, as if he had to devote all his attention to it or he might miss and scratch something he didn't mean to. "Um, so, you need to eat?"

"They fed us breakfast a couple hours before we landed." Not that he'd eaten much of it. He bent over and grabbed his pack, slinging it over his shoulder and using the motion to step away from Toby. Gomer and Danny noticed, and started arguing over who would carry Jock's suitcase.

"No man, you do it. You're a junior TAG brother," Danny was saying, pushing Gomer toward the cart.

Gomer tried to hold his ground, but he stumbled back when Danny pushed harder. "What're you talking about, dude? We're all seniors except Noah and Jock."

"Yeah, but I'm only a first-year senior—you're a *second*-year senior."

"How does that make me the junior brother? Besides, Ricky's a second-year senior, too."

Danny gaped. "Ricky's still using a cane, he can't carry a suitcase."

"It's got *wheels*, doofus!" Gomer stabbed his finger at the ground. "Right there."

"You're gonna make an injured man pull that thing? That's cold, man." Danny shook his head, pursing his lips. "Real cold."

Noah stepped between them and grabbed the handle of the bag, rolling his eyes at Jock. "This might be a long term, dude."

Jock's lips twitched, like maybe they'd like to bare his teeth, but he held them still and nodded before turning away. "Which way?" he asked no one in particular.

They answered as a group, herding him toward the exit, then toward a white van in the parking lot. As they loaded in, Jock couldn't help feeling like he was getting on a school bus. It didn't help when Toby told him quietly as they loaded his luggage in the back, "Only you, Gomer, and Ricky came in today. I tried to get the other guys to stay at the *gîte*, but they were all too excited about going on a 'field trip.'"

Jock shrugged and walked around to the side door to find that the guys had left him a decent spot. It was after he was settled in the second seat back that he realized Noah had taken the passenger's seat, next to the driver. In other words, next to Toby.

He tried to rest, balling up his sweatshirt and using it as a pillow, leaning his head on the window. But he mostly watched Noah and Toby talk. And laugh. A lot.

He was an aggressive guy, Jock knew that about himself. It came with playing center. Except he wasn't a hockey player anymore but he was still aggressive, so maybe he had that backward. Thing was, his aggression was getting worse. Little things fed into it, like Noah's flirty sideways glances at Toby, and it just kept growing. Enough that some people might call it anger. It was probably better if he removed himself from public until he got over his shitty mood and maybe adjusted some of his expectations about how he was going to get through the next twelve weeks with these guys. So when they finally got to "EuroTAG," he retreated into the cramped little room off the landing that he had to share with Noah—that'd teach him to show up last—and had bread, cheese, salami, and fruit for lunch while everyone else went up to the "main house" to eat.

"Don't fall asleep," Toby warned him as he headed up the stairs. "It'll take you a week to adjust to the jet lag instead of just a day or two."

Jock didn't respond. Better to say nothing than blow up at the dude.

Yeah, it's gonna be a long three months.

Jock didn't seem happy about the sleeping arrangements. Actually, the sleeping arrangements were only the most recent thing that he seemed unhappy about. He'd seemed unhappy about the van they all had to ride around in, and unhappy about the length of the drive from Marseille to the *gîte*, and unhappy about the attempts everyone made to talk to him. He'd mostly just grunted.

Toby suspected Jock's real unhappiness lay in Toby's presence. So much for that bubble of hope.

"He's gonna be more fun than a barrel of monkeys," Noah said, standing on the main floor and looking up the stairs. It had to be an illusion that the door was reverberating from the force of Jock's annoyance, didn't it? He hadn't slammed it or anything.

"It's probably just jet lag," Toby said. Noah rolled his eyes along with his whole head to give Toby some serious side-eye. "Or something," Toby added lamely.

"Oh yeah. I'm sure it has nothing to do with you," Noah muttered right before he walked off, leaving Toby alternately glancing up the stairs and then watching Noah's back, wondering how much he shouldn't read into that comment.

"Yo!" Danny yelled from right behind him. Toby didn't jump—he was getting used to the dude's enthusiasm and volume. It would be excellent training if he were ever on the front lines of a war. "It's time for *dejeuner*." He grinned when Toby turned to him. "See? Learning French already, dude. C'mon, Madame Bovinary is waiting for us."

He'd given up on trying to get them to call her Madame Bouvinet when he'd figured out they weren't being malicious. The problem stemmed from a few of them having read *Madame Bovary* by Flaubert in a lit class last year. Or, as Gomer called him, "Flow-bert."

That was the point at which Toby had started to think of Gomer as "Oxymoron," the least intelligent of his overgrown frat-dwarves.

For her part, Madame seemed to think they were cute. "The fratbros are amusing, no?" she'd whispered to Toby at yesterday's "*dejeuner,*" when the guys kept asking each other to please pass the "*pain*" and then flicking each other between the eyes shouting, "I got your bread right here!" She even found it amusing when Julian fell over backward in his chair trying to escape Turbo's overly enthusiastic (or actually, *that* might have been malicious) thumping.

"No," Toby'd answered, even though he kind of agreed with her. Mostly he found them taxing. He supposed he could spend less time watching over them, but he didn't trust them not to get themselves in trouble, which translated into Toby babysitting them the two days they'd been in France so far. He couldn't wait until the term started next week and he could have some time to himself to work on his thesis. There was something he never thought he'd be grateful for.

For now, though, he'd follow the guys up to Madame Bouvinet's huge kitchen table and eat his share of the huge lunch she'd made them. Hopefully he could get the bros down for a nap afterward.

The only one who napped that afternoon was Jock, and he slept right on through dinner. Toby didn't envy him the next week at all.

ΘΑΓ

Jock came to suddenly, jerking onto his back, trying to remember where he was—in a room so long and narrow the two single beds were placed end-to-end. The floor was warped, aged wood, while the dressers pushed up against the opposite wall were made of brand-new, laminated pressboard. Windows high in the wall next to him were bleeding the dim, bluish light of dusk.

France. Provence. Toby.

He wanted Toby. With the clarity of mind that came from sleeping well, Jock couldn't lie to himself about that anymore. He wanted to be with Toby, and it scared the hell out of him, because Toby might want more than he could give. Like his virgin ass.

Totally should not be that big a deal, dude. Oh, but here was that hollow feeling in his stomach again that came along whenever he thought about what it, like, *meant* for him to let someone do that.

"Get over yourself," he muttered, rubbing his eyes with the heels of his hands.

Noah walking in the door surprised Jock out of his moment of clarity, but not fast enough to stop himself from saying, "Sorry if I was a dick earlier." *Okay, random. The dude just wanders in and I'm apologizing.* He tried to cover up his gaffe with a stretch, but his hands hit the wall when he raised them over his head, and his toes got tangled in the pillow of the bed at the foot of his. Noah's bed.

His roommate shut the door softly and looked at him from under his brows. "You *were* a dick."

Jock let his arms thud back down on the mattress. "Jet lag."

"Yeah, that must be it," Noah said dryly, then sighed and leaned his shoulders against the wall. "If you want me to stay away from Toby, just fucking tell me, dude."

"Are you trying to hook up with him?"

"Honestly?" Noah straightened up, and Jock held his breath. "No. I mean, I wouldn't turn him down, but I wouldn't turn Turbo down if he offered me a handjob, either."

Jock nodded, holding Noah's gaze. "'Kay."

"If it makes any difference, I don't think he's into me."

Jock studied the windows in the wall above him. They were set so high up that even standing he'd probably barely be able to see out of them. "We got screwed on room assignments, man."

"I could've gotten a better room, but I wanted to room with you."

Jock had to smile at that. "'Cause the other guys are freaks of nature."

"Oh yeah, they are." Noah rolled his eyes and shoved a hand through his hair, then turned toward one of the dressers. "And I hadn't figured out how hot Turbo is yet. Help me look for toilet paper."

"What?" Jock stared at him opening drawers and riffling through the contents. "Did you say—"

"The bathroom's out and Gomer's trapped on the john until we find some." Noah huffed a laugh while he looked through both dressers—the second one was quicker, because Jock hadn't put anything in it yet.

"That's gotta be ugly," Jock muttered, sitting up and swinging his legs over the edge of the bed. This time he stretched for real, yawning and everything. "Can you even see? Turn on the light, man." It was getting really dark.

After Noah flipped the switch, Jock helped him search the rest of the room. They didn't have any cupboards or anything, but they checked under the beds, then in the single closet, which was totally empty. It was just a shallow depression in the wall with a door and hooks inside it to hang stuff on, so the chances that it'd been anything other than thin air were slim.

Jock stood in the center of the room, hands on his hips. "There's no toilet paper in here."

Noah flopped onto his bed, spreading out as much as possible. "Looks like it," he sighed.

"Guess Gomer's on his own, huh?" Jock sat also, but on his own bed.

"Yup." Noah shifted, getting more comfortable, it seemed. "What are you gonna do tonight?"

"Not sleep. I shouldn't have napped this afternoon, Toby was right." He'd been to Europe once or twice on family vacations, not to mention all the times he'd been dragged along on his mother's buying trips during the off-season. He'd known what Toby had said was true before the dude had even said it, but Jock had fallen asleep out of spite or some other stupid, self-harming urge. He had a vague recollection of Noah trying to wake him up a couple of times, but he'd fallen into that weird jet lag space where he just. Couldn't.

"You wanna talk about him?"

"Toby?" What did he look like, a girl? "Nope."

"'Kay. Lemme tell you how Turbo fills out a Speedo, then."

"He wears a Speedo? You sure that dude's straight?"

"He's straight, in spite of all my efforts. But dude, you need to get over the stereotypes. You believe in more of those things than a Bible Belt preacher."

Jock ignored him. "Maybe I should get a Speedo," he mused.

Noah clutched his chest, gasping. "I might not survive that. But if anything's gonna turn Turbo . . ."

"Yeah." Because seriously, pretending he didn't know he had a totally smoking body would be a big lie. "Except it'd turn him toward me."

"I'll stay away from Toby if you leave Turbo for me."

"You got a deal."

Chapter 11

The Calapooya satellite campus in Saint-Rémy-de-Provence was small, which meant there were only two courses of study, one beginning and one more advanced. All the bros were taking the beginning track, which probably meant learning a bunch of local history and some language. Toby didn't know because he didn't care enough to find out. Mostly he cared that he had five hours of uninterrupted time on Mondays, Wednesday, and Fridays (and three on Tuesdays and Thursdays) to drink *café*, write, watch people walk by, maybe wander around, stop for *une bière à la pression*, and write some more . . . then repeat.

Once he delivered the fratbros on the first Monday of the term, Toby left the van in the campus lot and walked into the center of town—a picturesque, antiquated area where a smallish ring road no more than a mile or two around circled the medieval city. He'd spent a term here early on in his program, then last summer he'd come up from Barcelona for a week when he was doing primary source research for his thesis. As a result he knew the town, at least this part of it, well. The Calapooya campus wasn't far from the asylum where van Gogh had been treated for mental illness, and only a little beyond that was the ancient ruin of Roman and pre-Roman Glanum. He'd revisit those sites another day, and probably a few times. Today he had an appointment with his favorite café on that tiny square across from the Musée des Alpilles.

The weather was still iffy as he walked into the center of Saint-Rémy. Last week it had been warm enough one day that some of the guys had tried to swim; they hadn't lasted long. Today it was sunny, but the mistral was blowing hard enough that Toby had to fight against it while he walked. Too warm for the wool peacoat he'd brought, too cool to shrug it off. At least, not until he'd found his café of choice and procured a seat by the window.

As powerful and pervasive as the mistral could be, Toby loved it. When it blew throughout Provence, it subtly affected everyone's mood, but it also defined the whole area. Sometimes when he met locals, such as Madame Bouvinet, he would swear the lines on their face had been grooved by the mistral.

You are sadly romantic, my friend. But he liked himself that way, didn't he? For the first time in many months, he felt like his old self. Not excited about finishing his thesis, but able to focus. Confident he could do the job, and meanwhile interested to see what the world around him would bring. *This could all work out.*

And amazingly, the day went according to plan. Even better than planned—he didn't feel the need to get up and stretch for a couple hours, and he finished more work than he'd outlined for the day. When he did quit, he ordered another *café* and went outside to enjoy it on the Place Favier, idly inspecting the chestnut and plane trees and the sand-colored buildings with the light aqua shutters for changes in the last year or two. It was late afternoon, and people were out, making a last stop at the grocer's before it closed until evening, going by the bakery, picking up their kids from school. Everyday things like that that he didn't have to do; the best part of any vacation. And of course, tourists wandered by regularly. Not as busy as it would be on market days—Wednesdays right?—or as the summer got closer, but definitely noticeable.

He should bring the guys out here tonight. Not late to the bars or anything, but for dinner and to experience what it was like to be in a French town, even a somewhat touristy one. There were a few brasseries that weren't too expensive. He'd wander by one or two on the way back to the campus and see. Toby had to admit he liked introducing them to this part of the world. They got excited every time something struck them as especially "French" and acted a little like kids. Or a lot, depending on the guy. At any rate, it wasn't as much of a burden as he'd expected it to be.

The rest of the guys were standing behind Jock, horsing around while they waited for Toby to show up, but he was still fighting sleep in the late afternoons. He sighed and leaned his head on the cool glass of a front window in the tiny admin/student center/library building of the Saint-Rémy–Calapooya complex, watching the road. Not looking for anything in particular, just tired and drained. Weird how the street was paved, but still gave the impression of being that same light beige color of the surrounding dirt.

The French class they'd started today would be easy, since he'd taken the language in high school, but French history could be interesting or not. Maybe when they got into the term it'd be cool, especially when they started going out to visit sites. Tomorrow was their first French lit class, and if he wasn't rested up for that it would probably bore him right into unconsciousness. Why couldn't they teach French math, for fuck's sake? He'd get into that. Or science. Physics. Now there was something he understood bodily. Nothing'd taught him that an object in motion tends to stay in motion better than being on skates half his life, and applying force to get the desired (equal and opposite) reaction learned from a hockey stick meeting a puck (or hooking a blade, or hitting flesh, whatever) was something he knew instinctively at this point. Repeat something enough and it became innate.

Jock's vision cleared suddenly, making him realize he'd been blurring out, eyelids drifting shut. He blinked, focusing to find whatever his brain had picked up on. A guy walking down the road. Hands in the pockets of his hip-length coat, left unbuttoned in front. Jock could just make out the gray straps of a backpack on his shoulders. The way the dude moved was mesmerizing. Confident, long strides in a swinging rhythm, but head down as if thinking. Dark hair whipped in the wind, just long enough to blow up off the top of his head, but the sides were clipped short.

Toby. Duh. Just then the dude tilted his head to one side, like he was in the middle of an internal debate and now arguing the opposite point. Jock could make out the upper edge of those heavy-rimmed glasses Toby wore sometimes. Why were they so hot on him? It kind of drove him nuts, the way he wanted to get close and personal with those eyes as soon as they were behind that shield.

Worse was when they weren't behind the glasses and anyone could get personal just by talking to the dude.

"Here he is," Jock said, straightening up and shoving out the door into the cold wind. It had only been cool earlier, but as they got past late afternoon into evening, it seemed chillier. He shrugged his bomber jacket up around his neck more and headed straight across the lawn and the dirt parking area until he stood in front of his quarry. "Hey."

Toby jerked his head up, expression going slack, then he squinted at Jock. "Your eyes are bloodshot. Jet lag's still getting to you, isn't it?"

Jock nodded and shifted his stance, not sure what to say, a little glow over Toby noticing heating him up.

"Driving back to the house would probably put you right to sleep now. I was going to suggest to the guys that we eat early in town tonight, hang out awhile, since Madame Bouvinet won't be providing dinner."

Jock was pretty tired of bread, salad, fruit, cheese, and salami in the evenings. One thing he'd forgotten about Europe was the way lunch was the main meal and dinner almost an afterthought. "That sounds cool."

Toby grinned, and the little glow inside Jock responded to the smile, upping its heat output. "I have a place in mind. It's not horribly expensive, but nothing around here is cheap. Too many tourists."

"But it'll broaden the cultural horizons of the guys?" Jock lifted a brow, smirking.

Toby's lips curved up even more. "Yeah. You get the idea."

"Not short on ideas," Jock said, eyes stuck on Toby's mouth.

"Hey!" Danny said, his outdoor voice booming right into Jock's ear, and Jock flinched forward, grabbing Toby's arm. Either to steady himself or steady the other guy or possibly just to touch him. Danny shoved his head between them, and Jock let go reflexively. "What're you guys talking about?"

Toby blinked, long and slow. Moving his attention from close-focus to wide-angle or something. He pasted a whole different smile on his face and turned to Danny.

"We're talking about food," he said, then a bunch of other stuff that Jock wasn't really paying attention to because he was trying to tease out the change in Toby's expression. Jock could pick out individual muscles in Toby's cheeks and jaw now—like Toby'd had to *make* them react in the appropriate ways. Had to school his expressions, where before he maybe'd just let them happen.

Jock was still thinking about the implications of that when they were loading into the school bus. Somehow, he ended up in the passenger seat without even trying. The brief drive into the center of Saint-Rémy zoned him out again, his mind wandering around and bumping into questions like, *Could I maybe just tell him I don't wanna bottom?* and *If I asked him to, would Toby blow me while wearing those glasses?* He sorta knew the answer to the first one, but the second question consumed his thoughts all the way to the parking lot in town.

"It's a hundred meters or so to the brasserie," Toby was saying as they got out, but Jock focused on the low hum of his voice more than the words. He opened his door, and the wind slapped him in the face and cleared the cobwebs and fantasies out, leaving him teetering there a few seconds, getting his bearings.

"C'mon man, let's go get some *bière*," Gomer said, walking up and slugging Jock in the arm. "I wonder how you ask for beer in French?" he continued in a hushed tone, as if pondering a religious mystery.

"*Je voudrais une bière pression, s'il vous plaît.*" Jock answered automatically, his four years of academic French welling up from the depths of his brain. Well, academic with a little extracurricular thrown in.

"That would be it," Toby said from his other side. Jock wasn't one hundred percent comfortable with how pleased that made him feel inside, like he'd gotten the approval of his coach. The dude wasn't his coach, and considering his last coach? He didn't want another figure like that in his life.

Dinner was in one of those places he never got to go into when here with his family because it was too local and down-market. Basically a bar, but the food was good. Jock ordered the classic *steak frites* and, on the advice of Julian, a white wine. According to him, if Jock drank white, he wouldn't get the headache red gave him. The other thing he learned from that conversation was that straight guys drank wine too, at least guys like Jules.

"Of course straight guys drink wine." The dude rolled his eyes. "Do you think the vineyards of the world could continue to run a profit on the amount women and gay guys consume?"

Jock nodded. "Yeah, I do."

Jules sighed theatrically. "Maybe it's because all your information is from straight guys who play hockey? I bet they aren't chugging wine in the locker room." He leaned back when the waiter came at that moment to deliver their drinks.

"Probably not so much," Jock agreed, watching Jules dig through his backpack under the table, pull out a wet wipe, and then carefully polish the rim of his glass with it.

When he was forced to turn away or laugh out loud at Julian's neurosis—totally cruel thing to do—he caught Toby watching also, then similarly looking elsewhere. Right at Jock. Was it random they could communicate with a look, or was it because they'd fucked? Thinking back to when they'd met, Jock had to go with random connectedness, because they'd totally been sending each other eye-messages that night too. And he didn't think he'd managed it with any of the other guys he'd been with before or since, but maybe that was lack of opportunity.

Nah. He and Max had blown each other tons of times, and hung out together, and he'd never shared any sort of private jokes with the dude, not like he and Toby were now, both suppressing smiles and both knowing exactly why. Or could he be reading into it? Maybe Toby was just trying to figure out what Jock's problem was, and that quivering lack of expression on his face was him trying not to make Jock feel weird?

But then Danny whined loudly next to Toby, "How come you didn't tell me steak tartar is raw meat?" and just before Toby turned away to explain once again that, since the menu had been in English, he'd thought Danny'd actually read it, one side of his mouth slid upward, and he rolled his eyes, just enough for Jock to see, but no one else.

Yeah, they had a connection.

ΘΑΓ

Jock looked like he was falling asleep at the table. He'd had two glasses of wine with dinner, and eaten everything on his plate, plus a salad, and now he'd propped his cheek on his fist, leaning on his elbow, eyelids drooping while around him the guys continued to have a good—or at least animated—time. Julian and Gomer were talking excitedly about that movie they'd seen the other night. Noah was still trying to flirt with Turbo, and Turbo was still mentally scratching his head over it, at least judging by his expression. Not offended or threatened, more like confused and not sure that what he thought was going on actually *was.*

Toby hadn't thought about whether Noah was into guys until Turbo had shown up in skimpy briefs the afternoon the bros had tried to prove late March was a reasonable time to swim in Provence. Noah had been sitting (fully clothed) on a lounge chair next to Toby (similarly dressed), making jokes about needing popcorn for the show, when he'd cut himself off mid-sentence. When Toby'd looked at him, Noah had been staring at the back porch of EuroTAG, mouth agape. Salivating over Turbo. The dude was hot, Toby wasn't blind, but his tongue hadn't been in danger of rolling out the red carpet the way Noah's was either. There was something . . . less about Turbo. Less tall, and less cut, and less broad-shouldered. Less light hair and more dark.

Toby hadn't delved into any secrets his inner self wanted to keep on who Turbo was lesser than. Instead he'd nudged Noah with his elbow. "He's totally straight, I can tell from here."

"So are all those gay-for-pay guys on the internet," Noah had murmured. "How much cash do you have on you?"

Since then, Noah had chatted up Turbo every chance he got. Toby figured another week or so of this and Turbo'd be about done. Which was probably about two weeks longer than the average frat boy would put up with it. At least that's what his innate assumptions about their kind told him. Although he was starting to wonder how accurate those assumptions were for any frat boys, not just these ones.

Movement to his left drew his attention from Noah and back to Jock. Judging by the way he was blinking and swaying while upright in his chair, his elbow had just slid off the table, jarring him awake. He was cute with his hair all messy like that and the squareness of his jaw somehow softer, like dozing off blurred all his sharp edges. He made a very sleepy, very sexy boy. Someone needed to take him to bed.

Put him. Put him to bed. Either way, Toby'd volunteer for the job.

Stop it.

He surreptitiously checked his watch. Almost seven. If he could keep Jock conscious a little longer, the kid would beat the forced exhaustion of jet lag for the day. He leaned across the table. "Want to walk back to the van with me?" Nerves fluttered in his stomach as soon as he asked, because to him it sounded shockingly similar to the time in tenth grade when he'd asked Lewis Maldonado if he wanted to walk over to his house after school since his parents wouldn't be home.

Was he seriously getting nervous about walking through a night-shrouded, very romantic European city with another guy? Even one he was very attracted to?

Yes. Yes he was.

Jock nodded heavily. "I should probably get up and move around."

Toby didn't let his eyes linger on Jock's, because he'd said yes now, and Lewis had said yes back then, and those memories led directly to the one about Lewis Maldonado being the first guy to touch Toby's penis that afternoon. *Chill. Jock's touched your penis.*

Wait, had he? Toby couldn't specifically recall it, although he remembered a lot of what happened that night and he'd definitely touched—oh, Jock was standing up. Maybe he should be getting ready to go too, instead of sitting here thinking about various dicks. He turned and told Danny ("Sorta Reliable" was Toby's current nickname for him) he'd come by with the van to pick them up in ten minutes and to make sure all the bros were *out front waiting for him* (repeated twice, for insurance), left money for his part of the bill, and steered his semi-somnambulant hunka hunka out the door with a hand between the dude's shoulder blades. Toby ignored the heated exchange between his palm and Jock's skin (under two layers of clothing), letting his touch fall away as soon as they were outside.

Jock stopped and took a couple of deep breaths. It was just cool enough that Toby could see his wispy exhalations in the streetlight. He shoved his hands in the pockets of his bomber jacket and tilted his head a few seconds later, indicating he was ready to go. They made it around the corner and into the narrow street that would take them back through the old village to the municipal lot before Jock spoke. "Good idea taking us to that place. The guys liked it."

"Yeah? What about you?" God, did that sound like he needed reassurance? Hopefully not, but the reality was he wanted to hear Jock's praise. *You're twenty-four. Get ahold of yourself.*

Jock smiled, but kept watching their path. “It was cool. Every other time I’ve been to France it’s been with my family, and Mom doesn’t go to places like that.”

“Too lowbrow?” Toby joked, then was attacked by more uncertainty. Was that insulting? Insulting the mother of a guy he’d like to sleep with again seemed in very bad form. *Shit.*

But Jock chuckled. “Totally.” He stepped around a barricade in the roadway that protected the new stones that had just been laid in this street, and Toby was forced to walk on the other side of it, separating them. As soon as they were past it, he overcompensated, drifting back to Jock’s side too quickly—almost careening—and bumping elbows with him.

What was this, his second puberty? “So, are you glad you came?” Toby blurted.

Jock shrugged, and Toby thought he was about to revert to his strong, silent, defensive wall, but then he answered. “Yeah. I needed to get away from all that shit, you know?” He stopped walking and turned to Toby, half his face in shadow with just a hint of dimple flickering in his visible cheek.

“I know,” Toby agreed, trying to console, then caught himself when Jock’s mouth turned down. “That’s not what I meant.” He was never saying what he intended to Jock, was he? “I meant that I can imagine.”

Jock’s nostril flared and his lips flattened out. “You can, huh?”

“No.” Toby shook his head, holding Jock’s gaze and his own breath a second. “Not on the scale you’re dealing with. If a picture of me blowing some guy surfaced, no one would care. Not even my mother, probably. Not to mention it wouldn’t end up on someone’s Tumblr because I’m just not as hot as you.” *Oh God.* He’d said that.

“Um, thanks?” Jock’s dimple reappeared, stronger and more solid this time.

Toby had to laugh at that, and at his own stupid nerves, and then he started walking again when Jock did.

“I’d put you on my Tumblr,” Jock said after a few seconds of silence.

“Um, thanks.” *I’d love to be on your Tumblr. Tumble me, baby.*

“Especially if you were on your knees and had your shirt off.”

Heat blasted through his chest on a tendril of mistral, but Toby did his best to ignore it. He swallowed. "The knees thing is important?"

"Yeah."

He might be reliving his teenaged angst over whether this boy liked him, but his somewhat more adult self had been around the block a time or two, and it knew an opportunity when it saw one. Before Toby's pimply, pubescent slice of psyche could stop it, that part of him reached out to take Jock's arm, stopping them both, and even bringing them a few inches closer together. "We could work that out. The shirt off and me on my knees. Your dick in my mouth." He took a shuddery breath, because between what he was saying and how Jock's shadowed eyes seemed to pin him down, he needed more air. "I'm not as into the camera part, but we could possibly negotiate that as well."

Jock's face went blank. Worse than blank. All the muscles in his cheeks went rigid, and one in his jaw kept flickering into prominence and then smoothing out. Fast enough to remind Toby of a strobe light.

The "experienced adult" part of himself was a fucking *moron*. "I shouldn't have mentioned the camera, huh?" he asked in a whisper.

"I don't want to see you like that," Jock announced, then wrenched himself backward, grazing the wall of a building before turning to walk along the road again.

"What?" Toby asked the air where Jock had been. It didn't reply, so he forced himself into movement, heart speeding up and tripping over itself, moving him forward until he was right behind Jock. "What was that about Tumblr, then?" He could pick up the thready note of anger in his voice, and it was such a relief to not be the fawning idiot he'd been since they'd left the bar. Or the hopeful guy who'd internalized every positive interaction they'd had, no matter how minor. "That was suggestive of someone who *would* like a blowjob, in case you're unaware." Jock halted, and Toby bounced off his back, faltering to catch his balance. "And you could simply say you aren't interested, you don't have to respond to me as if I've got a communicable disease." He'd had to say it, because he *knew* it would matter to Jock that he'd wounded Toby.

He could hear Jock swallowing before he turned around. They stood couple feet apart, looking at each other. "I'm sorry."

Toby couldn't respond with something like *It's okay* or *Thanks*, because it wasn't okay and he wasn't thankful. So he kept silent.

"Okay," Jock said, shifting suddenly, glancing away. "That picture, it's like I don't . . . respect myself for what happened, and I don't want someone I do respect in that position. It's not that I wouldn't want that. You to do that for me, it's just . . . Shit," he muttered, nudging the pavers with his toe.

"What *do* you want?" Toby asked after what had to be a full minute of silence. Which was a very long time when one was staring at someone who could crush one's ego with a word, waiting for him to utter said word. "I'm pretty much laying it on the line, Jock. I'd like to get with you again." And if he was going to lay it *all* on the line . . . "I'd really like it if you stayed in my bed next to me all night, and maybe even planned to come back other nights." Yeah, he'd said *that*. "What you do or don't want is the barrier here, and you're giving me some pretty mixed signals. I'll step off if you tell me to—"

"No." Jock swallowed again, watching his foot with brow-wrinkling focus. "I need to think about it. This is, I don't know, important."

Toby was tempted to cross his arms and tap his foot while he waited, but they could stand here all night, or a couple of days. Because something in the way the muscle in Jock's cheek bunched up suggested a whole load of indecision that wouldn't be easily resolved. So instead Toby backed up, and added in a much softer voice. "Take what time you need, but if you decide you don't want to be with me?" He waited until Jock's gaze met his before finishing. "I'd like you to let me know. Don't just . . . forget about me."

"Sure," Jock nodded quickly, with all the fervor of someone who'd avoided having to answer an impossible question. Then he frowned. "Is that what I did before?"

"It's okay." Toby waved off his question. "You had stuff to work out. It's not like you knew if you stayed I'd offer you more." Another thing he shouldn't have said. Implying that they could have created something relationship-like that night if Jock had given them the opportunity. *Way to scare him off.*

He could literally see Jock chewing on some thought, jaw working. "Okay," he said finally. "But, like, help me out here and tell me what you *are* offering or whatever, 'cause I'm not really sure what's going on."

"I guess . . ." *Huh*. He hadn't actually thought about specifics, because it had seemed too dangerous to let himself go there. "I like you. When I stand near you?" He stepped closer, partly to illustrate. "I want to touch you. Physically attracted to you, like we're magnets or something. When I talk to you, I feel like we connect." Jock nodded, but didn't interrupt, so Toby finished his half-formed thoughts. "I'd like a chance to find out how deep that connection goes. That's all I want." For now.

A smile flashed across Jock's face, then died down. "That doesn't sound too scary or anything." He took a breath and came closer, so they were inches apart. Then, so fast Toby didn't see it coming, he leaned in and kissed him. Just lips touching, and by the time Toby'd registered the shock of Jock's touch, regrouped and reacted to it with his own lips, Jock was pulling away. "I'll try and figure my shit out and let you know ASAP."

Not the most romantic thing he'd ever heard, but it'd do. Toby shrugged his eyebrows. "Sounds good to me."

Chapter 12

It took Jock about thirty seconds of reflection before he figured out the reasons pursuing Toby scared the hell out of him.

The first thing was the whole bottoming issue, but that wasn't any surprise—he'd already been thinking about it, and knew there was a work-around. At this point, he had just enough experience to be sure he could tell Toby he wasn't ready for that, and buy himself some time to figure out how to get over his squeamishness or whatever. Until now, he hadn't been putting any energy into working it out, because it hadn't come up. He didn't know if he just looked or acted like a total top, but no guy he'd been with had ever even hinted they wanted to fuck him.

But Toby was versatile, and if they got involved he'd for sure bring it up. Maybe Jock'd get lucky and it wouldn't come up until he'd successfully psychoanalyzed himself, but if it came up before then, he at least had a plan.

The second scary thing was kind of a surprise, even though it probably shouldn't have been.

He had to tell Toby about the picture and how he'd come out, because if he didn't it would be like lying to the dude. Not that he'd really be lying, but it would feel like a lie to Jock. When he'd admitted to Tank that he'd set himself up to be outed, he'd unloaded a ton of shame. So much that even under siege by the news media, he'd felt more at peace with the whole thing. Not okay with it, but no longer hating at himself as much. His brother was the one person he'd really owed the truth to.

Until Toby'd said that thing about the camera, and Jock realized he couldn't not tell *him* how it went down. Not if he actually wanted to try having some kind of relationship, and he thought he did. 'Cause thinking about the guy most of his waking hours had to be some kind of sign, right?

Did he have to tell Toby before they hooked up again, though? Like, could he maybe take this thing between them—relationship or whatever it was—for a test run first? Make sure it was really what he wanted?

Questions like that kept him from talking to Toby for days, even about little things, until he realized the reason the dude was in such a shitty mood all the time was his fault.

Toby had become too fucking reserved. Jock hated it. The guy wasn't like that normally, never had been, but now he didn't smile as much and he mostly only spoke after being spoken too, at least around Jock. The other guys were starting to notice, too.

On Friday, Toby found out their history prof didn't think they needed to see some protohuman site in Nice, and insisted he would take them to see it instead. "When are you going to be in this part of the world again—while taking a topical history class at the same time, no less—to see this? These are some of our nearest human ancestors, and that hack doesn't think it's important for you guys to explore it? Who *is* this douche, anyway?"

"That's Professor Douche to us," Danny said. Toby scowled. No one else tried to jolly him out of his annoyance, they just all agreed to go on the trip on Sunday.

It was exhausting, raining and so windy that Toby had to fight with the steering wheel to keep the van on the road. For once Jock didn't feel guilty not talking to him in spite of riding shotgun, because Toby needed to concentrate on driving. All two-plus hours of it each way. The weather got a little better as they went east, but Toby's mood didn't. By the time they got to the site, everyone was pissy, and as far as Jock could tell it was mostly dirt and some formations that people with letters after their name insisted were the remains of 350,000-year-old huts.

When they got back to EuroTAG, Noah followed Jock up to their room. Jock had figured it was so he could change out of his damp clothes, too, but judging by the way the dude firmly shut the door and then crossed his arms over his chest and glared, there was more going on.

"What?" Jock asked, dropping onto the edge of his bed and starting to strip off his soaked footwear.

"How long are you going to keep him hanging?"

He stared at the foot he'd just bared—it looked pale and wrinkly with the veins all standing out, the way feet did when they were too damp too long. Unattractive, kinda how he felt right now. "So, like, *all* you guys know?"

"That you and Toby are going to get together sooner or later? No. I think Danny has it figured out, but the other guys haven't noticed. Not yet, but they will."

"Fuck me," Jock said to himself, finally attacking his other shoe.

"Why is that so bad?" Noah asked. "That everyone knows?"

Jock threw his second sock at the dude, not really mad, just frustrated. Noah ducked but kept looking at him steadily until Jock answered. "Excuse the fuck out of me for thinking most of the world knows enough about my sex life already."

"So . . . what? You're going to never, like, date, because you don't want anyone noticing? Nothing but hookups the rest of your life."

"No. Just." *Fuck.* "I'll work it out."

Figuring out how much he cared or didn't about how much the guys knew took him another couple of days of not talking to Toby. So he left them both hanging for a week and a half, until Tuesday morning when he woke up and it hit him: *I'm never going to not be scared about this.* Which meant he had two choices: let his nerves stop him, or talk to Toby despite his nerves. It was totally against his nature to let nerves stop him, or at least it used to be, but without hockey—

Okay, fuck hockey, dude. Stop whining. He shoved himself out of bed, throwing off his blankets. They landed on Noah's head.

"Hey!"

"I'm gonna go work out. Breakfast is in an hour."

Noah rolled over and started snoring. Somehow he always made it to breakfast in time, in spite of never getting up until the last second. When Jock had gone through his routine, taken a shower and dressed, then arrived at the table, Noah was already there. Everyone was already there. The only seat left for Jock was next to his roommate, and two over from Toby.

Wasn't like Jock could try talking to him at breakfast. Wasn't like he had a clue what to say anyway, other than, "I'm dying to touch you." He'd like to find out if Toby's hoodie hugged his torso as tightly as it looked like it did, and he wanted to abrade his lips with the scruff on Toby's jaw and down his neck. He wanted a chance to see the fur on his chest and belly again, and—

Clink-clink-clink. Jock jerked his eyes off of Toby and saw Danny, tapping his fork against his coffee mug. Leave it to him to ruin a good memory. As soon as he had everyone's attention, he nodded and said, "As you all know, Jules had ulterior motives when he came along on this term abroad."

"*I* didn't know that," Toby said. He didn't sound happy about it.

"He came not only to soak up the culture," Danny continued blithely, "and to eat the excellent offerings from Madame Bovinary's table." He turned in his chair and took Madame's hand, kissing it gallantly and smiling at her. She giggled, but thank fuck she wasn't the type to blush. Danny turned back to the table, lifting both palms in the style of the great orators. "He also came to soak up some education in the language of *loooove*."

"Oh Jesus," Toby muttered.

Noah nudged Jock with his elbow, giving him a sly sideways look. "Told you," he mouthed.

"I thought he came for the same reason as the rest of us," Ricky objected.

"To go to school?" Toby sniped.

"For anti–beer terrorist training."

"Oh, yeah, totally, dude." Danny nodded. "But see, that's the thing—the antiterrorism agent is like a Renaissance man, isn't he? He's gotta be good at lots of shit, including being able to charm the babes. 'Cause he never knows when his life of cloak-and-dagger will demand it."

"Oh my God," Toby groaned.

It was drowned out by the sound of Jules gulping. "You didn't tell *me* that," he said to Danny in a strangled whisper.

"You'll be fine." Danny patted him on the shoulder reassuringly, then addressed the table as a whole again. "On Friday, I gave him a little 'homework.'" He air-quoted with panache. He had to have practiced that in front of a mirror. "And now he's ready to give a presentation of what he's worked up for his assignment." Danny nodded across Turbo to Jules, grinning with all his teeth. “Don’t be shy, dude. No one’ll laugh. We’re all here to support you.”

Jock had his doubts about that.

Julian stood unsteadily, picking up a stack of note cards lying next to his plate, shuffling them and then tapping them against the table to align them perfectly. Then again. “Um, you guys can keep eating, this isn’t a big deal,” he said, voice wobbling a little.

Jock took another of Madame’s croissants from the basket, but more to help Jules pretend that not everyone was dying to hear what he had to say. He’d already had four this morning, but he’d have another for the cause. Some of the other guys started eating again, too, but no one seemed to take it seriously except Turbo, who rolled his eyes at his food and then started shoveling it in.

Julian took a huge breath, chest expanding, then blew it out slowly, in the manner of someone who’d googled tips on how to relax before speaking publicly. “Okay, um, my assignment was to research ways that European men approach women. Which I haven’t really had a chance to do,” he gave Danny a bit of a stinkeye. “Because we haven’t been out a lot.” He very obviously didn’t look at Toby. Jock glanced at him in time to see Toby throw his napkin on the table and his eyeballs heavenward.

“What, I’m your social director?” the dude said. “Walk down to the village if you guys need to go out at night and conduct research on the mating rituals of the French.”

Danny frowned and pointed his fork at Toby. “That’s not very supportive,” he hissed. “Go on, Jules. Tobes didn’t mean to kill the atmosphere.”

Jock had his doubts about that, too.

Jules did the calming breath thing again, tapped his cards three times, stood frozen for a few seconds (Jock took a wild guess that it was three), and then tapped them three more times. “Okay, so, I went online and looked some stuff up, and this is what I came up with,” he rushed out before glancing around the table.

Jock did his best to look supportive.

“Um. Suave, European pickup lines.” He lifted the cards up to his nose and read off of the top one in the worst fake accent Jock had ever heard. "Your skin, she eez as smooth and creeeemy as cheese fondue. I would love to steeck my fork in zat."

Jock tried not to laugh, he truly did, which was more than he could say about some of the guys at the table. Ricky spewed a fine mist of coffee over everything before cackling so hard he had to clutch the table to stay in his chair. Toby had clamped his lips shut, but laughter kept erupting out of him, forcing itself around his attempt to take this seriously. Danny glared and yelled at everyone to be supportive, but Turbo and Gomer were guffawing so loudly they drowned him out. Next to Jock, Noah gasped like he'd laughed himself right out of air.

Jock caught Toby's eye, which was a total mistake, because they both gave in to the general mockery of Julian. At that point Jock could honestly say he was cracking up over the rest of the guys as much as Jules's come-on à la Emmentaler. Until Julian shouted over everyone, "What? I *like* fondue." After that it was more about laughing *at* the dude. Jock crouched over his plate with his head down, trying not to humiliate Julian more than necessary while he lost it. Noah jostled his arm, hard, then again, this time trying to push Jock out of his chair. Still chuckling, he turned to face his neighbor, and was met by the sight of someone's ass smashed into someone else's groin, the unknown pelvises—*male* pelvises—grinding against each other violently, in a jerky rhythm.

Noah and Turbo. *Never thought Turbo'd go for it.* And shit, especially not at breakfast, in front of everyone. Had Julian's pickup line had an unintentional effect? Turbo was all over Noah, arms around his waist, squeezing him so tightly it looked like he was trying to fist Noah's belly button.

Never thought Noah'd be into the rough stuff either. And he didn't look like he was enjoying it. His face was turning purple, and he was desperately trying to suck in a breath, body flailing and spasming as Turbo drove his fist against Noah's stomach again, up toward his diaphragm, like he was trying to force Noah's air out.

Wait a second—

"Shit, he's *choking*!" Gomer shouted, leaping out of his seat and reaching across the table, as if that could help.

A cough so soft it was anticlimactic was all the warning the dude got before a chunk of *fromage et croissant* flew out of Noah's gasping mouth and beaned Gomer directly in the forehead. Gomer jerked back, pawing at his face, falling against Madame's chair and toppling over the back of it. The *crack* of his head hitting the tile floor more than made up for Noah's lack of exclamation.

Noah's sucking breaths were the only sound for seconds after that, until Turbo let go of him and stepped away. Noah flopped to the floor with an audible thump.

"Okay." Toby stood up, chair legs screeching on the floor, perfectly calm. "The bus to the hospital leaves in five minutes. You two—" he waved his finger between Julian and Danny. "You're in charge of getting Gomer to the van. Don't jostle him more than absolutely necessary. Jock and Turbo, you've got Noah." Toby glanced down at the floor. "He's probably okay, but if he needs—"

"I've got it," Jock said, nodding. He'd seen enough trauma to handle this. There wasn't even any blood.

Toby's shoulders relaxed infinitesimally, and that gave Jock a rush he wasn't expecting at all. He'd never felt like this when he'd helped out his coach. *Seriously need to stop thinking about him that way.*

"Thanks," Toby breathed.

"What'm I supposed to do?" Ricky asked.

Gomer groaned, but didn't offer other commentary. Madame hustled over to him, crouching down, and Danny followed her.

"Ricky, call the school and tell them you guys won't be coming in today." Toby paused to sigh. "I'm going to take a wild guess you're all going to want to go to the hospital too."

"Well, I mean . . ." Danny said, looking up from where he knelt next to Madame Bovinary, arm around her shoulders to comfort her. "We can't really say it was a successful trip to Europe if we don't go to a hospital at least once."

Toby's eyebrows shot up, but he turned toward the door. "I'm going to get the van and bring it to the front entrance. You guys meet me there with your fallen comrades."

Madame took control as soon as Toby walked out, herding them all to the door and supervising their loading into the van. Jock had never seen it done so efficiently. Then she commandeered the seat next to Toby, which was a relief to Jock. The bros had gotten in the habit of engineering it so he always sat there. He'd tried to get someone else to ride shotgun, but no matter what he did, the guys were in and out of the vehicle, switching places like it was a clown car, until Jock took his place on the front passenger side.

Had he seriously thought the guys didn't notice he and Toby had something—whatever it was—going on? Thank God Madame Bovinary took precedence and sat in his regular spot.

Except as soon as her butt hit the seat, Jock realized he wanted it back. That was his spot, and it didn't matter what the guys thought, because it was his life, not theirs, and he'd sit next to Toby if he wanted to.

Fuck, he was a blind idiot when he wanted to be.

Madame began giving Toby orders. "The *clinique* in Saint-Rémy—"

"Clinique les Alpilles?" Toby asked. "That's where the college contracts for health services."

"*Bon*." She nodded, then slapped the dash with her palm a couple of times. "*Allez, vite*. I'll direct you."

An hour later, Jock found himself in the waiting room of what looked like a pretty American urgent care clinic, except for the signs in French, with Noah sitting near him, telling him what the doctor had said after they'd checked him out. "I'm gonna have the bruise on my abdomen for a few days. He said it's, like, internal. They did one of those scans on me, the kind they give pregnant women."

"Ultrasound," Jock supplied. He wanted to get up and move. He'd been sitting here too long, but it sounded like Noah needed to talk. He stretched his arms out, laying them on the back of the seats next to him. That'd have to do for now. Toby was pacing, sorta. Wandering to one side of the room, past the potted plants and the industrially upholstered armchairs to look out one bank of windows a minute. Then he'd wander on, past the rack full of some kind of medical literature to the other bank of windows where he'd stand a while. Then he started over. Jock was jealous of his mobility.

Noah cleared his throat, but it didn't help the raspiness. "And I got this spray for my throat. It makes it numb." He made a face, swallowing a few times. "I don't like it."

"You sound like someone throat-fucked the shit out of you."

Noah brayed. That's what nearly choking did to his laugh: turned it from a normal sounding thing to an echoing, high-pitched grating bark. Clamping his mouth shut, cutting off the sound, he turned to Jock. "That's *fugly*."

"It's not a good sound for you, man," Jock agreed.

Toby wandered up to them, hands stuffed in his pockets. Well, to Noah. That was who he halted in front of, not Jock. "You all right?"

Noah shrugged. "They let me go; I must be."

Toby sighed, glancing around the room. "I wish they'd tell me what's up with Gomer."

Jock almost asked why they'd tell him, but, duh, he was responsible for them, wasn't he? Madame B mothered them, but she wasn't in charge in the college's eyes. Sucked to be Toby. And Jock hated that he was adding to the dude's stress. *Gotta fix that.* "He'll be all right," Jock said.

Toby tilted his head, acknowledging what Jock said, and also that it was empty reassurance. But then Jock caught his eye, and he could read Toby's appreciation of the gesture in them.

"Monsieur Moore?" a guy in scrubs called out just then, holding a clipboard and looking around the room expectantly. Toby's shoulders slumped as he turned and walked over to the guy, but Jock couldn't tell if it was from relief, dread, or a mixture of both.

"He saved my life, dude," Noah said, reminding Jock he existed. And of course when he checked, Noah was watching Turbo talk to Danny across the room.

"I really don't think you should read too much into it." It was worth a try; he might listen.

Noah frowned. "Maybe you're right, because when he was pressed up against me doing the Heimlich, he wasn't hard at all."

Jock stared at the side of his friend's stupid, mooning head, willing Noah to take it back. He didn't. "You *noticed*? Maybe he had other things to think about, like keeping you from choking to death."

"So you think he might actually have gotten hard if he'd done that when I *wasn't* choking?" Noah finally turned his attention to Jock, but only because he wanted to believe.

"Reality check." Jock waved his hand in front of Noah's face. "It wouldn't have fucking *happened* if you weren't choking."

"Yeah." Noah turned back to his object of affection. "But if it *had* . . . ?"

"Jesus," someone muttered. It was Toby, standing behind them, pulling his coat on. "Give it up, Noah. He's never going to bone you."

Jock tilted his head back to see Toby. "So we're leaving?"

"Soon as they discharge Gomer. They don't think he has a concussion, but we have to keep an eye on him. Like I don't spend enough time doing that," he added in a mutter, straightening out his jacket collar in jerky movements.

When they all piled back into the van to return to the *gîte*, Jock found himself sitting in the front passenger seat again. He couldn't say how it had happened, but he didn't fight it this time. Besides, Madame B seemed happy sitting next to Danny. They were giggling together, having some kind of private conversation. A couple times, when Jock glanced back, he caught her patting Danny's knee and giving him a sidelong looks from under her lashes. The third time, Danny placed his hand over hers and squeezed it, smiling at her, before they moved apart again.

Huh. Under the guise of fiddling with the radio, Jock leaned closer to Toby, asking him quietly, "There's no Monsieur Bouvinet, is there? I mean, I've never seen the dude . . ."

Toby set his mouth in a resigned line. "No, he died in a farming accident, I guess. Thank God I don't have that to worry about, too."

Jock turned the radio to static instead of the pop rock they'd had on in the background, giving himself an excuse to stay right here. "Um, you don't really think Danny'd go for it, right? I mean, she's, like, old enough to be his grandmother." He kept fiddling until he found a new station. It sounded like more alternative rock than the crap the guys mostly listened to. Sweet.

Toby blew out an exasperated breath, gaze flicking to the rearview mirror. "Weirder shit has happened in the history of the world."

"Yeah, but—"

"Uh oh," Toby said, whatever he saw in the mirror making him widen his eyes.

"Okay, everyone." Danny clapped his hands for attention. "Since we aren't going to class today, I thought we'd continue Jules's education. Let's discuss where he went wrong this morning, shall we? Constructive comments only, guys," he warned.

Turbo snorted. "He came up with the *cheesiest* pickup line ever."

Noah's braying filled the van, and even through his own laughter Jock caught Toby's flinch at the sound of it.

"That's not very helpful, dude," Danny said loudly enough to drown out the donkey guffaws. "Does anyone *else* have anything to—"

"No," Toby barked, louder than Danny and Noah combined, effectively shutting everyone up.

For a couple of seconds. "Tobes, this is necessary for Julian's devel—"

"*Danny*," he snapped. "Do not make me pull this van over. If you don't drop this subject, I'll do it." Toby nodded emphatically, jaw set. "I swear I will."

Danny held his hands up, palms out. "Okay, okay, man. Sorry. Subject closed. Didn't mean to cause any problems, I was only trying to—"

"Shut. Up."

Danny did. Toby reached over and turned up the music, mumbling, "Told you there's more bizarre shit in the world," as he did so.

"Uh-huh," Jock agreed. Inside, he resolved to suck it up and talk to Toby. Because judging from what had just happened, the dude was going to a dark place, and Jock could at least let him know he wasn't going to ignore this whole situation.

Even if, after Toby found out all the details, he might decide he'd rather ignore Jock.

ΘΑΓ

If the bros didn't stop engineering it so Jock sat next to him in the van, Toby was going to string some of them up by their fucking balls. A few of the smaller ones probably. Gomer was about the same height as him, but he was a skinny little fucker, and Jules was downright Napoleonic. Ricky was a little bigger than him, but he'd be easy to catch with that limp, and Toby could just kick him hard in his injured leg if he gave him—

"Are you, um, busy?"

Toby turned around from where he'd been adjusting the stupid side view mirror on the van to find Jock standing behind him, hands buried in the pockets of his jeans, shoulders hiked up around his jawline, looking uncomfortable. It was as endearing as hell and Toby kind of hated him for it. Well, that and making him wait around for the guy to make a move or a decision. "Just fixing the mirror. The motor inside it broke or something."

Jock's brow wrinkled up. "Motor?"

"You know, so I can adjust it by pushing some buttons while I'm in the driver's seat." Toby thought for a second about asking Jock if he knew anything about motors, but that smacked far too much of damsel in distress—or possibly mansel in distress—so he returned to the job at hand. *Need to forget about him.*

"So you *are* busy?" Jock persisted.

Toby's fingers stopped, frozen on the armature that the mirror hung from while he tried to figure out what was happening. Possibly this situation wasn't precisely what he'd thought. He'd *thought* Jock had wandered by and felt like he *had* to say something, or things would be even more awkward than they'd already become . . . but maybe he'd sought Toby out? Toby's heart picked up, because after more than a week of being largely ignored—even when they sat next to each other in the van—he was ready for some news; even "Thanks, but I'm not interested," would be all right. *Really, it will.* Because then he could overcome this asinine secondary-adolescence crush he'd developed on the sandy-haired boy with the beautiful chesticles.

"Guess so," Jock said quietly, then his feet crunched on gravel as he moved.

"Wait." Toby faced him again. "You aren't just being polite?"

Jock's jaw clenched. "Polite isn't really my thing." He ducked his head, hiding behind his hair.

"I know you'd like people to believe that, but I'm asking seriously."

"So was I."

Toby tilted his head, trying to get a different view on Jock. "What is it exactly that you're asking?"

"Just . . ." Jock shrugged, squinting down at the vineyards below them. "Wondering if you have time to talk. I mean, we haven't really, not since . . . you know."

"If you're wondering if I'm okay with the way things have been between us, then not really."

Jock's face fell, sort of literally—his mouth turned down at the corners and Toby would swear his eyes drooped into the puppy dog look. "Sorry."

Toby studied him for a second, but if he wanted to know, he was going to have to ask, not try to read it off of Jock's expression. "Are you thinking you don't want—"

"I'm still thinking," Jock said.

"That's good to know." He shoved his hands in his pockets, afraid they'd tremble with the relief of knowing that Jock hadn't decided to just ignore this situation. He wasn't sure he'd blame the guy if he did—this was the weirdest not-quite-relationship Toby had ever been in. If his heart would let him, *he'd* ignore it. But his heart was firmly mired in the quicksand of Jock's packaging. Not just the package Toby usually focused on, but the whole thing. The way Jock loomed over him, and seemed so young sometimes while being so mature other times, and the way his hair was getting a little too long and almost breaching his eyebrows to tangle in his lashes, and the way he spoke, and the way they seemed to notice the same things, like the odd interactions between Danny and Madame B . . . and everything else, too. "Because I'm still waiting. And yes, I was worried you might blow me off again."

Jock didn't need to go for the obvious "blow" joke, because the knowledge of it sizzled between them, traveling through that eye-to-eye connection they had, making them smile in unison.

"You seemed kinda stressed today," Jock said instead. "I mean, I know the shit with Noah and Gomer was serious—"

"Ish."

Jock tipped his chin. "Yeah, but even after we left the clinic, you were kinda tense. I guess I was afraid it was, I dunno . . ." Jock kicked at the gravel. "Me."

You really think you're that important? But he was. "It's my thesis, too," Toby said, spreading the blame for his behavior around. "It's not really coming together well right now, and I have to be done with it by the end of the term, if not before." Just like the first time Jock had blown him off, Toby's mood had affected his ability to work.

Jock squinted at him, smirking lopsidedly. "So, you're here for school, too? You don't just sit around all day in town drinking, waiting on us?"

"Oh, I do." He answered Jock's smirk with a smile. "But I'm working on my paper at the same time. That's why I have a 'no beer before two' rule."

"What's it about?"

His thesis? "You really want to know?"

"Yeah, I do."

"If I'm going to talk about that, I'll need some wine. We could go to my place. Sit out front and have a glass or two, and I'll tell you about it."

Jock nodded, tilting his head and looking at Toby from under his bangs. "Yeah. I'd like that."

ΘΑΓ

Toby had a cool dark blue painted-iron table with two matching chairs that sat in front of his little *cabanon*, as he referred to it. Jock's French was rusty, and he'd never been to the country with the intent of learning it, but, "Doesn't that mean 'shed' or something?" he asked when Toby came back out of his little hut with a bottle of wine and two glasses.

"I think so," he said, grimacing. "I don't know why Madame B calls it that, but maybe it's a local colloquialism. They do say some things differently around here. When I was at the campus two years ago I knew a local guy named Gilles, but he pronounced it 'zhee-lay.'"

Jock had learned it was normally pronounced without the second syllable. At least he thought so. They learned names the first year or so, and he'd started taking it as a freshman. Three more years of a language he only heard for forty-five minutes a day tended to cancel out some of the early stuff.

"You all right with red?" Toby asked. "I have white but it's not open, and not cold. The fridge in that place is only so big."

"I can't believe you even have one." Jock eyed Toby's little cabin. It barely looked tall enough to stand in.

"It's about dorm-sized, at least if I remember dorms right."

Jock snorted. "I remember dorms well; let me have a look at it."

Toby met his eye. "Anytime you want an invitation inside, let me know."

Tension balled in Jock's gut, then migrated south to his groin. He licked his lip, staring into Toby's liquid brown eyes, considering the consequences of having a physical encounter while he was still thinking over the ramifications of emotional ones.

You've already decided you want it.

"Sorry," Toby said, breaking their connection by looking down at the village.

"I have to tell you something." Shit, was that really his voice? He sounded like he was at the bottom of a well.

Toby's attention was riveted back on him, eyes wide. "What is it?"

Jock traced the design on Toby's table a second, feeling the edges of the iron bite into his fingers. Listening to his pulse thump in his ears and trying to decide where to start. "What if I said that it wasn't, like, totally unexpected?"

Toby didn't answer right away, and when he did, his voice sounded very careful. "I guess I'd ask what you meant."

"When that dude took that picture." He had to stop and swallow. "I could have taken his phone away from him. If I'd held it over my head he couldn't have jumped high enough to reach it."

"But you didn't."

"No." He shook his head. When he glanced over at him, Toby's brow was wrinkled up.

"So, it wasn't a boyfriend or someone you were seeing who took it?"

"No." Jock slid his hands off the table, slumping back into his chair. "I had a friend, Max, and we sort of had an agreement. We traded blowjobs sometimes when we were desperate. Other than that it was pretty much dumb luck, finding some guy, and that only happened a few times."

"Is Max the guy that took the picture?"

"No." He closed his eyes, laying his head on the back of his chair. "I don't even remember that dude's name."

"Just some guy," Toby said, voice as soft as Jock's had been. "And you knew the chances of him outing you were good, didn't you?"

"Yeah. A guy Max had hooked up with was having a party, and we went because we knew there'd be lot of guys there, but, like, *anyone* could have gone. Anyone could have seen me. And seriously, I don't want to sound egotistical, but hockey is big at Avalon—"

"I understand."

Jock barely heard him. "But the thing is, no one did see me, or no one cared. And I was drinking a lot that night, which I wasn't supposed to do—I signed a contract with the athletic department and everything—but I was just kinda *done*." He straightened back up, opening his eyes finally and staring out over the vineyard. "I didn't want to hide it, or, like, *deny* it anymore—"

"I get it," Toby said, standing up, then walking behind Jock's chair. Jock held his breath, not sure what the fuck was going on, not until Toby laid hands on his shoulders, squeezing. "You don't have to tell me any more unless you want to." His voice wasn't loud, but somehow it reverberated in Jock's chest.

He gulped a breath, because he wanted to get it all out. "That guy was a prick. The one who took the picture. I think that's why I chose him, I mean, subconsciously. I picked the guy who was dissing the closet cases, eyeing me and Max because he *knew*. And then I let him take that picture of me while I was on my knees."

"Oh," Toby said. "The knees thing."

"I didn't, you know, *plan* it. I didn't even think about it after that, not consciously, but when I walked into the locker room after Christmas and that picture was everywhere? I wasn't surprised. At first I was . . ." He had to force the damn word out. "Relieved."

He felt Toby's body heat coming closer, then his arms sliding down, wrapping around Jock. "You regretted it later, though."

"About five seconds later and every minute since." Jock sighed, feeling the weight of Toby on him. Holding him even though Jock had confessed his most shameful secret. Which, now that he'd told two people, sounded like less of a thing than it used to.

And Toby was touching him. He hadn't gotten mad at Jock for lying or looked at Jock like he was dog shit on his shoe or any of the other things he might have done.

He'd done it.

"Everyone comes out in different ways, and some of us screw it up," Toby said, voice right next to Jock's ear. "It's not like anyone sits gay kids down when they're little and tells them how to go about it, or encourages them to plan it out like some girl's play 'wedding.'"

"That's for fucking sure," he murmured, reaching up to touch Toby's arm where it crossed his chest for a second. "Girls do that?"

"That's the way I understand it."

"Thank you." He dropped his hand, and Toby stood, his touch slipping away. Jock didn't know how to feel about that. He was still freaked, leftover adrenaline making him shaky.

Was he supposed to stand up now and get it on? Pull Toby into the little hut and find a horizontal surface? "So tell me about your thesis subject," he blurted.

After a second of silence, gravel crunched as Toby went back to his own side of the table, pouring them each a glass of wine and sitting. Then he started talking in a totally normal voice. Like he was telling the TAG boys some facts about a historical site.

It took a few minutes for Jock to be able to concentrate on what the guy was saying. Something about a basilica built inside the Roman amphitheater at Tarragona.

"In Spain?" Jock clarified. Welcoming distractions.

Toby nodded. "Southwest of Barcelona, an hour or two by train. Have you been to Barcelona?" he asked it carefully, as if not wanting to assume too much, but not wanting to insult Jock by suggesting he wasn't well traveled.

"Yeah. My mom's a women's clothing buyer for a major chain store in the US. She used to take me to *all* the fashionable places in Europe with her. No wonder I'm gay, huh?" Okay, weak joke, but he was trying to get things back on an even keel. Be normal. Ignore his still shaky nerves.

"Your mother is a style maven so she must have a gay son? What a disappointment for the parents who are into couture and have straight kids." Toby was smiling.

Jock took the comment like a gut punch, probably a little harder than he would have if he hadn't just confessed one of his deeper secrets. "What, like it's *not* genetic?" It'd fucking *better* be.

Toby reared back and looked at Jock from under his brows. Maybe he'd yelled? "Of course it's genetic—or at least it's prenatal—but it's not that simple."

"Sorry, not following." Jock took a full-on swig of his wine, then grabbed the bottle to pour himself more.

"My mom brought home the bacon and my dad fried it up in the pan."

Yeah, that still worked with his theory. "And?"

"I had a stay-at-home dad, and my mother worked. No wonder they had a gay son."

"Uh-huh." Still didn't explain shit. He took another slug of wine.

"My twin brother is straight." Toby tilted his head, like he was waiting for Jock to put two and two together.

"But you aren't identical." Toby'd told him that the night they met.

"And yet his father was a stay-at-home parent, too."

"Hate being outsmarted," Jock muttered, twirling the stem of his wineglass. Feeling calmer now.

Toby laughed. "I bet it's pretty rare. You're way too smexy."

"Huh?"

"Sorry, doing it again." Toby looked away. "It means smart *and* sexy." He drew in a breath and then exhaled slowly. "I've been on the scene too long. I mean, everything is an opportunity to come on to . . . someone I'm into."

"So you're still into me?" Jock asked, because Toby hadn't actually said it. "I mean, after what I told you?"

"Yes, but not casually," Toby answered immediately. Then he swallowed, his Adam's apple perfectly illuminated in the dusk, sliding down his throat and up. Throats were *so* suggestive.

"So Tarragona," Jock said, to give himself space.

"Yeah." Toby nodded at his lap. "It was the capital of the province in Roman times, and the amphitheater was really active. Lots of games and gladiators. And then after 313 AD . . ."

While Toby talked about the Roman Empire, and the fight between Arian and Athanasian sects ("normal" Catholicism, as Toby termed it) and which part of the Iberian Peninsula was under the rule of which belief system when, Jock saw him getting all intellectual and waited for the itching to start. It didn't. Toby cared about this shit, and that made it interesting. Or at least momentarily captivating. Besides, he got to watch the dude talk. Which he never would have thought he'd be into, but he liked how Toby's eyes nearly glowed when he got excited, and he liked the way Toby's jaw moved under his scruff-covered skin, and he liked to see him throw his hands up in the air or gesture with them. He had thin fingers, especially for a guy his size. He wasn't super skinny, but if someone only saw his fingers, they might think so.

Eventually he talked himself out, though, or talked himself out of his thesis. "So the question I'm looking at for my thesis is which parts of the basilica were built by the Visigoths and which were built by Romans before that." He frowned. "It's boring as shit."

"Can you change it?"

He shook his head and poured more wine. "I need to be done with it. My mom thinks I'm going to be a professor of history like she is, and finishing my master's is just a step on that road, but I'm going to have to disappoint her."

"So, *you* don't want the degree?"

"I used to, but lately? No. I'm too close though. It's stupid not to finish."

"You spend a lot of time telling yourself that?"

"Every. Freaking. Day." He half smiled at Jock over the table.

"What's the worst thing that could happen if you quit now?"

Toby winced. "I'd feel like a failure. It's getting dark out here," he said, standing and stretching out his arms.

Jock sat back in his seat, not sure he was ready to be done hanging with Toby, but not sure how to extend their time without saying something like, *I'd like that invitation into your place now.* Because he didn't know if he was ready for that, yet.

When did I become such a weenie?

Cut yourself some slack, dude.

"I'll get some illumination going," Toby said, turning toward his door.

So, they weren't done? Apparently not, because Toby came right back out with a wax-caked wine bottle that had a candle stuck in the top. Jock laughed at it. "Nice."

"You like?" Toby grinned, his teeth catching some ambient light. He set it down and started fiddling with a box. "I spent the first three days I was here dripping different colors of wax on it to make a pleasing design." The match he'd struck hissed and flared up, and as he held it to the wick, soft yellow and midnight blue picked out the different planes and lines of his hand. It looked like a cubist painting.

"I like."

Toby looked at him a long second over the candle, and Jock realized this was his moment. He could stand up and come around the table, place his hand on Toby's belly before kissing him, and then Toby'd invite him inside. But he didn't move.

You're still scared.

Yup. Petrified, obvi.

Toby tilted his chin, then sat back down, pulling his wine glass closer and idly tracing its curves with a fingertip. Effectively ending their moment. "What's this beer terrorist thing the boys are always on about?"

Jock forced his brain into this new gear. "It's kinda involved. And you know, if I told you . . ." Nice. Another lame, totally predictable joke.

"You'd have to kill me." Toby smiled. "So, just tell me, are we under imminent threat of beermageddon?"

"Beermageddon?" Danny's voice boomed out from somewhere in the dark. "That's awesome, Tobes." He waltzed right into their little circle of lamplight and togetherness. He had mad interfering skills. "Can I use it?"

"Be my guest," Toby answered, waving his hand. "I probably won't ever say it again."

"So you guys coming to eat with us? Families that eat together communicate more, you know. They've done studies and shit." He stood next to the table, head bouncing from one of them to the other and back. Over and over. "Uh, unless you guys want some alone time?"

Shit. He'd obviously decided something was going on. Jock's thigh muscles tensed like they wanted to vault him out of this chair, but the rest of him was annoyed. Annoyed with Danny, but also done with worrying about what the other guys thought about it if he and Toby wanted to start something.

"I think we've had plenty," Toby said, glancing at Jock before standing up. Jock got the message—Toby was doing him a favor. Letting him off the hook for the night.

He cringed inside at how grateful he felt about that.

Chapter 13

Jock wanted to be with him. Toby felt certain of that now. *Such a huge fucking relief.* He'd seen the evidence in Jock's eyes right after he lit that candle Tuesday night in front of his place. Toby had also seen what was holding Jock back: fear.

At least he could understand Jock's fear, or some of it. It had taken him a while, sitting in the dark by himself after dinner, but he thought he'd untangled the mystery. It wasn't an ex who'd fucked Jock over, it was *Jock* who'd fucked Jock over. Sort of. And if Toby's reasoning was right, Jock was afraid of fucking himself over again.

No wonder the dude was so cautious.

Unfortunately, only having that one psych class as an undergrad—which he'd barely managed a "C" in—he could be way off. But he knew something for certain: everything had changed. In a good way, he thought. Hoped. Jock had really opened up to him.

Hopefully he could help Jock surmount his fear. Because the sooner Jock surmounted, the sooner Toby could mount him. Thoughts of that kept him in the shower longer than normal every morning for the rest of the week. It also encouraged him to take a hard look at his situation. Ask himself what he wanted and what he was willing to settle for.

The answers were simple. He wanted as much of the boy as he could get, and he was willing to settle for humiliatingly little. He'd take friends-only (no benefits package), certainly. It was what he had now. He'd also settle for another night of sex with no promise of future nights. The one thing he wouldn't put up with was Jock leaving before morning.

In case he'd been wondering about himself, that confirmed the depth of the romantic nature he'd been stifling the last few years. Like the old Bonnie Raitt song, he'd take a night of lying next to Jock as a sop to his very involved heart. Then in the morning he'd do what was right. So yeah, he'd take pure sex with gratitude, and ask for next to nothing in return, just a few hours of pretend.

Plus he had a minimum orgasm requirement for that single night that he wasn't willing to negotiate. And he wanted Jock to fuck him. He could *see* it if he closed his eyes. Jock looming over him, that perfect body covered in sweat, panting, thrusting into him, watching himself fuck Toby with wide eyes. A do-over of their first time, but this time they'd both know the whole score.

Thinking of that night invariably led to the extra long bathroom visits. Not that he couldn't jerk off anywhere, but cleanup was so much easier in there. The spray from the shower pretty much covered the whole room, as long as Toby didn't hit any higher than about six feet, and he just hadn't been born with the necessary hydraulics for that. That led him to wondering about Jock's hydraulics, which led to the bathroom . . . it was a cycle that, while not vicious, consumed more of his time than it had since his teenage years.

Other things were looking up (so to speak) as well. His thesis, while no more interesting than it had been last week, was coming along. He agonized less and simply regurgitated his thoughts into his laptop more. He'd edit it into something intelligible somehow. Eventually. The whipped cream on his sundae was that the bros had stopped being so needy. One or two of them still came by each evening, giving him puppy dog looks and asking him when he was going to come over for dinner, but they'd started walking down to the village at night, apparently having found a bar there. Jock said they were practicing their French on the local farmers, which sounded entertaining enough that Toby sometimes considered going to watch. So far he'd only considered, though.

The cherry on top of his tired analogy was that he and Jock were communicating. No one had to manipulate the guy into sitting next to Toby; it was simply his spot now, and they took advantage of it. Talking to each other about inconsequential things, or sharing smiles when the bros did something new and stupid, or rolling their eyes when Noah kicked the back of Jock's seat.

Somewhat like a sullen teen, Noah had become silent and moody since the Heimlich incident. Toby and Jock both thought it was the result of the very obvious way Turbo had started avoided Noah at all costs. The rest of the boys seemed to know, and now the clown-car maneuver was regularly utilized to make sure those two guys sat as far apart as possible. Noah'd given up by Thursday and simply plopped himself behind Jock, pouty lip and all, glowering and *hmmph*ing every time Jock told him, "If you don't stop kicking the back of my seat, I'll cut your foot off and sew it into your ass."

They were becoming just like a real family.

Friday morning dawned beautiful after two days of a black mistral, where they were lashed with rain every time they stepped outside. They were coming up on the weekend, and he'd planned on not making the boys go anywhere. It wasn't his problem that Professor Douche was a lazy bastard who didn't see the point in visiting the historical sites the guys were learning about. He wasn't repeating last weekend's disaster. Instead, he was going to see if he could lure Jock away. He had the perfect place in mind, if the weather held. Nothing too serious, just a nice, relatively unvisited Roman aqueduct and grain mill ruin where they could climb around on the stones and sit looking out at the valley that led straight west to Arles. It was one of his favorite places in the area, and if he'd had half a brain (and no maternal demands), he'd have focused his thesis on it, instead.

He forced himself out of bed when his phone alarm went off, stretched, spent an extra long time in the shower, and came out extremely relaxed and, he was certain, with an immovable smile plastered on his face. Until he got to breakfast late and Turbo told him all the croissants had been eaten.

"There aren't *any* left?" he clarified for a second time. He stood behind his chair, wondering whether it was even worth sitting down without croissants. Madame B made them with real butter every morning, not shortening like most people. They were amazing. "No one even has a bite I can have?"

Gomer snatched something off his plate that looked suspiciously flaky and crammed it into his mouth until his cheeks bulged out, shaking his head violently.

"I know where some is," Ricky said, grabbing Gomer's face and squeezing it, trying to force his jaw open. Gomer started whacking Ricky's arm, frowning and making muffled angry noises.

"Stop it," Toby snapped. "I don't need it pre-chewed, thanks. I'll just have coffee."

"I'll save some for you tomorrow," Madame B said, coming past to pat him on the head after he sat down.

Jock was even later than him, or he'd already left, but Toby didn't ask. The guys had clearly figured out something was up between the two of them, and Toby didn't want any more attention focused on it. His patience was rewarded when he got to the van and found Jock already there, talking to Danny, who'd left breakfast just after Toby got there. Jock smiled when he caught sight of Toby, and they had one of those moments they now had whenever their gazes met. Well, most of the time. Recognition not just of each other, but (unless Toby was an overly sentimental fool) of something important growing between them.

Maybe the day would turn out all right in spite of his disappointing breakfast.

Toby hoped for that right up through his third coffee and a couple thousand words on his thesis. He was getting really close to having the rough draft done. Just a couple more chapters or so. Then he could start to revise it and fill in the holes. Before he started the next section, he stretched and considered moving outside. The man who owned the café was so used to him by now, he brought Toby coffee on a schedule. This morning he'd also had a croissant, not as good as Madame Bouvinet's, but it beat most of the ones in the United States all to hell.

Maybe he'd take a little wander outside and around. Philipe never minded keeping an eye on Toby's stuff if he just left it on his table. "I'm here whether your laptop is or not," he'd said the first few times Toby had asked. Then he said, "Stop asking. *Allez.*"

Toby caught Philipe's eye on his way out the door, and received a nod in return. Place Favier was one of the few well-shaded squares in Saint-Rémy, which was nice a lot of the time, but after two days of rain in a country where it wasn't supposed to rain, like, *ever*, Toby wanted to find a patch of sun. There was one over by the strange little tourist mercantile that sold tragically hip Provençalesque accessories for women, he thought. But when he found it, someone familiar was standing in Toby's sun, peeking in the windows of the little store, face screwed up in concentration.

Danny. "What are you doing here?" Toby asked.

"Oh, hey, I was looking for you," Danny said happily, turning to him.

"You're supposed to be at the campus."

"It's lunchtime, dude. I walked into town for a change."

"I thought you said you were looking for me."

"Yeah. That's kind of a change too." Danny nodded, beaming at him.

"How did you know where to find me?" If the boys could find him, his fratbro-free hours might be in serious jeopardy. *Fuck.* He'd have to find a new café, and break in a new Philipe.

"Jock told me you hung out here." Danny came toward him, two steps, then grabbed his arm before Toby even realized the threat. The next thing he knew Danny had shoved his face into the same window the guy had been staring into when Toby walked up. "Look at that big old purse, man. The, like, faded red one with all those little flowers and stuff? Do you think it'd make a nice gift for Monique?"

"Oh God," Toby groaned. "Please tell me that, if you did find some farmer's daughter to defile, he's not the type to want revenge. Or at least that you can take him."

"Monique doesn't really like to talk about her parents. They both died when she was still a teenager, then she married real young and—"

"She's *married*?" Toby jerked out of Danny's hold to round on him, brandishing his index finger in Danny's face. "That is *it*. No more French literature for you." He should have guessed Flowbert would be a damaging influence once they started calling Madame B by that name— *Wait.*

"Thank God, dude, I hate that French lit class. But I don't think my prof is going to let me skip without some kind of permission—"

"Monique who?"

Danny screwed up his face. "I don't know Professor Medcalf's first name. I mean, she's not the kind of lady I'd just ask. She's kinda bitchy."

"No. I mean who's this Monique you're thinking about buying a gift for?"

Danny frowned at him. "You know, Madame B."

"Oh no," Toby muttered, leaning against the wall of the store for support. "Okay, listen, I want to know *nothing* about this." He straightened again and held his hands out, curling his fingers to illustrate the huge ball of potential disaster that he didn't want to know anything about. "Nothing. At. All." He couldn't tell Danny not to see her, right? He and Madame B were both consenting adults.

Danny blinked a couple of times. "All right, dude. If I buy the purse I'll make sure you don't see it."

"Yes, that, and also? I want no details at all about any *extracurricular* contact you may have had with her. Just so we're all clear. I don't know her first name, or that you and she sometimes look at each other all calf-eyed, or that you aren't sleeping in your bed at night, okay? No. Thing." He punctuated his words by slicing his hand in the air, just in case Danny needed visual aids.

Oh Jesus. Danny's lip, was it . . . ? *Shit.* Trembling. But he sucked it in like a big boy, nodded, and turned away, staring into the window again. Not before Toby saw how wet his eyelashes were, though.

There were not curse words enough in the world to describe his inner pain. Toby's, not Danny's, because Toby knew what was about to happen, and he had to do it, because not only was he the resident advisor to this lovesick frat boy, but he was a decent person, and this was what he did. He helped people. So he took a calming breath and laid his hand on Danny's shoulder. "I suppose, though, if you *really* needed to talk to someone . . ."

"Thank you," Danny said shakily, grabbing Toby for a rib-cracking bro hug, sniffing up his tears. "Tobes, I'm so confused, I mean, I've never met anyone like her, she's so, like, *French*. And *mature*."

Please let this be an innocent boyhood crush, Toby prayed while leading a babbling Danny back to the café. *Even something oedipal but one-sided is okay, I can deal with that.* He knew a ton about *Oedipus Rex*. When they walked into the restaurant, he waved at Philipe and held up two fingers, then guided his charge to his table by the window and let the dude get it all out.

It took over an hour, and Toby switched to wine after the first twenty minutes when he realized it wasn't innocent. "You *slept* with her?"

"It just happened," Danny cried. When Toby shushed him, he managed to speak in a normal tone for a few sentences. "I asked her if she'd teach me how to make croissants, and she said I had to meet her really early for that, like the middle of the night, and I got there and her hair was down and she had this nightgown on you wouldn't believe, man—"

"OhGodno."

"It covered her from her neck to her ankles and it was all white and buttoned up and I couldn't think about anything but taking it off of her."

"Please, I'm begging you, stop."

Danny didn't hear him, too caught up in his memories. "I was doing all right though, you know, but then she made me knead the butter and it was all, like, slippery and squishy and it made me think about *things*, you know?"

"No, I don't. And I don't want to."

"Then she got out her rolling pin, and it's just this big . . ." Danny swallowed. "It's a shaft of wood, and she was cleaning the flour off of it, using her hand." He wrapped his fingers around an imaginary kitchen phallus, staring at them wonderingly. Then he started moving it back and forth, lovingly stroking the air. "And her fist was running up and down it—I couldn't stop myself," he finished in a bona fide whisper. "I don't even know how it happened. One minute I was kneading butter, and the next I had her on the counter and I was kneading her—"

"*No.*" Toby reached across and slapped his hand over Danny's mouth. "No-no-no-no-no-no. I will listen to your existential angst, and your relationship problems, and even your oedipal longings, but I *will not* listen to you describe any physical acts with any women, am I clear?" Especially not a woman old enough to be his grandmother.

Danny nodded, meeting Toby's eyes over his fingers. Toby took a chance and removed his hand.

"That was kinda too much detail, huh?"

"Yeah."

"Sorry." Danny ducked his head and fiddled with his coffee cup. "I just. I don't know what's going to happen now. I want to be with her again."

Toby chugged the rest of his wine.

"But what if it was just, like, sex to her? I mean, maybe she does this all the time with her guests."

"Oh God." They'd unknowingly walked into the den of a predatory cougar. Probably the grand high cougar of Provence. Who else would willingly take in a bunch of frat boys?

"I feel like there's something special between us," Danny continued, leaning forward earnestly. "Sometimes when I look at her and she looks at me? It's like, I can touch her mind or her spirit or, like, I don't know. *Her*. Is that stupid?"

Toby sighed. "No, it's not stupid." He patted Danny's hand, because the kid seemed to need the reassurance so much. "I understand exactly what you mean."

Danny nodded, then turned and stared out the window a while, quiet and possibly even contemplative for the first time since Toby'd met him. "So what do I do now?" he eventually asked.

Toby wasn't sure if Danny was asking him, or the window, or something outside, but he answered anyway. "You tell her how you feel. You prepare for the worst but hope for the best."

Danny nodded slowly. "Maybe I'll see if she wants help with her croissants again tonight."

"This time, make sure you guys actually get them in the oven, okay?"

Danny grinned suddenly, back from whatever introspective place he went when he had need. "I will. Thanks, Tobes. I really needed that."

It wasn't until they were walking back to campus that Toby thought to ask, "Is that why you came looking for me? To talk about, um, Madame B?" He just *couldn't* with calling her Monique.

"Oh yeah, dude." Danny snapped his fingers. "I was going to ask a favor—one of the guys needs to do some history extra credit or he might flunk, so he's going to need to go over to that big ruined castle tomorrow, you know? Les Baux or whatever. He's supposed to do some research."

"It's only the third week of the term," Toby protested. "How could he be failing already?"

"The professor's an asshole." Danny waved it off. "Anyway, can you give him a ride and stuff?"

It had to be Gomer. "How come he didn't ask me himself?"

"I told him if I saw you when I went in for lunch, I'd ask."

Shit. Maybe he could do something with Jock on Sunday. "Fine," Toby sighed. "Is it Gomer or Ricky?"

"It's Jock."

Danny kept moving even after Toby halted, staring after him. "Jock?" he called, then hurried to catch up.

"Yup. Jock. He missed an assignment, and he can't make it up, so . . ." Danny shrugged, stepping around Toby when Toby tried to get in his path to stop him.

"That doesn't sound like Jock." He didn't *think*.

"Everyone fucks up sometime, dude," Danny called over his shoulder. Toby couldn't be certain, but it looked like he picked up his pace, walking too fast for Toby to catch him and ask him any more questions.

Toby didn't say much to Jock about Les Baux on the way home from town. He didn't say much of anything, preoccupied not only with wondering why Jock needed the extra credit (which he wasn't willing to ask outright), but mostly with Danny and Madame Bouvinet.

"You okay?" Jock asked him at one point, leaning closer to his side of the van.

Toby smiled over at him, one of those quick ones everyone knew wasn't real, but rather was an attempt to reassure. "I just have a lot on my mind. Um, thesis stuff. So, we're going to Les Baux tomorrow?"

Jock nodded, sitting back. "Yeah. When Danny said you were going—"

"Hey, Jock-man," the person of interest himself called from his seat right behind Toby. "Did you take notes today in French class? I'm gonna need to figure out what I missed and try to make it up."

Jock and Danny fell into conversation—some of it in very academic, stilted French—and Toby sunk back into his thoughts. What did it mean for him if one of the residents he was nominally advising got involved with the woman at whose place they were staying? Was it really that big a deal? And yes, he'd essentially encouraged Danny to pursue the relationship, but what else could Toby do? He just didn't have the heart to tell someone else to put a lid on their pain. The dude probably wouldn't listen to him anyway.

That's my story and I'm sticking to it.

Friday night, Toby hung out with the guys instead of putting in more time on his thesis. He'd finally started making progress again after he and Jock had normalized relations or whatever.

But of course the fratbros started in about beer terrorism again. At least they weren't discussing tactics, like normal. Instead, Jules had a DVD one of his sisters sent him that Danny called a "training film." Toby groaned inwardly, but he started watching it anyway.

He'd kind of hoped Jock would walk him out later, but the guy had fallen asleep on the floor, just a pillow under his head. He looked utterly sexy with his shirt riding up and his jeans slung low, showing off a couple of his abs and a sprinkling of hair. If Toby craned his head just right, he could catch a hint of white waistband and the very masculine curve of Jock's hipbone.

Oh yeah, totally time for him to leave.

Saturday morning was beautiful again, and as Toby lay in his bed looking out the window at a few fluffy white clouds, he was fairly sure his heart floated up there with them.

Jesus, he really was kind of a sap, wasn't he?

There were croissants at breakfast. Many of them. Toby ignored the way Madame B fairly glowed, and the way Danny couldn't stop smiling or humming, and he didn't think about how the croissants got made. Instead he ate them with butter and jam, sitting next to Jock, their elbows bumping every once in a while, warm skin sliding against his. After he'd had three croissants and Jock had had God knew how many, he wiped his fingers on his napkin and said, "The sooner we leave, the more time you'll have at Les Baux."

Jock shrugged. "I don't hafta spend a lot of time there." He met Toby's eyes, and Toby had the sense that things weren't exactly what he thought they were.

Gomer interrupted his train of thought. "Where are you guys going? Do we all get to go? Is it cool? Is there a castle?"

"No, dude," Danny answered him. "We have beer terrorist business to get done today. We have to talk about fortifications they can work into the design as they rebuild the frat house. You know, we should have those things like they put along the tops of castles. Those walls with, like, skinny little openings that medieval knight dudes used to shoot arrows from? Yo! Tobes!"

Toby sighed. "Crenellations."

"How are you going to talk Kyle into that?" Noah asked.

"Yup," Danny half crowed. "Crenellations, that's what TAG House needs. Who's going to talk to Kyle? Jock, he takes you more seriously than the rest of us—"

"Nope," Jock said, focused on buttering a croissant. "He takes me seriously *because* I don't ask him about shit like putting crenellations on the frat house. You guys are on your own with that one."

"C'mon, Jock, you're part of this—"

"We could make a sort of spud gun," Ricky interrupted excitedly. "Except we'd shoot beer cans."

All the guys gasped and stared at him in shock. Ricky held up his palms. "No, *after* we drink the beer out of them. Then we fill them with, like, plaster and rocks. It's cool because it's not only self-defense, it's *recycling*."

Soft murmurs of awe followed.

"Absolutely not," Toby said quickly. "Talk fortifications all you want, but no weaponry."

"Cool!" Gomer pumped his fist in the air.

Shaking his head, Jock pushed back from the table. "I'll meet you out front in five?"

"Yeah, we're taking the car since it's just the two of us." Like a real date and everything. A study date.

It wasn't until he and Jock were sitting in the car, and Toby'd just turned it on, that he asked Jock, "So you know the site? Did you say you've been there before?"

"When I was a kid. My mom bought me one of those wooden swords and a shield they sell in the gift shop, and then we went and watched the siege engine demonstrations. After that, I climbed everywhere and fought off imaginary invaders." He was grinning by then. "There were a bunch of other kids doing the same thing, and I'd already been in hockey for years, so I started trying to organize the troops."

Toby laughed. "I bet you were good at it."

Jock threw up a hand. "I'll never know—none of those other kids knew what a defensive line was, and I couldn't get anyone to stay in formation. Maybe it was the language barrier."

"You're cute," Toby said unthinkingly. "Sorry," he blurted once he realized, then he turned to the steering column, trying to fumble the shifter out of park.

"You're cute too," Jock said, suddenly right in his ear, breathing on the side of his face. Toby turned to find him only a couple inches away, his Tom of Finland lips front and center.

"So," Toby asked softly. "Have you made a decision about what you want?"

"I want to kiss you. Is that enough?"

"Works for me," Toby said, fingers uncramping from where he'd white-knuckled the steering wheel, sliding up to Jock's face to trace the shape of his lips.

"I've never noticed this before," Jock murmured, breath falling on Toby's chin.

"What's that?"

"That there's a moment right before you kiss someone when you know it's coming and you can feel it everywhere. Like an electrical bond is forming between us, pulling us together. Polarizing the air or something."

"Maybe it's never happened before," Toby whispered.

"Maybe I never wanted to kiss anyone this much before."

Enough talk. Toby lunged those last centimeters and fit his mouth against Jock's, lips sliding and bumping until they hit that magical spot where it all fit. Locked together like two pieces of a puzzle. When Jock's tongue pushed into his mouth, wandering around and taking over, making itself at home, Toby welcomed it with his own, petting and cosseting and sucking. Doing everything so Jock would feel how much he wanted him there. He could move in permanently if he wanted; at that moment Toby wouldn't have objected.

But it was a short visit. Or at least not long enough for Toby's liking, although they were both breathing heavily when Jock pulled away, pressing one more kiss on his lips. His thumb stroked along the edge of Toby's jaw, and his fingers were tangled in the back of Toby's hair, and Toby had no idea when Jock had gripped him like that. "Yeah, just like lightning," he said softly.

"Hmmm?"

Jock smiled at him, but then looked over Toby's shoulder and jerked away, face muscles tightening up. "Someone's coming."

Toby sighed. "Which one is it?" Fucking fratbros couldn't survive ten minutes on their own, could they?

"Danny," Jock said, then pulled away further, back into his seat. Nothing for Toby to do but settle back into his.

Their intruder came walking down the driveway toward them with a picnic basket—a quaint wicker one with red and white checked fabric peeking out from under the hinged wooden lid. The quality of stillness next to Toby told him that Jock was coming to the same conclusions about why exactly Danny was bringing a picnic basket their way. He caught Jock's eye when Danny came around to the rear passenger side of the car, and yes, it was true.

Danny opened the back door and set the basket down on the seat. "Uh, just some, you know, nibbles or whatever you guys wanna call 'em. Case you get hungry. Oh, and Madame Bovinary put in a bottle of wine, case you get thirsty. Havefunbye!" He slammed the car shut and ran back to the house.

Toby eyed the basket. Were there croissants inside? Did he trust them?

"You get the feeling this is some kind of setup?" Jock asked, brows halfway up his forehead.

"Planned by a bunch of straight yet sensitive frat boys in dubious possession of subpar intelligence?"

"Uh, yeah." Jock nodded exaggeratedly. "So, like, they told you you *needed* to take me to Les Baux?"

"You don't have to write an extra credit paper to avoid failing history?"

Jock snorted. "I don't fail. And you aren't doing research at the Les Baux library for your thesis?"

"I'm fairly certain Les Baux doesn't have a library."

"So, like, we don't actually have to go there and do *anything*." Jock studied him a minute, while Toby held his breath. Staying here could be fun, too, if he wanted to continue the kissing and see what it led to, but Toby had wanted to hang with him. Socialize with clothes on. So when Jock continued with, "We could just go and have fun," Toby found that idea very appealing.

"Play invaders." Toby nodded. "Walk to the top of the fortress walls and look for Saracens."

"Did the Saracens make it into France?"

"Not this far, but we can pretend."

Jock grinned and nodded. "Sweet."

And Les Baux was sweet. Awesome. Toby's perfect fantasy ruin—a stark castle perched on a rocky promontory. The walls were built of native stone, and they seemed to rise out of the cliff face. Irregular, jagged geological shapes working into smoother, straight forms stretching into the sky. But the first clue that it was man-made was the windows up high, and as they got closer, a couple of arches appeared in the wall.

"That's exactly how I remembered it," Jock murmured, leaning forward to look out the windshield as Toby forced the car up the steep switchback road. Even early as they were, they had to park almost a quarter mile down from the main gate into the village. "I don't wanna pay to park in the lot." Toby grimaced. "It's a freaking fortune. Oh, you brought your historical site pass, right?" Paying to get into the fortress would suck worse than paying for parking.

"Got it," Jock said, already getting out of the car. Walking through the little village first, past all the tourist shops tucked into the medieval buildings, the heart of Saint-Rémy look positively modern in contrast. Jock didn't want to stop anywhere though, he just wanted to get to the castle. They had to enter through the gift shop (of course) and Toby saw him eying the wooden weapons.

He'd always liked Les Baux—it was a tourist's wet dream, as evidenced by the number of them around—but Toby'd never experienced it quite like this. Following along behind Jock, listening to him recognize something he'd seen ten years before, then finding something new. When they went out onto the small plateau to look at the siege engines, Jock knew all about them, and could explain in detail how they worked.

"The brochure says the demonstrations of them start in a couple hours. We could hang out for them."

Jock shrugged. "If we're still around." He turned back toward the fortress itself, looking over Toby's head. "Let's go check out the rest." And they checked it all out. The paths that clung to the cliff face which the on-duty guards had had to walk, and all the weird half-ruined rooms that were partly carved into the mountain and partly built of the stone that had been hewn out, and the "private" areas where the actual Baux family had lived. When no one was around for two minutes, Jock climbed a stone wall that someone had built to block out half of a huge archway. When he got to the top, Toby took a picture of him standing there, one hand braced on the surface of the barrel vault and the other shoved in his pocket, grinning down at him, light hair messy and eyes shining.

He was fucking *darling*.

The high point of the visit for Toby was also the high point of the fortress itself. The stairway up was in bad shape, and the majority of visitors didn't chance it. There was a spot about fifty feet off the ground, a single iron pipe guarding the open side, where three steps in a row were worn down to nothing but a rock slide with a few jagged spots on the sides. Jock could step right over that section, of course. Toby had to find a toehold.

They reached the top, completely devoid of other tourists, and stood on the watchtower where who knew how many guards had stood over time, looking out over the olive orchards and the Alpilles to the north. The wind gusted, and suddenly Jock was standing behind Toby, sharing his heat. As if he were sheltering from the breeze in Toby's body. Toby held his breath, scared to move, then let go of it when Jock's arms came around him, circling his waist and pulling him against Jock's chest, Jock's heart thumping against his back. Jock's cheek brushed along his hair, sliding through it until his lips were rubbing against Toby's jaw. "This scruff is so hot on you. Did I tell you that?"

"No." Toby swallowed. "I don't think you have." But of course, that was why he maintained it just like this, wasn't it? For how it looked, and for how much his partners liked to feel it. He was turning around, wondering about Jock's reaction if Toby were to scrape his neck with it, when Jock let go of him, stepping back so fast Toby swayed.

Voices. Other people coming up the stairs. Over Jock's shoulder, Toby saw heads appearing above the top of the roofline. Jock stepped back another foot or two. "I'm hungry," he said in a totally normal voice.

"Oh." He could understand not wanting to be caught mid-PDA, but it seemed annoyingly easy for Jock to just drop him like a hot potato. Or a girl. Jock shoved his hands in his pockets, and Toby couldn't help but check for evidence of how invested he'd been in that moment of affection.

"We could go, like, find someplace secluded and see what's in that basket," Jock suggested before Toby could decide. He kept flicking glances to the small group that had made it to the overlook, four Asians around their own age, then back at Toby, giving him puppy dog eyes. "Spend some time alone."

Yes, please. "Alone's good. Let's go." He didn't grab Jock's hand and pull him down the stairs at a run, but he wanted to.

Chapter 14

Starting something with Toby when they could be interrupted by any of the guys anytime was more than Jock could stomach.

After waking up the last three mornings wondering why he wasn't with Toby now that he'd gotten the whole thing with the picture off his chest, that's what it kept coming back to. So, when Danny suggested they go to Les Baux, he'd jumped all over it.

And yeah, he totally knew that eventually they'd be around the guys, but baby steps or whatever. That was his plan—get Toby away from the *gîte* and seduce him in private. He just hadn't had all the details worked out.

Turned out Toby had a more fully developed plan. Which wasn't going his way.

"This sucks," Toby said, pouting for the first time Jock had seen. He kicked a small rock in annoyance, staring out over a field of something some farmer had planted.

"What sucks?" It looked fine to him, as long as they weren't going to sit on this dirt road.

"This is supposed to be a field of red poppies. I mean, it *is* a field of poppies, but they aren't blooming yet. It looks so cool when they—"

"It's cool now." Jock grabbed Toby's hand, getting his attention. "What, you were all thinking you were gonna take me someplace romantic and seduce me?"

Toby turned as red as a poppy, choking on something a second before saying, "Well, 'seduce' might be a bit over-the-top, but um, maybe . . . put you in the mood?"

You *put me in the mood*. But he couldn't say that. He tugged on Toby's hand, leading him toward some trees. "You don't need to do anything at all." Hopefully Toby would understand what he really meant.

"Hang on, I forgot something." Toby pulled away as soon as Jock set the picnic basket on the ground, in a sort of grassy area with a few other scrubby plants. He went back to the car in that same confident gait that Jock couldn't stop noticing. He'd never even thought about anyone's walk before, but he was pretty sure he'd memorized Toby's—maybe could mimic it if he tried.

He dropped onto the ground next to basket and watched Toby dig through the trunk, smiling, and pull something out. A blanket.

"What are you laughing about?" Toby called over. Smiling even wider, he started back to Jock.

Jock waited until he got close enough to grab, then he yanked Toby down next to him by his wrist. "I'm laughing because you *totally* planned to seduce me." Which was awesome, because Jock had planned the same thing. Not like this, out in the middle of nowhere on the ground, more like when they got back, but right now seemed like a perfect time. He didn't let Toby answer, just started kissing him. Wrapping his hand in Toby's hair and leveraging Toby's mouth open with his lips, plunging in with his tongue to find Toby's and get it to twine itself around his and stroke.

Toby dug his fingers into Jock's back and drew back until they were lying on the ground, hand searching under Jock's shirt, feeling up his spine. Pushing and pulling to line up their bodies.

Jock thought he'd be crazy nervous, because this wasn't just sex and they both knew that, but he hadn't had time to get that way. There was none of the talking he expected would have to happen beforehand, or the fumbling to figure out who was going to touch whom first and where. The butterflies didn't flutter up in his stomach when Toby pulled away from him, saying something about the blanket, then trying to spread it out with one hand while using the other to slide into the back of Jock's waistband and grip his ass through his briefs. Jock kissed down Toby's throat, swirling his tongue around the Adam's apple that had been driving him nuts every time he looked at it, Toby's stubble poking him. Even then he wasn't nervous, just fucking eager. Dick throbbing against the buttons of his fly, digging into it, which made him wonder about Toby's dick, and how hard he was. Jock reached down and felt him through his jeans, squeezing the rod he found to test its ripeness.

"Fuck the blanket," Toby panted. "Take off your shirt." He started yanking on the hem. Jock pushed up long enough to whip it over his head, then he straddled Toby's thighs, sliding his legs alongside, bunching up Toby's T so he could rub their bellies together. His hard and ridged and Toby's furry and firm. He didn't get to, though, because Toby's cock was like a speed bump, slowing him down, distracting him. Making him groan when Toby lifted his hips and shoved his hardness against Jock's. His fingers were all over Jock's chest while he stretched up to bite his neck, then lick it. "You have the most perfect chest I've ever seen in my life."

"Thanks," he gasped. Toby pinched his nipple and Jock did it again, louder.

"Christ, your pecs are beautiful. Like all those childhood prayers were answered and my GI Joe action figure finally came to life."

That surprised a laugh out of him, but then Toby traced the underside of the muscle with his tongue, breathing all over everything he'd wetted, and Jock choked on it. At some point he'd started rocking his hips, pushing and prodding Toby's dick with his own aching cock, and it felt so fucking good, he didn't know if he could stop long enough to get their jeans out of the way, let alone hold Toby in his hand. But Toby was on it, working his fingers between them enough to flick open Jock's buttons.

"Fucking love a button fly," he murmured, lips back at Jock's throat, but when he dug under Jock's briefs and found his head, that wasn't good enough anymore. Jock dropped to his elbow, smashing Toby's arm between them, and grabbed Toby's chin, holding his mouth still for Jock's tongue to fuck again. Shoving his hips harder against Toby's hand, grinding him into the ground.

"You too," he panted, pulling away from the kiss for a second. Toby gripped him tighter, working his palm against the underside of Jock's dick, making him groan before he forced himself to stop long enough to get Toby's jeans open and his briefs out of the way.

Toby's cock was just the way he remembered. Darker than he expected on a white guy, with one of those mushroom heads made up of graceful curves and so perfectly smooth it looked like it had been animated by Disney. Jock ran his thumb down the big pulsing vein that stood out from the shaft, making Toby catch his breath and tighten his own fingers around Jock's dick.

"Never touched it last time," Jock said, feeling stupid and momentarily insecure. Was he even doing it right? But he had his own, and he'd practiced plenty on it, so—

"You're more than making up for it now," Toby responded, and then he let go of Jock, lifting his hand to his mouth and licking his palm before grasping Jock's shaft again, twisting and working his fingers right up under the head.

Jock swallowed. "That's hot." He let go of Toby's dick and held his palm up to Toby's mouth, watching as Toby slicked him up, too. Then Toby took Jock's wrist and pulled it down to wrap around him again.

Jock's self-consciousness dissolved, and he rolled them onto their sides to give them room to maneuver, maintaining his hold on the back of Toby's neck, kissing him again, working his tongue and hand in the same rhythm. Toby followed his lead, stroking Jock with the same tempo, moaning.

When Toby came, the smell pushed Jock over into his own orgasm. Salty and primal. His body instinctively responded, the same way he reacted to the smell of blood in the hockey rink, his pulse leaping around and priming him for something major. Some game-changing event. The penalty box or the medics or spilling his cum all over Toby's hand, shoving forward until his cock rested against Toby's furry belly and his nuts wrung out a few more drops in reaction. "Fuck."

Toby grinned, panting, his eyes closed and his head resting on Jock's biceps. "You're a curse-nutter."

"Huh?" Man he'd really done some damage to Toby's lips. They were slick and reddened and twice their normal size. "You're smexy."

"When you come, you curse. You did it the first time, too," he explained, then opened his eyes and met Jock's gaze, warm liquid brown. His pupils were huge and he looked half asleep and all happy. "Thank you."

Jock kissed him. Softly, so he wouldn't do more damage. He needed Toby to heal so he could do it all over again. "Thank you for what?"

Toby sighed, still smiling. "For thinking I'm smexy. For a good day."

"We could go back to the *gîte* and make it better," Jock suggested, and that's when his butterflies kicked in, because that was the threshold. Repeat sex meant going from casual to being *involved*.

Toby's smile slipped away and he met Jock's gaze again. "Is that what you want?"

"Yeah, I do." He kissed Toby again, harder this time, partly to distract himself from the way his stomach reacted to that. He'd been right, though. He'd never not be scared about this. But if he wanted more than just hookups, he had to get over the thing with the guys.

Suck it up.

Toby traced around Jock's lips with his fingertips when Jock let up on his mouth. "Works for me."

They used the blanket to clean up, then sat on it, avoiding the sticky spots. "I still want to eat before we leave," Jock said, pulling the food toward them.

"You worked up an appetite?" Toby asked, smiling fully at him, bending his legs up under his chin and wrapping his arms around them. They were sheltered from most of the wind, but it still occasionally ruffled his hair. He looked good rumpled up, sitting in the shade but spotted here and there with sunlight. He'd taken his shoes off—afterward—and Jock knew for a fact that he hadn't buttoned his jeans yet.

Yeah, he needed food and then they'd go back to the *gîte.*

Thank fuck, the picnic basket wasn't full of sausage and cheese. There was bread—there was *always* bread, but at least it was Madame B's homemade bread—and lots of little containers with various things to spread on it. And olives, of course. He'd never escape olives in Provence. Good thing he liked them. "Should we open the wine, too?"

"We may as well," Toby said. "I'm sure Danny and Madame B worked hard on planning this little meal."

Huh? "Why would Danny help her pack our lunch?"

Toby groaned and rested his forehead on his knees. "I probably shouldn't tell you . . ."

He dug around until he found a corkscrew, then leaned over to kiss the back of Toby's neck, right on a vertebral bump. "But you will because I'm your *luh-vah.*"

Toby laughed and leaned back on his elbows, straightening out his legs. His lips were still reddened, and reclined like he was, a small wedge of his skin peeked out at Jock, a few hairs curling toward him from Toby's half-zipped jeans. *I'm the man*. Because he'd totally put that look on Toby's face and loosened him up.

"You aren't going to believe it," Toby said.

"He's her *luh-vah*?" Jock handed Toby his wine.

"Okay, maybe you are going to believe it."

"Barely." Jock snorted. "I don't get it at all, but the way they act around each other—crazy."

While they ate, they speculated on what kind of future a twenty-something American frat boy and a fifty-something French widow might have. "Maybe it's just a vacation fling," Toby said eventually, but the frown on his face didn't look sure.

"It's gotta be more," Jock agreed with Toby's expression. "No guy as young as Danny goes for someone that much older than him unless it's, like, true love."

Toby glanced away, out over the non-blooming poppy field baking in the sun. "Maybe he's got an oedipal complex? Who knows what attracts one person to another. Maybe it really is all destiny."

Jock shrugged and spread some more of the artichoke stuff on a hunk of baguette. For some reason, Toby wasn't that into the bread. He kept inspecting each piece carefully before eating it. Actually, he kinda seemed done eating altogether. "I dunno, some things seem pretty universal."

"Like guys with torsos like GI Joe are going to pretty much get anybody revved up?"

"Wouldn't it suck if I'd had the groin of a GI Joe doll?" He shuddered.

So did Toby. "That would've been a nasty surprise."

"Bet I'd be hating it more than you."

Toby rolled onto his side and rested his head on his arm, facing Jock. "It would have been a disservice to all mankind."

Jock washed down his bite with the rest of his wine. "I don't work for it, I mean, not that hard."

"Your body? You work out every day. I see you guys. Doesn't Danny have you all on some beer terrorist physical training program? He keeps talking about it."

"Well, if training means we work out together, than yeah." Jock let his head fall back, watching the sky through the leaves and trying to figure out how to explain what he wanted to. "I guess that doesn't seem like much to me."

"Does it make you uncomfortable when I say stuff about how you look?"

"Not . . . exactly." He leaned back onto his elbows, reclining next to Toby. Parallel with him. "It's more like *I'm* not that impressed with it. And I dunno, it was cool I guess, when I figured out that most guys saw me and wanted me, but . . ." He shrugged.

"I dated a body builder," Toby began, and Jock stiffened up, because did he really want to hear about this? But Toby went on regardless. "But I only saw him a few times because he expected me to worship his muscles. He was boring as hell. You aren't." He pushed up from the blanket, brushing along Jock's jaw with his lips.

"That's good to know." He turned onto his side so they were parallel and only a few inches apart. Except Jock was tall enough that his elbow was off the blanket and resting in the grass, plus he had more to say. The stuff he'd kind of been thinking lately, now that he had some distance. Maybe Toby sensed that, because he lay his head back down and listened. "Before I came out, I was so focused on hiding it, but also on trying to, like, get my needs met. But after we hooked up the first time? All the sudden it was like there were guys everywhere and they were checking me out and responding to me." He couldn't watch Toby's face while he talked about this, so he inspected the grass at the edge of the blanket, brushing his palm across the top of it. "I had tons of offers after that picture went viral, but I couldn't do it." He shook his head and plucked a few blades of grass, throwing them up for the breeze to play with. "The fuckers who wanted to hook up with me after that were just . . ."

"They wanted to hook up *because* of the photo."

"Yeah." He shoved back up, sitting with his arms around his knees like Toby had been earlier, staring out over the fields and hills. Not too far away, Les Baux was visible, nearly white with the brightness of the day. "I don't know how porn stars do it, man."

"It's different," Toby said, sitting behind him and wrapping his arms around Jock's waist. Then he rested his cheek on Jock's back, and his voice vibrated in Jock's chest. "You may have chosen that, sort of, but that doesn't mean you wanted it."

"I guess I'll have to take your word on that, because I'll never know."

He could feel Toby's smile on his back, though his shirt. "Do you miss playing?"

Jock nodded, swallowing. "A lot. It wasn't a strategic move to eventually go pro, I just wanted to play hockey. I never thought it would be my career."

"Will you play again?"

He hung his head a second, watching the way Toby's thumb stroked his abdomen. "I wanted to compete against guys who are at my level; it's not any fun if you're better than everyone else. Maybe I'll find someplace else to play, eventually."

Toby squeezed him tighter for a second, then they fell silent, until Toby said, "Tell me about the beer terrorist thing."

"Uh, you know about the membership policy stuff?" That was probably the best place to start.

"About the alumni threatening to cut off the funding to the frat if you guys didn't take out the stuff about accepting gays?"

"That." Jock nodded. "They had this big meeting where Plant—he's the treasurer—had to tell everyone that if the TAG alumni association cut off funds, we couldn't afford to keep the keg fridge in beer."

Toby whistled at that. "Way to grab a bunch of fratbros by the short and curlies."

"It looked pretty bad," Jock agreed. "But that was right after Ricky broke his leg when someone tried to burn down the frat—you know about that, right?"

"Uh-huh. I saw Collin that night, he told me." Toby lifted his head from Jock's back, pulling away slightly as he said it.

Somehow that told Jock everything he needed to know about Toby and Collin's past. "I didn't know you were that close to him." The tension in his jaw transmitted to his voice.

"We're friends." Toby tightened his arms. "That's all we ever were. And that night he told me he wasn't interested in my benefits package any longer."

"Because of his boyfriend?"

"They weren't together yet, but they'd already met. I found that out the next night." A smiled crept into his voice. "We went to the Slaughterhouse and Eric showed up looking for him. That was the last time I saw Collin for a while."

"'Kay." Jock knew he sounded totally defensive, but he didn't care much. He just didn't like thinking about Toby with other guys, even when it wasn't anything serious.

"So what happened?" Toby asked.

"Huh?" Happened with who?

"Beer terrorists?"

"Oh, yeah." Jock nodded and sat a little straighter, running his hand through his hair like it could help him rub some brain cells together. "So the guys were pretty much ready to vote to go back to the old policy—they'd just voted me in as a member, knowing up front I'm gay—and Tank couldn't even threaten them into not changing the wording, but Ricky gets up there and starts going on about how he'd sacrificed his leg for this policy—"

"But he still has a leg."

"That's exactly what Collin said." *Forget about him.* "Anyway, then Ricky starts calling the alumni beer terrorists and telling everyone that if we let them hold the keg hostage, they'd control everything from then on. He, like, whipped them into a revolutionary frenzy." The memory of it made Jock smile, although at the time, just after he'd shown up at Calapooya, he'd been unable to. "Then everyone voted not to change the policy, and the guys are still stuck on fighting the beer terrorists."

Toby snorted. "Thank God they aren't allowed out in the real world. Theta Alpha Gamma might need to come up with a halfway house for when those guys graduate, so they can be introduced to society in small, manageable steps."

"I'll talk to Kyle about it when we get back."

"Good idea." Then came the unmistakable sound of Toby yawning.

"You wanna head back?" It was getting too hot, and Toby had started rubbing his chest, which reminded Jock they had business at the *gîte*. Like, *bidness* business. He trapped Toby's hand where it was tracing the curve of his pec and squeezed.

"If you're ready." Toby sat up, breathing in like he was trying to wake himself from a trance.

"I'm ready."

As Toby pulled in their driveway, around the main house to EuroTAG, he took one more look to see Jock's head turned toward the side window, as silent and contemplative as he'd been since they'd started back. As soon as Toby halted the car, Jock got out, before Toby turned the engine off.

His heart wobbled. Not sank, exactly, but urged caution. He was pretty sure this was a go, but Jock could get scared again or change his mind . . . *Oh, shut up*. Toby stepped out, too, watching Jock stretch as if he'd woken from a nap.

"Man, European cars are small," he said, coming around to Toby's side of the car. "It's not as bad as an airplane, but even twenty minutes and my knees are pissed off."

"You really have a thing about knees, don't you?" Toby asked, leaning against the side of the vehicle.

Jock smiled at that. "I guess."

Just ask. "Are you coming to my place?"

"Yeah." Jock rested his hand on the roof of the car, just behind Toby's shoulder, standing close enough that their feet touched. "If that's okay?"

"Definitely okay." Toby reached for Jock's shirt, pulling him closer. Jock didn't fight it, kissing Toby slowly at first, unlike before, but getting demanding within seconds, pressing Toby against the car with his body. Then suddenly he broke it off, pulling away and swiping at his mouth, turning toward the rosemary hedge that fronted the EuroTAG patio.

The suspiciously shaking, whispering hedge. "Shhh!" a very Danny-sounding plant hissed.

"I think the children are watching," Toby murmured to Jock.

"Uh, yeah." Jock kicked at the ground, not meeting his eyes.

"Spying on us to see if their picnic scheme worked, or training in stealth anti–beer terrorist maneuvers?"

"I'd say both, but they aren't good at multitasking from what I've seen." Jock shook his head, folding his arms over his chest.

"Hey!" a bush protested with Julian's voice. "I can totally multitask." He ended the mystery of the muttering shrubbery by popping up from behind it, holding a shoe in one hand and a very dirty cloth in the other. "I polished all my shoes while we waited for you guys to get back." He'd decorated his hair with rosemary branches, sort of like antlers.

"You're a *freak*, dude." Ricky stood, eyeing Julian sideways. He had similar herbal antlers, but more of them.

Jock sighed, turning back to Toby. "So, after dinner?"

Behind him, Danny bounced up, staring at them, cocking his head. Maybe he was wondering *Why not right now?* also.

"Yes." Toby nodded, suppressing the urge to lean forward and kiss Jock, even a quick one. He pretty clearly wasn't down with the public displays yet.

At least Jock gave Toby one of their communicative, reassuring eye-locks as he backed up a few steps, flashing his dimple quickly before turning and heading into the house.

"So . . ." Danny said after Jock had walked through the door. "It was a good day?"

Toby snorted. "I'm not telling you."

Danny trailed behind him as Toby started toward his *cabanon*. "C'mon dude, I told you shit about, you know, my love life."

"Yes, you did," Toby agreed, refusing to turn back. "And that was your choice. My choice is to *not* share."

"Well, you know where to find me if you change your mind, or, like, need to talk about anything."

Toby rolled his eyes to himself and hardened his heart to the wounded tone of Danny's voice. "Yep, I do."

His first order of business was to take a shower. Not the kind he'd been taking, but the more purposeful kind. Getting clean for Jock's visit later, because he knew exactly what he wanted, and he was pretty sure that was exactly what Jock wanted. And so what if Jock had taken a little break before getting it? He'd said he was coming over, hadn't he? Maybe the fratbro welcoming party had made him jittery. Or he simply wanted an opportunity to brush his teeth first. Lots of explanations that had nothing to do with avoiding Toby. *This level of insecurity is so unlike me.* Or it used to be, but since the advent of that boy, Toby had discovered new facets to his personality.

The bathroom was so small he kept catching glances of himself in the mirror. His body was nothing like Jock's, but he'd never been *un*attractive, he didn't think. He was pretty average, although definitely carrying less weight than a lot of Americans. And even less since coming to France, he could feel as he lathered his overly hairy abdomen. Jock *liked* all that hair. He seemed to like other stuff, too.

An hour later he was dressed again and stepping out the door to kill some time on his patio before dinner when he found someone sitting in one of the chairs in front. Someone whose hair was a little too light and whose shoulders weren't quite wide enough. *Noah*. And judging by the way his face was buried in his hands, Toby was about to be knee-deep in more bro-angst.

"What is it?" he asked, coming to sit next to the kid.

Noah lifted his head, pressing his steepled hands against his lips, knuckles white. "I need to talk to someone."

"Well Jock—"

"God," Noah groaned. "I can't tell *him* about this. He'll tell me how fucking stupid I am."

Lovely. "Do you want to go inside or sit out here?" *And can we make this fast?*

Noah looked at him beseechingly. "Can we go down to the bar in the village? I need to get away from this place."

Toby sighed. "Just let me tell someone where we're going?"

Noah nodded, and Toby jogged up to the house to find Danny sitting in the living room by himself, watching some part of *Carlos* yet again. He paused it and greeted Toby with, "He's in the shower."

Toby played dumb. "Who is?" Jock was showering too? *That sounds promising.*

"Your boyfriend."

"Don't use that word!" He waved it away, warding off potential jinx. "You'll scare him."

Danny lifted his brows, but was otherwise circumspect. "'Kay." Obviously, love had changed him.

"Can you just tell him that Noah has some kind of problem and I have to talk the guy off his ledge, but I'll be back later? Noah and I are going down to the bar."

"Oooh." Danny nodded exaggeratedly. "Yeah, *that* convo might take a while, dude, 'cause—"

"Don't tell me." Toby held up a quelling palm. "Give him the dignity of confessing whatever it is to me without my prior knowledge."

He escaped while Danny was still trying to decipher what he'd said.

Any hopes Toby had of getting through his "advising session" with Noah quickly died when he saw the dude waiting for him. He was standing at Toby's hut with his head bowed and his arms hugging his chest. When he looked up at Toby's approach, his face was pale and vacant. Not blank, just not there.

This was going to be worse than his talk with Danny yesterday. What was it Collin had said last term when he'd come out to at TAG? "God save me from straight, sensitive frat boys." Toby hadn't fully understood that until this week, but he totally comprehended it now.

Except Noah wasn't straight, so maybe it was just frat boys in general. Well, not *all* of them. Hopefully. Toby gave Noah his most reassuring smile and laid a hand on his shoulder, squeezing. "Okay, let's go. We'll get this worked out." Whatever it was.

Noah nodded, chin crumpling for a split second before he straightened his spine and started walking toward the trail the boys had discovered, worn by previous guests of Madame Bouvinet's, presumably with similar needs to theirs.

Beer, wine, and advice.

ΘΑΓ

"You *kissed* him?" Toby asked again, gripping his beer tighter, hoping that this time Noah would say "no." It had taken the dude utterly forever to admit the real problem, which had driven Toby insane and allowed him to drink enough that he was catching a buzz, but now he couldn't help wishing Noah hadn't told him at all.

"Uh-huh," Noah said, nodding slowly, staring down at his own glass in front of him. "I don't know what happened, but it was like my hormones took over. Or maybe it's Turbo's pheromones."

"Oh Jesus." He wanted to lay his head down, but the bar was nearly full at this time of the evening—not surprisingly, since by Toby's estimation it could only hold about twenty people—and they'd had to stand at one of the countertops built along the walls. Totally not the correct height for hiding one's face in defeat. One of the little round tables would have been perfect, but they were all taken.

He took a deep drink of his beer, then a deep breath, before continuing their conversation. "And what did he do when you kissed him?"

Noah swallowed, staring at the wall in front of him with blank eyes. "He pushed me away." He touched his shoulder with his fingertips, as if remembering the other guy's hand there.

Well, yeah. But now was not the time to point out the obvious, or to give Noah a lecture on the fruitlessness of pinning his hopes on "turning" a straight boy. *Well, what time* is *it?*

It's damage control time.

"Did he say anything to you after that?"

Noah ignored the question, burying his face in his hands, then slipping even lower, until he gripped his own hair, his nose inches from the countertop. "I couldn't *stop* myself," he moaned. "He wasn't wearing anything but that towel, and his hair was all wet from the shower and he smelled *sooo* good and the hallway was deserted—"

"*What*? You assaulted him when he was almost naked?"

Noah straightened up, but couldn't look at Toby. "I . . . I'm not sure I'd call it *assault*, exactly."

"Noah." Toby leaned forward, enunciating, wanting this to be very clear. "If Turbo was a girl, and you'd done that, what would be happening right this second?"

His eyes went wide. "All the sororities would be marching on TAG House and throwing things through our windows and ripping up our lawn and spraying penis slurs on our walls? And they'd hunt me down mercilessly on campus and scream abuse until I had a nervous breakdown and left college? Oh God, I don't want to go like BLO, dude."

Toby had his doubts if kissing a girl—even a half-naked girl—against her will would bring down the kind of wrath that had been heaped on the Beta Lambda Omicron brother after he'd drugged and raped that girl fall term, but it helped Toby's case to play along with it for now. "If we were at Calapooya? Maybe. You'd also be facing *assault* charges. Or at the minimum, a complaint to the college and the Greek council."

"But he's a *guy*."

Toby leveled his sternest expression at Noah. "A straight guy, who didn't in any way invite you to come on to him. He's been avoiding you like—like you're a gay guy he knows has a crush on him."

"Um, I'm actually bi," Noah said.

"It doesn't. Matter." Toby used his index finger to make his point, tapping the counter with it. Maybe a bit hard, if the beer sloshing in his glass was any indication. "You may as well be an alien offering him a bioprobe. He wants it about as much."

Noah's face fell. "Isn't that a little harsh? I mean, the internet told me most straight guys will actually—"

"Porn is not reality!"

Noah scrunched up his forehead. "But I read it on Facebook."

Toby grabbed Noah's biceps, making the dude pay close attention. "Facebook is not reality, either. Anything that glows, chimes, chirps, pings, or rings to get your attention? Not a reliable source of information."

Noah's brow wrinkled up again. Toby began to interpret it as a sign of mental exertion. "Okay, even if you're right . . . this is different. It's not—it's not just *lust*. I didn't assault him so much as express my overpowering emotions."

"Okay, first thing is, that's what stalkers say in court and the judge finds it as worthy an excuse as I do. In other words, *your feelings don't matter*. I mean, they *matter*, but not to Turbo. Not in this situation. You cannot do anything you want and then excuse it by saying you were overpowered by some primitive, limbic response." He shook Noah slightly, hoping that would somehow help what he was saying to penetrate his skull. "That's why they call them 'crimes of passion.' It's still a *crime*."

"What's going on?" Someone asked, looming far too close to them. Close to Toby, in particular. *Jock. Did he come looking for me?*

Focus on the problem at hand.

Noah turned to speak to Jock. "I committed a crime of passion."

"Oh my God." Toby dropped his hands from the guy's arms. *This might be hopeless.*

"Yeah?" Jock drawled, staring at his roommate, eyes downright icy. "Which one would that be?"

Noah's thinking wrinkles appeared yet again. "As far as I know, the only straight guy I assaulted today was Turbo."

Jock squinted at him a moment longer, then turned to Toby. "You guys missed dinner." Either the lighting in this place was bad, or Jock was pouting.

"We've been here that long?" Toby craned his head but couldn't find a clock anywhere. He stretched to see around that post over his shoulder and bumped into Jock, who'd moved even closer to him. Standing with his arm braced on the bar—Toby could feel the heat on his back. Closer than one guy generally stood to another in public, which Toby couldn't help but see as a positive sign.

"You've been here a couple hours." Jock answered Toby, but Toby was fairly sure his focus was on Noah. "Uh, I think."

Toby tipped his head ever so slightly to the annoyed hulk behind him, then widened his eyes.

"Um, can I just talk to Toby another minute?" Noah asked Jock, looking over Toby's shoulder. "Alone?"

Toby felt Jock's huff more than heard it. "I'll be sitting out front with the other guys," he said after a few seconds. The heat of his arm dissipated, and then he stood next to them again, giving Noah one more hard look before turning to go.

Oh he's totally *into me.*

"Wow, uh." Noah gave one of those laugh-snorts of disbelief, staring after Jock. "He possessive much?"

"I don't know." Toby stared after Jock himself, watching the muscles in his back. "It just started today."

"Well, congrats, dude." Noah sounded utterly wrecked.

Shit. Toby diverted his energy, putting it back into this kid. If he fixed the problem well enough, he could forget it for a while. "I'm sorry things aren't working out for you, but seriously, you have to believe me when I tell you that—"

"No, I get it." Noah nodded, twirling his beer glass. "Sorry about before, I was just . . . I guess I wanted to believe."

"You'll recover," Toby said, knowing that was an easy platitude in his position, even if true. "I've been there, I—"

"You were in love with a straight dude?" Noah jerked his head up.

"Not exactly." *Not at all.* Although he'd definitely done the unrequited lust thing in his high school PE class. And many, many other times. "I mean, I've had crushes on unattainable guys." Okay, it was disturbing that Noah's eyes drifted over his shoulder, in the direction Jock had just gone, but Toby forced himself to ignore it, reaching to grasp his advisee's arm. "I know it might feel like, you know, 'love,' but it's not. Real love isn't one-sided."

"But I'm not sure it's one-sided." Noah leaned forward, earnest in his belief. "I mean, there were times when he—"

"It *is* one-sided." Toby firmed his jaw and nodded after a second of Noah staring at him. If the poor kid had looked wrecked before, he was destroyed now.

"You think I really scared him?" Noah swallowed.

"Um, well, it depends on how you define 'scared.'" *Total evasion.* "Let's just say I think he was very concerned for his safety." Not exactly pulling his punches, but he had to be cruel to be kind and all that.

"I probably owe him an apology, huh?"

"Um, I would say so, yes."

Noah nodded quickly, shuffling his feet. Toby hated making him so unhappy, but it had to be done. He clapped Noah on the shoulder with false cheer. A totally fake "Well, glad we resolved that" gesture. "Okay, then. Let's go get another beer and find the guys."

Noah made a face, but followed along when Toby led the way to the bartender.

Chapter 15

Waiting for Toby in front of his place, Jock had some time to think. A lot of time. More than he wanted, for sure. But he was the coward who'd run this afternoon when they'd gotten home and the guys had caught them kissing. He was also the dumbass who'd gotten all territorial when he'd seen Toby with Noah, even knowing nothing was going on. Danny'd filled him in about Turbo, and he could see why Toby was the obvious guy to go to.

Still, he'd decided against waiting with the guys at the bar for Noah's crisis to end, because he was sick of their never-ending beer terrorist crap. And because he didn't want anyone else to waylay Toby. Now that he was certain he wanted more, he wasn't interested in letting anyone get in the way.

Everyone wanted a piece of him, didn't they? It didn't matter that Jock didn't feel like sharing. He'd never been good at sharing. He was the kid who'd whacked others for taking his toys in preschool, and the kid who'd always wanted to make up the rules of the game. It was part of the reason his parents had started him in hockey early, to "channel his aggressions" and "help him learn discipline."

Hockey'd done that, but it hadn't rid him of those personality traits, had it?

Whatever. Jock sighed and slouched further in Toby's patio chair, stretching his legs out in front of him and hanging his arms off the sides. The thing was only comfortable for so long, at least when he was sitting here by himself waiting for its owner. It was too straight-backed, and it didn't support lounging.

The sun had just set when he'd gotten here, but it was full night now. The wind had died some—it did that at the end of the day—but there was still enough of it to chill him. Toby said the mistral was the reason Provence had a unique climate, but still, it could be warmer and it wouldn't hurt, would it?

Probably, what did he know? That wind, the mistral, definitely *felt* unusual. Nights like this with a full moon, looking out over the landscape, Jock almost thought he could see the way the air currents swirled. Like watching cold and warm water mix, little disturbances that were barely detectable.

"Was that necessary?"

Jock nearly fell off the chair onto his ass when Toby's voice came out of the darkness. How had he snuck up on him? He shoved himself up onto the seat, then stood, watching Toby pass through the glow of the yard light mounted by the pool, that same confident walk, but slower, approaching warily.

"What?" Jock asked.

"The way you acted toward Noah, was that necessary?"

"Um, what way?" He didn't have a lot of hope that Toby'd buy his act, but he didn't have any other answer, either.

Toby smiled; Jock caught his mouth curving up just before he passed from light into darkness again. "Like you were a dog protecting your bone."

He shrugged. "If you're my bone, I guess." He forced himself to stay still as Toby came closer, not shifting his weight. "Sorry," he mumbled when Toby stood just in front of him.

"For calling me your bone or treating me like one?"

Jock shook his head because he wasn't sure if he was sorry at all. Toby stepped forward until he stood so close not even the wind could fit between them to blow away the smell of him—a hint of salt and something else that Jock's brain labeled caramel, even though it wasn't anything like that. Before he knew it, he had a hand on Toby's waist, pulling him closer. "You don't wanna be my bone?"

"Do you wanna be my dog?" Toby pressed his body against Jock's, wrapping his arms over Jock's shoulders so they were as close as they could be with clothes on.

"I wanna feel you naked, all over me."

Toby's heartbeat reacted immediately, picking up speed, thumping against Jock's ribs. "You gonna fuck me?" he asked, barely louder than the sound of Jock's lungs working to bring in air.

Jock swallowed. "Yes."

"Thank God," Toby said, right before Jock kissed him.

Toby let them into the cabin, Jock standing right behind him, prickling Toby's skin from the brush of breath on the back of his neck while his key slid into the lock like a lover. He took that as a good sign. A shiver worked down his spine, feeding the building ball of tension at the base of his dick.

Once he got the door open, Jock followed him in, stepping out of the entry so Toby could shut it, moving silently, then clamping Toby's wrist in his hand and pulling Toby toward him. He didn't say anything, but that eye-lock connection they shared told Toby a lot. Jock wanted this, and he wanted it because it was Toby.

Toby pulled Jock's head down, getting things underway, making the first move but knowing it was probably the last moment of real control he'd have. This kiss was his, and Jock would take what he wanted after that. Toby'd never had a clue nervous tension balling in his gut could be so exciting.

Jock was pushing Toby's coat off and then pulling his shirt over his head within seconds, looking at Toby, running his hands down Toby's sides, then bending to kiss his neck. Using teeth to scrape along the side of Toby's throat, bringing up goose bumps everywhere.

The way Jock undressed him made Toby forget all about his physical insecurities and shortcomings. He didn't think once about how his body compared to GI Joe's, not with the way Jock touched him, using his whole hand to feel every molecule of Toby's skin. Molding and kneading and finding obscure parts of Toby's body. The spaces under his scapula, and where his ribs curved around his torso. Jock's touch gave him a buzz, disorienting him enough to tell Jock, "You aren't leaving until we're both sweating, panting, wrung out, and drunk on sex."

Good lord, he'd even made himself swoony with that line. He had to rest his forehead on Jock's collarbone, and then he had to trace the line of it with his tongue.

"I fucking hope so," Jock said, voice so deep it resounded in Toby's ear, small vibrations infiltrating his body and adding to the great big pile of arousal building inside him.

Fingers slid down Toby's abdomen, searching out the top button of his jeans, then flicking it open before skimming around to his back and working under his waistband. Jock pulled his head up then, eyes catching Toby's again before he cradled the back of Toby's skull in his other hand and kissed him. Tongue lunging into his mouth at the same time Jock shoved into his briefs, fingers gripping his ass, forcing Toby's jeans down until they hung up on his hipbones. Jock barely had room to maneuver inside Toby's clothing, but he managed to wedge his thumb between Toby's cheeks, hooking it on Toby's tailbone for leverage and working down further.

Toby pulled out of the kiss. "You can't feel me naked all over you if you're still dressed," he panted, bunching Jock's shirt up his back, under the coat he still wore. Jock let go of him long enough to shrug his jacket onto the floor and yank off his tee, then he pulled Toby close again, gasping when Toby slid his chest along Jock's, stretching up on tiptoes and letting Jock's abdominal ridges caress his own belly, until they were almost the same height and Jock's pecs skimmed his nipples. Jock cupped and kneaded Toby's ass, kissing him while walking them toward the bed. Pushing Toby down until he lay on his back, stripping off his shoes and jeans, then standing to get rid of his own.

When Jock shoved his white briefs over his hips and his dick sprang out, Toby had to sit up and catch it. Wrap his fingers around it and slide just the head into his mouth, ignoring all thoughts of condoms because he wanted to feel Jock push between his lips. He traced the corona with his tongue, following it around until he found Jock's pulse and could taste the excitement throbbing through his veins, carried along with his blood.

"Fuck," Jock gasped, gripping Toby's hair in his fist. "That feels so good, but I wanna be in your ass."

Toby moaned and pulled off, glancing up when Jock tightened his hand. Their gazes locked.

"On your stomach?" Jock asked softly. In total contrast to the look in his eyes—he didn't do requests, he did commands. But he was trying to make this different. *They* were different, and even though

Toby'd tortured himself wondering who and how many guys Jock had fucked between the first time and now, he let go of it all right then.

None of those guys had been him.

He lay back on the mattress, holding Jock's stare until the last second before he rolled over, relinquishing any claims to control over what was about to happen. Jock's breath hitched in his lungs before he climbed on the bed, crawling on his hands and knees over Toby, caging him. He stayed like that for long seconds, energy building between their bodies, before skimming one palm down Toby's flank, tracing a line alongside Toby's spine with his thumb, then sitting back on his haunches and grasping Toby's ass in both his huge hands. Toby's hips lifted off the bed, and his toes curled with expectation. Jock was being so careful, still holding back. He could feel it in the fingertips digging into his muscles, and the slight tremble in Jock's thighs where they brushed his. He hadn't understood the "take me, I'm yours" message.

So Toby made it clearer. "Fuck me," he whispered. "I've been waiting for you for months."

Those were the magic words. Far more effective than a simple *please.* Jock grunted something, and then he was everywhere at once. Fingers shoving between Toby's cheeks, lips and tongue on Toby's neck, heavy dick rubbing between Toby's thighs. "Where're the—"

"On the windowsill. Right next to the bed." Inches away from Jock's free hand. It still took him too many seconds to scrabble around for the lube. Even more seconds before his hands were back on Toby's skin. Spreading his ass open, cool slick, fingers sliding down from his tailbone, making only the most cursory trip around his asshole before one shoved inside. Toby hissed.

Jock froze. "Hurts?"

"No. Don't stop."

"You feel so good," he mumbled. "Warm and squishy and slick. Like I'm actually *inside* you."

"Yeah." Toby understood exactly what Jock meant. As if he were exploring Toby internally. He gasped when Jock introduced a second finger, going deeper, knuckle pushing past Toby's resisting muscle like it wasn't there.

"Is this it?" Jock asked, sliding across Toby's prostate and making his whole body jerk. He hoped a moan was enough of an answer.

"Guess so." Jock massaged his gland while Toby tensed until he shook, pushing up from his toes and wrapping the sheet in his fists.

"Gonna fuck you now." Jock's voice thrummed, done with asking permission. He pulled out and moved to kneel between Toby's legs, extending long fingers across Toby's butt cheeks, holding him open and down on the bed at the same time, the heel of his hand against the small of Toby's back. All while Toby could hear the sound of a condom wrapper ripping open. Then Jock rested his weight on his arm, pressing Toby's body into the mattress hard as he brought his cock to Toby's asshole and began pushing inside.

Toby's body almost couldn't contain the force. Not the physical mechanics of Jock entering him, filling him too full, but the way sensation swept all over him, making him shiver and tremble and tighten with just the first inch or two.

Jock grabbed his hips and pulled him up onto his knees, adjusting them until his cock was working deeper, almost going too fast, but Toby encouraged him, pushing back and spreading his thighs wider.

Within minutes he was exactly where he'd wanted to be since that night in February. Completely surrounded, inside and outside, by Jock. He was so long. Standing up he was tall, but it was the length of his body while he was pressed up against Toby's back, chest to his spine, that Toby was aware of in a new way. Jock could bury his dick deep in Toby's ass while resting his arms on the bed alongside Toby's, jaw scraping Toby's cheek. When Toby took a breath, his lungs filled with the scent of Jock.

Jock rocked them both forward, moving Toby's body with the force of his own, and apprehension curled through Toby's stomach as lust shivered its way up from his tailbone. His brain had relinquished control, but his body still had to get with the program. Accept what Jock was doing with him.

"Tell me how it feels," Jock said in his ear.

He swallowed, arching his back as Jock slid out, then back into him. "Full."

Jock kissed his cheek, rubbing his lips along Toby's stubble, hips working still. "Good kind of full?" He pulled out slowly, spreading his thighs between Toby's legs, holding them open. His arms moved in tighter, bracing Toby's body in that same subtle way.

He captured Toby, held him in position, kept him from rocking too far forward when Jock shoved inside him, or pushing too far back when he slid out.

Not thinking, wrapped up in the frighteningly hot feeling of Jock holding him in place as he shoved into Toby's ass, Toby said, "It's scary."

"Can't believe I'm inside you like this," Jock whispered.

They'd done this before—Toby shouldn't be scared and Jock should believe it. But he knew exactly what Jock meant. It was about the moment, the intensity of this kind of closeness, and the way Jock had taken control of things.

And therein lay the root of Toby's fear. Jock engulfed him, bigger than him and able to move Toby like a doll. When Jock pulled out, Toby followed only as far as Jock let him, keeping him where Jock needed him, primed for his next thrust. Working him by force and muscle, keeping Toby open to him. It wasn't the physical reality of that which scared him, it was the emotional one. He was more than just receptive, he was submissive. Willingly. Letting Jock take him the way he wanted rather than the way Toby allowed him to.

"Oh God," he whispered, the apprehension curling through him mixing with lust and desire, creating the best kind of tension. The *out of control, driving down a dark highway at 100 mph* kind. He spread his legs a little wider and arched his back a little more. "Feels so good. Fuck me."

Jock grabbed his hands, lacing their fingers together, increasing his mastery of Toby's body, fucking him faster, grunting in Toby's ear each time he shoved inside his ass.

"I'm fucking you," Jock panted. His next thrust forced the breath out of Toby, in counterpart to Jock's soft "uh." "Gonna keep fucking you until I make you come all over the sheets. Stroke the cum out of you with my cock."

"Jesus." No one had ever talked to him like this during sex. It sounded lame in a porno, but Toby's skin prickled in response to Jock's words, and the intent behind them. His hips canted up on their own, answering Jock's thrusts. Jock's sweaty chest slid along Toby's back, making his skin burn where they touched and shivery where they didn't. When Jock shoved inside him the next time, he pushed a groan out of Toby's chest.

Jock was as good as his word, riding Toby harder and faster until Toby exploded, teeth sunk in his pillow and ass in the air. His orgasm filled every atom of his body, possibly even expanding his boundaries, blurring him on the edges. It lasted forever; each time Jock shoved into him he wrung out more, forcing cum out until Toby was pretty sure he'd emptied out a year's supply before Jock plunged in one more time, hard enough to bow Toby's spine, shaking and groaning curses and shooting inside him.

Just like the first time, Jock didn't pull out until he had to. He maintained control of Toby's body, adjusting them both until they were lying on the bed again with him on top, still inside Toby.

Jock kissed his neck, then finally rolled off. Toby zoned out, muscles throbbing everywhere, pulse surging through him, hugging his bed. Not even annoyed about the wet spot on the mattress under his belly. His skin hummed where Jock stroked his back, and he found Jock's jaw with his fingers, tracing the shape of it, eventually moving closer, until Jock had wrapped an arm and a leg across his body.

They fell asleep just like that.

Toby slept like the dead. It was a good thing, because Jock slept like it was a blood sport. When he and Tank were kids, if they had to share a bed on vacation or something, he'd regularly given his brother bruises.

At least, Toby slept like the dead except for when he woke up every couple of hours for more sex. Jock got a lot of what he'd been fantasizing about that night, and he was pretty sure Toby felt the same way. He got Toby on his knees, glasses on, blowing him while looking into his eyes. He got his first long, lazy fuck, Toby straddling his hips and riding him just before dawn. He got to taste Toby's dick, and for the first time ever he didn't suck cock with a condom.

Semen tasted gross, turned out. But he was pretty sure he hid his reaction.

Toby fell asleep again after that, but Jock lay awake, not really thinking. Drifting around in his head, sort of like the dust motes drifted in the sunlight starting to stream into the windows. Shining first on the upper wall and ceiling across the room from the bed, then slowly creeping down, over the blue wood door, slipping into the wall cubby next to it, lighting up some stacks of clothes. Shirts, maybe, just visible over the naked curve of Toby's shoulder rising up next to Jock's pillow.

Thank God he'd ignored the fears of getting together with him again. They were still balled under his breastbone, putting tension on his rib cage, but it was manageable. He scooted closer to Toby, spooning him—another thing he'd never done before—stroking his hip until Toby *mmm*ed and pushed back into Jock's groin, smiling. But then Jock let him rest more. He'd just needed to feel that for a second. Needed a little bit of a reaction, reaffirm that Toby responded to him in more than physical ways.

He'd totally made the right choice.

Chapter 16

At breakfast Sunday morning, the table overflowed with baked goods, and both Danny and Madame radiated weary satisfaction. Toby showed up a little after Jock, in a poorly concealed attempt to not look as if they'd been going at it all night. It wasn't as if Noah couldn't verify to anyone who asked that Jock hadn't slept in his bed.

Except Noah wasn't at breakfast. He *never* missed breakfast. None of the boys did. "Is Noah feeling all right?" Toby asked, sitting down next to Jock. Had he taken the thing with Turbo that hard?

Of course he had.

Danny grinned at him, though, nodding slyly. "Noah met a chick at the bar last night and no one's seen him since."

"A *girl*?" Turbo half yelled through his bite of croissant.

"There are just *so many pastries*, dudes," Gomer said, staring at the table with all the wide-eyed glee of a kid on Christmas morning who woke up and found out he'd gotten all the presents and his sister had gotten coal.

"Yeah." Danny's grin widened until it nearly split his face. "Madame baked *aaall* night long." He turned to her, hovering just behind him, to take her hand and kiss it.

Well, everyone got some last night, didn't they? Toby glanced at Jules, Turbo, and Ricky, all of whom seemed a little put out, if well rested. *Well, half of us.* Gomer didn't count, because he either hadn't figured it out, or he saw Madame's baked goods as a very adequate substitute. Under the table, Jock bumped their knees together, and when Toby looked over, he was smirking, sharing his amusement through his blue eyes.

It filled Toby with a warm fuzzy. One of those things from that book his mother had read to him and Nathan when they were kids, about small balls of fluff that would dissolve into one's chest and fill it with a sense of cozy contentment. *Oh no.* He'd become utterly sentimental, hadn't he? Next thing he knew, he'd be writing odes to Jock's penis, or possibly his testicles.

Warm fuzzies; twin circuitous snarls of seminal conduit,
hanging side by side in your fortress of shirred flesh,
joined by single purpose,
I salute your silent, undemanding vigilance.
Oft forgotten, yet never forgetting, ever standing ready
spewing forth the milk of your labors when called upon,
urgently summoned by the pulsing shaft that leads your charge.
Stalwart in thy ringleted hirsutitude . . .

Oh Jesus, that was horrible. Never mind, he wasn't a poet. Although with some tweaking, it might make a good riddle.

He shook himself out of his little moment and tried to concentrate on breakfast. Next to him, Jock wasn't having any problem with that—he was working his way through most of the pastries without a breather. Toby hadn't had the heart to tell him about the nocturnal baking fetish he suspected Danny and Madame B had developed. Why ruin it by warning him to inspect each croissant for a filling of little black curly hairs?

All morning he kept waiting for the guys to say something about him and Jock, and they never did. Other than some puzzled looks from Gomer, they were almost alarmingly circumspect at breakfast. Afterward, when he and Jock stood outside Madame's house and had a murmured conversation about their mutual need to do homework, no one butted in once. It was abnormal.

"I'll see you later?" Jock asked before they parted, giving Toby the eye-lock he'd started to expect as a substitute for a good-bye kiss when they were around other people. The kind one might give a guy he was seeing.

Noah showed up at lunchtime, and with him the guys weren't circumspect at all.

"So, a chick? Seriously?" Turbo asked in lieu of a greeting, scowling across the table at Noah.

Noah unfolded his napkin and put it on his lap, giving it more attention than it needed. "I'm bi, not gay," he finally answered.

Gomer needed help with the concept. "By what?"

Other than flaring his nostrils for a split second, Noah explained it calmly. "I'm attracted to men *and* women. Any gender."

"I never get that bi thing," Jock said. "How do you decide whether you're going to be with a guy or a girl?"

Toby tried not to wince. The boy's need to categorize the world neatly into boxes wasn't his most endearing flaw.

Noah rolled his eyes and sighed. "Do you want to get with every guy you ever met?"

All eyes at the table turned back to Jock, waiting for his answer. "Noooo."

"Yeah." Noah nodded. "So how do you decide who you *do* wanna be with?"

"I'm attracted to him." Under the table, he bumped Toby's leg with his knee, rubbing a second. More warm fuzzies.

"Same same, dude," Noah said shortly. "Can someone pass me the butter?"

"Oh. Sorry, that was kind of a dick question, huh?"

"S'okay."

It was a beautiful day again, even warmer than the day before, and soon the guys were talking about trying out the pool that afternoon. "I got different swim trunks," Turbo announced many times.

"Yeah? I got a Speedo." Jock smirked. On the other side of him, Noah made a choking noise. Or possibly that was Toby himself.

After lunch, Jock walked slowly back toward the EuroTAG with him, talking, and still no one butted in. It was getting eerie.

"Did you really get a Speedo?" he asked.

Jock snorted. "Nah, I was just giving Noah a hard time."

"I bet you're giving him a hard time right this second." Toby couldn't not go for the joke, even an easy one. It was like a compulsion with him.

Jock chuckled and changed the subject. "So . . . like, when you said a while back that you'd like it if I wanted to come and stay with you again—"

"Yes." Toby's heart *ker-thump*ed. *Please come back.* "Tonight?" Shit, was that too eager?

Jock stopped walking, turning to face him, giving him the eye-lock again. "Yeah. Tonight."

Jock's other fear reared up and grabbed him by the nuts that night in Toby's bed, when Toby told him they couldn't fuck every night. Brad had neglected to mention that little detail, but maybe he'd figured Jock was smart enough to think of that on his own. Not so much when all the blood had fled his brain for regions south. Not to mention he'd been so focused on the issue of Toby not asking to fuck *him* that he'd pretty much used up all his brain cells on that.

Because there was something Brad *had* told him, but Jock had been trying not to think about. Toby was versatile, and would want to fuck him eventually.

He blinked down at the guy, heart pounding, trying to think of what to say. How to start this conversation, because he knew he had to buy himself some time to figure out what his problem was with bottoming and get over it. Since this was looking more and more like a real relationship, he probably actually needed to, huh?

Toby shoved his torso up off the bed, propping himself on one elbow to kiss Jock, then work his lips and tongue down the line of his throat. "I have another suggestion."

Shit. This was it, wasn't it? Toby'd ask and they'd have to have that convo and the—

"Because I get the feeling you aren't ready to bottom."

"Oh thank fuck no," Jock breathed, falling back onto the mattress.

Toby laughed again, then placed a sucking kiss on Jock's breastbone before moving down under the curve of his pectoral. "It's cool." His voice thrummed in Jock's chest, then he started swirling his tongue around Jock's nipple. No one had ever played with his nipples before, and he'd totally been missing out. "I can wait."

No one had ever pulled him over them and let Jock drive his dick against their groin before, either. Another thing he'd been missing out on, but the only person he'd been with before who he might've done this with was Max. And thinking about Max while he slid himself against Toby's skin, working up sweat and friction between them, was impossible. The distant memory of that guy had no staying power while he was in the physical presence of this one. He only wanted to do it with Toby. Just Toby's tongue working in and out of his mouth in the same rhythm Jock was using to thrust against him.

That was his introduction to exactly what "rubbing off" on someone really was. Before, he'd figured it was a poor substitute for fucking, but he understood after that why he'd want to do it again, although not with just anyone. Because it was almost more intimate than fucking, and he couldn't imagine letting anyone but Toby grip the back of his skull and control the movement of his head so he'd be in just the right position, unable to end the kiss until Toby allowed it.

Maybe that kind of closeness was enough for Toby, and Jock would never have to sacrifice his virgin ass.

ΘAΓ

Jock pretty much moved into the *cabanon* with Toby. By the end of his first week or so of spending every night there, he'd brought over everything but his clothes—there just wasn't enough room to keep them there, at least not more than a few things. Whatever he planned to wear the next morning.

It wasn't until the day Noah asked him, "Don't you want some of your own space, dude?" that it hit Jock that maybe he should have asked Toby how he felt about it before unpacking his toothbrush, package of razors, laptop, and textbooks on that counter built into the wall. But by the third day of hanging out with Toby while they both did schoolwork in the evening, or hanging out by the pool with the guys (which was closer to Toby's place than Jock's room) and leaving EuroTAG after dinner with Toby for bed, it had seemed stupid to not just keep his stuff there. It had seemed like a practicality, not moving in.

But he didn't *want* to pack his stuff back.

"Um, I think I'll do my homework up at the house," he told Toby Thursday when they returned from campus. The dude was sitting on one of those iron chairs in front of the cabin, alternately typing like crazy on his laptop, or chewing on the pen he'd stuck in his mouth while staring at the screen. Every once in a while he'd run his fingers through his hair, yanking on it, stretching his skin, until it looked like he was trying to give himself a facelift. Then he'd drop his hands and sigh, or even motorboat his lips.

"Toby?" Jock asked when he didn't respond.

"Wha'?" Toby jerked his head up, blinking. If he were a cartoon, his irises would be swirling spirals of "I'm not really paying attention."

He'd probably be happier if Jock wasn't around distracting him from working on his paper. Toby'd told him last night he was going to start editing it today. Which was apparently more than the spell-check thing *he* did when he edited. "I said I'm going up to the house."

"Oh." Toby nodded vacantly. "'Kay." He turned back to his computer. "I'll see you later."

Jock had expected a little more of a farewell. Maybe a kiss, or one of those looks Toby gave him sometimes when they were around a bunch of people and they couldn't touch. Asking when he'd be back would have been cool. Jock nearly said something, but that'd be pathetic, so he turned and walked toward the house.

"You're in a fucking foul mood," Noah told him an hour later, when he came into their room to put on swim trunks. Jock had pretty much done nothing but glare at him whenever Noah spoke. His excuse was that he was reading their assigned section of the history text and he needed to concentrate. He might've believed that himself if he could remember any of the last four pages that it had taken him forty-five minutes to get through.

Noah was either stupid or had a death wish, because he didn't shut up after Jock growled at him.

"What's'a matter, Toby didn't put out today?"

Jock was off the bed and halfway to Noah before he realized he was about to punch the dude. He halted so fast he swayed, staring at his roommate, trying to figure out how something that minor could make him this mad. When he was in the rink, he'd been famous for keeping a cool head. He hardly ever overreacted to trash talk, and those guys could sling some serious shit. What Noah had said was nothing, but Jock was ready to break his nose for it.

"Um, dude?" Noah interrupted his thoughts. He had his trunks on and a towel over his shoulder, watching Jock carefully, his weight balanced like he was prepared to defend himself. "What're you doing?"

What *was* he doing? "Sorry," Jock rasped. Then he cleared his throat. "Just, you know . . ." He shook his head and then shrugged, because he didn't know, but hopefully Noah wouldn't figure that out.

Noah huffed through his nose, but turned to go. "Come out and swim if you think you'll be able to play well with others." He slammed the door behind him.

Instead, Jock did what he always did when he was confused: he went for a run. It was dusty and still too hot, but he didn't go far, just did a lazy circuit of Madame B's son's vineyards. The fields stretched down to the village with the steepest sections at the top. Running hills was always a bitch. He ended up running down and walking back up to the halfway point before his preoccupied mind got control and he halted, staring down at the designs his shoe was tracing in the dirt, like he might find answers in the patterns.

A chance to see how deep their connection could go, that's what Toby had said he wanted. But what did *Jock* want? The same thing, right? It wasn't just about getting laid regularly, even he knew that at this point; but other than thinking he'd be giving Toby what the dude had asked for, Jock hadn't decided anything. Hadn't set any goals for himself or them. Hadn't identified a single thing he wanted out of this relationship.

I'm in a relationship. Wasn't he? Weren't they?

Was that how Toby saw it?

"Fuck me," he muttered to himself, sinking down onto a handy boulder, hanging his head and letting his hands dangle between his knees. He had a goal, at least: find out if this was a real relationship. He could only think of one way to discover what Toby thought was going on between them.

They'd have to talk about it. He could do that. The other talks had been successful, right?

On his walk back up to the cabin, he tried to figure out what to say. Should he just ask outright where Toby thought their "connection" would go? Had gone? It would have been fucking nice if Brad had decided to share some of these details with him. He and Sebastian had figured it out; maybe the dude could have, like, shared some intelligence with him about how to successfully negotiate a relationship.

They were gonna have words about this when Jock got back to the US.

Meanwhile, he had some words he needed to have with his man. In the next few minutes, because he was on the trail that led to Toby's place—cut into the apex of the hillside a few feet below EuroTAG and the pool, overlooking the farm and the village. It was getting to sunset, and the guys were probably done swimming now. Anytime now they'd start looking for Toby, wondering where he was. Worrying like senior citizens about whether he'd come to dinner—something they did every night. Jock had lain on the floor in front of the television and listened in on many discussions about who needed to go check on Toby and when.

"Where did you go, babe?" Toby's voice floated out of the dusk, right in front of Jock when he came around the last row of grapevines. He ignored the endearment, or rather the little jolt it gave him, because Toby did that with his friends—called them "babe" or "hon."

"For a run." Jock kept walking, until he had to stop or trample over the guy, standing in the middle of the trail. Toby had his hands shoved in his pockets, as if trying to fake indifference, but the glimmer of worry in his eye eased Jock's nerves. Soothed his anxiety over the whole thing. He couldn't say now why he'd thought Toby was dissing him earlier by not asking him when he was coming back. The dude had been concentrating on his paper. Jock had just . . . overreacted.

Toby glanced away, to the spot on the horizon the sun was angling toward, then back to him. "Needed a little time for yourself?" he asked.

Jock found himself answering truthfully. "Not really."

Toby licked his lower lip, then sucked it into his mouth before releasing it. "Okay." He squared his shoulders.

"I thought *you* wanted some time to yourself," Jock said before he could go on. Positive that wasn't the truth, now.

Toby's jaw moved, chewing on words, then he dipped his head and said very quietly, "I prefer it when you're around."

"Me too." He reached for Toby's wrist, pulling him forward until Toby's arms came around his waist and his chin tilted up toward Jock's mouth, their gazes locking for a second. "I wanna stay with you."

Toby didn't say anything, just slid his hand up Jock's body, cupping the back of his head and kissing him. Which was everything Jock needed to know. Toby wanted him, he could feel the assurance of it soaking into him from Toby's skin and lips, making him ache inside—not that pre-sex ache he got, or not only that, but something working its way through him like a musical note. Like Toby had discovered Jock's resonance frequency and was sounding it.

Toby broke away for a second, breathing heavily. "Come back with me. Stay as long as you want."

Jock fisted Toby's hair, meeting Toby's eyes before drawing in a deep breath to ask, "This connection or whatever between us, it's a relationship, right?"

A little bit of uncertainty flicked across Toby's face, the counterpart to Jock's over what was happening between them. "Well, that's how I think of it," he said.

"Me too." He pulled Toby into another kiss. And thank fuck, because he knew with certainty in that minute that this was what he wanted. Even if it meant having a relationship with an audience of frat boys, and him having to work out being the girl. He could man up for that if it was what Toby wanted.

Seriously, this talking about the relationship shit was easier than he'd expected. No wonder Brad hadn't thought he needed guidance.

ΘΑΓ

Within minutes after Toby figured out Jock didn't want some distance any more than he did, they were back in Toby's cabin, half-naked and working up a sweat, grinding, trying to make each other come as fast as possible. Or at least that's what Toby was trying to do, using his arms and legs to wrap and press Jock's weight into him on the bed, as if gravity alone wouldn't work. It wouldn't, of course, because gravity was all about the natural attraction of one body to another, and Toby had a supernatural attraction to the body he was holding, and more importantly to what was inside it. Hiding that was pointless, and he couldn't have if he'd wanted to. But he *wanted* Jock to know how he felt. He wanted Jock to pin him to the bed and take whatever he needed in order to understand that yes, Toby craved being with him all the time.

"Give it to me," he said when Jock freed his mouth for a second, using his palm to press Jock's prick against his abdomen. Again with the porn talk, but it worked for them. Jock groaned, curling long fingers over Toby's neck and gripping his jaw, holding on as he shot all over Toby's stomach. Coming first for once, and just in time because Toby thought he'd lose it again. Let the sex pull him under to that place where he'd dissolved into sensation, unable to gauge his partner's needs and only able to respond.

Jock lay next to him, working his arm under Toby's neck and pulling him closer. They stayed that way, half-dressed and half-entwined, while the room got steadily darker and their breathing slowed. Toby pulled his shirt off the rest of the way and wiped up the cum with it, but otherwise they were still until the sky outside the window only showed the faintest glow above the peaks of the Alpilles.

"Maybe I should take a shower," he murmured into the space between his pillow and Jock's ear, not entirely sure Jock was awake.

"Huh?" Jock yawned and rolled onto his side, scooting down the bed until his feet hung off and his chin rested on Toby's shoulder, nose against his neck. "Why? I like the way you smell now."

Toby finger-combed Jock's hair. "Because you just hosed me down with your scent."

"Oh yeah," he mumbled. Toby could feel Jock's lips stretching into a smile.

"So . . . do you understand what I'm saying? About the shower."

Jock's sudden alert stillness told Toby he got it. He moved after a second, wrapping his arm around Toby's side, stroking the small of his back. "Yeah, I get the shower thing." Then he rolled on top of Toby again until his shadowed face nearly touched Toby's. "If you're asking me if I want to fuck you, the answer is yes."

"Good." Toby hooked his legs around the backs of Jock's, cradling Jock's pelvis between his thighs and stretching up for a kiss. He probably hadn't needed to say it, but they hadn't fucked since that time last weekend, and he'd missed it. Was hungry for it, actually, and surprised himself with a need for reassurance that Jock wanted it, too.

In spite of not usually being the passive one in the past, Toby didn't find himself wondering when Jock would be ready to bottom or with a major desire to fuck him.

He did find himself with a major desire for Jock to take what he wanted. Wanted to know what Jock's body thought of his when he took his own instructions out of the equation. Find out what Jock would do to it if Toby let him have at it. Let him own Toby's ass.

ΘAΓ

Jock refused to share Toby with the bros that night. As soon as he was out of the shower, Jock pulled him toward the bed, caressing all his naked skin, loosely stroking his cock and kneading his ass. Shoving him down on the mattress, Jock stripped his briefs off before climbing on also. Toby reached for Jock's dick, but Jock grabbed his hand and pushed it away. "I get to run this show," he said, pressing Toby flat into the sheets, resting most of his body weight on him from his calves to his chest.

Toby's pupils dilated, and his lips parted on a shaky exhaled breath. Jock couldn't have asked for a clearer reaction—Toby wanted him to take control. He started with Toby's mouth, because he loved that part of Toby. The way Toby's scruff rasped his chin, and how Toby's breathing changed, matching his, sometimes even breathing through him. The way Toby liked to suck Jock's tongue into his mouth, opening wider as Jock worked in farther. Toby tasted like sex, especially at that spot far back, when Jock was nearly to his throat.

Someone knocked just then, when Jock was so deep in Toby's mouth it felt like fucking, and he was wondering how far he could go. Toby didn't even notice the first knock. By the third he was trying to pull away from Jock, but Jock wasn't going to let Toby's overactive sense of responsibility end anything.

He let Toby's mouth go, tonguing that spot just below Toby's ear, around the back curve of his jaw. Toby was incredibly sensitive there. He moaned every time Jock even touched it with his breath. "Ignore them, they'll think we're gone."

Toby's Adam's apple bobbed next to Jock's chin as he swallowed, and he stretched his head to the side, giving Jock more access.

The doorknob rattled, and Toby's shoulder muscles tensed up.

"I locked the door," Jock whispered, then ran his teeth down the side of Toby's neck, making him hiss.

But Toby hadn't totally forgotten about the guys. "The lights're still on, they'll know we're—"

Jock smothered the rest of his words with a kiss, pressing hard against Toby's lips and gripping his hair tightly, until he could feel Toby give in. He broke away long enough to say, "They'll think we did it accidentally."

He didn't think either one of them believed that. The guys knew they were here and knew what they were doing, and if they didn't have a death wish, they'd leave now.

"It's time for dinner, don't you want to eat with us?" Jules called through the door.

Toby dropped his hands from Jock's back, like he was giving in. Jock pulled away, waiting for him to decide who he was really giving in to.

"Go away," Toby called, looking up at him. He ran his thumb across Jock's mouth, lifting himself up toward it. "We're busy."

After that, Jock didn't mean to get so rough, but Toby choosing him over the guys made his normally bad possessive streak worse, and he let it have its way. He rode Toby into the upper atmosphere. Like a fucking rocket booster launching him into orbit, until they both dropped their payloads. Coming down, thrusting lazily inside Toby and eating at his mouth as Toby stroked his back, pausing to knead his muscles, something in the way he touched Jock communicating satisfaction. Happiness even.

Jock didn't know whether to trust his instincts about that. He kissed Toby with all the gentleness he hadn't shown earlier before rolling off. "Good?"

Toby shook his head, legs flopping onto the bed while he gasped, staring up at the ceiling. "It was fucking incredible."

Jock rested his head on Toby's shoulder, combing fingers through his stomach hair. It was incredible, but uncertainty crept back into him in spite of what Toby'd said. "Not too rough?"

"No." Toby turned toward Jock, but Jock wouldn't tilt his head up to look at Toby. "I mean, it was rough, but it felt . . . honest, I guess. As if you . . ." Toby paused for a breath. "Needed me like that."

"Good."

Toby wrapped his arms around Jock and squeezed him, holding him until he fell asleep and rolled away. Jock pulled him back, fitting Toby's body against his, Toby's back to his front, and drifted off himself.

Chapter 17

Jock's hand smoothing down his hip woke Toby up at dawn. That and the tingle of Jock's jaw stubble on the back of his neck. "Mmmm, what're you doing?"

Jock didn't answer verbally, he demonstrated. Sliding his hand around to trail fingers down Toby's stomach, he gripped his cock, using teasing strokes to make Toby squirm while kissing along his jawline. Then he let go, feeling Toby up in other places. His chest and then his shoulders, gliding around to his back, then lower.

"Morning breath," Toby mumbled.

"Ignore it," Jock whispered, working his leg between Toby's, then using his knee to push Toby's thighs apart. Toby rolled onto his stomach and hugged the sheets, letting Jock touch him wherever he wanted. Kisses down his spine, palms tracing his flanks to his ass cheeks. There Jock kneaded him a few seconds before placing his fingers on Toby's tailbone, then working them into his crack slowly, searching.

"Do you want to fuck me again?"

"Yeah," Jock said into the skin of his back. "I'll go easier on you this time." He followed the line of Toby's shoulder blade with rough lips.

Toby shivered. Did he want easier?

Jock wasn't practiced or suave or smooth; he was exploratory and fascinated. Just like last night, but devoting more time to it this morning. Spreading Toby's ass open to touch everything carefully from his balls up, feeling it all out as if he were blind. By the time he'd fetched the lube from the floor and slicked up his fingers, Toby was going insane. His whole body tensed up, hips hovering inches over the bed, waiting for Jock to push inside him. "You don't need to work up to it," he said. "Just fuck me."

Jock groaned, so softly Toby didn't think he knew he'd done it, and then he forgot about it when the condom wrapper crinkled.

He could feel Jock's restraint—his attempt to "go easy"—when Jock kissed his lower back, drawing a design with his tongue right at the top curve of one of his cheeks before pressing the head of his dick against Toby's hole, pushing in carefully, by centimeters, taking forever to enter him fully, then rocking against him, gradually building a rhythm.

This might be the end of him, death by orgasm. And it was nearly too much, having Jock fuck him slowly, taking his time and being careful. "Let me know if it hurts," he murmured in Toby's ear at one point. "I did you so rough last night."

Toby gurgled, angling his hips up more. *Oh I know, believe me.*

But gentle wasn't an easily accessible part of Jock's nature, and it wasn't long before he was thrusting harder, straddling Toby's pelvis and drilling into him, knuckles white where he gripped the bed next to Toby's face. "Are you gonna come?" he gasped.

Toby groaned and shoved his hand under his body, gripping his dick even though he barely needed it. "Do it, baby."

They came together, Toby as tuned in to Jock's orgasm as his own. Jock came in waves inside him, each one heating Toby's insides up even more. As if the friction from Jock riding his ass hadn't been hot enough. Making his moan build to a wail by the time Jock shoved home one last time, grinding against him.

Gentleness came easier to Jock afterward. He kissed Toby's back and caressed Toby's ass muscles, then pulled out, rolling onto his side, leaving Toby unprotected in the breeze as sweat dried on his skin and he shivered.

"Okay?" Jock asked in his ear, arm resting on his back.

"Very much okay."

"You called me baby."

"I did?" *Was that a bad thing?*

"Yeah," Jock murmured, rolling closer to rub his leg against the backs of Toby's.

He didn't sound horribly upset about it.

Toby turned his head just in time to see Jock's eyes flutter closed, and watched him drift into sleep, lips parted, breathing softly.

Wondering if Jock defined "relationship" the same way Toby did. He should ask, but looking at Jock right now, no worry or anger on his face, he didn't care. Just having this was worth it. He'd go with the original plan: let things happen and see where they led.

Jock had to share Toby with the guys again on Saturday. He resolved not to be too growly about it, but in the end it wasn't that hard. He knew a part of Toby none of them ever would.

On Friday afternoon, riding back to the *gîte*, Jock had told Toby about their history homework for the weekend, all while having a pretty good idea of what Toby's reaction would be. As a matter of fact, the guys had asked him to broach the subject, and they were now all conspicuously silent, waiting for Toby's reaction. At least, it seemed conspicuous to Jock, but Toby was too annoyed by the news to notice.

"*What*?" He jerked the wheel when he turned to stare at Jock, and had to refocus on the road to get back in their lane. It didn't stop him from having a mini-rant, though. "That hack of a professor is sending you guys on a *self-guided* tour of Glanum? You can walk to it in five minutes from campus, and he can't take you himself? Those self-guided tours are for *tourists*, not history students."

Jock didn't point out that the average tourist was probably better-versed in history than two-thirds of the guys in the van.

Besides, Toby wasn't done with his rant. "I can't *believe* that prick." He threw one hand up in the air. "Well if he's not going to do his job, I guess I'll have to do it for him. You're all going to tour one of the finest examples of a provincial Roman city in the region, and you're going to have a real fucking guide."

"Yay!" Gomer yelled from the back. "We're going on a family outing."

Toby glanced at Jock again, eyebrows raised and chin tilted. In response to Jock's smirk he rolled his eyes, but he couldn't hide his smile.

For dinner they all ended up going down to the village bar. Everyone except Danny, that was, who'd claimed to have a date. Most of the guys didn't make any comment about that, except Noah. "I wonder who he has a date with?" he mused after Danny walked out.

The silence that answered him seemed as conspicuous as the earlier silence in the van, but Noah picked up on it about as well as Toby had. Jock and Toby laughed about it later, in Toby's cabin, lying naked on the bed with the blankets tangled around their legs. "I can't believe the second smartest frat boy is the only one who hasn't figured out about Danny and Madame B."

"Second smartest?" Jock teased. "Who's the first?"

Toby kissed him. "You are, smexy."

Jock would be lying if he said it didn't make him feel good to hear someone like Toby say he was smart.

Glanum turned out to be as cool as Jock remembered from when he'd visited as a kid. He'd fought off at least twice as many invaders there as at Les Baux, and he'd done it all on his own, mostly from a small hill overlooking the former town.

The guys seemed impressed as Toby took them up the town's main street, pointing out details left in the ruins that showed how the houses became more opulent the closer they got to the center. "All the major civic spaces are in this compact area, and they've all been excavated. It's not that Glanum was a particularly impressive city, although it was very important—"

"Oh! Oh!" Gomer jumped up and down, hand raised high in the air. When Toby looked at him, he said, "Because it was along a major trade route, right below an easily defendable pass over the mountains, right? Right?"

Toby smiled. "Excellent, Gomer. You get a gold star."

Gomer beamed like Toby'd just given him his own basket of Madame's croissants he didn't have to share with anyone.

The morning went on like that, with Gomer and Ricky at the forefront of their group, and every time one of them would excitedly announce some detail, like which temple they were standing in front of, and whether those walls were Roman or dated from earlier, Toby'd praise them like third graders and then catch Jock's eye, smiling with him.

It was fun, as much as Jock had expected to just suffer through it. Madame showed up in her car with a picnic lunch and they ate on the hill overlooking the ruins where Jock had fought off barbarians ten years before.

In the present day, the other guys spent most of an hour after lunch playing anti–beer terrorist agent. “They are such freaks,” he said to Toby as they watched the bros work their way down the hill, running crouched over from shrub to boulder to shrub, pausing behind them to send each other hand signals.

“They’re obsessed with this thing.” Toby shook his head wonderingly. “I almost hope beermageddon’s a real thing.”

“I’m kinda hoping that too, for their sakes. I mean, think of the crushing disappointment if they ever figure out they aren’t really some kind of antiterrorism task force.” Jock waited for Toby’s laugh. When it didn’t come, he turned to see Toby’s brow wrinkling up.

“Do you think I should put a stop to it?”

“You really think you could?”

He snorted, then winced as Julian tripped, somersaulting his way down the hill. Fortunately, a small tree trunk stopped him. “God I hope we don’t have to go back to the clinic,” he muttered.

Julian hopped up from the ground, arms in the air, shouting, “I’m fine guys. Don’t worry, I’m fine. I planned that.”

Jock laughed. “Yeah, that’s what a real spy would do, because it’s *stealthy*.”

This time Toby laughed with him. “Did you notice who’s *not* playing commando?”

“Danny.”

Toby smirked. “I saw them go over the other side of the hill together. Supposedly he was helping her put the stuff back in her car, but they seem to have misjudged which direction the parking lot was in.”

Jock lay back on his elbows and lifted his chin, closing his eyes and soaking in the sun—one of the best things about this trip, in his opinion. They sky here really was different. “He’s really into her.”

“It’s like you said—he’s gotta be, or it wouldn’t have happened at all. Unless he has a fetish or something.”

Jock grimaced. “What, like a sagging skin fetish?”

“Stop.” Toby threw his palm up, inches from Jock’s face. “Seriously, I can’t hear any more.”

Laughing again, Jock reached for him, just about ready to pull Toby down onto the grass next to him, when he remembered where they were and froze. Toby never said anything, but Jock knew it got to him that Jock had some weird phobia about touching him in front of others. He'd sorta gotten over the guys seeing him touch Toby, but this was public. With, like, people.

Toby's gaze was locked on Jock's hand, hanging there in midair, inches from Toby's arm. Then he met Jock's eyes. "It's okay," he said.

Jock dropped back onto his elbows, feeling anything but okay. "Sorry."

Toby stretched out next to him. Not too close, but close enough to speak softly. "You can only do what you're comfortable with, baby."

Fuck it. Jock did it before he could think it through, leaning forward and kissing Toby quickly, his heart exploding in his ears, drumming away. He couldn't stop himself from glancing around, but they were basically alone on this hill, everyone around them focused on the ruins or the freaks skulking in the bushes.

"Hey," Toby said, drawing Jock's attention back to him. He didn't say anything else, but his smile told Jock everything.

Now Jock felt far more than okay. And he felt as if he'd done something substantial. Just as sharing wasn't in his nature, neither was hiding, and he'd finally broken through whatever had stopped him from doing it.

This time he pulled Toby closer to him with less hesitation. Not doing anything other than giving him another small kiss, because making out here would be a little beyond his comfort zone. But still, anyone looking at them had to know they were more than friends.

Jock would own up to a little anxiety about that, but mostly he just felt freer.

"Uh-oh," Toby muttered, then shot up onto his feet, skidding down the gravel path. Seconds later, Jock heard screeching.

The fratbros strike again. He got up and followed, just in case Toby needed some muscle or something.

It wasn't as bad as it could have been. Just a simple case of Gomer jumping out from behind a bush at the wrong moment and scaring a group of nuns touring the site. It said something about their situation with these guys that a bunch of sisters in black habits screeching and clinging to each other didn't seem like much of a problem.

Things got a little weirder when Danny showed up, panting and towing Madame B by the hand, then tried to "help Tobes" by explaining about the beer terrorist thing. "See, it's like this: the frat boy's relationship to beer is as the nun's relationship to God—"

"Okay, that's it, everyone in the van!" Toby started yelling, clapping his hands. He dragged Danny away with the help of Madame B, shouting "*Désolé*" at the pack of nuns, squawking and running around like penguins.

Just another outing with the fratbros.

Toby never thought he'd describe his life—or any period of it—as idyllic. It simply wasn't a word he thought would apply to the modern way of living, for anyone. But the next week was best described as exactly that. He hung on to the moment, living in it, because they were in one of the most beautiful, evocative places in the world (that he'd been, although scores of artists agreed with him) and he had the most perfect bed partner he'd ever imagined.

Or not imagined, as the case happened to be.

They fell into a routine that worked for them. As the days got longer and hotter, it was as if they had more time to laze around in bed. He spent his days in Saint-Rémy, working on his almost-finished thesis and sometimes meeting Jock for lunch, and in the afternoons they'd all swim, and before long he and Jock would make their way to the *cabanon*. Sometimes they'd join the guys for dinner, but often not. Mostly they indulged in bed sports, and talking.

And many times in the morning, Jock would suck him off. He could give an amazing blowjob. Toby's favorite way to wake up, ever, bar none, was when he did so with his dick in Jock's mouth.

Even better, Jock made noises. Low grunts that vibrated the head of Toby's cock, and soft, higher pitched moans. Noises that were a constant affirmation that he wanted this. Wanted to get Toby off in his mouth.

Once Toby did, Jock would haul himself up the bed while the orgasm still echoed through Toby's nuts, grabbing Toby's hand and holding it to his dick. Toby obeyed the implied command, wrapping his fingers around Jock's shaft and holding it against his stomach. Often Jock came less than a minute after Toby did, shooting until he'd gummed up Toby's body hair, not ready to stop until he was limp in Toby's hand.

Then he'd roll off, breathing in gasps, working his arm under Toby's neck, using one huge palm spread across Toby's back to pull him close, until Toby took full advantage and wrapped himself around his frat boy.

"You like that," he murmured into the skin of Jock's shoulder after their blow- and handjob session the Friday morning after their trip to Glanum.

Jock squeezed him. "Like what?"

"Giving head."

"Yeah." Jock ran a hand down his back and up again. "No guy is more under my control than when I have my mouth on his dick."

He couldn't argue with that. He didn't like thinking about it that way, but he couldn't argue with it.

"You're the first guy I've ever done that for without a condom," Jock went on, chin grazing Toby's forehead.

Toby did his best to hide his surprise, because he didn't know if Jock understood how significant that was for him. At least that explained the look on Jock's face the first couple times after he'd sucked Toby off.

He closed his eyes and asked in his most casual voice, "I am? What do you think of the taste?"

Jock shifted, rolling to face him, although still with his chin at Toby's forehead. "If it wasn't you, I probably wouldn't have done it again after the first time."

He could understand—he'd sort of hated it at first, too. "It's not like anyone's clamoring for them to make ice cream that flavor." But he did love the taste of Jock, for the same reason Jock kept letting Toby come in his mouth. Because it was him. *Warm fuzzy.*

"There are people who'd love it, though," Jock said. "They'd buy that ice cream by the gallon."

Toby nodded, hair catching in Jock's chin stubble. "Smearing it on themselves and begging people to lick it off. I think we just started a whole new kink."

Jock laughed with him, then kissed Toby's forehead.

Such a boyfriend thing to do.

"It's not my kink. The way some guys go on, I was expecting something more like cotton candy and less like slimy baking soda."

Toby lifted his head. "Really?" He *hated* disappointing Jock.

Jock smiled and used his finger to shift hair off Toby's brow. "Not really, no. I mean, that's what it tastes like to me, but I didn't expect a night at the carnival."

"You don't have to swallow, baby. I can warn you next time." It was only polite, and who cared if it left him a little bit emotionally raw? More of that insecurity from the other day rearing its head. The whole conversation was a little too menacing to his carefully constructed shell of "now."

Jock cupped his face, oblivious to what was going on inside him, and stretched up to kiss his mouth. Using his perfect, poster boy lips to shape Toby's, and his very assertive tongue to soothe Toby's blip of emotional vulnerability. "But . . . doesn't it seem like I should be able to suck off my boyfriend?" he asked when he was done. "I don't have to like the taste, but I can like doing it for you, right?"

Okay, fuck being casual and cool about this. Jock *had* to know that word was significant, right? He tangled his hands in Jock's hair, holding him loosely while Jock continued to caress him. "Do you mean that?"

Jock swallowed, eyes suddenly uncertain. "That you're my boyfriend? Only if it's all right with you."

Toby tightened his grip in Jock's hair and pulled his head up. "It's all right with me," he said, just before kissing him.

Chapter 18

That weekend, Toby took the guys to Barbegal. He'd originally wanted to go with Jock only, but the guys whined if he and Jock went off alone too often, and they tended to get in trouble if left to themselves too long. Noah would sneak off with that girl from the village, which wouldn't have been a big deal if it didn't result in Turbo having some kind of competitive reaction and dragging whomever would go with him down to the village bar to try to "pick up chicks." Toby had to impose a strict "buddy-system" rule for trips to the village, just from the fear of Turbo going too far someday. According to Danny's reports and the occasional time he went down to the bar, Turbo was mostly the butt of a lot of local jokes. Fortunately, he couldn't speak enough French to figure that out.

Speaking of jokes, it was finding out their joke of a history professor hadn't even discussed Barbegal with them that pushed Toby into taking the guys. It may not be a major tourist destination, but it was the sight of one of the greatest hydraulic mills ever built. Plus it was a great spot for a picnic.

Jock just shrugged when Toby suggested bringing them, too. "They'd probably like it. Besides, they'll just play commando, right?"

Unfortunately, Toby couldn't argue with that.

At breakfast, Danny said, in the manner of one inviting a guest lecturer to speak, "So, how about we let Tobes tell us about this place we're going."

Toby ignored Jock's soft snort. "Well, it's part of an old Roman aqueduct system."

"Cool," Danny said, nodding encouragingly.

Toby didn't roll his eyes. "This isn't a tour, guys, we're just going to hang out."

"Sweet!" Ricky gave the table a fist pump. "More field exercises."

They really were taking this beer terrorist thing too far, but Toby'd decided to pretend it was perfectly normal. Apparently that worked with similar behavior in children, like imaginary friends. Research showed that kids whose guardians didn't make a big deal of it were better adjusted in the long run.

At least, according to what he'd read online. Toby was hoping that was the case here.

He really should have worked harder in that psych class. Or at least paid attention. But how was he to know at the time that one day he'd be responsible for a pack of mutant fratbros and the information would come in handy?

The guys loved Barbegal. They weren't sure about it at first, when the parking area turned out to be a wide spot on the road, but even from there the brick arches of the former aqueduct were visible. Two of the old waterways had been put in side by side here, the original and the second, larger one built for Arles at the beginning of the fourth century. At the site of the grain mill, about a quarter mile from where they'd parked, the original aqueduct had driven the production of enough flour to feed the entire population of Arles, while the second one took a sharp turn west toward the city.

He and Jock hiked out to the mill site, losing guys along the way as they found cool things to look at, calling to each other. Only Noah made it to the channel cut into solid rock that had fed the mill. This was Toby's favorite thing about the site. Walking through this narrow, man-made gorge and reaching the other side, where the hill fell away steeply and the ruins of the mill overlooked a huge flood plain. It was dramatic. Not in the way Les Baux or Glanum was, and he could see that Noah and Jock thought it was kind of cool, but neither one of them got how amazing it was until Toby explained how the mill worked.

Noah wandered off about five minutes into Toby's explanation. Toby could understand that—he'd probably try to escape some shining-eyed zealot going on about some subject he had no interest in as well. Jock stayed though, asking questions and getting gradually more impressed. Toby could see it in the way his eyebrows drew together just slightly, and the set of his lips. His thinking frown. "It shouldn't be that hard to believe they engineered this, considering all the other stuff they did, but no one ever talks about it."

"It takes a lot of imagination to see it." Toby climbed up the slope a few feet so he could reach the top of one of the columns that used to support a waterwheel. It was covered with rubble and shrubbery grew out of it, but he found a clear spot to sit on a small ledge, letting his legs dangle over the edge a couple feet off the ground. From here he was mostly hidden from the aqueduct hikers. "I think that's part of what I like about this place. A few thousand people come here every year, but most of them only take pictures of the aqueduct, then they leave, and a minority of them make it through the rock-cut channel to see these ruins, but most people don't understand how it worked or how significant it was. Only a chosen few." He sighed. "Maybe it's the elitist in me."

Jock turned toward him, grinning. "It's the intellectual in you. You like knowing shit others don't even care about figuring out."

Toby sniffed and stuck his nose in the air. "*Someone* has to be the repository of historical knowledge."

Laughing, Jock came over to the wall Toby was sitting on, and placed his hands on Toby's knees, head just about level with his shoulders. "You're smexy." He ran his palms up Toby's thighs slowly, building tension in Toby's gut with every millimeter he traveled. Toby's dick had totally taken notice of Jock's proximity and touch. He was the perfect height to simply lean forward and rip Toby's jeans open with his teeth. Equally exciting was the pressure he exerted to spread Toby's legs open until he could stand between them, clasping Toby's hips and smiling up at him.

Jesus, he was going to suffocate in Jock's eyes someday. Atmospheric blue and capable of holding him captive until he didn't even notice his surroundings. Well, surroundings that weren't part of the Jock package. Toby very much noticed his boyfriend's heat and firm muscles where they pressed into him. Jock's fingers on Toby's pelvis were impossible to forget. Toby took a chance, even knowing they were in a public area, and any one of those people *ooh*ing and *aah*ing over the aqueduct might wander out here and see them. But there was no one below them, and anyone coming from above would make noise. Shoving the possibility away, he reached for Jock, tracing along his jaw and tilting his head up, bending forward for a kiss.

Maybe it was the position, with Toby above him, but Jock didn't muscle his way in and take over. He let Toby coax him into the kiss, responding to him even when Toby drew Jock's tongue into his mouth with his own. Toby realized then what he'd been doing. What he wanted. That he hadn't just fallen into this sexual dynamic with this boy because it made Jock happy and it worked for Toby—he *desired* it. Was possibly addicted to letting Jock have his way. Even like this, with Toby in the nominally superior position, he let himself sink into Jock, almost unconsciously encouraging him to take over.

And Jock was doing it, fingers working up Toby's spine under the hem of his shirt, pressing Toby closer to the edge. Using his other hand, he cupped Toby's jaw, adjusting the angle of their kiss. Pressing forward until Toby's cock was right against his abdomen.

Toby slid his hands down, following the contours of Jock's pectoral muscles through his shirt to just above where his dick rubbed against him. *Fuck.* It so perfectly matched the fantasy he'd been having, one that was too out there to share easily, but as he found Jock's nipples with his fingertips and Jock groaned softly, pressing hard enough to qualify as grinding, Toby began to think that maybe it wasn't so impossible to ask if he could rub off on Jock's chest sometime until he came all over his very muscular neck.

The noise of a rock skidding downhill made Jock pull away, and Toby jumped too.

Jock hadn't leapt away, at least; he'd only stepped back, still touching Toby, hands on his thighs. The kiss at Glanum hadn't been just a fluke. "We could find someplace more secluded," he suggested, looking around quickly.

"Where do you think that rock came from?" Toby asked, lifting his brows. The TAG commandos could be lurking around, infiltrating their privacy right now. Probably were.

Jock made a face. "If they see anything, it's their own fucking fault for sneaking up on us. But yeah . . ."

"I don't want to, like, scar them for life or anything. Between us, I'm fairly certain their brains aren't fully formed yet. They're still at an impressionable age."

Jock arched his brows and pressed his lips together, looking away toward that utterly European manor house on the flood plain.

"What?" Toby asked.

He shrugged. "Nothing."

"I can tell you're thinking something."

Jock's dimple flashed in his cheek. "Just, you know, wondering if you'd really turn down a blowjob."

"People have survived worse trauma. They'll get over it." They could find a more secluded spot in the bushes and—

"*Toby*!"

"Oh no," he groaned, hanging his head, holding on to Jock for one more second. Another moment of pretending he didn't have to watch over the most trouble-prone college students in Europe. He could tell by the pitch of the voice calling his name that this was going to be a problem.

Jock sighed, leaning to the side to see uphill. "It's Jules."

Toby bowed to the inevitable, standing up and heading for the dude scrabbling down the slope toward him. "What is it?"

"Someone broke into the van," he panted.

Following Jules, they started back, but unlike him they didn't run. Whoever had smashed in the window would already be gone. As soon as he cleared the last arch of the aqueduct and saw the group of downhearted boys staring at the broken-out glass, Toby started his lecture. "I told you not to leave *anything* in the vehicle."

"It was just my sweatshirt," Turbo protested.

"And my sketchbook," Julian admitted. "And drawing supplies." Ever since Jules had decided chicks were into artists, he'd been carrying those around. Not actually using them, just toting them everywhere.

"And that case of Heinie we picked up when we got the stuff for lunch. What?" Danny protested when Toby glared at him. "It was still warm."

"Lovely. I'll tell the police to follow the trail of beer cans to the drunk *artiste* wearing the TAG hoodie."

The police in Fontvieille weren't interested in that much detail. Not that they didn't file the report, or promise to look for the perpetrators, but tons of people had their cars broken into at Barbegal. Toby knew it was almost useless, but he went through the motions.

Driving back to EuroTAG, cardboard taped over the window, Toby glanced in the rearview mirror just as Danny opened his mouth. Toby stomped his foot on the brake, like that could keep Danny quiet, but of course he didn't manage to say anything useful, like *Shut up!* before the guy uttered his words of wisdom.

"Well, it wouldn't have been much of a trip to France without visiting a police station."

ΘAΓ

He was so close to done with his thesis. And that was what it was about at this point, simply being done with it. Good or not as good, Toby didn't care anymore (although bad wasn't an option if he wanted to graduate). He'd finish, get the degree, break the news to his mom, and then . . . do what all the other overeducated, underqualified guys his age did.

Friday went really well—he was totally in the zone. When they got back from Saint-Rémy and the guys decided to go swimming before dinner, he put on his swim trunks and sat out by the pool with a glass of chilled white wine and his laptop. He had to unpeel the skin of his bare back from the chair every once in a while, and occasionally the fratbro antics would make him look up—especially those of Jock in his trunks. He had such an amazing body, and Toby found himself wondering how he'd gotten so lucky.

Coming back from his little house after refilling his wine, Danny called out, "Hey, what's that on your back?"

Toby sat on the edge of his lounger, looking around, trying to figure out whose back had something on it.

"Tobes!" Danny said. "You got some, like, dirt on your back."

Oh, they were talking to *him*? He whipped his head around to see Danny and Turbo walking toward him. Ricky and Jules were either uninterested or lazy—they only leaned forward in their chairs and squinted at him. Toby craned his neck, trying to see over his shoulder to his back. That worked about as well as it ever had—not at all. "What does it look like?"

"Like a streak of dirt," Danny said, nose wrinkling up.

Toby shrugged. "I'll take a shower later." He started to lay back in his deck chair, but Danny's hand on his shoulder stopped him. "Why is this so fascinating to you?"

"'Cause it just looks like . . ." Toby couldn't see his face, but he could feel the intensity of Danny's mental ruminations in the air behind him. Then his finger poked Toby's spine, and that's when it hit him what it was they were looking at. A token of Jock's possessiveness he'd forgotten about once it'd stopped hurting.

He tried to shrug Danny's hand off and lean back, but the guy had a good grip. "Danny, just drop it."

"Dude! Is that a *friction* burn?"

Toby closed his eyes and sighed, jerking them open again when a spray of cool water droplets hit his foot. Jock stood next to him, soaking wet, shoving his sopping hair off his forehead and glaring at Danny. "Leave him alone." He reached for Danny's wrist and yanked the hand off of Toby's shoulder, then straddled the lounge chair behind him, sitting and pulling Toby's back against his front.

Goose bumps erupted all over Toby's skin, but it wasn't from the cool water—it was from being held like this by Jock in front of all these guys. He shifted, trying to adjust to it. Not that he cared about them seeing, but he couldn't help his conviction that *Jock* cared. He'd jerked away that time the guys had caught them kissing. Obviously, he was getting more comfortable with it, but Toby hadn't imagined he'd be more than willing to hold hands in front of them yet. The only reason he was doing it now was to protect Toby.

More goose bumps.

"How do you get a friction burn on your back?" Danny mused. He was either stupid or had a death wish, but since he'd already proven his stupidity many times over, Toby didn't have to devote a lot of energy to figuring out which. "What do you think, Turbo?" he turned to the other guy.

Jock growled. Toby was fairly sure he was turning red.

"Uhhhh . . ." Turbo gurgled, definitely turning red. "Dude, let's just—"

"Oh my God!" Danny slapped himself in the forehead, unfortunately not knocking any sense in. "You have a rug burn on your back from *fucking*!"

"Oh Christ," Toby moaned, covering his face.

"C'mon," Jock said, pushing on Toby's shoulder until he leaned forward. Jock climbed out from behind him and picked up Toby's laptop, then held out his hand. Waiting for Toby to take it.

Which of course he did. Letting Jock glare at all the guys while they walked toward their hut. He should probably protest Jock's behavior, but he didn't. Sometimes, when a guy was embarrassed by a rug burn on his back, he needed a champion.

"Sorry, babe," Jock whispered, kissing under his ear, bumping his nose against Toby's cheek as they walked along. "I didn't mean to be so rough."

"You know I was into it," Toby said. "That's not the issue."

Jock halted, pulling Toby to a stop with him. "What's the issue?" They were right below the pool deck, visible to all the guys still, but out of hearing range, Toby thought. He refused to turn and find out how many of the boys were watching.

"Do you ever feel like we're in some kind of unnatural relationship pressure cooker?" he asked before he'd fully thought it through. "All these guys around us, practically shoving us together sometimes, and we'd be running into each other all the time even if they weren't. And now they're, like, prying into our sex life."

Jock frowned. "Yeah. I mean, it bugs me, but I guess I thought you were okay with it. Like, freaking over them watching us was my thing."

"That's not the issue."

Jock tugged gently, getting them moving again. "'Kay, so let's go talk."

Toby followed, focusing on their hands, his chest filling up with dread, drowning him slowly. Now that he'd let himself say that, know it, he couldn't lock the thoughts back up in whatever box he'd been hiding them. Jock stopped again, setting the laptop on the patio table in front of the *cabanon*. He turned to Toby.

"Tell me."

Toby shook his head, not sure where to start, and ashamed of himself for feeling this way. He was normally a confident, laid-back guy, but with Jock he was tied up in knots half the time. Adding in this unnatural situation where he had so much responsibility for so many people who could barely get themselves dressed in the morning . . . "The way we are here may not be the way we are at home." Judging by Jock's expression, which hadn't changed, he didn't get it, which wasn't surprising since Toby wasn't displaying his usual powers of clear communication. Desperate, he took the first analogy that popped into his brain. "Okay, um, my mom told me once that when she goes on a trip, she almost always ends up buying clothes that seem perfect for where she's visiting, but are totally wrong for when she's at home. Even knowing she's done it in the past, she'll go ahead and do it again, convincing herself that this time it's right. But then she gets home and that shirt that looked so exuberant and chic in Paris looks tacky in central California."

Jock frowned even harder, really working his brow into it. "Are you saying I'm the shirt you shouldn't have bought in France because I won't fit right once we're in Oregon?"

"No." Toby placed his hand on Jock's chest, still a little damp from the pool. "I'm saying *I'm* the shirt *you* bought."

"So . . . this is about whether we're actually going to stay together once we get back to Oregon?" Some of the wrinkles in Jock's forehead eased. "I don't get why you'd think we wouldn't."

"Because." Toby swallowed, trying to work moisture into his throat. "When we were in Oregon, you didn't think I fit you right."

Jock massaged the back of his neck, looking into Toby's eyes a while, but Toby couldn't read them like he often could. He had to wait until Jock spoke to discover what was going on in his head. "In Oregon, I *did* want you. Even after we hooked up I did, but . . . I didn't get it. Everything was so confusing with all the shit going on. I mean, that sounds like a lame ex—"

"It doesn't." Toby shook his head.

"I thought about you a lot. When I got here, that's when I figured out I wanted more, and I guess, you know . . ." He shook his head. "I got scared."

"This isn't just sex." Toby could barely speak above a whisper.

"Can you really be wondering about that?"

"Well." He forced a shrug. "I mean, I guess you wouldn't give just anyone a friction burn."

Jock smiled. "No, only guys I'm serious about."

"I feel like an idiot," Toby whispered. "I know it's not just sex now, but someday we have to go home, and what if it's not the same?" Jesus, what did he think he was asking for? Promises? Jock would be convinced this shirt would be fit him just as well and be just as comfortable at home as here, and be as wrong as Toby's mother always was. "Never mind."

Jock used the hand on his neck to guide Toby closer, pulling his forehead onto Jock's shoulder. "I don't think it's just being here. I think, if we were still at home, we'd have gotten together by now, or we would soon."

He could believe that, or he could go on torturing himself. Toby chose to believe, nodding his head and wrapping his arms around Jock's waist. Relief soaked through him, along with the enormity of what was happening. He was falling in love with this frat boy and he wanted it to be mutual so badly. That was the root of his insecurity. Jock was so young, regardless of how much control he took in bed or how mature he seemed sometimes. He didn't have Toby's experiences. It wouldn't stop him from falling in love with Toby if he was going to, but it might stop him from recognizing it.

And really, was that so bad? It was all a gamble, regardless. He'd told himself he was going to see what happened, float with the current, and that's what he'd do, moments of doubt aside. It was exhilarating. But of course the "B" side of exhilaration was terror. Given the choice between experiencing neither of them or taking both, Toby knew he'd take both every time. And giving up on Jock now was simply not a choice at all.

"I don't get what that had to do with the burn," Jock said in his ear, still rubbing the back of Toby's neck.

"Honestly? Neither do I."

ΘΑΓ

Hours later, making out lazily, Toby was soaking in sensation. Provençal scents from the soft breeze drifting through the window tickled his naked skin. And Jock, similarly naked, was utterly bursting with potential stimulation. For example, lips like his boyfriend's needed special attention, nibbles and sucks and thorough exploration.

After a while Toby moved on, testing Jock's jawbone with his teeth, until his tongue could work its way up behind Jock's ear and make him moan.

"Wanna make love to you," Toby mumbled into Jock's hair, half to himself, more caught up in the slide of his thigh between Jock's than what he was saying.

Jock froze, then jerked away from him, pushing himself up to kneeling on the bed, leaving Toby blinking and a little motion sick. Until his words replayed themselves in his mind, then he just felt sick. Fuck, had he actually *said* that? Judging by Jock's wide-eyed horror, yes, he had.

How did he take it back?

Did he *want* to take it back? Those particular words—and the sentiment—they weren't really a bad thing, were they? Not if he meant it. When he prodded at the feelings, both sensory and emotional, that had prompted him to say them, it confirmed that yes, he'd been sincere. They didn't sound bad. They sounded *true*.

His heart thumped extra hard, a happy burst of emotion radiating through him, and he started to reach for Jock again to make the words happen.

But Jock still looked horrified. Terrified.

Obviously, his feelings weren't nearly on a par with Toby's own. Toby dropped his hand, propping himself on his elbow. "That just slipped out."

Jock swallowed, adjusting himself on the bed, sitting and pulling the sheet over his lap, making it really obvious he wasn't going to erect any tents over what Toby'd said. He'd *so* fucked this up. Assumed way too much about how Jock saw the relationship, and how deeply it went for him.

"I don't want . . ." Jock began.

Toby tried to quell the sick feeling in his gut with the power of his rational mind. His rational mind was outgunned, though. Sick feeling had his heart on its side. "You don't want what?"

Jock's eyes were pinging around the room. *Looking for an escape.*

"Maybe you should leave."

Jock huffed out a breath like Toby'd punched him in the stomach. "You mean, if I don't, like, put out, we're done?"

"No." *What?* "I meant if you aren't comfortable with what I said, I understand if you don't want to stay." *Tonight.* "I don't . . ." He *had* to finish the thought. "I don't want to end things, though."

Jock wrapped his fists in the bedding. "Even if I never let you fuck me?"

Toby's brain recalibrated, zeroing out everything he'd been thinking and starting over. *So it isn't the love thing, it's about bottoming.* They'd never even talked about it again since that night Jock had said he wasn't ready, and Toby hadn't cared because he hadn't been missing it. Yet. He'd just sort of assumed one day it would happen.

"That wasn't what I meant," he said. Except maybe it kind of was. Possibly. He didn't know exactly what he'd been wanting, not in physical terms. Only emotional ones. *Shit shit shit.*

"What did you mean?"

Oh, this wasn't a potential minefield or anything. "I simply said it, like, sort of an endearment. I wasn't thinking of any particular *act*."

Jock furrowed his brow. "So, you don't want to fuck me?"

Toby took a moment to settle his back against the wall, next to Jock. Trying to figure out how to answer. "I do, if you want me to." He reached for Jock's hand, unwrapping it from the sheet and stroking his fingers. "I've never bottomed this much for anyone in my life."

Jock swallowed. "If you didn't want to—"

"I did. Every time. Do you think I could fake it that well?"

He nodded once, staring down at the bedding. "Um, you know, before we ever hooked up, I was talking to Brad . . ."

Toby waited him out.

"He said you were versatile, so I knew that you liked it both ways."

Jock had talked to Brad about him? Before, when they were still in Oregon. So maybe that shirt *would* fit when they got home. Toby squeezed Jock's hand. "He was right. I used to top more than bottom."

Jock looked at him blankly a second. "You did?"

"Yeah."

His eyebrows scrunched up. "You don't seem like a top to me."

Toby sighed. "I don't *feel* like one with you."

The edges of Jock's lips turned down, weighted by the hurt anger that he was sometimes prone to.

"I kind of want to bottom with you," Toby said before the frown could grow, turning to face him more fully, sitting next to him and keeping hold of his hand. "I mean I *do* want to, I don't know why. It's just . . ." He shrugged. "We work together best that way. It feels good to me. Physically and otherwise."

Jock was still frowning at him, but it wasn't the hurt-angry one anymore. It was the frown that tried to make sense of things. "You prefer it with me? But didn't before, with other guys?"

"Yeah." Toby swallowed. This shouldn't be so hard to admit, should it? "It's different with you. *Everything* is different with you. Sometimes I feel like a different person."

Jock jerked his head back, fingers squeezing into a fist around Toby's for a second.

"Not like I'm not *me*," Toby said quickly. "Just as if parts of me are becoming more prominent, and others that *were* at the forefront are becoming less so. If that makes any sense."

"So . . . you don't like that?"

Toby ran his hand down Jock's face, trying to figure out what and how much to say. "I don't really care," he said. Jock kept looking at him as if waiting for more. "I like *you*. And I like myself when I'm with you."

Jock reached for him, working his fingers into Toby's hair and cupping his cheek. "I like you too. And I like the way I feel with you." He took a breath and added, "You make me feel understood."

"I'm trying, baby," Toby whispered, leaning closer for a kiss, up on his hands and knees and then straddling Jock's thighs, holding his face. "I understand being scared to let someone fuck you. Lots of guys are."

The way Jock's eyes flickered away was his first clue that he might not have this quite right. But he met Toby's gaze again. "Can I ask you something?"

"Of course."

"How does it feel?"

Toby half smiled, stroking Jock's jaw. "Well, I like it now, I think you know that."

Jock smiled back at him, although it was on the faint side.

"But the first time wasn't so great. It hurt, but that's because the guy I was with knew as little as me."

Jock rested his palms on Toby's thighs where they straddled him, watching them. "That's not exactly what I was asking, I guess. Um, how does it feel, like, to let someone . . ."

It took a few seconds for Toby to figure out what he meant, but of course it was about one thing with his boyfriend. "Let someone have that kind of control over me?"

Jock nodded quickly, pursing his lips.

"It depends," Toby answered carefully. "With you, it's like . . . riding a roller coaster. I'm a little scared, but mostly I'm excited."

"Do you ever feel like . . . the girl?"

Toby's fingers tightened on Jock's face, then he let them drop away. The sick feeling came rushing back. "I'm not a girl."

"I know, I know that," Jock said, squeezing Toby's thighs. "But, I mean, you let me, like, *have* you."

"Wait, you think of it that way? With me? Like I'm, I don't know, lesser or something because you stick your dick in me?" Toby shoved off Jock's legs, pulling out of his hold, then off the bed. Fuck, where were his briefs? He couldn't stand here naked right now.

Jock followed him, standing also. Toby backed up when he got too close, finding his underwear when he stepped on them. "I'm sorry," Jock said. "It's not like that. I don't think less of you, I just . . ."

Toby planted his hands on his hips, glaring at him. "You just think it would emasculate *you*."

Jock swallowed, looking at the floor and shifting his weight.

"Christ," Toby muttered, dropping onto the edge of the bed and burying his head in his palms. "So, like, every time you fuck me, you think . . . what? I'm not a man?"

"No!" Jock said. "It's got nothing to do with you."

"It's got *everything* to do with me. I'm the one you're fucking." Toby dropped his hands and stared at Jock, trying to figure out how to explain. What Jock had said about feeling understood? It was true, Toby understood him, which made things difficult right now, because a lot of Toby was pissed off and hurt and wanted to storm out, but the rest of him could see it from Jock's point of view.

Then suddenly he was seeing Jock from a new point of view. Dropping to his knees in front of Toby, holding him the way he had at Barbegal, arms around his hips and head at Toby's shoulders. "I'm *sorry*," he said, and his eyes were utterly sincere. "It's not about how I think of you, though. It's about how I think of *me*."

Which was exactly what Toby already understood. "I know," he admitted. He stroked Jock's hair off his forehead, sighing. "But, baby . . . why did you get pissed off thinking I'd put myself in the same position you did when that guy took the picture?"

Jock's brow wrinkled up. "Respect," he whispered.

Toby nodded. "If you don't want to do it because it emasculates you, than how can you respect me when I let you fuck me?"

"It's not like that," Jock objected. "It's like, something *I'm* scared of for reasons I don't even understand." He swallowed, gripping Toby tighter. "I even sometimes want it with you, but it's like there's something holding me back. Instinct or training or something. I don't mean to always bring it back to hockey, but I got sort of indoctrinated into thinking being in control all the time was absolutely necessary. Or maybe it's my personality, I dunno. But it's got nothing to do with how I feel about you."

"I get it," Toby said, stroking Jock's jaw. "I know you mean it, but I don't know if I can let you do it again knowing how you see it. How could you think it makes you less of a man, but *not* see me that way, even just a little? It'd be different if you just weren't into bottoming, I could work with that, but this isn't that. This is about self-worth."

"I don't want to lose you over this," Jock whispered. "Just, give me time, okay? I'll work it out."

Toby nodded, pulling in a shaky breath. "I might . . ." Ugh, saying this was going to gut him, but he couldn't *not* say it. "I need some time too, baby. If I let you keep fucking me, it might destroy everything we have."

Right before Jock dropped his head, hiding his face, pain rippled across his eyes like the tide coming in. And there it was, the gutting of Toby. He didn't want to hurt like this, and he really didn't want Jock in pain over it. He'd do almost anything to avoid it, but even thinking about letting Jock top him right now . . .

Jock could say, and even believe, that he didn't think any less of Toby, but how much weight did his words carry when his actions didn't follow suit?

Toby leaned forward, bending over his boyfriend and resting his cheek on the top of Jock's head, heart bleeding for both of them.

"What are we going to do?" Jock's question floated up to Toby's ears.

Toby lifted his head, and Jock met his eyes again. His irises had turned dark blue, weighted down with whatever was going on inside him. "Um . . ." Toby took a deep breath, trying to think. "I guess you have to dec—"

"Dude! Tobes!" Danny's voice blasted through the doorway, making both of them jump, followed quickly by a pounding fist.

"Oh no."

"Ignore him," Jock urged, fingers digging into Toby's thighs.

"Tobes, we got some serious shit happening, here. If you don't open the door, they'll bust it down like they did at the frat."

"What?" Toby stood up, Jock moving quickly out of his way, before finding his briefs and hopping around on one foot, yanking them up, but he'd barely regained his balance when something else started slamming into the door. Something much, much heavier than Danny's fist. The door shook with each blow.

"What the fuck?" Jock said, stepping forward, but Toby grabbed his hand, yanking him back just as the door burst open, a bunch of guys with black ski masks on spilling through after, guns pointing at them.

"Dude, it's the cops," Danny was yelling over the confusion and orders being barked at them in French. Toby caught "*Restez ou vous êtes!*" and his brain supplied the translation—"Stay where you are!" Neither he nor Jock was having any problems complying—they were too shocked to move.

Someone gripped his arm, twisting it behind his back and wrenching his hand from Jock's, then snagging his other wrist. Before he knew it, he was standing in the middle of his formerly cozy little *cabanon*, staring at his similarly cuffed boyfriend. *Thank God he got briefs on, too.* Toby was too shocked to think about practicalities for the first few seconds, but the flexing of Jock's jaw muscles and the way he stared icily over everyone's head forced Toby into dealing.

"English," he said to the guy speaking to him in French, gripping his arm still. "We need a translator." They had to provide one, right? Should he ask for a lawyer now?

"Okay." The office nodded and waved to another guy in a ski mask near the door, of about the same build. Looking around, Toby finally registered three black-clothed officers, "DCRI" printed on the breast of their jackets. *How do they tell each other apart?* Glancing outside, he saw a fourth clone guarding Danny. His hair stuck up everywhere, hands behind his back, eyes wide and mouth hanging slightly open.

As soon as Toby caught Danny's eye, before the new officer could say anything to him (presumably in English), Danny yelled out, "They're arresting us for terrorism."

Toby locked his knees against a wave of dizziness. "I *never* should have let you guys believe in beermageddon."

Chapter 19

Jock should have been focused on his arrest, but sitting in the holding cell in Marseille, he mostly thought about Toby. Wondering if his room also had a bench built into the wall with a thin vinyl pad on top. Jock had a feeling he was supposed to be able to lie down on it, but it looked about a foot too short for him.

He knew they'd all been taken here—each of the guys in a separate black, tinted-window car with two officers in the front and a cage barrier between the backseat and them—so Toby was probably in a similarly uncomfortable room with similarly bright white walls and high-wattage fluorescent ceiling fixture.

Or being questioned. Alone. Jock had fantasies of punching through the wall and finding his boyfriend on the other side, cuffed to a chair and being questioned by a cigarette-smoking Frenchman with sallow skin. He'd punch the guy out and escape with Toby, chair and all.

Unlikely. He knew it logically, but his hands kept bunching up into fists whenever he wasn't forcing them to relax. A month ago he might have actually tried it, but things had changed. He'd changed, because of Toby.

But not enough, or he wouldn't feel like an anxious rat was gnawing its way out of his stomach every time he thought about their last few minutes together before the cops had shown up.

He rubbed his eyes, forcing himself to think about something else. Wondering what time it was. Way past midnight, definitely. It might have been that late when the cops broke down the door. They'd uncuffed him and let him get dressed in the clothes he'd had at Toby's, but he hadn't been allowed to talk to or really even see any of the other TAG brothers, and they'd separated him and Toby immediately, leading Toby outside and away. For all he knew, Toby was still in navy-blue briefs with white trim.

Hope not. He'd be cold—they had the AC on in this building. And other guys might be checking him out.

The worst thing about being arrested: he was stuck alone in this holding cell where he could only keep his mind off of Toby for short periods. It kept drifting back to their conversation. To Toby asking how Jock saw him when they were together, like, sexually. A few more seconds and maybe he could have told Toby what he'd figured out, kneeling there in front of him. It had been hearing himself ask, *What are we going to do?* that jogged sense into his brain, but he'd still been absorbing it when Danny had started yelling outside. His mind hadn't quite made the connection yet, hadn't quite worked out what his heart had already known.

I'm not in this alone. That was it, right there. The irony of it was killing him—he'd only realized that being in a relationship meant working through stuff together when the issue was all his. Having a boyfriend meant he *got* to let somebody help him deal.

He was the one with the problem, but it affected both of them, and he needed Toby's help. Or he really wanted it, at least.

But Toby wanted time to himself, thinking Jock didn't . . . what? See him as an equal? Respect him?

Love him?

Of course he didn't know that. Jock had only figured it out himself in this holding cell. And the longer he sat here, the more things kept occurring to him. Like, if being the receptive partner was so bad, why *did* he let the man he loved do it? Because he didn't really love him? But Jock's heart got pissed off at the suggestion and had a hissy fit, so it had to be something else. Like maybe he knew somewhere inside that it wasn't a demeaning thing.

Had he really thought of it that way? Like, if it was demeaning to bottom for a guy, what did that say for girls in general? Or rather, how he thought about them? And what the guys on his hockey teams thought of them, the way they talked about the almighty power of owning a penis.

Every new thought set up a cascade of other realizations. And most of them led to him feeling like a fucking douche bag.

He sat there forever, repeating the cycle. Realization, douche bag. Realization, douche bag. Eventually he just cut out the middle man and realized he was a douche bag.

Then he was on the ice, skidding to a stop, crystals spraying up from the edges of his blades, and right there was the puck, waiting for him. He had a clear shot at the net, and no one was defending him. His teammates were keeping the opposing guys busy, even the goalie. And the crowd was screaming for him to score.

Perfect setup. He reached up and grabbed his stick—because for some reason he'd taken to carrying it in a holster strapped to his back, which didn't sound regulation—and slapped that fucker in, watching it sail through the air . . . right over the top of the net.

Then everything rewound in high speed and it happened all over again. Over and over, just like realizing he was a douche bag.

Jock came to with a jolt, nearly pitching off the bench.

Holding cell. He'd been dreaming.

Okay, subconscious mind. I get it. Shut up already. Change the game plan or lose it all.

"Can you tell me where my boyf— the guy I was with when I was arrested, where he is?" Toby asked as soon as the spook in the gray suit walked in. He doubted this guy was actually a spy, more like the FBI at home from what he understood, but he looked like a "spook." Or at least what the movies told him was a spook. Tall, thin, expressionless, dark suit. He just needed sunglasses and an attractive face and he'd be the questionably motivated "good guy" in the next blockbuster. They could call it *Frat Boys Take Provence.* It'd be half gay porno and half action flick. This interrogation room—well, that's what Toby assumed it was called—would make a great set. It was as blindingly bright as the cell they'd had him in before, but the pale tile floor was grimy, and the single plant in the corner was dying. The table he was seated at didn't fit, though—instead of being scarred faux-wood laminate, it was nearly pristine gray laminate.

"Your boyfriend is not being mistreated, I assure you," the man said, sitting down across from him. He had a very American accent. "I'm Monsieur Faustin, it's a pleasure to meet you, Mr. Moore."

"You aren't a cop?" Should he have asked that? But he'd decided a while ago that trying to strategize about the best way to answer questions was pointless. They hadn't done anything wrong, so unless those same action flicks were right about most cops being nefarious, this should all be cleared up soon.

"I am an agent of the *Direction centrale du renseignement intérieur*. You may call me Officer Faustin, if it eases your mind any."

"Being released with all charges dropped would ease my mind more. Speaking of which, what *are* the charges, exactly?" He'd already tried asking for a lawyer a few times, and was informed that under French law, they could be held for up to seventy-two hours without being allowed attorney privileges.

"Ah." Faustin smiled pleasantly and looked down at the file he'd carried in with him, as if he needed to refresh his memory. "For now, it is as you've been told already: you are suspected of having committed or preparing to commit an act of terrorism."

Toby drew a calming breath. "Does this act of terrorism have anything to do with beer? Because I think I can clear that right up."

"Yes, maybe you can," Faustin mused, lifting a sheet of paper from his file. "'The frat boy's relationship to beer is as the nun's relationship to God,'" he read from it.

"Oh no," Toby muttered. "I was afraid of that." He was going to fucking *kill* Danny. At least then he'd deserve the jail time. "Okay, it's really very simple. You see, the guys have this membership—"

"Mr. Moore—may I call you Toby? *Merci*—I'd prefer to begin with your exact relationship to these 'guys,' specifically the one with you when you were taken into custody, the young man going by the name of Gavin Jacques Gervaise."

This just kept getting worse. "Um, I probably should have looked into this before, but what's the legal age of consent here?" This was *France*, though. Nineteen had to be old enough, didn't it?

Faustin tilted his eyebrow, just on one side. Toby'd never seen that trick before. "It's fifteen, unless the sexual partner is in a position of influence over the minor."

Oh, *of course* that would be the case. He was going to rot in a French prison. "What's the age of consent if one partner *is* in a position of influence?"

"Eighteen. Mr. Gervaise is nineteen." He leaned forward to whisper, "I believe you are safe."

So utterly fitting that he'd get the smart-ass cop, wasn't it? Toby nodded, clasping his hands on the table, gathering his thoughts. "Yeah, um, Mr. Gervaise . . . Gavin is my boyfriend, as you've already surmised, and the other guys are in the same fraternity as he is. Um, that's like a—" Shit, what was the term? "—*bureau des élèves*."

"I attended university in the US. I can assure you I'll be able to follow along. Are you a part of this fraternity as well?"

"Um, no." Toby had the distinct impression that Officer Faustin already knew exactly what his role was. "I'm the, uh, resident advisor for them during their quarter in France. They had to live off-campus, you see, and the college felt it was necessary for them to have a . . ." *Jesus*. He cleared his throat. "Responsible party at the place they'd made arrangements to stay."

Faustin regarded him blankly.

"They're pretty good at getting themselves in trouble." He smiled tightly. "Case in point would be this arrest."

"Yes, it would be. Unfortunately for everyone, you—the 'responsible party'—have also been arrested."

"I had a feeling you might bring that up." His advisor was going to string him up by the balls. But she'd have to get in line behind his mother. "You see, I let them continue the beer terrorist thing because, after researching child psychology"—*on Wikipedia*—"I thought it best not to challenge their fantasies. Working on the theory that they still have some, well, *maturing* to do, I judged this to be a relatively normal stage of their neural development. I think in the long run they'll be more well-rounded human beings if we nurt—"

"Let's move on."

Oh thank *God* Faustin put a lid on any further ass-talking. Toby nodded attentively, waiting for him to continue.

"Are you familiar with the term 'beermageddon'?"

Oh no. Toby knotted his fingers together even tighter. "I might have heard it once or twice."

"Ah. Where is it that you heard it?"

Sooo, so tempting to blame the fratbros. "Well, actually I coined the term when Jock was explaining the guys' fascination with the concept of beer terrorism to me. I meant it as a joke, but Danny overheard me and he may have, um, taken up the banner."

Faustin nodded, making a quick note in his file. "And where else have you heard the term?"

Toby couldn't claim his brain was at peak performance, but he felt pretty confident in saying, "I may have mentioned it while I was being taken into custody, but Danny was the only one I remember discussing it with."

"Hmmm. How did that discussion go?"

"Well . . . he overheard me, and then he asked if he could use it, and I said it was fine."

"Use what?"

"The word. Beermageddon."

"Simply use the word? This wasn't a discussion of how to bring about this 'beermageddon'?"

"Um, I'd like to point out that the boys aren't trying to bring on beermageddon, they're trying to *prevent* it." Wait, was he seriously arguing this?

"So . . ." Faustin leaned forward, narrowing his eyes. "You *are* familiar with their plans?"

"If by 'plans' you mean 'delusions,' then yes, I'm familiar with them."

"Let's talk about the *taverne* in the village."

Toby sighed. "If you'd like."

"I'd like." Faustin smiled.

"What do you want to know?"

"Did the 'boys,' as you call them, visit it frequently?"

"A few times a week for the last few, I suppose." He wasn't sure it was relevant, but he thought he'd save time, since Faustin would invariably get to this detail. "I told them they're not allowed to visit it alone. At least two guys have to go together."

"To watch each other's backs against threats?"

He crossed his arms and sat back to view Officer Faustin more completely. "I understand it's your job to find out the truth by whatever means, but I'd think deliberately misunderstanding me is counterproductive."

"Not at all." Faustin waved off the comment. "I'm not misunderstanding you, I'm asking you 'leading questions,' as they say. Now, why exactly did you incorporate this buddy system?"

Toby pinched the bridge of his nose, trying to figure out the most concise way to explain. *Just start.* "Okay, you see, Noah had a bit of a crush on Turbo—um, his real name is Graham Libutzki—and one day his hormones got the better of him, and even knowing Turbo is straight, Noah kissed him. I talked Noah through it at the bar—"

"What about this Turbo? No one talked him through anything?"

"Oh." Toby sat back a second, blinking. "That was an oversight on my part, wasn't it? It's just that, when they have a problem they need my help with, they come to me. I mean, you've met them, I'm sure you can understand I can't go chasing around after their problems."

Faustin folded his brows into a V, frowning.

"For example," Toby went on quickly. "When Danny and Madame Bouvinet began *their* relationship, and Danny had some confusion over his feelings for her, he came to—"

"*Pardon*?" The officer's eyes had gone wide, which Toby had a feeling was the closest the man ever came to gaping. He bent his head, riffling through his papers, then pulled one out. It looked sort of like a curriculum vitae, with a picture of Madame B on the corner. He pointed at the picture, holding it right in front of Toby's face. "This is Madame Bouvinet?"

Toby cleared his throat. "Yes."

He let that sheet flutter to the table. "*The* Madame Bouvinet," he began, madly shuffling through his pile again, "who this man—" he yanked out an image of Danny that looked remarkably like a mug shot "—is conducting an affair with?"

"Well, um, I sort of think you should be asking him about this, I mean, it's not really my news to share . . ." Even though he'd already done so.

"*Merde*." Faustin dropped the picture and sat back, gripping the edge of the desk as if holding on, but at the same time shoving the rest of his body away.

Toby nodded. *Fascinated repulsion*. He understood that ambiguity very well.

It took a few seconds, but Faustin settled himself again, clasping his own hands and resting them opposite Toby's, mirroring him. Was this some kind of interrogation technique? If he'd had any idea how much he'd come to depend on the stuff he'd failed to learn in that psych class—

"I'll be straight with you," Faustin said.

In spite of the gravity of the situation, Toby couldn't suppress a smile. But seriously, the dude had said "straight."

"I could quite easily present a case to the court wherein you are the mastermind of a group of student activists."

Toby opened his mouth, but Faustin stalled him with a palm in the air.

"Let me finish, then you may voice objections." When Toby nodded he went on. "Using the somewhat farcical idea of 'beer terrorism'—"

"*Somewhat* farcical?"

Faustin tipped his head, conceding that point. "After the interviews we've conducted with your 'boys,' it begins to look almost like a cover for an attempt to further the—as your politicians call it—'gay agenda.'"

"*What*?" Toby shot up from his chair.

Now Officer Faustin had both palms out. "I'm not saying anyone investigating this case thus far believes this is true. After all, we've met these boys, as you said, and I find it hard to believe they have the necessary intellect. However, we're legally obligated to present these interviews to the judge, who will make the decision whether to continue the inquest. It would help your case very much if you could give me some specific details to clear up some discrepancies. Please sit down again."

Toby did, muttering to himself. "This is utterly insane."

"Quite," Faustin agreed, nodding. "However, shall we begin?"

"Bring it on," Toby sighed.

ΘΑΓ

"No," Jock said firmly for the hundredth time, or around there. He clenched his jaw before going on, trying not to lose his temper. "We were sitting on a hill overlooking Glanum, talking, and Toby saw Gomer—James Nierada—scare a bunch of nuns while he was playing, you know." Jock waved his hand in the air, because this is where his story got weak. Factual, but weak.

The officer—whose name Jock had totally forgotten—said something to the interpreter (whose name he'd never been told). "Beer terrorist?" she asked Jock.

"Okay, it's not like it sounds. The guys are, like, *abnormal*, you know?" He leaned forward and lowered his voice, for no real reason since they were in here alone. "We kind of think some of them are a few IQ points short of average."

"Who is 'we'?" the officer asked through the interpreter.

It couldn't be good that he'd already mentioned Toby's name so many times, could it? "Um . . ."

"Toby Moore?"

Jock squeezed his eyes shut and nodded.

"Mr. Gervaise, could you please explain the nature of your relationship to Mr. Moore?"

Jock's eyes popped open, glaring. "He's my boyfriend." If they wanted to make an issue out of it, he'd *show* them issues. Both the officer and the translator lifted their eyebrows and nodded in unison. Jock lowered his and crossed his arms over his chest. "Is that illegal or something?"

"Of course not, we're just trying to understand. It is imperative that we have all our facts in a row. This college you attend, Calapooya—"

"Cal-ah-*poo*-yah," Jock corrected her, just because it made him feel like he had a tiny bit of control.

"*Oui, bon*. Calapooya. From this institution, who funded your term abroad? Was it this Greek organization, Theta Alpha Gamma?"

"It's not *actually* Greek," he tried to explain again. "It's called a Greek letter organization because the name is made up of *Greek letters*. It's a student association."

They nodded in unison again. Jock got the distinct feeling they weren't that interested. "Your funding, Mr. Gervaise?"

It went on and on, Jock explaining things that didn't mean much to anyone but that the DCRI wanted to know the minute details of. Yes, the idea of "beer terrorists" began in the United States, but it wasn't an official group or anything, and it wasn't sanctioned by TAG. "It's a bunch of maturity-challenged guys who bought into the college fantasy," he said in exasperation at one point.

That led to questions about who bought what from whom for how much. They seemed to want to follow the money. "Okay, just . . . can I just start from the beginning, you guys take notes and then you ask me questions afterward? Please?"

The interpreter had a long discussion with the DRCI agent. Jock had the feeling the officer understood most or all of what he was saying, but used the interpreter to make certain there weren't any miscommunications. A few times he'd asked questions directly. Jock couldn't follow their discussion, though, just little bits and pieces here and there. Both of them said, "I don't know," a few times, and there were lots of words such as "*incroyable, bière, très stupide*," and he could swear the translator said "wankers" once, followed by stifled laughter from both of them.

By the time she turned back to him, Jock could actually see his annoyed brows hovering at the top of his vision.

"Please." She waved her hand. "Share your story with us."

About fucking time. He sat up, trying to ease the tension in his shoulders with a couple of deep breaths. It would be good to not start out by biting their heads off. "Some of this happened before I was a member, so you'll have to talk to the other guys to confirm it—not Toby, he's not a member of Theta Alpha Gamma at all." He'd told them that already, but he was as interested in keeping their facts in nice, neat rows as they seemed to be. And protecting his boyfriend.

They nodded. Did they practice together or something? He shook it off. "About a year ago, one of the TAG brothers—that's what we call each other, 'cause, you know, fraternity—never mind. Anyway, this dude, Brad Feller, he came out."

Wrinkled foreheads met that. "Came out of where?"

"The closet. Okay, uh, like, he announced he's gay."

"Ah, of course. We are familiar with the term." The translator waved him on.

"Just making sure," he bit out, then he took a second to consciously relax his neck and jaw muscles. They were nearly vibrating with the effort of storing all his anxiety and anger. But he had to keep it somewhere, because he was trying not to let it out and jeopardize their position. Or Toby's. "Anyway, so the fraternity wanted to make it clear they supported their gay members, even though at the time Brad was the only one everyone knew was gay. Sorta. I mean, pretty much everyone knew Collin was gay, I guess, but Collin didn't know they knew until later."

The translator's brow wrinkled up again. "Who is Collin?"

As he went through the story, he began using his fingers to represent different people. Kyle was his pinky, Collin his ring finger, Collin's uncle Monty his middle finger (fitting), Tank his index finger . . . soon he was going to have to start using his right hand also.

"*Arrêt*," the officer said, standing up. He dug in his pocket, pulling out coins. "Collin, Monty, Kyle, Brad, Tank," he named each one as he set it down on the table.

It made things a lot easier. He sailed right through the explanation of TAG voting for a new, inclusive membership policy, but then he started describing the fire and he had to introduce Eric, Ricky (at least they knew him personally, he supposed), and Sparky.

The agent ran out of pocket change. But once they got to the bombing, neither he nor the translator cared. "Who bombed your TAG House? A rival Greek faction?"

"No, no." Jock waved his hands in the air, palms out, trying to get them to calm down. They'd gone from bemused interest back to alert status. "It was Sparky, because he was angry with Collin's uncle Monty." He moved the appropriate coins into position, opposite the pen cap that represented Sparky. "Well, Monty and the rest of the Alumni Association."

They all stopped, heads swiveling, searching the room for something to represent the new players. The officer ended up ripping the blank bottom half of a sheet of paper from his file and handing Jock the pen so he could write "alums" on it. Then he kept the pen, in case he needed it to represent someone else.

"At which point of this story did you arrive?" the interpreter asked him.

"Um, actually this all happened before I showed up."

Altogether, it took hours. Plus seven coins, the pen cap, the pen (Danny) and various smaller scraps of paper (the rest of the guys), and one of the interpreter's earrings (Toby). The narrow windows set high in the wall of the room showed full daylight by the time he was done.

"Thank you, Mr. Gervaise," the interpreter said, nodding sharply as she stood.

Jock stayed in his seat, gripping the edges with his fingers. "What happens now?"

"The interviews of you and your companions will be reviewed by the judge, and she'll make a decision about whether to continue this investigation."

"So, are we, like, still in custody? All of us?"

She nodded expressionlessly, but then added, "Someone will bring you food when you're back in your room."

"I'd rather see my boyfriend," he said quickly. "Toby."

For the first time since she'd walked in, she looked mildly sympathetic. "I'm sorry, that's not possible."

Jock squeezed his eyes shut a second, exhausted by the long night and the questions, but mostly by the disappointment that he couldn't defend himself against. He didn't know how to deal with not being able to do anything about this situation. How to deal with not being able to protect Toby. "Please."

The DCRI agent said something, and the interpreter told him, "We don't have the authority to grant you that."

Jock hung his head. He couldn't look at them, so he watched his fingers try to strangle each other. Even the ones with names. "When you guys broke down the door, we were in the middle of, um, a discussion. Like, I'd just told him something that really bothered him, and I didn't have a chance to . . . apologize I guess. I just want to talk to him for a minute. I don't even care if someone's listening—" he swallowed the rest of his words. Fuckers were choking him anyway.

"I'm sorry," she repeated, voice much softer. For a fleeting second she laid fingers on Jock's shoulder. "Someone will arrive to take you back in a moment." Then he heard them both walk out of the room.

He'd had a lot of low points in his life. Probably too many for his age. Defeats in major championship games, injuries, being outed to the team, the picture hitting the public. This was worse. The other times his default reaction had always been anger, because it was easy. Anger didn't hurt like this, it wasn't a gelatinous glob of shame and nausea that just sat, immovable, in his stomach—what did he even do with that? He couldn't fight it off *or* digest it. It was like radioactive oatmeal or something. How long could he live with it eating at him?

Shoes walked into his periphery, coming across the room at him. Jock steeled himself and started to look up, but his attention was arrested by the piece of paper and pen being set in front of him.

"I will have to read whatever you write to your Toby." It was the translator.

Jock swallowed and glanced up, meeting her eye. "Thank you . . . um—"

"Corinne."

He nodded. "Thanks, Corinne."

It took him a few minutes, because even when he'd said he'd be willing to let someone listen in on a conversation with Toby, he hadn't actually thought they'd let him do it. He couldn't go with anything too graphic, like, "I'll let you fuck me," even if he'd wanted to say that. That wasn't the real issue anyway.

So yeah, it took a while. But finally he had it.

You're the only shirt I'll ever want to wear.

Corinne frowned down at it. "This isn't a code phrase?"

"No, I swear." Jock tried to look extra innocent, force some dew into his complexion.

She tilted her head, inspecting it a few seconds longer. "Does this have something to do with coming out from your own closet?"

Close enough. He nodded. "Yeah, it does."

"*Bon*. I'll deliver it, I promise."

"Thank you," he breathed.

Toby was, not surprisingly, exhausted. But he couldn't get comfortable in his little holding cell, even after he'd convinced them to turn off the light, and he was hungry. What passed for coffee and croissant in their prison made him horribly homesick for the *gîte*. And his little *cabanon*.

And Jock. Toby never should have said that, about Jock's issue destroying everything they had. It sounded so *final*, but if Jock wanted to try to work it out, Toby'd be there. He believed in his frat boy's ability to overcome.

But he'd left his frat boy thinking he didn't.

Fuck, they could at least give him a pillow to hold in here, but there was nothing. Nothing to cling to, unless he wanted to hug a half-eaten pastry.

He lay there, watching the room get lighter as the sun came up, and thought about the situation he was in. If he knew how it would end up, would he do it again?

Yes. All of it. Come to France, fall in love with Jock, support the fratbros in their illusions (for their emotional welfare). They may make him nuts, but he had an odd sort of affection for the boys now. Possibly it was because they'd forged bonds through proximity and diversity, but did that matter? Not really.

Besides, if he hadn't come, who would have in his place, and would he have been as nurturing as Toby? Unlikely.

Of course, if he ended up incarcerated over this, his feelings on the matter might change. But Officer Faustin had seemed confident that they would be freed soon, and Toby decided to have some faith in that. It was better than worrying.

Besides, he had Jock to obsess over. Because however they ended up, he wouldn't choose to undo what had happened between them. It was too special. Jock was too special, even with all his stereotypes and lack of experience. Toby'd been lucky to have him.

I sound like I'm preparing to let him go. Toby squinted up at the ceiling, trying to decipher the odd feelings. He felt calm, and even a little serene—although very little—but overlaying it was that deep aching sadness that came from knowing that things were out of his hands. Jock either would or wouldn't work through his issues, and Toby's only choice was to stand by his man regardless of the cost to himself, or to give his man space and hope for the best, thereby retaining some of his own self-respect.

The light fixture suddenly came on, blinding him. Toby jackknifed up, rubbing the spots out of his eyes. He put the pieces together when the electronic lock buzzed. Someone was coming in. To let him go? It was still early, and on a Saturday. But Faustin had sworn the judge would make a decision today, hadn't he?

When the door opened, a woman walked in, and for a second Toby thought that she might be the judge. The impression was reinforced when she handed him a piece of paper. Were these his release orders or something? But it was a single sheet, with a single handwritten line.

"Mr. Gervaise requested that I give you this." She smiled at him.

"Mr. Gervaise?" Toby stared at her.

She arched her eyebrows questioningly. "Your boyfriend?"

"Oh, I mean, I know he's my boyfriend, I just didn't expect . . . anyone to let us pass notes, I guess."

The woman shook her head. "There will be no more note passing. Just this one. You will have to keep whatever you want to say to him to yourself until you're free to go."

"Okay." He nodded, still watching her.

Her eyes flickered down to the note in his hands. "Are you going to read it?"

"Um . . ." Was it weird that he felt shy about doing it in front of her?

She tilted her chin. "I'll leave you alone with it." Then she turned, knocking softly on the door before someone buzzed her out.

Toby stared after her. He'd really thought the French FBI would be less matchmakery and accommodating, and more militant and hard-nosed. *Huh.*

Taking a deep breath, he finally read Jock's note. One line. He hadn't even signed his name.

You're the only shirt I'll ever want to wear.

"Oh baby." Toby stroked the words with his fingertips. His frat boy did want to work it out.

Chapter 20

The end came not with a whimper, but with a bang as the door exiting the bowels of the DCRI and leading into the small lobby area slammed behind Toby. It had taken another five hours or so, but the judge had determined there was nothing to the charges, and they were free to go. In fact, according to Officer Faustin, they would be returned by the same officers who originally arrested them.

Toby was far more interested in finding Jock and the bros than he was in his ride home at the moment. The small room he'd been shown to was full of people, and it took him a few seconds of concentrating before he began to recognize any of them. Danny was smiling, talking to Jules (very much *not* smiling) about something, hand clamped on his shoulder. Turbo was leaning against a wall, sulking. There were a couple of officers near him, guys in black with the white DCRI letters.

Jock should have been easy to find in here. He was taller than everyone.

The door behind Toby opened again, and before he'd fully turned to see who'd come through it, Jock had grabbed him. Pulling Toby around by his arm, then holding his face between his palms. Their eyes locked, like always, and Jock's were so full of relief and fear and something else. "I love you," he said. "I'm in love with you—"

"Baby—" Toby's own hitching breath stopped him from continuing.

"I can't lose you over this. I'll let you—"

Toby cupped his neck, pulling him forward into a kiss. Partly to shut him up, but mostly because Jock loved him. He pressed himself closer, stretching up and initiating full-on contact, trying to dissolve himself into his boyfriend. Become a warm fuzzy and melt into Jock's heart. Or something ridiculous like that. Jock was everywhere, hands on Toby's back, crushing them together, lifting Toby onto his toes and directing their kiss with his tongue until Toby was breathing through him. Cupping the back of Toby's head, holding him right there even after ending the kiss.

"I'm in love with you too," Toby whispered against his cheek.

A palm slapping him between the shoulder blades jolted them both, and then Danny's voice shouted from too damn close, "Well, that was a lovers' reunion scene if I ever saw one."

"Oh Christ." Toby dropped his forehead to his boyfriend's shoulder.

"Danny, you're ruining our moment. Get the fuck away," Jock snapped.

"Just thought you guys might want to put it on hold for now and continue this in private, later," Danny said in the quietest voice Toby'd ever heard him use. "I know that's how I'd want it to be with Monique." He beamed at them.

"That's so . . . perceptive of you."

"Yeah," Jock said, face screwed up in confusion. "Thanks."

"Don't say I never did you a solid, dudes."

"I wouldn't," Toby promised.

Danny grinned, then turned and addressed the room in general. "Well, it wouldn't have been much of a trip to France if we hadn't gained some intimate knowledge of their legal system."

"I hope he never becomes a tour guide," Jock muttered.

Danny did them another solid, too. The DCRI returned them to the *gîte* in fewer cars than they'd used to transport them to Marseille. Presumably because now they wouldn't collude with each other in the furtherance of their beer agenda. The officers took them out to the parking lot and began divvying them up into three vehicles. That was when Danny whistled loudly and barked, "Clown car maneuver, men."

Toby and Jock ended up alone together in the backseat of their own ride. They hadn't had a private moment together since Danny'd broken into their unprivate moment earlier. Toby was trying to decide if he was willing to have a serious discussion in the back of a spy car—he'd be stupid to think they weren't bugged, right?—when Jock settled in on the other side of the bench seat from him, then pulled him close.

"Um, they'll probably want me to have a seatbelt on. It's the law here, and they're, you know, law enforcement."

"Wear the one for the middle seat if you have to, but you're staying right next to me." Jock stretched out his arm behind Toby's neck, wrapping his hand over the ball of Toby's shoulder.

Toby couldn't come up with a compelling reason to protest. He dug out the center seat's lap belt instead. Jock didn't say anything until they were moving, pulling out of the parking lot between the two other government vehicles in their caravan. Then he turned his head and buried his nose in Toby's hair, kissing his temple.

"Did you get any sleep?" He kept his voice low, adding to the intimacy already created by their closeness and the warmth and strength of his body.

"No," Toby murmured, tilting his head, laying it on Jock's shoulder. "I couldn't stop thinking. Did you?"

"I fell asleep as soon as Corinne took that note to you."

"That was her name? She seemed nice."

"Yeah, she was the translator for my interview."

Toby snorted. "Interview." He turned enough to rest his hand over Jock's heart. "Thank you for the note." He could feel Jock swallow.

"Did you understand what I meant?"

"Yeah." He lifted his chin enough to kiss Jock's neck. "We're still going to have to talk about it."

"I know." Jock wrapped his arm tighter, squeezing Toby to him for a second. "And I know this isn't the time, but I need to tell you I want to figure out this, you know, bottoming thing, and I want to do it with you. If you're willing."

"I'm so willing." Toby nodded, hair rubbing against Jock's jaw, catching strands in his whiskers. "I wanna be your favorite shirt." He had more to say, but a yawn interrupted him, and then he forgot.

Jock kissed his hair. "They didn't let you bring your glasses."

"I didn't need them. I'm not driving." Toby tried to blink the buildings zooming by outside back into focus. *Too hard.* He let them blur out again.

"But you look so hot in them."

He smiled and wanted to lift his head for a kiss, but he was too tired, so he rolled forward to press his lips against Jock's clavicle. "I don't think they were concerned about that, or they wouldn't have let me get dressed."

Jock kissed his forehead. "Go to sleep, babe."

"'Kay," he mumbled, letting his eyelids shut, sinking into Jock's heat.

He slept the whole way back to the *gîte*, waking just as they were pulling into the driveway. He sat forward to stretch and look around with interest. As if something might have changed since they were taken into custody. "Was that just last night?"

"That we were arrested? Yeah, it was."

"Weird." He could tell by the position of the sun that it was late afternoon now. The cars stopped in front of Madame B's house, and before Toby could direct their driver around back, Madame was flying through the front door, arms outstretched, calling out something to someone.

Danny bolted out of the car next to them and ran toward her. They met, Danny picking her up and twirling her around and kissing her, in the middle of her herb-filled patio. It wasn't quite a field of flowers, but the effect was the same.

As Jock and Toby climbed out of their ride, Toby overheard Noah saying, "Whoa. Didn't see *that* one coming."

"Ha," Gomer scoffed. "That's because you don't pay attention to life's smaller details."

It was an awesome homecoming. Madame B got over greeting Danny, then started haranguing the officers who'd brought them back. It was all in French, but Jock caught a lot about doors, and damage, and someone needing to replace stuff. They bore it pretty well—in fact, they kind of looked bored. They must have heard it a few times before. Finally the DCRI left, and the guys stood around in front of Madame's house, talking and laughing, everyone kind of delirious with their freedom. It was a beautiful, sunny day, with the bonus that there was only a mild wind, which added to the party atmosphere. Jock kept Toby's fingers wrapped in his, and every once in a while Toby'd smile at him, or lean over to kiss him quickly. Madame Bouvinet was telling them about the many the things she'd spent all day making for them to eat when they got home. "They cannot have fed you well," she declared.

"You cooked without me, cupcake?" Danny pouted.

"It helped me keep my mind off of what might be happening to you, *mon cher*. I was so agitated."

"Seriously can't believe that still," Noah muttered behind Jock.

"Hey man," Turbo responded quietly. "Dudes fuck dudes. Why can't he date someone's gramma?" He sounded like he was joking around, not needling Noah. Good, maybe they'd get over what had happened.

Toby squeezed Jock's hand and smiled, flicking his eyes toward them to indicate he'd overheard Turbo and Noah. Jock tipped his chin and smiled back.

Madame B raised her voice, addressing them all, but nodding at Toby. "Someone from your institution is here to welcome you as well."

Jock's hackles went up, and Toby swallowed before asking, "Someone informed the college of our, um, adventures?"

"*Oui*," Madame B said. "Not me." She set her mouth in a flat line. "I believe the DCRI involved them in their investigation."

"Shit," Toby whispered. Jock gripped his hand tighter. Louder, looking around at all the guys, Toby said, "I guess we should find out what he wants and get this over with."

"Maybe he really *does* just want to welcome us home," Gomer offered as they all set off, walking around the main house to EuroTAG.

As they got closer, they could see a gray-haired, thin man sitting in a chair on their patio. Jock didn't know why, but he'd sort of assumed Madame B would let the guy in. But why would she? It was their place, they were paying for it. "I wonder how long he's been waiting for us?"

"Hours, I hope," Toby said. "Whatever he's here for can't be good news."

The administrator caught sight of them, then, and started speaking before he'd even stood up fully. "Ah, gentlemen, so glad to see you made it back from your, um—"

"Incarceration?" Noah suggested. Toby reached behind Jock and hit him in the arm.

"I believe he means to say 'wrongful incarceration,'" Danny added. The guy looked as if he had been about to say more, but when he turned to Danny, his eyes went wide. Probably because of the way

Madame B was plastered all over Danny's side, arms wrapped tightly around his waist.

"Guys," Toby said through clenched teeth. He waited a second, but no one else offered anything. Then Toby stepped forward, pulling Jock along with him. He halted suddenly, shooting Jock an apologetic glance, and let go of him before pushing to the front of the pack, between Gomer and Ricky. "Hi there, Dean Ursine. Toby Moore, we met once a couple of years ago when I was a student here. I'm sure you don't remember."

The dean nodded, shaking the hand Toby offered him. "No, I'm sorry to say I don't recall meeting you, but we have so many students and they stay for so little time I can't possibly remember them all."

That was it. Jock couldn't stand him.

"Yeah, well . . ." Toby tilted his head and half shrugged. "I assume you need to talk to us. Would you like to come inside?"

"Certainly. Thank you. And yes, I do need to speak to all of you, in light of today's events."

"Great." He sounded like he was grinding his teeth. Danny and Madame led the way around the house to the back—the front door was boarded up. It looked like it had come out on the losing side of a law enforcement battering ram.

"What's he the dean of?" Jock asked, taking ahold of Toby again once he caught up to him.

"Students." Toby rolled his eyes. "This could get ugly. I'll take all the blame."

"No, you won't," Jock whispered as they started inside. Behind them, Noah and Turbo voiced similar opinions.

Standing in front of the television with everyone seated in their usual spots—except Madame B, who squeezed onto the long couch with Toby, Jock, and Danny—Dean Ursine started with the good news. "First, I need to inform you that, due to the stress of your recent experiences, we've cancelled all your midterms this coming week."

"Woot!" Gomer shouted. Some of the guys murmured appreciatively, but Jock could feel the tension in the room. They all knew it was about to go downhill.

The dean nodded at Gomer, clasping his hands behind his back. "As a matter of fact, we've unenrolled you from the sections being taught at the Saint-Rémy satellite campus."

"*What*?" about three guys yelled. Toby put his hand on Jock's knee, stalling him when he started to sit forward.

"So what're we supposed to do for the rest of the term?" Danny asked.

"Well." Dean Ursine smiled tightly at them, pacing a couple of steps closer. "You'll use this week to travel back to the main campus and finish your sections there."

The silence lasted for about two seconds, until Noah said, "The main campus is in *Oregon*." He hit Gomer with some squinty-eye as he continued. "That's kind of an important detail, Dean."

Gomer was oblivious to Noah's diss. "What, you mean we have to *leave*? You're kicking us out?"

The dude held up his hands. "Not precisely. You have the option of dropping out and staying here for the rest of your term, but not under the aegis of the college. We're simply reassigning your classes to a different campus, where you'll have to relocate to if you wish to continue."

"In Oregon," Danny said quietly. Next to him, Madame let out a small, hurt noise.

"Yes, well, under the circumstances, the college felt it was better for you all. I'm sure you don't want to remind the authorities of your . . ."

"Antics?" Noah suggested. Toby didn't try to hit him this time. "They dropped all the charges. It's not like *they're* kicking us out of the country."

The dean's lips were stretching thin, trying to hang on to his polite smile. "We're not 'kicking you out,' per se, so much as encouraging you to leave."

"Don't punish them," Toby said. "Dean Ursine, I'm the one at fault here. As resident advisor—"

"It's *not* your fault." Jock clamped down on Toby's hand where it still rested on his knee, stopping him from getting up this time. "We're all adults." Legally.

"Yeah, Tobes," Danny jumped in. "Besides, you had other things on your mind."

"No, really guys. You all came to me when you needed stuff from me, but I didn't make the effort to actively reach out to you—"

"Yes you did!" Ricky shot up, lip going pouty. "What about all those weekends when you took us places because our hack of a history professor was too lazy to do it?"

Toby blanched. "Um, I'm not sure I'd call him *lazy*, exact—"

"Yeah." Gomer stood too. "And when you took us *all* to the emergency room when Julian tried to pick up that chick with fondue and then Noah choked on a croissant and I got a concussion?"

"It was a *possible* concussion," Toby said, addressing the dean.

"Plus, you made sure we had unique experiences," Jules piped up. "Like taking us to our first French tavern, and when we parked on the side of the road and someone broke into the van and stole all our beer."

"And your art supplies," Toby blurted. "Don't forget your art supplies. It's not as if we only used the van to transport alcohol."

"And dude," Danny said, some note in his voice drawing the attention of everyone in the room. He picked up Madame's hand, staring into her eyes as he kissed the back of it. "You totally encouraged me to go after the woman I love."

"Yeah," Toby sighed. "I did do that, didn't I?" When Jock caught his eye, he smiled faintly. Jock twined their fingers together.

The dean cleared his throat, reminding everyone he was in the room. The dude had gone shifty-eyed, gaze pinging from Jock's hand engulfing Toby's, to Jock's face, then to Toby. "Um, I hope I'm reading this wrong, but Mr. Moore, are you *involved* with one of your advisees?"

"Yes," Jock announced, sitting forward and fixing the dude with his most intimidating frown.

"Well . . . yes." Toby said at the same time, squeezing Jock's hand.

Dean Ursine took a deep breath, rising up on his tiptoes before planting his heels on the floor again. "I see."

"Is that going to be some kinda problem?" Jock asked.

Dean Ursine tilted his head to one side, then the other—one of those motions between a nod and a shake, a *well no, but yes* sort of gesture. "He *is* in a position of power over you."

The room was filled with the collective snort of all the guys.

The dean licked his lip. "It's frowned upon for resident advisors to have romantic relationships with their advisees."

"Heh," Noah scoffed. "When I was a freshman, I was doing the RA at my dorm and everyone knew—and I mean *everyone.* No one ever said shit to us."

A vein fluttered in the Dean's temple. "Well, it's not *specified* in the rules, exactly, yet—"

"Was your RA a guy or a girl?" Turbo asked Noah.

Noah squinted at the dean. "A *girl.* Maybe that's why no one cared."

Turbo stood slowly, stare never wavering as he jerked his head to the side and loudly cracked his neck. Half the room winced, including the dean. "Whaddya think, guys, is this dude a homophobe? Is that his issue?"

"Okay, wait." Toby stood up. "I appreciate what you're trying to do, but it's not necessary."

"Uh, *yeah.*" Danny nodded his head vigorously, then stood also. "I think it is necessary. If this so-called *administrator* is engaging in discriminatory behavior, it's necessary for me to know before I file my complaint." He crossed his arms over his chest, sidestepping until he stood shoulder-to-shoulder with Noah and Turbo. "So, mister dean person, how *do* you feel about the LGBT community?"

Madame got up and walked over to him, looking down her nose at the enemy.

"Oh no," Toby muttered.

Jock rose to his feet slowly, consciously using his size to fill the room—it was all in the attitude. "Chill, guys." He may have been talking to the bros, but he was watching the dean. "We don't want to cause any problems for anyone. Not unless it's warranted. And I don't think that's the case here, is it? We'll all go home to save the college from any further 'embarrassment' . . ." He waited for any objections, but there were none. "And mister dean person will accept that and leave, saving *himself* from any further 'embarrassment.'"

"Works for me," Dean Ursine called, halfway to the exit. "Thanks for being so—"

Whatever he was grateful for was cut off by the slamming door.

"I really could have gotten in trouble for being with you," Toby said on their way out to the *cabanon* after a huge dinner at Madame's house. She'd gone all out and made bouillabaisse. "It doesn't matter that Noah's RA was a girl. It's like when your coach kicked you off the team because you're gay, but he had grounds because you were drinking. Dean Ursine has grounds to make problems for me because I *am* in a position of power. Not much power, but still."

"I know," Jock said. That was *all* he said. It took Toby a minute of silent walking through the night before he figured it out. Jock was worried about their upcoming talk. Toby couldn't claim to be calm about it, but he'd managed to forget for a while over dinner. Jock probably had a plan for what he wanted to say, and Toby should probably let him do it his way, but . . .

He yanked his boyfriend to a standstill, just before the yard light from the pool deck spilled onto the path they were on. The moon was full tonight, and if Toby looked downhill he'd see row after row of grapevines shining blue and silver, marching down the hill. But he didn't; he focused on Jock.

He's still my boyfriend. It was amazing how good that felt, to know that. He'd thought he'd be able to let go of Jock if things didn't work out, but standing here, feeling Jock's fingers smooth down his neck as he gave Toby a questioning look, he couldn't say that with certainty. If Jock really did think of Toby as lesser than him because he let Jock fuck him, would he be able to accept that?

No. "We don't have to talk tonight if you don't want." *Buying ourselves a little time, are we?*

"Don't you think we should? I mean, what I said last night was kinda harsh." Jock's fingers dug into Toby's shoulder as he turned away a second, toward the grapes. Toby had a feeling he wasn't enjoying the view. Or even seeing it.

He touched Jock's face, and instantly all attention returned to him. "What do you want to tell me?"

Jock's mouth turned down. "Nothing, I just want to . . ." He swallowed. "I want to do this."

Toby attributed his confusion to the amount of wine he'd had. He'd had a pleasant buzz before, but now he had a disorienting light-headedness that was making it hard for him to follow what Jock wanted to do.

It. He wanted to do *it.* "So instead of talking, you want fucking?"

Jock swallowed, ducking his head.

"I don't want to fuck you."

Jock jerked back upright, staring at Toby, mouth hanging open.

"I don't want to fuck you to somehow make things *even* between us." He cupped Jock's face between his hands, holding on tightly so Jock had to look right into his eyes. "Last night, the thing I said that started all this was that I wanted to *make love* to you. Me topping you to make things equal would be the opposite of that. It would take all the love out of the act and make it only about sex. I don't want that."

Jock drew in a deep breath. "I don't want that either."

"It probably doesn't seem like it right now, but you have something that a lot of guys throw away because they just want to get it over with. You have the opportunity to do it right. Your first time *should* be special. If not with me, then with someone else."

"With you," Jock corrected.

"That's how I'd like it to be. Maybe, if we did it right your first time, it would make up for my first time."

"Your first time was *that* bad?"

Oh God, should he say the first thing that popped into his head? He shouldn't, because it was incredibly sappy, but standing here in the French moonlight, overlooking a French vineyard, about to go get naked in a French *cabanon* with his (American) boyfriend? *France is for lovers, after all.* "My biggest regret is that my first time wasn't with you."

Jock nearly swallowed him into a kiss, taking his whole mouth at once and cupping the back of his skull to hold him steady. A replay of the kiss in the police station, but better because it was in the moonlight and there were no frat boys watching. "Let's go to bed," Jock said as he pulled away, both of them breathing heavily.

Toby resisted when his boyfriend took his hand and tried to get them going toward the cabin. "Wait, we still need to talk."

"Can't we do it later?" Jock asked. "Like, after we . . . do that thing you said?"

"Make love."

Jock nodded, stepping close again and tunneling his fingers in Toby's hair. "Make love."

"We need to talk about one thing first. I know you might think you can do this tonight, bottom, but I want to wait. Is that okay?"

The relief that flashed through Jock's eyes told Toby he'd been right about him not really being ready for this. "That's all right."

He probably wasn't going to be as relieved about the next thing Toby was going to say. "And, I think maybe we need to put a moratorium on fucking altogether for a while."

Jock nodded slowly. "Like starting over, kinda. Reboot."

"That's it exactly."

Jock pulled Toby through the door of the cabin, ignoring where the police had splintered the jamb, and led him to the bed—which Madame B must have made. Everything was tucked in and the pillows were plumped and the coverlet had been smoothed out. It looked almost virginal.

Jock sat down on it, nudging Toby until he stood in front of him. Then he consciously gave up control. Lying back on the bed and spreading his arms. Toby smiled at him, then toed off his shoes before kneeling to remove Jock's.

When Toby'd said, "I don't want to fuck you to somehow make things even between us," the load of apprehension and anxiety that Jock had been carrying around since this morning just fell away. He'd almost thought he could hear it hit the ground. Then Toby'd said all that other stuff that was almost too embarrassing—too precious—to remember, and it had filled up the raw spaces inside him left exposed, like that expanding foam or something. Or caulk. Toby'd caulked up his heart.

Watching Toby undress in front of him, it became clear that giving up control was just like choosing to start this relationship in the first place. He'd never not be scared to do it. And when Toby climbed onto the bed, beginning on Jock's clothes, it hit him that he'd never stop trying to take control. Toby massaged Jock's dick through the denim while opening each button on his fly separately, and as every extra centimeter of freedom eased the constriction of his jeans, Jock had to physically hold himself back from just ripping his pants open.

He could shuck them and his briefs in seconds, then roll Toby over onto his back and . . .

"Pretend your arms are glued to the bed," Toby whispered before kissing Jock's now-exposed abdomen, tongue swirling into his belly button. "If you're a compliant boy now, you can do whatever you want to me later."

Jock shivered from his words and his breath blowing on the skin he'd wetted. "Except—"

"Except that."

Jock was compliant. Fighting his instinctive need to direct things and letting Toby do what he wanted. Even when Toby straddled Jock's torso, pinning him arms between his thighs and laying his dick on Jock's chest. Anyone who thought cocks weren't their own entities had never had one naked and pulsating over his heart. The beat in Toby's vein echoed the thump of Jock's blood, sending some kind of Morse code through his body, making him ache everywhere and not care what Toby wanted—he could shove himself down Jock's throat and choke him, pinning his arms like this the whole time. Do whatever he needed.

"You okay?" Toby whispered.

"Yeah."

Toby smiled, circling his hips so his cock dragged across Jock's skin, drooling pre-cum on him and leaving little shivers in its path. "I have a thing for your chest," he whispered, as if it were a secret.

"I know," Jock said.

"It's beautiful," he went on. "So defined I can see the sinews holding your muscles together, and I want to rub my dick all over it until I come on your neck."

Jock sucked in a breath, his gut clenching.

Toby stilled his rocking. "Is that too weird?"

"It sounds kinda hot." Jock swallowed. He wasn't lying, but it was definitely a frightening kind of hot.

But that's not what Toby did at all. "Another time." He slid down Jock's body until they were pressed fully against each other, then grasped Jock's wrists, still lying on the bed. Jock didn't smother the little noises that he usually bit back when Toby started rocking against him, his hairy belly rubbing and caressing Jock's dick. Tickling him. Teasing his nerves and senses until he got confused and actually believed Toby was holding him down and would stroke him until he came, leaving him no control over the outcome, which somehow fed his anxieties and his excitement at the same time, and both of them were fueling his building orgasm. When Toby took over Jock's mouth, directing the kiss and feeding Jock his flavor and the scent of him, it fogged his mind. Disorienting him, so he didn't realize he was about to come until he was flying through unknown space with it, half in terror and half in joy.

"I love you so much," Toby whispered afterward, while they were still shaky from coming so hard and he was still lying on Jock, kissing him with soft lips. On his eyelids, and temples, then down his jaw to find his mouth.

"I love you too." So much it made his eyes sting and his heart fill up his chest. He finally pulled his arms off the covers, wrapping them around Toby and pressing him against his ribcage. Toby sighed happily.

They did talk more, eventually. Once they were under the blankets and holding each other. "I can't believe I thought that was okay."

"What?" Toby asked, head pillowed on Jock's arm, fingers tracing his pecs.

"That it was okay to fuck you—or anyone, but mostly you—while I still thought it was demeaning if someone did me."

"'Still thought'? You don't anymore?"

"I don't know for sure what I think, but it's like I flipped a switch or something. I look back at that attitude and . . ." He shrugged. "I don't blame you for not wanting to be with me."

"But I did want to be with you, even then. I just knew that if I stayed, knowing you thought that, it'd destroy us someday."

"I get that now." He kissed Toby's head. "You know what's weird? I miss hockey less. Like, I kinda think, for me, it wasn't just the game, it was how I saw myself."

"Even once you figured out you were gay?"

"Yeah." He rolled onto his side, facing his boyfriend. "Which is extra weird. Because once I figured that out, it seems like I would have started questioning everything, doesn't it?"

Toby turned onto his back, rubbing his forehead and staring intently at the ceiling. "I should have taken more psych classes," he muttered. Before Jock could ask, Toby returned, facing him again. "Okay, so, this is my amateur take on things, but it's like we get told stuff, about what it means to be a man or a woman, and most kids buy into that early on. Sometimes even the kids whose parents are consciously trying not to force gender norms on their kids. Then as people grow up, some of them start to figure out that that cultural ideal they were sold? It's not *their* version of being a man or a woman. But it takes a while for most of them to, like, shed the chrysalis of society's gender stereotypes. And that's not even touching the subject of people who feel like a mixture of genders, or another gender altogether."

"So, like, you're saying that I could accept that I was gay, but it took me longer to accept that . . . that might mean doing things that didn't fit into the 'male' box. The box I feel like I fit in." Because even now, he knew instinctively that he was all boy. The difference was that he could see how being masculine wasn't as restrictive as he'd thought. He got to define it for himself.

"Yeah, that sounds about right."

"I like that theory." It gave him comfort, oddly. Answers should have given him comfort, but after nineteen years of other people's answers, he was good with not knowing everything now and figuring it out as they went along.

"So, do you think you'll ever play hockey again?"

"I still don't know, but I'd like to do something like that. Maybe I'll check out some other stuff. I hear rugby's cool."

Toby lifted himself up on his elbow, grinning down at Jock. "Rugby's not cool, baby. It's *hot*."

"So . . ." Jock felt his own smile break through his attempt to be serious. "You'd encourage me to do that, huh?"

"I'd be your favorite athletic supporter." He smirked. "I'd come to every game just to see you get all muddy and worked up and wrestle around with other guys."

"As long as you come home with me. I don't share well."

"You do with me," Toby said.

"Yeah, but that's because you're *mine*."

Toby snorted. "I should probably protest how possessive you are, shouldn't I?"

Jock shrugged, combing his fingers through Toby's bangs and then gripping his head, pulling him closer for a kiss. "I think you like it though."

"I do," Toby said, almost to his mouth. "But only because you're *mine*."

There was only one answer for that. Jock kissed him.

Chapter 21

Someone was banging on their *cabanon*. Toby didn't even flinch, but it woke Jock up. He blinked and felt around for his phone to look at the time. 9:28; he'd totally slept in.

Bang bang bang.

"What?" It couldn't be the cops again, they'd just shove the door open. The only thing holding it closed now was lack of wind.

"Danny's calling a meeting." Ricky's voice came through the wood.

Jock snorted. "So?"

"So he says he has an important announcement to make, and he wants you guys there."

"This isn't a beer terrorist meeting, is it?" Toby croaked from beside him. "Because if it is—"

"It's not," Ricky said far too quickly. "Really. It's not that."

Toby groaned. "Should we go?" he asked quietly.

"Probably," Jock sighed, then raised his voice so Ricky would hear. "Give us fifteen minutes and we'll—"

"A half hour," Toby yelled. "I want to take a shower," he muttered.

"I can help with that."

It was more like an hour before they made it to EuroTAG. Everyone was waiting for them, sitting in the great room. They'd left Jock and Toby's space on the couch open, although they had to squeeze in with Danny and Madame again.

"Sweet, you're here," Danny said, rising and moving to stand in front of the flat-screen. "I'll get started, then." He stayed silent though, looking at each of them in turn.

"Think he'll start soon?" Toby whispered loudly.

"Men," Danny intoned before falling silent again for a second. "I've called you here today so we could have a few moments of reflection. Look back at where we were just over a month ago, and compare it to how far we've come. When we showed up in Provence, we were a ragtag bunch of frat boys without a frat house, but we've worked hard since then. We've come together into a unit, man. A *unit*!" Danny punched his fist into his palm. "An honest to God *team*."

"Danny," Toby said through clenched teeth.

The dude held up his hands and lowered his head, acknowledging the warning. "I know, Tobes. You said we can't say the *name* of the team anymore, and I'm gonna respect that, because you're like our general. You're the leader of this little—"

"I'm *not* the leader." His leg muscles tensed up, pressing into Jock's thigh.

"The *secret* leader." Danny leaned forward and whispered. "The one no one knows is really calling the shots."

"I'm not calling any shots!"

Jock stretched his arm out along the back of the couch, behind Toby's head. Trying to show his support without shutting Danny down. Because seriously, all signs indicated that this was going to make a great story to retell. Toby'd appreciate it later.

"You're really messing with my analogy, dude." Danny pouted.

Toby's nostrils flared, and he sounded like he was trying to breathe fire through them and reduce Danny to cinders, but he eventually nodded, waving a "go on" hand at him.

"Okay, so, yeah. I'm saying that we have this unit, and we're led by a shadowy figure—"

Toby grunted in the back of his throat.

"But we have a visible leader too, don't we? Someone directing the ground troops, keeping up morale."

"That's you, Danny," Ricky said. "We all know that."

Danny halted, swallowing audibly and turning away from his audience, just far enough to brace his arm on the TV, swiping his other hand down his face. "Thanks, Ricky," he choked out. "It means a lot to me that you can see that, man."

Rocky nodded solemnly.

After a moment of silence while Danny gathered himself together, he turned back to them, planting his feet shoulder width apart and clasping his hands behind his back. "So, if Toby's our general, I guess that means I'm the sergeant." He waited for the murmurs of agreement from the other guys to die down before going on. "But, men, I've got some news that's going to affect our little troop."

More murmurs, questioning ones this time.

Danny took his time telling them, first looking around, focusing on each guy in turn, meeting everyone's eyes. Jock tried very hard to appear as if he wasn't finding this cray-cray entertaining when Danny got to him. He even tilted his chin, hoping that it'd read to Danny like him showing respect, rather than trying to hide the barest edge of a smile.

Finally, he took a breath and soldiered on. "I won't be going back to Calapooya with you."

"So?" Turbo asked. "You'll be there next fall, right?"

Danny bowed his head a moment, somehow silencing all the questions with the gesture. "I'm dropping out of school," he announced when he had quiet. "Permanently."

"Are you fucking *insane*?" Toby snapped. He started to push off the couch, sitting forward, but Jock clamped his hand on his boyfriend's knee, pinning him there with that and the arm he had around Toby's shoulders. It didn't keep Toby from expressing his opinion, though. "A college degree is the only hope you have of— Jesus." Toby huffed, falling back on the cushions again. "Never mind," he muttered, crossing his arms over his chest. Jock totally got what Toby was upset about, but Danny was a trust-fund kid, so maybe he figured it didn't matter. It wasn't as if academia would be losing one of its finest young minds or anything.

"But *why*?" Jules nearly wailed.

Danny nodded, taking a couple steps to one side, then the other, pacing contemplatively. "We'll get to that in a minute, Julian. But first, we have some official business to take care of." He stopped, straightening and throwing back his shoulders again. "Our unit—*your* unit—needs a new leader for the ground troops. Someone to fill my shoes. Now, I'm out of it, so the decision's yours, but I've been thinking about who the best possible successor would be."

He let the suspense build.

"Who?" Noah finally asked, and Jock almost thought he sounded hopeful. As if he were buying into this.

Danny took a deep breath, puffing out his chest, and intoned, "Ricky."

"What the *fuck*?" Turbo spit out. "Him? Why not me?"

Danny sighed, pacing in measured steps to Turbo, clamping a comforting hand on his shoulder. "I understand your questioning my choice, but I gave it a lot of thought, and when it comes right down to it, Ricky has shown true valor under fire. He's got the right stuff, Turbo. So do you, don't get me wrong, but you didn't have the chance to prove yourself the way he did against that staircase at TAG House."

Turbo muttered something but acquiesced.

"Man, Danny," Ricky choked out, standing up. "I just don't know what to say. I'm not sure how I'll fill shoes as big as yours." He paused to swipe at his eyes, then threw his shoulders back, taking a deep breath. "But I'll try to do you proud, sir."

"Sir?" Jock mouthed to Toby. Toby rolled his eyes.

Danny shook Ricky's hand, clapping him on the shoulder. Gomer took a picture of them standing there like that, smiling at each other. Commemorating the changing of the guard for posterity. Jock thought he heard someone sniffle, but he really didn't want to know who it was, so he ignored it.

"So why aren't you coming back with us?" Jules asked.

Danny motioned Ricky to sit down, and then he took up his stance front and center again. "I know you guys are saddened by my leaving you, but for me personally it was motivated by a positive force in my life. I came here thinking my job was to look out for you all, but I found someone who needs me more. Someone relying on me, and no offense to any of you, but she's more important to me than all of you put together."

"Um, *I'm* offended," Julian interjected.

Danny ignored him, and beamed over at Madame on the couch. Madame blushed and smiled back.

"Monique, would you join me?" Danny held out his hand to her, and she stood and came to him.

"Oh no," Toby breathed. When Danny got down on one knee and pulled a small black velvet box out of his pocket, Jock totally got Toby's concerns.

Jules gasped, clapping his hands over his mouth, muffling his exclamation of "Oh my God."

"Monique, my love, cupcake, you're the woman for me, I know that like I know the eyes in my face. I'm madly in love with you, and you've said you love me, too."

"Oh, *mon cher,* I do," she sighed, covering her trembling lips with her palm.

Danny swallowed and opened the box, revealing the expected: a ring with a big rock on it. "Would you do me the very great honor of becoming my wife?"

A tear rolled down Madame's cheek as she said, "Oh, *oui*! But of course, nothing would make me happier." She held out her hand, and Danny fumbled the ring out of the box and got it on her finger after a false start or two, then stood and crushed his fiancée to him, kissing her.

Amid all the cheers and backslapping of the other guys, Toby turned to Jock. "I guess it wouldn't be much of a trip to France without a marriage proposal, huh?"

"I'm sure Danny agrees."

They didn't have anywhere to go or any homework or much to do beyond swimming. Well, he and Toby could go to the cabin and mess around, but Toby was finishing up the last of his edits, and besides, it got really hot in there by afternoon now. The warmth made for some interesting and rewarding experiments in using sweat as a lubricant, but they had to be in the right mood for that.

Bored, Jock checked his old email address for the first time since he'd arrived in France. Being arrested and sitting through that whole interview had made him realize he was handling his aggression better. Maybe as well as he had before. If he could handle that, he could probably handle the emails.

He wasn't surprised when he logged on to find over three thousand emails. It could have been more, easily, but after scanning the dates, it looked like no one had contacted him for a few days. Deleting them all was kind of satisfying, and he got into the swing of it, not even really looking at who they were from before he clicked the "trash" button. But when he was nearly done, one caught his eye. It was from an individual, not a nonprofit or a media outlet or anything. Probably some skeeze propositioning him again. It came from sinbindiva1997, which could totally be a porn star looking to raise his profile by dating a guy with some notoriety, but "sin bin" was hockey slang for the penalty box, and if the dude who sent the message was born in 1997, that'd make him only sixteen or so, right?

So what the hell, he could delete it when the giant picture of the guy's dick started loading. Or after it loaded, if it was hot.

There wasn't a picture, though, just a short message.

Hi Mr. Gervaise—

My name's Evan Coulters, and I hope you don't mind me emailing you like this and all, but I kinda need to tell someone something and I don't have anyone else. You probably get lots of messages like this, so if you don't want to answer that's cool. I just need someone else out there to know.

I'm gay. I mean, I've slept with a girl, and it wasn't that great. But the guys on my team? When we're in the locker room I've got the good wood ALL THE TIME. And, you know, other stuff. I mean, I think about our goalie a lot in bed at night, you know what I mean? But I can't tell anyone because they'd do to me what they did to you, and hockey's all I care about.

So I guess that's it. I'm sorry you can't play out here anymore. I saw your game against Cornell in November. Dad took me, and he kept telling me if I worked hard I could be as good as you. He won't say your name, now, though. I looked it up, and there are some teams in Oregon, so maybe you can play out there, and someday I can catch a game.

Well, anyway, thanks for listening.

Evan

After checking his trash file, Jock found out he had three more similar emails from teenaged guys. The first one was almost a month old, and it was like a punch to the gut, knowing this high school football quarterback in rural Mississippi had reached out to the only guy he thought would understand and Jock had ignored it. Not intentionally, but still. He wrote back to all four of them, giving them his new email address and telling them why he hadn't responded earlier. But he couldn't figure out what else to say, because he didn't want to say too much and talk down to them, and they already knew he understood their situations.

In the end he went with the tried-and-true cliché. *It gets better. No matter what happens to you or how bad things seem, even those times when you don't see how it's ever gonna work out, just believe in that. Email me anytime you need to talk, or we can set up a chat or whatever.*

He hadn't been fighting going back to Oregon, but he did wonder how things were going to be. He'd heard from Brad that a forty-something philosophy professor had shown up to class stumbling drunk and wearing only a flotation device around her midriff, so most of the Calapooya campus was focused on her potential lack of sanity right now. Jock didn't expect to draw a lot of attention anymore. But he wouldn't have minded staying here, either.

Now, though, he suddenly felt like it was time to go home.

ΘΑΓ

The next few days were a blur for Toby. The college somewhat successfully imposed a sort of house arrest on the guys. They still walked down to the village, but Danny was the only one who didn't do so furtively. "What're they gonna do to me? I've already been arrested as a terrorist and dropped out of school."

Then Toby had to start shuttling guys to the airport. Everyone but Danny had decided to go back. Toby'd be the last to leave, and whether by accident or design, Jock was the second to last. He accompanied Toby every time they had to say good-bye to another one of the bros—all the remaining guys did—and in spite of his conviction that it wouldn't be sad when they departed, it was.

"Do you think I actually kinda *like* these guys?" he asked Jock on the way back from dropping off Turbo and Ricky for their flight home. They were the last to leave before he took Jock down tomorrow afternoon.

"Babe, I know you do."

That night, they could have rented a hotel room in Marseille, or stayed in the now-empty EuroTAG—Danny had moved into the main house, of course—but they chose to stay in their *cabanon*. Toby tried to temporarily suspend their "fuckatorium" as they'd started calling it, but Jock talked him out of it, mostly by the means of a blowjob.

Toby tried to argue. "But I want you to do *me*."

"Let's wait," Jock said. "It's only been a few days, that doesn't seem like long enough to, you know, reboot. Make it special."

At least that's what Toby thought Jock said, but some of it was muffled by his dick.

Afterward, before round two, Toby lay on his boyfriend's chest, playing with the few light hairs that ringed his nipples. "I don't have any place to live when I get back," he said.

Jock kissed his head. "You can stay with Brad and Sebastian for a while. I already talked to them."

"You did?" He rested his chin on Jock's pectoral and looked at him. "How did you know I needed—"

"You told me. You were bitching about how you thought living with Larry the Breeder sucked, but now that you didn't even have that option it was starting to look not so bad. I happened to be chatting with Brad and I know you've barely had time to think the last two days, so I asked him."

"That's so sweet, baby. Thank you." Toby rested his ear over the steady thump of Jock's heart again.

"Just taking care of my man," Jock murmured, fingers massaging Toby's scalp.

"You've been online a lot. Did you hear from any of those kids that contacted you yet?"

"All but one," Jock said. "He's the one I'm most worried about. He's a black kid in rural Mississippi, says his parents are conservative Christians. I mean, my mom's a Jesus freak, but she's one of those liberal Christians, so she didn't have a problem with me being gay. Not once she adjusted, at least."

Why had they never talked about this before? "What about your dad?" Toby asked.

"I don't know how he reacted at first, because Tank told him."

"What, did he take it upon himself to tell *everyone* for you?"

"When I was seventeen and he came home for the summer, he asked me if I wanted him to and I took the easy way out and said yes. Tank waited until I went off to hockey camp and told Dad the day I left, so he had a week to get over it before I saw him again. I'd already told Mom, so that helped. He was kind of uncomfortable for a while, but once the season started up again and I was still playing, things started to return to normal."

"So he didn't take it well when you got kicked off the team?"

Jock snorted. "He called the school and threatened to sue. He was, like, breathing fire, going on about discrimination. I don't think, if the same thing happened to Clancy—the kid in Mississippi—that he'd have as easy a time of it as I had."

Toby lifted his head up, dislodging Jock's hand from his hair. "Baby, I don't think many people would consider what you went through with the picture an easy time."

Jock smiled and stretched for a quick kiss. "But look at all the good things that came out of it. Those kids have someone to talk to, and I got you."

"I'm going to miss you when you leave," Toby whispered.

"It's only two days, babe. Then we see each other again."

The next afternoon, standing in the Marseille airport, playing with the zipper of Jock's hoodie, trying not to pout or sulk or—God forbid—get teary, Toby repeated himself. "I'm going to miss you."

Jock bent and kissed his temple. "Two days and we'll be together."

Toby lifted his head to look in his boyfriend's eyes, knowing full well he was pouting. "But we won't have our little cabin."

Jock smiled at him. "We'll have something else." He cupped Toby's cheek, holding him for a kiss. A long, explicit one that a month or even two weeks ago Toby never would have thought Jock would have indulged in in public. "I love you," he whispered against Toby's mouth.

"I love you too."

Jock smiled one last time, then let go of Toby and headed toward security, waving once he got in line.

Two days.

Two days later, Brad picked Toby up from the Eugene airport, surprising the hell out of him. When he saw the dude standing next to the baggage claim carousel, he couldn't help but lean over and try to see behind him, in case Jock might be hiding back there. He wasn't, of course, and it would have been nearly impossible anyway. Jock was a few inches taller than Brad, and at least as broad-shouldered.

"Jock couldn't make it," Brad said, giving Toby a brief hug. "He said he'd see you once you get home."

"Home," Toby confirmed. He couldn't exactly say where home was. He didn't feel like Brad and Sebastian's spare room could be called that, but he couldn't imagine any other place it might be. He was too fucking exhausted to figure it out. "Hope I have time to take a nap before he shows up." He was pretty sure he was swaying on his feet. Brad stepped to his side and gripped his arm.

"Dude, when's the last time you slept?"

"Ummm . . . has to be at least twenty-four hours, but I bet more. We didn't get a lot of sleep the night before Jock left—"

"I bet."

"—and the last couple of nights I've been having crazy dreams that wake me up."

"What kinda dreams?

"Every time I fell asleep, I dreamed someone was breaking down my door about to arrest me for having sex with a minor."

Brad scowled. Not at him, he didn't think, just in general. "Jock's not a minor."

"Yeah, it doesn't make sense, but I couldn't convince myself of that, I guess." He must have been swaying again, because Brad grabbed him and the luggage stopped tilting in that funny way. "Oh, there's my suitcase," he mumbled, watching it slowly glide by.

Brad hauled it off the belt. "C'mon dude, you can nap in the car on the way home."

Toby fell asleep once his butt hit the seat and his head hit the window.

What seemed like seconds later, Brad was shaking him awake. "We're here, dude."

Toby rolled his head back onto the headrest, slowly opening his eyes and taking visual inventory. Cars, fir trees, rain, asphalt, manicured grass, meandering paths. It took him a few seconds, but he would swear this was a campus parking lot. "Where are we?"

"Oh, I gotta stop by the frat for a minute. It's important."

Toby rolled his head to the side and stared at him uncomprehendingly.

"Jock will be there. He's waiting for you."

Toby comprehended *that*.

It was a loooong walk to the frat-dorm from where Brad had parked though, or at least Toby thought it was as he stumbled along, but when he mentioned that, Brad looked at him funny and said, "It's the closest lot. It's, like, two hundred yards."

Seriously, if he didn't know Jock was in that dorm, he'd have lain down right here in the rain and told the dude to do whatever he had to do and pick him up on the way back to the car. But seeing his boyfriend superseded sleep. Although seeing him in bed would be the best of both worlds.

"We're here," Brad announced. He grabbed Toby's arm when he tried to keep walking, pointing up to the sign over the door. Toby had to close one eye to be sure, but there were two banners—one said "Welcome to the temporary home of Tau Alpha Gamma" but with the "Tau" crossed out and a "theta" scrawled in above it, and underneath that banner . . . "Welcome Home, Tobes," the hand-painted sign read, colors starting to run in the rain.

He had to clear his throat, and he couldn't swear the moisture in his eyes came from the clouds. "Those freaks did something *nice* for me."

Brad grinned. "Yeah, they did."

"Awesome," Toby mumbled. "Now take me to my boyfriend."

Brad laughed and led him inside. They had to take an elevator up to the third floor, and Toby leaned against the rear wall, directly across from the doors, so that when they slid open after the short ride, Jock was standing front and center. Blue eyes smiling at him, hair still long in front, hands in his pockets, legs braced wide.

Toby jumped him, fully prepared to climb his boyfriend in front of a large audience of straight fratbros. It took him a few seconds after he'd wrapped his legs around Jock's hips, still kissing him, to realize they were alone. He pulled away and looked over his shoulder just in time to see Brad's waving hand disappearing behind the elevator doors. "We're alone?"

"I love you," Jock said, kissing him hard and fast. "I'm in love with you."

Toby hitched himself up higher on his boyfriend, pressing their chests together. "I'm in love with you, too."

Jock cupped his ass and smiled. "That was the way it should have been."

"The first time you told me? Yeah. That was the most perfect reenactment ever, baby."

Jock smiled at him, letting Toby slide down his body and stand on his own two feet. "I have something to show you."

"You do? Is it a bed?" Toby could feel his eyes getting heavier, like finally seeing Jock was akin to eating most of a turkey on Thanksgiving. It made him warm, content, and sleepy. "You're the L-tryptophan of love."

Jock bit his lip, still smiling broadly. As if he had a most excellent surprise. "It *is* a bed, as a matter of fact."

"Can you carry me?"

"Uuum . . ."

Toby sighed. "I'll walk." He did, but barely. Jock held him so tightly around the waist, pulling him so close, that it was more like a very sedate three-legged race than a lovers' stroll down the long hall to the left, nearly to the last door. Jock opened it while Toby watched his face. He had an odd smile, almost smug. Or at least satisfied. Like things were going his way for once.

"I missed you." Toby stroked his neck.

Jock turned to look at him, eyes going heavy and soft, leaning down and skimming Toby's nose with his before kissing him. "I missed you too, babe. Now here's your surprise." He lifted his head, eyes focusing somewhere beyond Toby.

So, of course, Toby had to turn and look.

It was Jock's dorm room. At least Toby assumed it was Jock's. And front and center, right under the windows, was a bed so large it almost skimmed the wall on either side.

It looked *sooo* soft. Toby found himself walking toward it in some kind of hypnotic trance. Like it had bewitched him and called him forth. When he got to it, he dispensed with pleasantries and pitched himself over the foot of it, landing on its pillowy, welcoming, non-airplane-seat-shaped surface, hugging it tightly. "Oh Jock," he breathed, eyes closed. "It's beautiful."

He felt Jock's weight settle next to him, laughing. "I'm guessing you don't get the significance of this."

"Of course I do," Toby objected. "It's a significantly comfortable *bed*."

"It's a queen-sized bed in a dorm room, hon."

Huh. That did seem unusual. Toby lifted his very heavy eyelids. "This is your dorm room, right?"

Jock propped his head on his elbow next to him, watching him. "It's *our* dorm room," he said after a few seconds. "If you want to stay here with me."

Toby pushed up from the bed, trying to blink sense into what Jock had just said. "You mean, like, I could . . . what about Collin? Isn't he technically your roommate?"

Jock tilted his head. "Technically, yeah, but he said if you wanted to stay, he'd move out to Eric's. Then he said if you didn't want to stay, he'd move out to Eric's."

"So . . ." Toby had to swallow to dislodge his heart from his throat. "You're asking me to live with you?"

"I am," Jock said softly, holding his gaze. "And I know we can live in a space this small, because we just spent the last few weeks in the cabin."

"Our cabin," Toby echoed. This was a lot like their little cabin. It had a dorm fridge and windows and a bed. So, pretty much the same. "Can I really live here? I'm not in Theta Alpha Gamma."

"Yeah, well." Jock made as if he were trying to wipe the smirk off his face, but it was still there while he finished speaking. "Ricky successfully petitioned the brotherhood to make you an honorary member for 'valor under fire.'"

Toby dropped back to the bed. "I don't know whether to feel happy about that or not."

"Be happy, because I talked them out of having an induction ceremony for you." Jock smoothed one of his huge palms down Toby's spine, spreading lots of shivers in his wake.

"I'm very, very happy about that."

Jock lay down next to him, nearly touching Toby's nose with his own. "Well?"

Toby just had to make sure he understood, because his brain was fuzzy and so much had happened and now he had so many warm feelings lying next to his boyfriend like this. He didn't want to make a mistake and get it wrong. "So, you're saying we're going to live together? Here?"

Jock nodded. "If you want to."

He bit his lip a second. "Of course I want to, but, like, what if things don't work out in the long run?"

Jock sighed. Exasperated but not really upset, Toby didn't think. "Why do you keep implying that we aren't going to last? I don't get it. You did that a couple of times in France. The whole shirt thing was about that."

Toby traced around Jock's mouth, following his finger with his eyes. "I don't wanna offend you, but baby, you're only nineteen. A lot could happen for you over the next few years."

Jock took hold of Toby's and kissed it, then scooted just a little closer, sliding one hand over Toby's waist. "There are a lot of people who meet the right person at nineteen and spend their life with them. Brad met Sebastian when he was only a little older than me, and they're planning on being permanent."

"Yeah. But there are many, many more who don't."

"Are you saying I'm not going to be your favorite shirt for the rest of your life?"

Toby had to smile at that, but he also had to be realistic. "I'm saying I might not be your favorite shirt forever. What if I go out of style?"

"This is the way I see it." Jock pushed himself up again, rolling Toby over so he lay on his back, looking up at his boyfriend looming right over him. "If you can't go into a relationship thinking it's going to last forever? Maybe it's not one you should be in. I'm going into *this* relationship thinking it can last forever." He paused to take a slow, deep breath. "And, I guess I'm asking if you think that too."

"I do think that." Toby lifted his hands and cupped Jock's face, maybe a bit too tightly, but he was trying to contain the wobbly feelings inside, the ones that made him swallow hard and his eyes get misty. "I want that."

"So, say yes," Jock urged.

"Yes. I'll live with you."

Jock's smile was radiant, and his kiss was just as strong and dominant as always, but slower, like they had the rest of their lives to kiss if they wanted it.

As much as he loved this man and as warm and fuzzy as his chest had gotten, Toby was exhausted, and mixed with this much happy it made him almost delirious. "Baby," he whispered, when Jock pulled away to find that spot below his ear.

"You need to take a nap."

"Kinda, but before I do, I need to tell you two things."

"Anything," Jock breathed into his ear, rolling so he was blanketing Toby's body, but not crushing him. Holding him close.

"First, I'm ending the fuckatorium. When I wake up? I want you to make love to me. It'll be special, I promise."

"Very special," Jock agreed, skimming his lips down Toby's neck.

"And second, we're not living in this dorm room next year. Yes, it's just like our little *cabanon*, but I want to be alone with you. I've learned to like frat boys, but I don't want to live with more than one at a time."

Jock lifted his head and came back to Toby's mouth. "Just the frat boy you love," he murmured before giving Toby one more gentle kiss. Then he rolled onto his back, pulling Toby onto his chest.

"Yeah." Toby yawned hugely, settling into his boyfriend's heat. "Just the frat boy I love."

Epilogue

Jock organized Toby's birthday weekend with all the care he'd devote to his own deflowering.

Which it would be, if all went as planned.

"Deflowering is such a lame-ass word," he told Brad while they were sitting in the dude's living room one afternoon in mid-July a few days before the big event. Jock had pretty much told Brad everything, because Brad had been free with the advice and personal experiences so far. And seriously, after the "let Toby make friends with your prostate" conversation, he was feeling like he owed Brad a little gratitude. Or a lot.

"Guess you could call it 'stemming,' like from 'stem the rose.'" Brad shrugged, as if most of his attention was on his new guitar and putting his fingers in the right spots on the fretboard.

"I've never heard 'stem the rose.'" Jock grimaced, because seriously, he could never hear it again and be happy about that.

"It's from *Brokeback Mountain*," Brad said absently, holding his tongue between his teeth as he stretched his ring finger into different position.

"Short story or movie?"

"Dunno. I heard it in the movie, but I never read the story." Brad smirked at him. "Not all of us are as academic as you."

"Whatever." Jock snorted. "Think I'll stick with 'deflowering' until something better comes along. So glad we aren't still using condoms," he added in a mutter, resting the back of his head on Brad's chair. It wasn't so much that he was dying to bottom, but he was dying to get it over with. No matter what Brad and Toby said, he didn't need to wait to make it special—wasn't letting Toby do it special enough already?

"Waiting'll be worth it," Brad said, convincing Jock that the dude could read his mind. It wasn't the first time Brad had done something like that.

"You didn't wait."

"Nope, but if I'd done it the way you are? I could've saved myself some emotional pain."

"You said you wouldn't change anything."

Brad stopped plucking at his strings and met Jock's eye. "No, I wouldn't. I'm just saying if we'd done it after I knew how he felt about me, it would have made it even better."

"You know we're guys, right? We're supposed to be able to separate sex from emotions."

Brad snorted at him. "Just 'cause we can doesn't mean we should. That's like a primordial holdover or something. You know when guys come, the signal originates in our spinal columns, not our brains? And you know what else? For the first three months in the womb, we're all girls. It's the default sex."

Jock held up his palm. "Um, I don't wanna talk about girls with you."

Brad laughed and went back to his guitar.

"I didn't know that though. Guess some of us aren't as academic as you."

Other than flipping him off, Brad ignored him.

Jock threw his leg over the arm of the chair and relaxed, listening to Brad try to make music. He was going to miss hanging out here. Being in the dorm was getting seriously old, even with Toby there, and they'd ended up at Brad and Sebastian's a lot. It would be even better to have their own place though. Which they'd have as soon as Brad and Sebastian turned over the lease to them.

"When do you guys move again?" he asked when Brad took a break, setting his instrument on the coffee table.

"End of July. Sebastian has to be at Berkeley by mid-August, and we need time to find a place and stuff."

"You're still staying with Toby's parents until you do?" They were only an hour or so away from the Bay Area.

Brad smirked. "Yup. Toby's mom just loooves Sebastian. I think she sees him as a substitute son since neither of hers is continuing on to get a PhD."

"You'd think Tobes deciding to get a Master's in Social Work would be good enough for her. He finished the one in history for her first."

"Yeah?" Brad said mildly. They'd had this conversation before. He stretched his arms and then laced his hands behind his head. "He only did it for her?"

Jock ignored that. "He's totally serious about the MSW though."

"He still thinking it would be cool to have a camp for queer youth someday?"

"Yeah." Jock shook his head. "Being with those guys in France and helping them work through their crazy did something to my Tobes. He's all driven to help people now."

"Your Tobes," Brad murmured, calling Jock's attention to the fact that he'd said it—probably on purpose, knowing the dude. "All those guys that email you, like Clancy? The kids in high school who're trying to figure their shit out, that motivated him too. It's not just France."

"I know," Jock sighed. For every part of him that didn't like sharing Toby, an equal part of him loved his boyfriend's dedication to the idea. Plus, he understood it. "Every guy out there like us who needs someone to talk to? Or a place to, like, fit in for a while? It'd be awesome."

"Yeah." Brad nodded. "But would you have gone to a camp like that if it was an option?"

"No."

"Me neither."

"Toby says that's my job, to figure out how to get the kids like you and I were to go." He'd been talking to Clancy about that a little, once the kid had finally emailed him back.

"Toby's sure changed a lot," Brad murmured, staring at the wall.

"Not really," Jock protested, his shoulders tensing up. "Just some parts of him sort of came to the forefront. Parts he didn't share with you."

"I'm not saying it's out of character, dude. I'm saying I never picked him for a guy to get all fired up about some grand plan."

To be offended, or not to be offended? That was the question for Jock.

"Gotta tell you, man," Brad continued, shifting on the couch and blinking out of his spaciness. "I thought he'd be good for you, you know? But you're just as good for him."

Be not offended. But seriously, "Do you spend a lot of time thinking about your friends' love lives?"

Brad nodded, totally not showing any evidence of embarrassment.

"Bet you didn't see Danny's happy ending coming."

Brad chuckled. "When's his wedding again?"

"Next June. Almost a year." Jock was starting to get it. "And yeah, we're all planning on going."

"I could probably get my boyfriend to take me to that," Brad said, smiling.

"Cool. I'll show you the *cabanon*." Which he'd already told Madame B he and Toby would be staying in when they came for the nuptials.

The cabin Jock rented in Oregon wine country was nearly perfect. It was a "studio" cottage, a single room with a bathroom, and the walls were faintly yellow. Bigger than Toby's little hut in France, though. It even had a kitchenette. Nearly one whole side of the building was made up of windows that looked out onto a vineyard sloping away before them. They could lie in bed and watch the grapes grow if they wanted.

One thing it did have that the *cabanon* hadn't was a hot tub on the deck. After a day of checking out the wineries around the place and eating at a local French restaurant, they returned to the studio and watched the sunset while soaking naked in the warm water. Jock leaned against the side and Toby sat between his legs, back to his chest.

"Happy birthday, babe," he murmured in Toby's ear. Then he kissed that special spot that always made his boyfriend sigh and tilt his head for more.

"Best birthday ever," Toby said. He played with Jock's toes under the water, which was a weird sensation. Sort of ticklish in an erotic way.

It's time. He'd done everything—all the stuff that would make Toby happy on his birthday—except let Toby fuck him. But it was time, because just like every other milestone they'd passed, Jock would never not be freaked out about it. So he had to take his balls in his hand and do it. "It's about to get better," he whispered. Easier to hide the tension in his voice that way.

Toby sat up, splashing a little, and turned around to face Jock. "What's your plan?"

Easier to hide the tension, but not necessarily successful. Jock stretched his arms out on the edge of the tub and shrugged one shoulder. Beyond being able to explain, because he'd tied himself up in knots over this, and he was afraid that once again Toby'd sense that and insist they wait until he was ready. Jock had thought he'd be able to hide it this time, but—

Toby stood up, water sluicing down his body, dick level with Jock's mouth. But before Jock could reach for it and get his lips around the head, Toby had a hand between them, out for Jock to take. Looking down at him and holding Jock's gaze.

He'd be lying if he said he wasn't a little bit excited by what he saw there. Toby thought it was time, too. Jock let Toby twine their fingers together and pull him up, then take his hand again when they'd toweled off. Following when his boyfriend led him silently to the bed.

Using only touch to guide him, Toby had Jock lie on his side, facing the nightstand where he'd left the lube. Staring at it, with his boyfriend lying right behind him, palm smoothing down Jock's side, Jock had a little bit of a panic. "We made too big a deal of this," he said over his pounding heart.

"Maybe," Toby said quietly. He kissed a line across Jock's shoulders. "But can you honestly say there's been a better time than right now?"

"No," Jock breathed, heart slowing as he closed his eyes and let Toby's touch soothe him. First stroking his arms and kissing the back of his neck, then Toby's fingertips trailing across the contours of Jock's chest. Jock let it all happen, pushing his need to take over away and enjoying the sensations. Small bolts of desire raced to his groin when Toby played with his nipples, making Jock groan. "Love the way you do that. Feels so good."

"Love to make you feel good," Toby said against the skin of Jock's neck, twisting closer and rubbing against him, chest and belly hair caressing him. Then the end of Toby's cock nudged Jock's lower back, and Jock instinctively arched, tilting his hips to give Toby more acreage to work with and himself more contact. Shivering when Toby's thighs rubbed his ass cheeks.

Toby was so much slower than Jock was. Maybe because it was his first time, but Toby'd searched out a response from every possible inch of skin above Jock's waist before his fingers finally reached between Jock's legs. He hadn't taken this long the times he'd furthered his relationship with Jock's prostate, or the sensitive nerves of his asshole. They'd done that enough that Jock was prepared for this. Even welcomed it with a groan, straightening one leg out and rolling half onto his stomach to give Toby better access. Let Toby take care of him, and let him see how much Jock loved it.

Toby tortured him, rubbing his taint and cupping his balls while reaching around to stroke his dick. Building up the tension until Jock flung his arm out for the lube and held it behind him for Toby to take. "C'mon, please. Toby. Please."

"'Kay baby," Toby whispered, circling his thumb around Jock's hole, then dribbling a couple drops of cold lube on it and rubbing that in. Pushing in and pulling out, a little farther each time. Jock didn't need it that slow, but being touched this way was too good to fight against. Too delicious to skip over by shoving his hips back and forcing Toby deeper. Letting Toby do what he wanted, Jock gave him his reactions in turn, because he'd finally figured that out—Toby needed to have control sometimes, and it made Jock happy to give him what he needed. So he didn't stop himself from groaning, or smother the jerking gasps Toby elicited from him. He didn't try to keep his hips nailed to the bed either. Instead he opened up further, rolling onto his stomach and pushing his ass into the air a couple of inches, then more as Toby introduced other fingers.

But he couldn't stop himself from asking for more then, either. "Babe, now."

Toby halted, fingers buried in Jock's ass, up on his knees. "You're sure? I don't want to—"

Wrapping his hands in the sheets, Jock groaned. "I want to feel you fuck me." And for the first time, he one-hundred percent meant it. He had a deeper understanding of Toby when he was at this point—widening his legs and tilting his hips, showing everything, trying to entice him inside. Needing to get to the next step, because the anticipation was starting to break him.

Toby's shaky breathing almost drowned out the sound of more lube being slicked all over something. His dick. Then Toby's fingers slid out and his head was pressing against Jock's ass.

Jock had another second or two of panic because it felt so much bigger than it looked, and for the first time he got it—he was afraid, at least somewhat, of the pain—but Toby kissed his spine and held himself there, letting Jock adjust to the idea. Until he nudged against Toby's cock. Like his asshole was feeling a little curious and wanted to play.

It didn't really hurt, but there was so much more to a dick than just being bigger than a finger. He flashed back to that night Toby'd laid it on his chest and Jock had thought it was its own entity.

He'd been right, or close. Jock hadn't quite believed this could be the life-changing moment everyone swore it was, not until he was being penetrated by his boyfriend. His eyes flew open, gaze fixing on the wall in front of him, while chills raced up and down his body, spreading goose bumps over his skin in waves as Toby worked farther into him. Thoughts and feelings he couldn't name or describe built into a big swirling jumble, filling him up as much as Toby's dick slowly was. Overwhelming and confusing him, and he didn't know if the physical sensations were causing the emotional ones or if it was the other way around. It all raced through him and back over and over.

Right now, the last thing he felt like was a girl.

Once Toby was all the way in, balls pressing against Jock's taint, Jock was more out of control than he'd ever been in his life, and he totally got it. Why guys wanted this, and it wasn't just because they wanted to make their boyfriends happy. It was exhilarating and terrifying all at once. It made him feel alive.

"Okay, baby?"

Gasping, Jock nodded.

Toby dropped down onto his elbows, forehead resting on Jock's upper back a second, trembling. "I don't know how long I'll last, but I'm going to try and make it good."

"It's already good," Jock managed to say. "It's you."

Toby swallowed and started rocking. Slowly, pressing his groin into the muscles of Jock's ass. Totally different from the way Jock fucked him—pulling Toby up on his knees and angling his strokes for maximum effect. Toby was gentler, but Jock felt swamped by the act just the same. Unable to think straight and only able to feel and enjoy as Toby thrust into him and slid out, each motion pushing Jock's excitement a little higher. Winding him up for the big finale.

"I'm gonna come," Toby panted, and Jock's hand moved to his own dick without thought, stroking himself a few times before he felt Toby pulsing, then the heat of his cum flowing into him, triggering Jock's own orgasm, and even that was different than he expected. Stronger and deeper inside him, like an undersea quake that created a tidal wave, washing through him in a rush and carrying him along with it until the water ebbed and left him shuddering on the bed, lying in the damp sticky glory of it all, with Toby half on top and half beside him.

The sticky glory slowly got gross, but Jock didn't feel like moving, just staying there with his eyes closed, not quite asleep but not totally in touch with reality. He couldn't remember the last time he'd been this loose, muscles too lethargic to move. In a good way. Toby's occasional kisses on his shoulder and the soft glide of his palm over Jock's back added to the tranquility.

"Do you feel any different?" Toby asked after a while, voice soft and falling right into his ear.

Jock smiled. "Huh-uh. Should I?"

"I don't think so." Toby stroked back Jock's hair, massaging his scalp with his fingertips, then kissing his temple. "I love you."

Jock pried up his eyelids to see his boyfriend looking down at him, forehead bunched up. The sun had set, but ambient light picked out the planes of Toby's face in dusky blue and a tinge of pink. For a second it took Jock back to that night in front of the *cabanon*, when he'd not quite been ready to take the plunge into a relationship. He lifted his hand and smoothed out the lines in Toby's forehead. "I love you too." Rolling over onto his back, he pulled Toby's head onto his chest. "I'm glad we did that. I get it now."

Toby didn't want to stay where Jock put him. "Get what?" He propped his cheek on his hand, still watching Jock.

"What I've been missing." He blinked heavily. "Letting you get that close to me. That . . . intimate." He rolled so they faced each other. "Show me how much you love me."

Toby kissed him, long and slow, then finally settled down on the bed. "No regrets?"

"Never. Not with you." He had to yawn before adding, "I'm kinda stupid, though."

"Why?"

"Because I made such a big deal out of the bottoming thing without having a clue what it would really make me feel."

"How's that?" Toby's mouth wasn't quite a frown, more like his lips were on the precipice of going for it, but not quite ready to leap.

"Just, right now? About the last thing I feel like is a girl."

Toby's face melted into a smile that made it obvious how much he liked hearing that. He stroked Jock's face a second before kissing him quickly. "Take a nap. You need to rest up for later."

Jock blinked open eyelids he hadn't realized he'd shut. "What's gonna happen later?" As if he didn't know.

Toby grinned at him. "You're gonna make me feel like a man."

Explore the rest of the *Theta Alpha Gamma* series:
riptidepublishing.com/titles/universe/theta-alpha-gamma

ΘΑΓ

Dear Reader,

Thank you for reading Anne Tenino's *Poster Boy*!

We know your time is precious and you have many, many entertainment options, so it means a lot that you've chosen to spend your time reading. We really hope you enjoyed it.

We'd be honored if you'd consider posting a review—good or bad—on sites like **Amazon, Barnes & Noble, Kobo, Goodreads, Twitter, Facebook, Tumblr,** and your blog or website. We'd also be honored if you told your friends and family about this book. Word of mouth is a book's lifeblood!

For more information on upcoming releases, author interviews, blog tours, contests, giveaways, and more, please sign up for our weekly, spam-free newsletter and visit us around the web:

Newsletter: tinyurl.com/RiptideSignup
Twitter: twitter.com/RiptideBooks
Facebook: facebook.com/RiptidePublishing
Goodreads: tinyurl.com/RiptideOnGoodreads
Tumblr: riptidepublishing.tumblr.com

Thank you so much for Reading the Rainbow!

RiptidePublishing.com

Acknowledgments

This would be a very different—and inaccurate—story without the help of a number of people. In particular, thanks to Bénédicte Girault and Indra Vaughn for help with France and French law enforcement, and to Mike Garzillo for sharing his knowledge of hockey. Thanks also go to my beta readers, Andrea, Steve, MC, Thorny, Alec, and Ellen, for making this a much better book with their feedback. And, of course, much thanks go to my editors, Sarah Frantz and Rachel Haimowitz, for having such high expectations of me. Most importantly, I'd like to thank The Husband for introducing me to France (and then taking me back again).

Also by Anne Tenino

Theta Alpha Gamma series
Frat Boy & Toppy
Love, Hypothetically
Sweet Young Thang
Good Boy

Romancelandia series
Too Stupid to Live
Billionaire with Benefits (coming soon)

Task Force Iota series
18% Gray
Turning Tricks
Happy Birthday to Me

Whitetail Rock
The Fix (Whitetail Rock, #2)

About the Author

Raised on a steady media diet of Monty Python, classical music and the visual arts, Anne Tenino rocked the mental health world when she was the first patient diagnosed with Compulsive Romantic Disorder. Since that day, with her trusty psychiatrist by her side, Anne has taken on conquering the M/M world through therapeutic writing. Finding out who those guys having sex in her head are and what to do with them has been extremely liberating.

Anne's husband finds it liberating as well, although in a somewhat different way. He has accepted her need for "research," and looks forward to the benefits said research affords him. He thinks it's kind of cool she manages to write, as well. Her two daughters are mildly confused by Anne's need to twist Ken dolls into odd positions. They were raised to be open-minded children, however, and other than occasionally stealing Ken's strap-on, they let Mom do her thing without interference.

Anne's thing is writing gay romance and erotica.

Wondering what Anne does in her spare time? Mostly she lies on the couch, eats bonbons, and shirks housework.

Check out what Anne's up to by visiting her site, annetenino.com.

www.ingramcontent.com/pod-product-compliance
Lightning Source LLC
Chambersburg PA
CBHW030342020726
47493CB00003B/654

* 9 7 8 1 6 2 6 4 9 1 3 1 1 *